THE RAVISHING
OF LADY MARY WARE

DENNIS WHEATLEY

DENNIS WHEATLEY

THE RAVISHING
OF LADY MARY WARE

Frontispiece Portrait by
MARK GERSON

Original Illustrations by
ANNE KNIGHT

Distributed by
HERON BOOKS

Published by arrangement with
Hutchinson and Co. (Publishers) Ltd.

© *1971, Dennis Wheatley Ltd.*
© *1974, Illustrations, Edito-Service S.A., Geneva*

DEDICATION

As several chapters of this book concern Marshal Bernadotte, the founder of the present Royal House of Sweden, I take great pleasure in dedicating it to my friend

IWAN HEDMAN

who has done so much to popularise the Swedish translations of my books.

CONTENTS

I	Wanted for Murder	1
II	The *Gamin* Marshal	13
III	The Forged Letter	25
IV	Roger Faces the Emperor	39
V	The Imperial Divorce	52
VI	A New Mission	64
VII	At the End of the Road	78
VIII	Resurgent Germany	88
IX	Death Stalks at Midnight	103
X	A Limited Compensation	120
XI	The Trap	131
XII	'He Who Laughs Last'	153
XIII	The Forwardness of Lady Mary Ware	178
XIV	The Devil with Blue Eyes	197
XV	The Serpent Enters Eden	213
XVI	England, Home and Beauty	231
XVII	A Call of Conscience	252
XVIII	Caught in the Toils Once More	274
XIX	Caesar versus Caesar	292
XX	Advance to Desolation	313
XXI	A New Problem	332
XXII	Napoleon Signs his Army's Death Warrant	344
XXIII	Death Takes Something on Account	360
XXIV	The Grim Reaper Gives No Respite	377
XXV	Old Soldiers Sometimes Die	404
	Epilogue	430

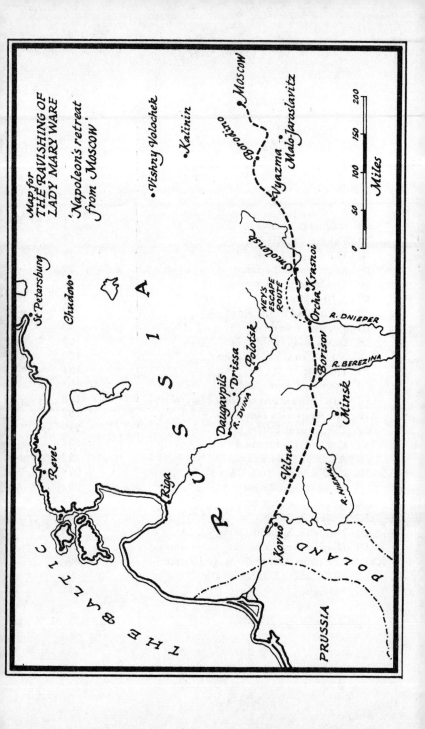

Map for
THE RAVISHING OF
LADY MARY WARE

'Napoleon's retreat
from Moscow'

ATLANTIC OCEAN

Coruña

R. MIÑO

0 20 60 100
Miles

Valladolid

Oporto

R. DOURO

SPAIN

•Cuidad Rodrigo

Subugal•

Madrid•

PORTUGAL

R. TAGUS

Torres
Vedras
Cintra
Lisbon

•Santarém

R. GUADIANA

R. GUADALQUIVIR

•Seville

Map for
THE RAVISHING OF
LADY MARY WARE

•Gibraltar

CHAPTER I

WANTED FOR MURDER

On a lovely morning in late September 1809, a man and a woman were sitting at a table on the vine-covered terrace of the inn at the little village of Winningen, on the Moselle.

The man was forty-one and the woman just a year older. Their clothes were of the finest quality, but slightly rumpled from hasty travel—which was not to be wondered at, since forty-eight hours earlier they had been fleeing for their lives, and had with them only the garments they were wearing. But now they were lazily partaking of a bottle of good wine, their faces as serene as the river which flowed swiftly past to join the Rhine, eight miles downstream at Coblenz.

Apart from them the terrace was deserted, and there were few passers-by in the street, for the vintage was in progress and every hand needed to get in the grapes before the coming of the first frosts. Yet anyone catching sight of them could not have failed to be struck by the strong, resolute face of the man and the voluptuous beauty of the woman.

He was Roger Brook, the son of the late Admiral Sir Christopher Brook; but he was wearing a French uniform and had spent more than half his life on the Continent. Circumstances had led to his assuming a second identity as *le Chevalier de Breuc,* a native of Strasbourg. For many years Billy Pitt had looked on him as his most

1

resourceful secret agent. He had served the Prime Minister well all through the French Revolution and later, as an A.D.C. to General Bonaparte, he had risen to become *Colonel le Baron de Breuc*, a Commander of the Legion of Honour and one of the most trusted members of the Emperor's personal staff.

His companion's name was Georgina, and she was now the very recent widow of Baron von Haugwitz. But she too was English by birth, the only daughter of a Colonel of Engineers who had made a fortune from inventions, and a gipsy mother. It was to the former that she owed an exceptional education and a fine intelligence; from the latter she inherited her superb dark beauty, her abundant vitality and, at times, the gift of foretelling the future.

Roger took from his pocket a news sheet that had been printed in Coblenz the previous day and given to him by a waiter when they had been breakfasting in the coffee room earlier that morning. For the dozenth time he read the leading article, which ran:

MOST MYSTERIOUS TRAGEDY OF THE CENTURY

It is reported that the Herr Baron Ulrich von Haugwitz and a French lady, the Baronne de Breuc, were found dead yesterday in the most extraordinary circumstances. The questioning of the servants at the Herr Baron's Schloss Langenstein leads to the belief that the two were lovers. For some utterly inexplicable reason, they elected to consummate their passion for one another in a wine press. Presumably they fell asleep there, and failed to wake when, in the late afternoon, vintagers tipped hods of grapes into the press upon them. Or it may be that they were swiftly suffocated.

Their presence at the bottom of the vat remained undiscovered until the must running from the press

2

took on an unusual pinkish colour. The Kellermeister
*ordered the press to be emptied. Only then, when a
ton of grapes had been removed, there was revealed, to
the amazement and horror of those present, the naked,
flattened corpses of the Herr Baron and the French
Baronne.*

The dead woman had been Roger's third wife, Lisala :
the beautiful but incredibly evil daughter of a Portuguese
diplomat, the Marquis de Pombal. Roger had met her in
Tehran when a member of a mission that Napoleon had
sent to Persia, and her father had been Ambassador to
the Shah. They had entered on a hectic love affair. Many
months later they had sailed together to Brazil, when the
Portuguese Royal Family had gone into exile to escape
from the French, who were about to enter Lisbon.

In Brazil, Lisala had told Roger that she was pregnant
by him. They had planned to elope, but had been
betrayed by a Negro slave. In the mêlée that followed,
she had driven a stiletto through her father's back and
killed him. Roger had got her away to a British frigate
lying in Rio harbour. He already knew her to be a nym-
phomaniac and utterly unscrupulous in gaining her own
ends; but, as he believed her to be carrying his child, he
had felt bound to marry her.

In Europe, matters had gone from bad to worse. Once
more in the service of Napoleon, Roger had accompanied
him to the Conference of Erfurt. There Lisala had given
birth to a black baby. The child's father had been the
Negro slave who had betrayed them. Horrified, Roger
would have rid himself of her, but she knew the double
life he was leading and threatened to reveal that he was
an English spy.

At Erfurt, Roger had again met Georgina : the first
and only truly great love of his life. He and Lisala had
gone to stay at Schloss Langenstein with Georgina and

her husband. Her marriage had turned out most unhappily. Von Haugwitz was a homosexual, but his fondness for boys did not prevent him from becoming Lisala's lover. In lust and depravity, they proved to be a pair. By then Roger found it impossible to restrain her. For her amusement, financed by the Baron, she secretly opened a brothel.

Sent on a mission from Vienna to Paris by the Emperor, Roger had returned unexpectedly and overheard the Baron and Lisala plotting to murder him and Georgina. Lisala was boundlessly extravagant. She had a great fortune in Portugal but, owing to the war, could get no money out of that country. Von Haugwitz was also at his wits' end for money. Georgina, too, was very wealthy, but her money was in England. Her death would enable von Haugwitz to claim her fortune as soon as the war was over. With Roger also dead, Lisala and the Baron would be able to marry and share this great wealth.

To save Georgina, Roger had again gone to Langenstein. But to get her away from the Schloss had presented a most difficult problem, as the Baron's retainers were under orders to keep a watch on her and prevent her from leaving. Roger had decided that the best chance of doing so was to suggest that they should all go on an expedition to Frankfurt, about which the servants would be told the previous night; then, during the night, to drug the Baron and Lisala. In the morning Georgina would say that her husband and Roger's wife were not going on the expedition after all. Instead, they had gone out early to see the vintagers at work. She and Roger would not then be prevented from driving off in the coach that had been ordered.

But they dared not leave their would-be murderers lying drugged in their beds, for it was certain they would be found there before the escapers could get away. So the question remained of where to hide them. As no-one went

4

into the *weinstube* until late in the afternoon, they had decided to conceal the unconscious Baron and Lisala in one of the big presses.

The plan had worked, except that when Roger had forced the coachman to turn the coach about and drive in the direction of Coblenz instead of Frankfurt, a footman had jumped off the back of the vehicle and run up to the Schloss to tell the Baron's steward what had occurred. The Baron's men had pursued them, but they had managed to get away. Had they remained on the Prussian side of the Rhine, the Baron could have had Roger arrested for carrying off Georgina; but, by crossing the river at Coblenz, they had entered French territory, so could consider themselves safe from his fury when he had sufficiently recovered to realise how he had been fooled.

Roger had had no means of assessing the power of the drug which he and Georgina had forced von Haugwitz and Lisala to swallow at pistol point; but he had quite reasonably assumed that its effect would wear off in twelve hours, so they should have come to soon after midday or, in any case, well before the vintagers came to the *weinstube* for the evening pressing. But evidently it had proved more potent than he had expected. That it had resulted in their deaths did not distress him. Even had he deliberately killed them, it would not have weighed heavily on his conscience, for both were given over to every form of evil and would, in due course, have brought pain and grief to many other people. So it was well that they were dead. Moreover, their deaths had altered immensely for the better the prospects of Georgina and himself.

Not only was he now free from Lisala for good and all. Had she continued to live, it was certain that, within a week or so, she would be back in Vienna, and revenged herself by denouncing him as an English secret agent.

So securely had he established himself over many years as a distinguished French officer that, at first, few people would have believed her. But, on returning from Brazil, she had spent some time with him in London. In consequence she knew so much about his English connections that it needed only for her statements to be checked by a French agent for them to become proven facts. That would have put an end for good to his activities as *Colonel le Baron de Breuc*; and, when the Emperor realised for how long he had been fooled, his fury would have known no bounds. Roger would have become a hunted fugitive in a Europe swarming with Napoleon's secret police.

Georgina, too, was no longer the wife of a husband whom she detested, and from whom she might have had great difficulty in freeing herself. Being English-born, she could expect no sympathy from the French, and her late husband's brother was Chief Minister of Prussia. His influence was great enough to have had her hunted throughout the French-dominated Continent and, if caught, sent back to her husband.

After the desperate anxieties of the past week, they had spent the previous day at the inn, quietly recovering. During that time they had discussed the future as it then appeared to them. In view of Lisala's almost certain denunciation of him, it was essential that Roger should not be recognised by one of the many hundred French officers with whom he was acquainted, and his whereabouts become known. As a first precaution, before arriving at the inn he had removed his rank badges, decorations and A.D.C.'s sash, and given their names as Captain and Madame Bonthon. As soon as he could, he intended to procure civilian clothes and get rid of his uniform; then make his way with Georgina by little-used roads from the Rhineland to Pressburg in Austria.

Ultimately, they were both anxious to get back to England—Roger to escape Napoleon's police, and Georgina to rejoin young Charles, her dearly-loved son by her second husband, the Earl of St. Ermins. But, although Roger had had himself smuggled many times across the Channel and the North Sea, he doubted his ability to do so with a woman companion, and was greatly averse to exposing her to such a risk.

An alternative occurred to him, owing to the fact that no great while since Georgina had had a brief but passionate affair with the Archduke John, youngest brother of the Emperor Francis of Austria. Hostilities in the war of the Third Coalition had temporarily ceased in July by France and Austria agreeing an armistice, which still continued. Meanwhile, Austria maintained diplomatic relations with her ally, Britain. Therefore, the Archduke was in a position to secure Georgina's safe passage to England, escorted by a diplomatic courier. So it had been decided that Roger should take her to the Austrian headquarters at Pressburg and, having handed her over to the Archduke, make his own way home.

They were now re-discussing the matter. Having laid aside the news sheet that gave them the welcome tidings that their marriages were at an end, Roger said:

'For me this means that I no longer have to go into hiding from the French; but for you, my sweet, it makes only the difference that I can escort you openly to Pressburg, so be certain of getting you there safely and more swiftly. The good offices of your dear friend John remain the best method of conveying you back to England.'

Georgina nodded, her dark curls stirring slightly on either side of her rosy cheeks. 'I think you right; though I regret that our parting should now be the sooner. I had looked forward to our making a long, circuitous journey together, with a spice of danger and many joyous nights spent at wayside inns. But what of yourself? Now that

you no longer have anything to fear, do you intend to rejoin the Emperor?'

'That depends on yourself,' he replied, his bright blue eyes holding hers intently. 'Do you at long last agree to marry me, wild horses will not stop me from joining you in England with all speed imaginable.'

'Oh, Roger!' she protested. 'We have talked of this so often through the years, and always reached the same conclusion. Our joy in sleeping together has never lessened since we first became lovers as boy and girl. But solely because fate decreed that we could share a bed only for brief periods, at long intervals. You have ever been the dearest person in my life, and so will ever remain; but had we married, our mutual passion would long since have waned, and we'd be no more than a humdrum couple approaching middle age.'

'Ah, but that is just the point! I grant you that with our virile natures and lust for life, had we married when young we might, after a few years, have become satiated with each other and sought pastures new, or thwarted our instincts and settled into a dreary, joyless domesticity. But we are older now. Both of us have sown our wild oats, and far more abundantly than most. To my daughter, Susan, you have for many years played the part of a sweet and devoted mother. But your boy, Charles, needs a father to bring him up, and who better than myself? 'Tis time that we put casual lechery behind us and entered on the quieter joys of life.'

For a long time Georgina was silent, then she said, 'You are right that Charles needs a father. How wrong I was to imagine that brute, Ulrich, would fill the role. And no-one could make a proper man of Charles more surely than yourself. I agree, too, that I have had my fill of lovers. How lucky I've been in that: a score or more of men, all handsome and distinguished. But now I feel the time has come when I could be a faithful wife. I make no

8

promise, Roger dear; but before we part at Pressburg I'll think seriously on it.'

'Bless you for that, my love,' he smiled, as he refilled her glass with the golden wine.

When she had drunk, she asked, 'Should I decide against letting you make an honest woman of me—what then?'

He shrugged. 'I hardly know. I've been monstrous fortunate in that, during seventeen years of war, I have had many narrow escapes from death. But, on the law of averages, such luck cannot last indefinitely, and I'm much averse to throwing my life away on yet another of the Emperor's battlefields. On the other hand, I am much tempted to stay on with him, so that I may witness the final act of the drama he has brought upon the world.'

'Meseems then that, should you survive, by the time you come tottering home the grey hair above your ears that now gives you such a dashing look will have spread to cover your whole head. England will never make peace with Bonaparte, and he is now more powerful than ever before.'

'Most people suppose so. And with some reason, as his word is now law from southern Italy to the Baltic Sea and, except for severely wounded Austria, from the Atlantic coast to the borders of Turkey. Russia alone on the Continent of Europe retains her independence; but she is his ally. So, on the face of things, it does now appear that his position is impregnable. Yet it is well said that "all is not gold that glitters."

'No man is more greatly hated. There is not one of that horde of subject Kings and Princes who fawn upon him wherever he holds his Court who would not, given half a chance, knife him in the back. For the moment they are tied to his chariot wheels and forced to send their troops to fight and die in his campaigns, because all the fortresses in their countries are garrisoned by French

troops. Moreover, his demands on them for contributions to his war chest are insatiable. He is sucking their countries dry. A time must come when their people will revolt against this terrible drain upon their manhood and the intolerable burden of taxation.

'That has already happened in Spain, and it will in other countries. Enormous as his army is, he'll not have enough troops to hold them all down. This vast Empire he has created is a house built on sand. Does he make one false move, and it will collapse about his ears.

'He is, too, not only faced with this danger from without, but also a swiftly-growing canker in the very heart of his Empire. His personal magnetism is immense, so that whenever he appears, his own people are still hypnotised into giving him a great ovation. But no sooner has he turned his back than they now curse him below their breath. There is not a family in France that has not lost a father, a husband or a son in his wars. In every city, town and village, one cannot walk a hundred yards without seeing an ex-soldier who has lost an arm, a leg, or is blind. He has bled the manhood of France white, and is now scraping the bottom of the barrel by calling to the colours boys of sixteen.

'Time was when, as the Paladin of the Revolution and new Freedom, he was defending France from invasion. Then the people gloried in his victories; but, in recent years, they have come to realise that all the terrible sacrifices they are making can bring no benefit to France, and that the wars he wages are solely for his own aggrandisement. Even his own troops are losing faith in him. Europe now swarms with French deserters. They can be numbered by tens of thousands.'

Roger paused for a moment to finish his wine, then went on, 'And that is not all. Realising the desperate straits to which he has reduced their nation, many of his most trusted lieutenants have secretly turned against him.

All but a few of his Marshals are utterly sickened by his endless wars. They long for peace, so that they may return to France, live on the great estates he has given them and enjoy the vast fortunes they have acquired by looting the wealth of a dozen countries. Given a lead, they would betray him.

'And that lead will come. The two most powerful men in France are Talleyrand and Fouché. As you well know, the former has been my close friend since my first years in France, while the latter, who at one time was my most bitter enemy, agreed with me to let bygones be bygones at the time of *Brumaire*. Up till that time they, too, were enemies; but it was I who brought them together and, between them, it was they who made possible the success of the *coup d'état* that raised Bonaparte to First Consul and Dictator. Now, as they have both told me, they are again leagued together, and have vowed to bring Napoleon down.'

Roger had been so engrossed in what he was saying and Georgina in listening to him, that neither of them had consciously heeded the clatter on the pavé of a number of rapidly approaching horses. A moment later a small cavalcade came into view. It consisted of a large travelling coach escorted by a troop of French Hussars.

The coach came to a halt in front of the low terrace of the inn, immediately opposite the place where Roger and Georgina were sitting. The door swung open, and a tall, lean officer jumped out. He was clad in the resplendent uniform of a Marshal of the Empire. Above the gleaming black, gold-tasselled Hessian boots and white doeskin breeches, the blue tail coat was heavily embellished with gold braid. His chest was a blaze of diamond-studded decorations. Above his hawk-like face his cocked hat carried waving ostrich feathers a foot high. As he glanced up, Roger instantly recognised him as Pierre Augereau, Duc de Castiglione.

11

Recognition was mutual. Staring at Roger in amazement, the Marshal exclaimed:

'Blood of my guts! What in the devil's name are you doing here, Breuc, taking your ease with your woman? Why are you not making the ground fly beneath a horse's hooves? Do you not realise that the authorities are after you for murder?'

CHAPTER II

THE *GAMIN* MARSHAL

ROGER had come to his feet. Staring down at the tall Marshal, he exclaimed, 'Murder! I have committed no murder.'

'Should you be brought to trial by the Prussian authorities, you'll be hard put to it to prove you have not,' Augereau retorted.

Picking up the news sheet from the table, Roger said, 'I take it you refer to this—the deaths of the Baron von Haugwitz and my wife?'

'What else? All Coblenz is agog with it. Last night in the Mess at headquarters, they did naught but make wagers on whether or not you would get away.'

'They were not murdered,' Roger insisted firmly. 'They met their deaths by accident.'

'You say so; but what other interpretation can be put upon the facts? The servants declare that you were having an affaire with the Baron's wife.' Belatedly, Augereau lifted his plumed hat to Georgina, as he added, 'and as tempting a piece as a man could wish to see. For that who could blame you? But 'tis another matter when you make off with her and, within a few hours, her husband and your own wife are found to be corpses. It stares one in the face that, fearing the Baron would put the police on your track and have them bring his wife back, before leaving you to decide to make certain of keeping her by

13

taking his life. How otherwise could it have come about that his body and that of your wife were found hidden at the bottom of a wine press? There is evidence enough that they, too, were having an affaire; but both, it emerges had their own rooms, so could have bounced each other in the bed of either. Who could conceivably believe that instead they elected to have a romp in a wine press, and both walked downstairs stark naked for the purpose?'

'For that, Marshal, I can offer no explanation,' Roger declared. 'I can only assert that when the *Frau Baronin* and I read this news sheet a few hours ago, we were utterly amazed by its contents. Upon that I give you my oath. Naturally, we had expected that, as soon as von Haugwitz learned of our flight he would take such steps as he could to get back his wife; and had we been caught on the far side of the Rhine, I would have been compelled to give her up. That is why, as soon as we possibly could, we crossed into French territory, where the Prussian authorities have no jurisdiction.'

'You are right that they have none in civil matters. And, had things been as you say you supposed them to be, von Haugwitz would have been powerless to prevent your getting away with his Baroness. But you are wanted on the criminal charge that you murdered him and your wife. By now the Prussians will have applied to the French authorities for your apprehension and extradition. It was believing you must realise that which caused me such amazement to come upon you placidly sitting there enjoying the autumn sunshine.'

Roger's face had become grim and he said, 'I'll admit that the marriages of both the Baroness and myself were most unhappy. In the circumstances this morning's news that we were free of them came as a relief. Since receiving it we have thought of little else, so the possible consequences to us of this tragedy had not entered my mind.

But I see now that our situation may soon become a desperate one.'

While they had been talking, the escort had dismounted and were helping an ostler, who had run out of the stable yard, to change the horses drawing the coach. From its far side, an A.D.C. had emerged, run up the steps to the terrace and was shouting to the waiter to bring a bottle of the best wine.

Augereau now followed him and, his great, gold-hilted sabre clanking on the stones, came striding toward Roger's table. Roger presented the Marshal to Georgina and, as he bowed over her hand, said quickly, 'In view of what you tell me, Marshal, you'll excuse us if we leave at once. Fortunately, the few things we have with us are already packed, as we had intended to set off after an early midday meal.'

Augereau waved him back to his seat. 'You have no need to bust your guts now. D'you think I'd stand by and let your handsome head be lopped off because you've given the *congé* to some pissing German Baron? The Emperor would never forgive me, let alone the Army that speaks of you as "*le brave Breuc*". Nay, I'll take you both with me, and under my protection you can spit in the eye of any official who attempts to detain you. All Europe knows well enough that anyone who interferes with Pierre Augéreau courts death.'

In that he made no idle boast. Augereau was the most redoubtable swordsman in the whole of the Grand Army. Even Roger, who was also renowned for his swordplay, would not have dared challenge him to a duel. He had killed scores of men and, given the least provocation, never thought twice before drawing his sword and driving it through a man's body.

With a sigh of relief, Roger exclaimed, 'Indeed, Marshal, for this generous act the Baroness and I will forever be your debtors!'

Georgina, who spoke French fluently, had followed the whole conversation. Smiling up at Augereau, she said, 'Fortune has truly smiled on us in sending you here at this moment, *Monseigneur le Duc*. I would not take the Emperor himself in exchange for you as our protector.'

Returning her smile, he casually chucked her under the chin, and replied, 'De Breuc asserts that he did not kill your husband; but I would have for the chance of playing his part with such a peach as you, Madame.'

The A.D.C. had joined them and Augereau introduced him as Colonel Laborde. At that moment the waiter hurried up with two bottles of wine, and glasses. Instead of waiting for the wine to be poured, the Marshal took one of the bottles, put the neck to his mouth, tilted it and swallowed half the contents without drawing breath. Setting the bottle down, he gave a gasp, licked his lips and said:

'Ah! That's better, it's laid some of the dust from these infernal roads. Now, I have no time to lose. I halted only to change horses and give my men a chance to quench their thirsts. In five minutes we must be on our way. Go now, collect your baggage and pay your score as swiftly as you can.'

As Roger and Georgina had left Schloss Langenstein on the pretext that they were driving into Frankfurt only for the day, he had had to leave all his things behind; while she had with her only two medium-sized valises. The Baron's steward had believed that they contained silver articles her husband had asked her to take into Frankfurt to be valued by a goldsmith. Actually, she had packed in them her jewels, toilet things and a few under-clothes. The waiter fetched them down, Roger paid his bill and, with Augereau and Laborde, they got into the big coach. At a sharp order from a sergeant, the escort mounted; and, with a clatter and a jingle, they were off.

Augereau had told them that he was on his way to

16

Paris, so their route lay through Trier, Luxembourg, Longwy, Rheims and Château Thierry. As the crow flies the distance was only some two hundred and fifty miles, but the roads were far from being direct highways from city to city, and this applied particularly to the road that ran alongside the Moselle. Between Coblenz and Trier, it not only followed over two dozen great bends but, in places, actually ran back for several miles in the direction from which it had come; so, with other divergences they would have to travel close on five hundred miles before they reached Paris.

The events of the morning had forced Roger to abandon his intention of taking Georgina to Pressburg; and, when they got to Paris, having her with him there would raise new and difficult problems. But, in the meantime, Augereau's having given them his protection was a piece of miraculous good fortune.

The road they were travelling could not have been more picturesque. Alternately, as the smooth-flowing river curved for mile after mile through the corkscrew valley, on one bank there were lush water meadows where cattle grazed in the autumn sunshine, on the other steep hills covered with tall vines, among which the colourfully-clad peasants were gathering the grapes.

Moreover, Augereau proved a most entertaining companion. As a child he had been a *gamin* playing in the Paris gutters. He was still a *gamin* : shrewd, resourceful, contemptuous of the laws of both God and man, full of the lust of life, foul-tongued and bawdy-minded. Within a quarter of an hour he was telling stories that would have turned the cheeks of most women scarlet and, as he did so, he watched Georgina with cynical amusement. But she listened unabashed, then after a while bested him by remarking quietly :

'*Monseigneur le Duc*, I would find your stories even more amusing if, when telling them, you made your point

17

without using words that are offensive to well-bred people.'

Unused to being rebuked, he stared at her with a frown, then he gave a great guffaw of laughter and cried :

'God's boots! You are a woman in a thousand. Madame, for baiting you as I did I freely apologise and for the future, while in your presence, will endeavour to remember to call a spade a garden implement.'

That night they slept at Berncastle, dined and wined off the best and went up to bed tired but cheerful. Before they fell asleep, Roger told Georgina something of their rumbustious protector's extraordinary history.

At a very early age he had got himself a job as junior footman to a Marquis, but had been dismissed for seducing the Marquise's personal maid. His next job had been as a waiter in a gaming house, but he had lost that through seducing a waitress. He had then enlisted in the cavalry, but had been discharged for insubordination. However, a Colonel of Carabinières had been attracted by his splendid physique and taken him into his regiment. He proved an excellent trooper, a good companion and, before long, had acquired a reputation as the finest swordsman in King Louis XVI's Household Brigade. As, by nature, he was intensely quarrelsome, that had led to his fighting a dozen duels. He had never been worsted and most of these encounters had ended in the death of his opponent.

His days in the old Army had ended abruptly. A young officer had struck him with his cane while on parade. Augereau flicked the cane away. The foolish youth drew his sword. Augereau's blade came out like a streak of lightning and, a second later, six inches of it were sticking out behind the officer's back. Before Augereau could be seized, he was galloping off to Switzerland on a stolen horse.

From Switzerland he made his way to Constantinople

as a pedlar of watches. Turkey then being at war with Russia, he decided to enlist in the Russian Army, and served under Catherine the Great's famous General, Suvarov. But he found his Russian comrades uncongenial, so he deserted and made his way north through Poland to Prussia. There he was accepted into Frederick the Great's crack regiment, the Prussian Guards. Soon afterwards, to his indignation, in a fit of pique Frederick decreed that no Frenchman in his service should receive reward or promotion; so Augereau again decided to desert.

But to do so from the Prussian Army was a far more risky proceeding than from the Russian. So, for his own protection, he secretly persuaded no fewer than sixty of his comrades to desert with him. Leading this band of desperados, he had fought his way out of Prussia into Saxony.

Having had his fill for a while of military life he then became a dancing master and, in due course, wandered down to Athens. From there he travelled to Lisbon where he was imprisoned for enthusiastically acclaiming the Revolution that was about to sweep the Monarchy away in France. A sea captain secured his release and, at long last, he returned to his own country. There he joined a battalion of Revolutionary Volunteers in the Vendée. He proved such an excellent leader that he was enthusiastically elected *chef de bataillon.*

That was in '92, and from then on his promotion was rapid. The following year he was commanding a division in the Pyrenees, and in '96 he was one of the three divisional commanders of the Army of Italy when Napoleon arrived from Paris to take it over.

In that amazing campaign he did more than cover himself with glory. During this time there occurred one of the very few occasions on which Napoleon lost his head. The ragged Army of the Republic was greatly outnumbered by Austrians and Sardinians and partially sur-

rounded. Retreat could have proved disastrous, yet to attack the Austrians up on the heights of Castiglione appeared equally dangerous. Napoleon could not make up his mind which to do; so Augereau took charge, stormed the heights and won a great victory.

He was no strategist but a brilliant tactician, and always had his divisions in the right place at the right time. He was utterly fearless and, like Ney, Lannes and Murat, was a front-line commander who always personally led his men into battle. Although he was a strict disciplinarian, he never tired of looking after their welfare, so they adored him.

In spite of the fact that he was now a Duke, with great estates and a huge fortune piled up by wholesale looting in a dozen countries, he was at heart still a revolutionary and atheist; and he lost no opportunity of treading on the toes of the returned émigrés whom in recent years Napoleon had been welcoming to his Court, or showing his contempt for everything connected with religion.

Such was the strange, forceful, unscrupulous, gay, greedy man in whose company Roger and Georgina spent the next five days. On October 1st they arrived in Paris and, with heartfelt thanks for his most timely protection, took leave of the Marshal Duke after drinking a last bottle with him in his great Paris mansion.

From there Roger took Georgina to his old haunt, *La Belle Etoile*, not far from the Louvre. Long ago, in the days before the Revolution, as a youth and the secretary of a wealthy Marquis, Roger had lived at the hostelry. The patron, Monsieur Blanchard, and his wife were an honest Norman couple. They had sheltered Roger during the Terror and seen him rise in Napoleon's service to fame and honour.

Although for many years past Roger could have afforded better accommodation, whenever he was in Paris he always stayed at their inn. Up in the attic they

kept for him a big trunk containing a considerable variety of civilian clothes, and a reserve of money.

It had become a custom that, whenever Roger arrived in Paris, on his first night there he should dine with the Blanchards in their parlour. Now, having been presented to Georgina, they realised at once that she was a great lady and hesitated to invite her to share a meal. But Roger swept away their diffidence by saying that he had told her with such gusto about duck cooked in the Norman fashion that, all the way to Paris, she had been looking forward to this speciality of Madame Blanchard's.

A few hours later, rested and refreshed, Roger and Georgina were happily despatching a pair of fine ducks with their host and hostess; and washing them down with a good vintage Burgundy. Innkeepers have their fingers more firmly than other men on the pulse of public opinion and Roger never failed to get a sound assessment of feeling in Paris from Maître Blanchard. When asked about it now, he replied:

'*Monsieur le Colonel Baron*, I cannot complain. There is plenty of money about and no lack of food to be had at reasonable prices. But the people are not happy. In the bad old days, when the churches had been turned into gaming-hells and brothels, the populace were half-starving and the city one great slum, but at least the citizens did not lack *joie de vivre*. As the ragged bands of volunteers marched to defend France from the armies of the Kings who would have crushed the Revolution, they laughed and sang. Later, as you will know, when the news used to come in of victory after victory gained by the "Little Corporal", we had good reason to cheer and, whenever he came to Paris, the people went wild with excitement. But that is so no longer.

'Apart from that short break in 1803, we've been at war for seventeen years. And what good has it done us? Saving your presence, it is no doubt a wonderful

21

experience for the Emperor, his Marshals and high officers like yourself to ride in triumph into Milan, Berlin, Vienna, Madrid and all those other cities. But, for all but a few, these great campaigns mean death, to be crippled for life or, at best, years at a stretch marching with heavy equipment, along endless roads, living in great discomfort, often existing only on vegetables stolen from some wretched peasant's garden and, above all, separated from those they love.

'Time was when my wife and I used to think that *Le Bon Dieu* had treated us harshly by denying us sons. Today we thank Him that He did not. By now they would be dead, handicapped by some awful injury or far away with but only half a chance of our ever seeing them again.

'For two years past a great part of the drafts to the colours have been made up of youngsters who should still be finishing their schooling, instead of being sent to fight and kill their fellow men. And even the supply of these is drying up.

'Yet, on the Emperor's return to Paris, he insisted that the gaps in his armies must be filled. For the purpose he ordered Marshal Moncey to take special measures. As you must know, deserters have become legion. No-one reproaches them any more. On the contrary, everyone helps them to get back to their homes, or hides them and gives them work to do at night. Now they are being flushed out by the thousand. In every city, town and village throughout France, Moncey's *gendarmes* are carrying out house-to-house searches, and thrusting their bayonets into the hay in the barns. Every man between the age of sixteen and sixty has to give a satisfactory account of himself. If he can't, he gets a brutal beating and is dragged off to the nearest barracks. Can you wonder that people no longer cheer the Emperor, and that many wish him dead?'

The duck was followed by a flaming *omelette au rhum,*

and they rounded the meal off with pre-Revolution Cal-
vados. When they went up to bed, Georgina having every
confidence in Roger's ability to take care of her, was
tired but happy. He, on the other hand, although their
cheerful evening with the Blanchards had caused him for
the moment to put aside thoughts of the future, was far
from being so.

The mysterious deaths of von Haugwitz and Lisala
were so sensational that the story might already have
reached Paris. In any case, it was certain that when the
voluble Augereau paid his respects to the Emperor he
would give him an account of the affair. What view he
would take of it was quite unpredictable. Napoleon
justifiably prided himself upon being a great law giver
and, provided it did not conflict with his own interests,
was a great stickler for the law being carried out.

When Roger reported for duty, as he must the following day, he felt sure that the Emperor would question
him about his doings at Schloss Langenstein. If he insisted
on his innocence, Napoleon might well decree that he
must be sent back to stand his trial. On the other hand,
the case against him being so black, the Emperor, who was
notoriously indulgent of faults committed by his old
friends, might, if told the truth, rather than expose *le
brave Breuc* to the risk of being condemned and
executed, decide to deal with the matter himself. Yet, if
he did, as Roger's victim had been the Prussian Chief
Minister's brother, he might feel it politic to appease the
wrath of his Prussian allies by sentencing Roger to a year's
imprisonment in a fortress.

And, should that be the outcome, what would become
of Georgina? Gone would be all chance of getting her to
England. Still worse, apart from the Blanchards, she
would be friendless in Paris and, although they had told
Augereau and his A.D.C. that she was Dutch by birth,
she might at any time run into someone who had known

her on one of her earlier visits to Paris, when France and England were not at war.

If that happened, things could go very badly indeed for her. After the brief Peace of Amiens in 1802, Napoleon had horrified the world by initiating an entirely new measure against nations with whom he was at war. Previously, hostilities had been confined to armies and navies; civilians living in enemy countries had been regarded as harmless and were never interfered with. But the 'Corsican brigand' held in contempt ancient customs dictated by chivalry. He had decreed that all British citizens resident in France should be seized and thrown into concentration camps.

For a while, as Roger lay in bed with Georgina curled up and sleeping peacefully beside him, he contemplated leaving Paris with her the following morning and going into hiding in some small village on the coast, until an opportunity came for him to attempt to smuggle her over to England.

But it was certain that the swashbuckling Augereau would tell the Emperor that he had brought Roger to Paris and, if he failed to present himself at the Tuileries, he would be promptly sent for. When it was learned that he had disappeared, Napoleon would be furious, have him posted as a deserter, and half the police in France would be put on to hunt him down. With only a few hours' start, his chance of getting away for good would be extremely slender. On his own, he might have managed it, but not with a strikingly beautiful companion like Georgina.

Filled with miserable thoughts about what the morrow might bring, he at last dropped off to sleep.

CHAPTER III

THE FORGED LETTER

AFTER a bad night Roger woke early and again wrestled with the problems of how he could protect Georgina and save himself. Eventually he decided that his best hope lay in consulting his old friend, the wily Talleyrand. So, at nine o'clock, clad in his brilliant uniform, he had himself carried in a sedan to the Prince de Benevento's splendid mansion in the Rue du Bac.

Charles Maurice de Talleyrand-Périgord came from one of the most ancient families in France. The neglect of an injury he had sustained when young had caused him to become permanently lame, and so unfitted to enter on a military career, with the result that his father had forced him, against his will, to go into the Church. Handsome, charming, witty, at the Court of Versailles he had seduced innumerable beautiful women, and became known as the *Abbé de Cœur*. When the Revolution erupted he was Bishop of Autun, but had strong liberal convictions, so he had abandoned the Church and played a leading part in opposing the continuance of an absolute Monarchy. The Terror had forced him to go into exile in America, but during the Directory he returned, and started his career as a great statesman by advising on foreign policy. He had been swift to recognise in young General Bonaparte a potential force for restoring France from the destitution and chaos into which she had fallen,

and had planned the *coup d'état* that had raised Bonaparte to First Consul.

For the eight years that followed, he had been using his great talents most successfully as Foreign Minister. He was venal, licentious and unscrupulous and had amassed a great fortune by taking bribes from foreign Ambassadors; but, above all, he was a patriot. As time went on he realised that Napoleon, having earlier restored France to order and prosperity, had begun to ruin her by his ceaseless wars; so, in 1807, he had resigned his portfolio in order to be free to work secretly for the Emperor's downfall. But, such was the fascination that he held for Napoleon that the Emperor still continued to consult him, although rarely now taking his advice. On his retirement he had been made Vice Grand Elector, one of the great dignities of the Empire, shared only by Napoleon's brothers, his brother-in-law Marshal Murat, now King of Naples, and Cambacérès, once Second Consul and now Arch-Chancellor.

He had always held the belief that there could be no lasting peace and prosperity in Europe until the two great protagonists, France and Britain, buried the hatchet once and for all. He had learned as far back as 1787 that Roger was in fact an Englishman, but kept his secret because their minds were as one, and he believed a time might come when Roger could prove a valuable link between their two countries.

Even way back in '96, when he had returned from America and Paris was still seething with ex-*sans-culottes* sworn to maintain the doctrines of the Revolution, he had boldly reassumed his status as a great noble, dressed fastidiously in the finest silks and lace ruffles, and wore his hair powdered.

Roger knew that it had long been Talleyrand's custom to give frequent lavish breakfasts at which he entertained the great men of the Empire; so it was no surprise when

he arrived in the Rue du Bac to find half a dozen men holding high office, all of whom were known to him, assembled there. Leaning slightly on his diamond-studded malacca, the elegant Talleyrand limped forward, welcomed Roger most amiably and insisted that he join them for breakfast.

Among the guests were Gaudin, Napoleon's brilliant Minister of Finance, who had miraculously lifted France out of her state of bankruptcy in 1800; Decres, the able Minister of Marine, who was engaged in a vast building programme to replace the French battle fleet, almost entirely destroyed at Trafalgar; and Marshal Bernadotte. To Roger the last was of most interest, as he knew him only slightly, although he had heard a lot about him.

Charles Jean Bernadotte was the son of a lawyer, and a Gascon of Gascons. He was a fine, tall, handsome man and, to the Emperor's annoyance, defied the prevailing fashion by continuing to wear his hair long. That was far from the only way in which he had annoyed Napoleon.

In '96, towards the end of Bonaparte's first great campaign, Augereau had been sent off to command the Army of the Rhine, and his division was replaced by that of Bernadotte. The soldiers of the Army of Italy were ragged *sans-culottes*; those of the Rhine old regulars who were, by comparison, gentlemen. The latter regarded the Revolution as over and, instead of addressing one another as *'citizen'* had reverted to the use of *'monsieur'*. This had resulted in much bad feeling and scores of duels, which had tended to hamper operations. Bonaparte had done his utmost to get Bernadotte recalled to Paris, but had failed.

That, however, was not the worst result of the exchange. The Army of Italy had fought its way magnificently up through the Carnic Alps and was within a hundred miles of Vienna. It needed only a strong thrust south-east by the Army of the Rhine to join up with Bona-

parte, and Vienna would have fallen like a ripe plum into his hands. But Augereau was no strategist and he bungled matters. Winter was fast coming on, Bonaparte was hundreds of miles from his base, so dared advance no further on his own. Thus he was robbed of the finest spoils of victory and deprived of entering the Austrian capital in triumph until many years later.

When Napoleon was in Egypt and his Italian conquests had been overrun it was, after Masséna, Bernadotte who had played the major role in saving France from invasion; so he had become a popular hero.

When peace with Austria was signed, he had been sent as Ambassador to Vienna, and there hung the Tricolour out from his Embassy. The sight of the Republican flag had so infuriated the pro-monarchist people that a riot had ensued; but Bernadotte had come out on to the steps of the Embassy, sword in hand, and later the Austrian Government had been forced to apologise.

As Minister of War at the time of Napoleon's unauthorised return from Egypt, sensing that the ambitious little Corsican might make trouble, Bernadotte had proposed that he should be arrested and court-martialled as a deserter. But Napoleon's exploits had already made him such a national idol that the Government had feared to take so dangerous a step and that had led to its own downfall. As a staunch Revolutionary, Bernadotte alone of all the senior Generals, had refused to support Napoleon in the *coup d'état* of 18th *Brumaire* which, it could be foreseen, would lead to his becoming a Dictator.

The Jacobin faction that stood for Government by the People, Atheism and Equality in its fullest sense, had then still been very powerful; so, for a time, Napoleon had had to proceed with caution. Moreau, Lannes, Jourdan, Augereau and Bernadotte were all Jacobins, and it would have been dangerous to quarrel with these pala-

dins thrown up by the Revolution. It was largely for this reason that, in 1804, Napoleon included a number of them in his original creation of Marshals, and the cunning, inscrutable Bernadotte had been one of them.

In order to minimise opposition to his autocratic rule, Napoleon sent the Marshals he disliked and distrusted away from Paris. Bernadotte was made Governor of the important state of Hanover, and later other German territories were added to his Viceroyalty. He proved as able an administrator as he was a soldier, not only pacifying the considerable part of the new French Empire but bringing contentment and prosperity to its people.

He had thus made himself one of Napoleon's most valuable lieutenants. Moreover, he was almost one of the Imperial Family, because he had married Desirée, the younger daughter of a rich Marseilles silk merchant named Clary, and Julie, the elder daughter, had married Napoleon's eldest brother, Joseph. The tie was rendered even closer by the fact that, when a penniless young officer, Napoleon had been in love with and engaged to Desirée, and still had a strong affection for her.

Feeling, no doubt, that Desirée's handsome, subtle-minded husband had become one of the main props of his Empire, Napoleon decided to elevate him still further. To the fury of the other Marshals, who remained Dukes, when Napoleon made his invaluable Chief of Staff Berthier, Prince of Neuchâtel, he made Bernadotte Prince of Ponte Corvo, with a revenue of a million francs a year.

Despite his antipathy to the creation of a new upper class Bernadotte, unlike Lannes and Augereau, was a gentleman. His manners were faultless and he had great personal charm. He was greatly beloved by both his officers and men, and worked ceaselessly for their welfare. Prisoners who fell into his hands could also congratulate themselves, for he treated them with great

courtesy and took care to see that they enjoyed every reasonable comfort.

No-one could question the fact that he was among the most able of Napoleon's Marshals, but he was far from popular with the others, and more than once he had been accused of failing to support his colleagues in the field. A particularly flagrant case of this had occurred during the Prussian campaign of 1806. The irresolute and cowardly King Frederick William had, that autumn, at last been pushed by his military advisers Scharnhorst and Gniesenau into declaring war on France. They had under their hand what they believed to be the finest military machine in Europe: no less than the army trained by Frederick the Great.

With incredible swiftness Napoleon had marched against them and formed one of his superb concentrations in the neighbourhood of Jena. Believing the main body of the enemy to be immediately ahead of him, he despatched the corps of Davout and Bernadotte far out on his flank in an encircling movement, so that when he drove in the Prussian centre, the two Marshals would be able to fall upon and annihilate the retreating enemy.

But, for once, the Emperor had made a serious miscalculation. His attack at Jena was completely successful, but it was only one wing of the Prussian army that he had defeated. The greater part of it remained intact and fell back on Auerstadt, where it encountered Davout. Against overwhelming odds Davout's three divisions fought desperately all day. Bernadotte's corps was only four miles distant and he could not have failed to hear the guns blazing away at both Jena and Auerstadt; yet he came to the assistance neither of the Emperor nor, in spite of appeal after appeal, of Davout.

He had shrugged this off afterwards by saying that he had obeyed the Emperor's orders by remaining in the position to which his corps had been assigned. But every-

one was convinced that he had deliberately remained out of the battle because Davout was the Emperor's man, body and soul. For that reason he loathed Bernadotte and Bernadotte loathed him.

The Prussian Army was almost annihilated. Its remnants were pursued and butchered by Murat's cavalry. The other corps advanced by forced marches. Fortress after fortress fell, until the victorious French reached the Baltic. After only twenty-three days of battle Murat reported to the Emperor, 'The war is over, because there are no more Prussians left to fight.' Davout had earned undying glory and was made Duke of Auerstadt.

Bernadotte was a most fluent talker and held the table for a good part of the time while they made inroads into the oysters, lobster pasties, sturgeon in aspic, quails stuffed with foie gras, truffled capon and other delicacies provided by Talleyrand's chef, and washed them down with Montrachet and Château Latour. As there were few secrets from the men who were asked to the statesman's breakfast parties, the conversation at them was always fascinating; but on this occasion Roger's mind was so occupied with his own anxieties that he took little heed of it.

At last, to his great relief the other guests took their leave. Leaning on Roger's arm, Talleyrand led him into a small, richly furnished library, as he said, '*Cher ami*, it is an age since we met. Tell me, how has the world been treating you?'

'Well enough,' Roger replied, 'until recently. But now I am landed in a pretty mess. And I am come to crave your Exalted Highness' advice.'

The Prince lowered himself into an easy chair and waved Roger to another. 'You are, as ever, welcome to it.'

Roger then gave him a full account of his dealings with von Haugwitz, and their outcome. Talleyrand heard him out in silence, took a pinch of snuff, and said thoughtfully,

31

'This is certainly a bad business. Had you killed this unsavoury Baron in a duel, you'd have no cause to worry.
But murder is another matter. Your wife having been
found dead with him and your having made off with his,
provides such strong circumstantial evidence that one
can hardly doubt that you'd be convicted on it.'

'I know it. But what hope do you think I have of the
Emperor's giving me his protection?'

'In spite of your secret activities, you have served him
well in many ways, and he'll not hand over so old a
friend to the Prussians. But, seeing the Baron was own
brother to the Chief Minister of Prussia, he will almost
certainly feel it incumbent on him to make some gesture
of appeasement.'

'That is what I fear. And the prospect of kicking my
heels in a fortress for a year or two is damnably un-
attractive. Even more, I am concerned for the safety of
the Baroness; for she is of English birth and my life-long
friend.'

'On her account you have no need to worry. I will see
to it that no harm befalls her.'

'I was about to ask Your Highness' protection for her,
and I am more grateful than I can say.'

Talleyrand shrugged. ' 'Tis nothing. I'll send her to my
château of Valencey. To implicate me in his folly in
going into Spain, the Emperor has foisted on me there
that idiot ex-King Carlos and his licentious old Queen.
They are by no means the type of fellow guests I could
have chosen for your lady; but at least she will be safe
at Valencey from anyone knowing her to be English.
Your own situation is our real concern, and needs some
thought. Give me a while to think.'

Closing his heavily-lidded eyes, the man with the most
subtle brain in Europe remained motionless for a good
five minutes, then he opened his eyes and said, 'Somehow we must endeavour to make it appear that you killed

32

the Baron because you believed that doing so was in the service of the Emperor. Does the name von Stein mean anything to you?'

Roger nodded. 'He was a Minister in 1806, and one of the men who pushed Frederick William into going to war with France. After Jena he was the leading spirit in bringing about the regeneration of Prussia by the abolition of serfdom and many other liberal measures that made the common people feel that they now have a stake their country. His object, of course, was to arouse the patriotic feelings of the nation, so they would rise *en masse*, free themselves from the burden of taxation imposed by Napoleon and drive the French out of the territories stolen from Prussia after her defeat. Am I not right?'

'You are. But his zeal proved his undoing. The Emperor saw through his manœuvres, demanded that Frederick William should dismiss him, deprive him of his estates, outlaw him and, if caught, have him shot as an enemy of France. The spineless King complied. But Stein escaped to Bohemia and, from there is still inciting the Prussians to rise against us. I think we might make use of him.'

Stretching out a beruffled hand, Talleyrand tinkled a gold bell on his desk. When a secretary appeared, he proceeded to dictate a letter in French. It purported to be from the *Freiherr* von Stein to Ulrich von Haugwitz, and its contents implied that it formed part of a regular correspondence between them. The letter conveyed that von Haugwitz had for some time been opposed to the pro-French policy of his brother the Minister and that he was secretly in touch with other German nobles in his district who, among them, believed that they would be able to raise a force of two thousand men when the time was ripe to attempt to throw out the French.

When Talleyrand had done, he said to the secretary,

'Give that to Monsieur Oster. Tell him I wish him to translate it into German and write it out in their script.'

As soon as the secretary had left the room, Roger asked, 'How go things here? Are there any signs of this long armistice with Austria coming to an end?'

Talleyrand took another pinch of snuff, flicked the fallen grains from his lace cravat and nodded. 'Yes. The Emperor Francis has become weary of being kept out of his capital for so long, so he has at last given way to our major demands. As you know, I am in secret communication with Prince Metternich, and I received the news from him only yesterday. The Peace Treaty will be signed at Schönbrunn in the course of a week or so.'

'Then Britain will be the only nation left in arms against the Empire,' Roger remarked.

'Not quite. You forget Spain,' the Prince smiled. 'And I have considerable hopes that it is those ragged, nebulous hostilities in the Peninsula that will eventually break our little man's back.'

'You really think that likely?'

'I do. It is just on two years since Junot was sent into the Peninsula, and there has been fighting there, with a constant drain on French forces, ever since. If Napoleon had not panicked after he had put his brother Joseph on the throne of Spain, and returned to Paris because he believed that Fouché and I had joined forces with the object of bringing about his downfall, he might long since have brought the Spaniards to heel. But, as he then became occupied with his war against Austria, he had to leave the Peninsula to his Marshals. Some of them are very able men, but they are not used to this type of warfare in which everywhere the common people have taken up arms against us and fight with furious fanaticism. Moreover, during the past year the British have established themselves firmly there, and now a very

large army indeed would have to be sent to the Peninsula to drive them out.'

'Agreed. But now the war with Austria is over, that will have freed at least two hundred thousand men, and the Emperor could again go to Spain to direct operations.'

Talleyrand shook his head. 'I judge you wrong in that. The peace will, of course, free large numbers of troops, but so many must be retained to garrison the fortresses all over Europe and hold the Emperor's conquests down, that I greatly doubt if a sufficient reinforcement to make any material difference could be sent to Spain. As for our little man going there himself in the near future, I'd wager my Principality against it. His mind is no longer occupied by war. It is entirely absorbed in this prospect of a new marriage.'

'Then the divorce has been definitely decided upon? I gathered at Erfurt that he was seriously contemplating ridding himself of Josephine; and I am greatly distressed for her.'

'You count her, I know, a dear friend.' Talleyrand spread his long, beautifully-kept hands. 'But what would you? As long as he believed himself incapable of fathering a child, her position as Empress was secure. Since there can be no reasonable doubt that Elenore Denuelle's son was begotten by him, the situation is entirely changed. His dearest wish has long been to found a dynasty, and he is now so powerful that he contemplates adding still further to his grandeur by an alliance with one of the great Imperial houses.'

'We may, then, have as Empress a Hapsburg or Romanoff Princess?'

'It will be one or the other. Which, is still in the balance. He sounded the Czar at Erfurt; but Alexander fobbed him off by saying that his sister's marriage was a matter for her mother. Recently he has reopened the question

and is hoping that the Dowager Empress will give her consent. The alternative is Marie Louise of Austria, and both Metternich and I are pulling every string we can that would favour the match.'

Roger smiled. 'I know well Your Highness' antipathy to the Russians; and a closer alliance with them could mean yet another series of ruinous wars. The project formed at Tilsit would be revived. The two Emperors would almost certainly march against Turkey and divide the Sultan's dominions between them. Then Napoleon would set about his long-cherished plan for a descent on India.'

'That is exactly the danger as I foresee it, and whether or not he succeeded in driving the British out, the strain of such a vast campaign would prove the final ruin of France. Therefore, no opportunity must be lost to press both for the Austrian marriage and sow dissension between Napoleon and the Czar.'

For another half-hour the two old friends talked on, then the secretary brought in the forged letter. Handing it to Roger, Talleyrand said, 'How you bring this to his notice I must leave to your ingenuity. I can only pray that it will serve to excuse the part you have played in this most unfortunate affair.'

Having expressed his deep gratitude, Roger took his leave and returned to *La Belle Etoile*. There he found Georgina in Mère Blanchard's kitchen, showing her how to make the famous British dish, Cornish Pasties. Such condescension by a great lady, and to find that she was an accomplished cook, filled the good, buxom Norman woman with surprise, and a respectful devotion that she would not have given to a Queen.

They all made an excellent midday meal off the dish, followed by a fine variety of cheeses. Then Roger took Georgina up to their room and broke to her the dangers of their situation. Although he made as light of matters

as he reasonably could, over the years her mind had become so closely attuned to his that she sensed how gravely apprehensive he was about the outcome of his meeting with the Emperor.

She said that, should the worst happen, she meant to remain in Paris, on the chance that she could find some way to help him; as his freedom was more precious to her than her own. But he told her that he had secured Talleyrand's protection for her and eventually made her promise that she would place herself entirely in his friend's hands.

As he prepared to leave her, she suddenly thought of the crystal ball that she had brought with her jewels, and insisted that he should remain while she looked into it, in an endeavour to see what the future held for him. Getting it out, she set it up on a small table. They sat down in chairs on either side of it, and held each other's hands while she gazed into the smooth, shining sphere.

For a time they sat perfectly still and remained absolutely silent, while Georgina concentrated. At length, in her sight the ball misted over. The mist dissolved into slowly whirling wisps, then figures appeared in it.

Her big, dark eyes widened and she gave a sudden gasp of dismay. 'Oh, Roger, I see you in a cell and you are not in uniform, but . . . but in prisoner's clothes. A man is speaking to you. He is a parson . . . but not a Frenchman. My psychic sense tells me that this place is not France. You are in Germany and . . . oh, God! Can it be that you are in a condemned cell and . . . and being prepared to go to your death?'

Pushing the crystal from her, she burst into a flood of tears. Roger did his utmost to comfort her, but his efforts were of no avail. When she had become a little calmer, she begged him not to go to the Tuileries, but to leave her in Talleyrand's care and seek safety in immediate flight. Knowing that Georgina's predictions were rarely

wrong, he was greatly tempted to agree; but he hesitated because he knew that if he failed to report he would have burnt his boats. While he was still trying desperately to make up his mind which course to adopt, there came a knock at the door.

Roger opened it to find Maître Blanchard standing in the passage. The landlord bowed, 'I regret to disturb you, *Monsieur le Colonel,* but there is an officer below. He has a carriage waiting, and he says he has been sent to fetch you because the Emperor requires your presence.'

With a nod Roger closed the door and, giving a pale smile, turned back to Georgina. Taking her in his arms, he said softly, 'There is no escaping fate, dear love, and it looks as though I have tempted it once too often. But I beg you not to despair. Maybe I'll cheat it once again. And now, before I go to meet whatever is in store for me, I pray you grant me a boon. It is something that beyond all else will inspire me to fight death. Do I succeed in surviving this peril and get safely back to England, will you marry me?'

The tears streaming down her lovely cheeks, she nodded. 'Roger, my own. How could I possibly refuse you? I have been the veriest fool to reject you for so long.'

Ten minutes later he had joined the officer who had been sent for him, and was on his way to the Tuileries.

CHAPTER IV

ROGER FACES THE EMPEROR

La Belle Etoile lay in the Rue de l'Arbre Sec, which was in the oldest part of Paris, to the east of the Louvre. The streets there were narrow, with the wood-framed upper storeys of the houses projecting beyond the gutters. There were no pavements, and the cobbled ways were a seething mass of people, dashing beneath horses' heads or squeezing themselves against the walls to make way for drays and coaches, which could proceed only at a foot pace and were frequently brought to a halt.

It took the carriage in which Roger sat with his escort nearly a quarter of an hour to reach the Place du Louvre; but, having crossed it, they were able to drive at a better pace down the broader thoroughfare that ran alongside the Palace and, not long since, renamed the Rue de Rivoli in honour of Napoleon's victory.

Beyond the Louvre lay the big garden where, on the terrible 10th August 1791, the first scene of the Terror had been enacted by the massacre of Louis XVI's Swiss Guard. Turning left into it, the carriage pulled up in front of the Palais de Tuileries. Two minutes later, Roger was mounting the splendid grand staircase, up which he had often so gaily gone to participate in magnificent fêtes and Imperial ceremonies.

The fact that he had not been asked to surrender his sword and so was not actually under arrest, caused him

some relief; but he was far from taking that as a sign that he had nothing to fear. At the door of the big ante-chamber on the first floor, his escort, with whom he had exchanged no more than a courteous greeting, handed him over to the Chamberlain-in-Waiting, and left him.

In the lofty white and gold salon, a number of people, mostly officers, were sitting about or talking in small groups. Roger knew a number of them, but had too much on his mind to wish to enter on idle conversation; so, after nodding to a few acquaintances, he sat down on a *fauteuil* at the far end of the room.

He had not been there long when Duroc, Marshal of the Emperor's Palaces and Camps, came into the room to speak to the big, black-bearded General Montbrun who, with Lasalle, St. Croix and Colbert was, after Murat, one of Napoleon's four finest cavalry leaders.

The Marshal was one of Roger's oldest friends. Getting up, he crossed the room toward him. When Duroc had finished talking to the General, he turned, raised his eyebrows and exclaimed with pleasure :

'How good to see you, *mon cher ami*. I had no idea that you were in Paris.'

'You surprise me,' Roger replied. 'I got back only yesterday. But the Emperor has sent for me, and I felt certain you would be able to inform me of the reason.'

'No. He has made no mention of you to me.'

'What sort of mood is he in today?'

'There has been nothing so far to put him out of temper. But he is, of course, as busy as usual; so it will probably be an hour or two before he sees you.'

'I suppose he and Berthier are hard at it making plans to put an end to the trouble in Spain?

'Oh, no. He is not worrying himself on that score. He still regards it as no more than risings here and there by ill-armed rabbles, stiffened by an English army of no great size. It now looks as though a peace with Austria

will soon be signed. Then he'll be able to withdraw his legions and send an army of a hundred thousand men to clean up the Peninsula. But you must forgive me now, as I have much to do. Unless he sends you off on some mission, we must agree a night to dine together.'

When Roger returned to his chair, he was in two minds whether or not to be pleased that a long wait lay ahead of him. On the one hand he was anxious to get his audience over, and so learn the worst; on the other he had had little time to think out how he could most effectively use the forged letter, and the delay would give him a chance to do so.

He had been pondering the matter for three-quarters of an hour when Marshal Brune came in and took a seat near him. Brune was the son of a lawyer: a well-educated man with literary pretensions, who prided himself particularly on his poetry; but it was so indifferent that he had had to buy a printing press to get it printed. Like Lannes, Augereau and Bernadotte, he regretted the ending of government by the people, so was not well regarded by Napoleon. Unlike those Marshals, he had little ability as a soldier, and his only claim to military fame had been in 1799 when Bonaparte was in Egypt.

Bonaparte's absence had led to the loss of Italy, and France had been threatened with invasion from both the east and north. Masséna had held the bastion of Switzerland and won undying fame by defeating the Russians under the redoubtable Suvarov; while Brune had been despatched to repulse an English army that had landed in Holland. It had been commanded by the hopelessly inefficient Duke of York, and at Alkmaar Brune had compelled him to surrender. But every General knew that, given sufficient troops, any fool could have done that.

Nevertheless, the public had acclaimed him a hero, so Napoleon had thought it politic to include him in the original creation of Marshals; but there his elevation

had stopped short. When the other Marshals, with the exception of Jourdan, Serurier and Perignon, had been made Dukes, Brune had received no title. Many people believed that this omission was due to his having, while Governor of Hamburg, gravely offended Napoleon by referring to himself as a Marshal of France, instead of a Marshal of the Empire. In recent years he had been employed mainly on administrative duties.

Greeting Roger pleasantly, he remarked anxiously, 'I would I could guess why our master has sent for me. I hope to God it is not to despatch me with a corps into Spain.'

'Indeed,' Roger replied noncommittally, still occupied by his own uneasy forebodings. 'I would have thought that after all this time you would have welcomed a command in the field.'

Brune passed his hand over his tall, bald forehead. 'I would; but not in Spain. The war there is not war as we understand it. Every hand there is against us. Rather than let us buy their food and fodder, the peasants burn them. Even the children are used to carry intelligence to the English, so that General Wellesley is kept informed of our every move, which makes it impossible for us ever to take him by surprise. Our armies are isolated, each hundreds of miles from the others, and separated by countless thousands of murderous brigands. They take no prisoners. Instead, they flay or roast alive any Frenchman they can catch. The women are as bad as the men, and at times pretend friendliness in order to poison our troops. It is certain death for fewer than a score of our men to venture a few miles from their camps. Do you know, if one General wishes to send a message to another, he now has to provide his courier with an escort of two hundred horse to make certain of his reaching his destination?'

Roger nodded. 'How awful for our people. I had not realised that things were quite so bad as that. But I gather

that Austria is on the verge of agreeing a peace. Once that is signed, the Emperor will be able to send a great army into Spain and subdue it.'

'You think so? Well, perhaps you are right, but I doubt it. No-one would dispute his genius. I tell you, though, the war there is utterly unlike those he hás been accustomed to waging. He has always relied for his victories on skilful combinations with each unit reaching its appointed place on time before the opening of a battle. To do so in Spain is an impossibility. That clever little devil, Berthier, can pore over his maps and get out schedules of march till his great head bursts like a pricked balloon; but it will be all to no purpose, because Spain is cut up by a dozen ranges of high mountains, and there are no roads by which guns and baggage trains can cross them.'

Having been in Spain himself on several occasions, Roger knew that the tall, gloomy Marshal was right, and that even Napoleon would have to surpass himself to subdue all resistance in the Peninsula. They talked on for a while about the state of Europe generally, until Brune was summoned to the presence. Roger sat on for another hour; then, at last, he in turn was called on to face the unpredictable Corsican.

A corporal of the Old Guard stood rigidly on either side of the tall, gilded, double doors. The Chamberlain-in-Waiting tapped sharply on the parquet with his white wand of office; two footmen in liveries bespangled with golden bees and eagles threw the doors open and, as Roger was announced, he advanced into the great room, his head held high, his befeathered hat under his arm.

At the far end, the Emperor was pacing slowly to and fro, his hands clasped behind his back, his big head thrust a little forward. He was dressed, as usual, in the white and green uniform of the Guides, and presented a very different figure from that when Roger had first met him at the

43

siege of Toulon. Then, he had been a lean-faced scraggy fellow, with long, untidy hair, wearing a shabby uniform, who appeared hardly more than a youth and was remarkable only for his aggressive jaw and dark, flashing eyes. Now he looked much older than his age. He was scrupulously clean, and his hair was cut short. Both his unnaturally pallid face and his body had filled out. He had become corpulent and stooped a little when he was not consciously holding himself erect in public. His powerful jaw remained his most prominent feature, and his fine eyes held their old intensity, as he suddenly turned his head and snapped at Roger :

'Well, Monsieur Casanova Breuc! What have you to say for yourself?'

Roger had already bowed three times as he crossed the room. Smiling, he bowed again. 'Nothing, Your Imperial Majesty, except that I am happy to have been received again into your august presence.'

'Ha! As smooth-tongued as ever, eh! But this time your honeyed words will not save you. You have indulged in your eternal pursuit of women once too often.'

For years past Napoleon's constant infidelities to Josephine had been notorious; so Roger said amiably, 'It is a pleasure, Sire, in which I have endeavoured to emulate you.'

Napoleon's broad forehead creased in a frown. 'You impudent rascal! How dare you compare your licentiousness with my occasional peccadilloes? I am a man apart, and carrying the burden of Empire, have every right to seek such relaxation.'

'By "endeavour", Sire, I meant only to pay you a compliment. I have to exert myself mightily to succeed with women; where it needs only a glance from Your Majesty for them to swoon with delight and fall into your arms.'

'Enough of this! To obtain your ends by murder places you beyond the pale.'

'Murder!' Roger exclaimed in feigned surprise. 'What mean you, Sire? I have done no murder.'

'Liar! Augereau was here this forenoon and told me all. In order that you could make off with the Baron von Haugwitz's wife, you killed him; and your own wife into the bargain.'

'They met their deaths by accident, Sire, although I'll admit that I was responsible for bringing that about. As for the Baron's wife, she is an old friend of mine, and the least I could do was to escort her away from the scene of the tragedy, lest she be accused of having had a hand in it.'

'You admit then that you brought about their deaths?'

'I do. But you must know me well enough to be certain that never would I have done such a thing had it not been in your service.'

'Ha! The same old plea that you have so often made to excuse your wild escapades and neglect of your duties. I'll hear no more.'

'I protest, Sire! I have ever served you well, and in this matter have done so yet again. Since you rightly pride yourself upon your sense of justice, you must hear me out.'

'Speak then, but be brief.'

'Your Majesty may recall that, while at Erfurt, you gave me leave so that I might pay a visit to Schloss Langenstein. While I was there, Prince Metternich came one day to luncheon. Afterwards, I chanced to overhear a brief conversation between the Prince and the Baron, which led me to believe that the latter was secretly an enemy of France. With the intention of endeavouring to verify my suspicions, I went on another visit to the Schloss in mid-September. On my second night there, when everyone had retired, I stole along to the Baron's cabinet and

went through his papers. Among them I found a letter incriminating him up to the hilt.

'I must now reveal to you the truth about my wife. She turned out to be a most evil woman. The black infant she gave birth to while we were at Erfurt was not the result of rape, but of her having given herself willingly while in Brazil to a Negro slave. Although I would admit this to no-one but yourself, on her return to Europe she *trompéd* me with numerous men, among them von Haugwitz.

'The Baron's cabinet was adjacent to his bedroom. She had been in there with him, but came out to return to her own room just as I was abstracting this incriminating letter from his files. I attempted to stifle her cries before she could bring her lover on the scene, but failed. Among her crimes was the appalling one that, in my presence, she had knifed her own father in the back and killed him. Knowing her ferocity, and that I stood little chance of overcoming both her and von Haugwitz, if they attacked me together, I struck her senseless. Next moment, the Baron was upon me. Fortunately, he had been drinking heavily. One blow to the jaw and he fell senseless to the floor.'

'What then was I to do with their two unconscious bodies? By ancient right, the Baron maintained in the Schloss a small bodyguard under the orders of his steward, Big Karl. When they learned what I had done, they would certainly have killed me. The only possible course was to hide the bodies and tell Big Karl in the morning that the two of them had gone out early to see the vintagers at work, then make off as swiftly as I could, with the Baroness.

'For that they had to be kept quiet until we had got well away. Had I gagged them they might have suffocated; so I found some laudanum in a medicine cupboard and drugged them both. Then I carried their bodies

down to the *weinstube* and lowered them to the bottom of one of the big wine presses, feeling confident that they would not be found there, but regain consciousness by midday.

'The Baroness and I succeeded in escaping to Coblenz. It was not until forty-eight hours later that we learned that I had drugged them too heavily, and they had been crushed to death under a load of grapes.'

With set face the Emperor had listened to Roger's account. Now he burst out, 'Liar! Liar! Liar! I know of old your ability to invent specious excuses for your doings. 'Tis a tissue of lies from start to finish. I'd wager a million francs that you could not produce that letter.'

'Then you would lose your wager, Sire,' Roger retorted sharply, and he took the letter from his pocket, adding, 'It is from the *Freiherr* von Stein.'

'What! That recalcitrant German cur!' Napoleon exclaimed. 'Give it me! Give it me!' And he snatched the parchment.

Swiftly he ran his eye over it. Seeing it was in German, he read it through twice, until he had fully grasped its contents. Then he threw it on the floor and stamped upon it, cursing furiously.

'May hell take these *Deutschlanders*. The trouble the swine give me is endless. I make a treaty with their King and *crapauds* like Stein have the insolence to set the people against it. Von Haugwitz's friends will raise two thousand men, will they? This is conspiracy. It will not be war but rebellion. I'll hang every one of them. I'll line the banks of the Rhine with their dangling corpses.'

Roger gave an inward sigh of relief. Unless matters now took some unforeseen twist, Talleyrand's trick had worked. Two minutes later, his new optimism was confirmed. Recovering his temper, Napoleon said:

'Clearly, it was your life or that of this scum. Since he was a traitor, he had already forfeited it. By your action

47

you did no more than anticipate the sentence of a Court. As for your wife, she was a most ravishing creature; but, from what you tell me, a positive demon in human form. In attacking you as she did, she brought her death upon herself. You are well rid of her.'

Roger bowed. 'I thank Your Majesty for your renewed confidence in me. I am, however, still troubled by one possibility. Seeing that Baron Ulrich was own brother to the Chief Minister of Prussia, the Prussians may make an issue of it, and request you to hand me over to them. Even should they not, I'd still be in danger should you at some future time send me on a mission into Germany.'

'Have no fears on that score. I will send an instruction to the Prussian Ambassador, Baron von Brockhausen. I'll say that he is to inform his Government that I am averse to any further investigation into the Schloss Langenstein affair; and that any proceedings being taken against you are to be quashed.'

'I thank you, Sire. And now I have a request to make. This last business has placed a considerable strain upon me, and you know of old that my weak chest requires that I spend as much as possible of the winter in the sunshine. I pray you allow me leave to proceed to the South of France.'

The Emperor stared at him in surprise. 'But 'tis scarce yet October. And you have already been away from me for too long. Unlike the majority of my *beaux sabreurs,* you are a well-educated man and have brains in your head. I've found you useful to me in a thousand ways. No, no! A week or so before Christmas will be time enough for you to go nurse your health. Now that a peace with Austria is as good as concluded, I'll be sending an army south to put an end to this Spanish nonsense. You have often assisted the Prince of Neuchâtel to work out troop movements. Report to him tomorrow morning. And now, *au revoir.'*

It had been worth trying for immediate leave, although Roger had thought it unlikely that he would get it. And there could be no arguing about the matter. Drawing himself to attention, he made his three bows and backed out of the room, only too thankful to be still a free man.

As an A.D.C. of the Emperor, he was entitled at any time to take a horse, and mounts were always being walked up and down outside the Palace, in case one was required by a courier carrying an urgent despatch. As the swiftest means of rejoining Georgina, Roger took a chestnut from the nearest groom, then imperilled the lives of several pedestrians on his way back to *La Belle Etoile.*

Georgina's joy knew no bounds when she learned that they no longer had anything to fear, except the not very likely possibility of her being recognised and denounced as formerly English. But it was a danger that had to be guarded against, and Roger said to her :

'As you know, Napoleon believes me to suffer from a weak chest, so grants me leave to spend a part of most winters at my little château at St. Maxime. It is while I am supposed to be there that I have often made my secret trips to England; and, for a moment, I hoped that by again practising this deception I could get you home. But as it is still autumn, the Emperor would have none of it. I must remain here on duty, but I am anxious to have you out of Paris, and I think I have hit on a means of doing so. Now I must wait on Talleyrand, and thank him for what he has done for me.'

'Oh, Roger,' she protested. 'Must we part so soon? I would as lief remain here with you; and the chances of my being recognised would be virtually nil if I spent all my time up here in one room. That I will do most willingly for the joy of our being able to spend our nights together.'

He smiled down on her. 'I pray you be patient, dear

love. Give me an hour or two and maybe I'll have a way by which we may both eat our cake yet keep it.'

Hastening to the Rue du Bac, he enquired for the Prince. Talleyrand was at home and, after a short delay, received him. Greeting Roger with a happy smile, he said :

'*Mon vieux,* congratulations. The fact that you are still free tells me that our ruse succeeded.'

'Indeed it did,' Roger laughed, 'and I am once more eternally your debtor.' Then he gave an account of his audience with Napoleon. When he had done, he added :

'And now I have to ask Your Highness yet another favour. That is, if you still have your *petite maison* out at Passy. Should my fair lady remain in Paris, there is the risk that she may run into someone who knew her as the Countess of St. Ermins. But, could we for a while make that charming house our refuge, out there she would be in no danger.'

Talleyrand waved a beruffled hand. '*Cher ami,* you are most welcome to do so. By occupying it for me during a great part of the Terror, you prevented the house from being confiscated and its contents looted by some mob. Ever since I have regarded the place as being as much yours as mine. I wish you and your charmer a very happy sojourn there.'

A quarter of an hour later, Roger was again on his way back to Georgina. When he told her of this solution to their problem, and that they could look forward to several weeks in a charming love-nest, she could hardly contain her delight.

As Georgina's predictions had previously always proved well founded, they were puzzled that, in this case, her vision seen in the crystal was no longer a cause for apprehension. Having talked it over, they came to the conclusion that, in this case, she must have gone backward, instead of forward, in time, and seen him when,

some years previously, he had been imprisoned in England and the prison chaplain had, at times, visited him in his cell.

That evening, after a last glass of wine with the Blanchards, they drove out in a hired coach to Passy: an outlying suburb of Paris that lay in the direction of St. Cloud.

Passy was a pretty village of farms and attractive little houses in which, in pre-Revolution days, nobles used to keep ballerinas and the ladies of the Comédie Française. In those times Talleyrand had been far from rich and had made one of the houses his home. There, at his buffet parties, Roger had met many men who were later to become famous: Mirabeau, Louis de Narbonne, Mathieu de Montmorency, among them, and heard them talk enthusiastically of the Liberal Revolution by which they planned to bring democracy to the French people.

The little house was looked after by a couple named Velot. During the Terror, Roger had paid their wages and, in those dark days when food was scarce and expensive, seen to it that they lacked for nothing. In consequence, they had become devoted to him, and looked after his welfare as though he were a cherished son.

The Velots were old now, but they received Roger and Georgina with surprise and joy. Madame Velot killed a chicken, and got out her most treasured preserves for their supper; while her husband lit a fire in the best bedroom and filled warming pans for the big bed. An hour and a half later, the two life-long lovers lay in it, naked, embraced and without a care in the world.

CHAPTER V

THE IMPERIAL DIVORCE

NEXT morning Roger duly reported to Marshal Berthier, Prince de Neuchâtel. The only virtue of this ugly little man, whose head was too big for his body, and who made himself ridiculous by wearing fantastic uniforms of his own design, was that, in all history, no soldier had ever equalled him as an efficient Chief of Staff. His great, top-heavy head was packed with facts and figures. He could, from day to day, give the effective strength of every division in the Army, and the position of every unit. He could plan the movement of vast masses of troops across hundreds of miles of country, without their jamming the roads or running short of food and ammunition. At the criticial stage of a campaign, he was capable of going without sleep for several days on end. As he was habitually rude and dictatorial to the other Marshals, all of whom were junior to him, he was far from popular. But, knowing Roger to be a level-headed and competent assistant, he greeted him with a fair show of politeness.

The following day the Emperor set off for Vienna, as usual travelling at great speed, with frequent relays of picked horses. As he was not going on a campaign, he left Berthier behind him, to plan the transfer from Austria of the divisions that had been earmarked for Spain. This meant for Roger many hours spent working out endless calculations; but he managed to find time to pay his re-

spects to such members of the Imperial Family as were in Paris.

First he waited on Josephine. On one occasion she had saved his life, and on another saved him from imprisonment; while on two occasions he had saved her marriage, so they were very close friends and, in private, she always treated him without ceremony. As he felt certain that by now she must know that she was to be divorced, he had dreaded her raising the subject, but she made no mention of it. On the other hand, as Lisala had been one of Josephine's ladies-in-waiting, before his departure Napoleon had told her about the affair at Schloss Langenstein, so she made him give her a full account of it. When he had done so, she said:

'What ill fortune for you that you should have married such a terrible woman. Of course, I greatly admired her beauty; but there was something about those big, widely-spaced eyes she had that made me vaguely distrustful of her. I am so glad that you are now free, and hope that you may soon find another wife more worthy of you.'

His next call was on *Madame Mère*. Napoleon's mother was a tall, gaunt, once-handsome woman, deeply religious, and parsimonious from the belief that her great son's Empire might not last; so that one day he and her other children would need the money she saved out of the huge income he gave her. She had great courage, despised all pomp, was very shrewd, but of limited intelligence and lived only for her family. Many people dreaded her sharp tongue, but she had always treated Roger pleasantly.

Joseph, the Emperor's elder brother, was in Spain. He had, until the summer of 1808, been King of Naples, but Napoleon had sent for him and, without even asking him, insisted on his mounting the Spanish throne.

Of the younger brothers, the firebrand Lucien had quarrelled with Napoleon and was living in self-imposed

exile in Rome. Louis, having been pushed unwillingly into marrying Josephine's only daughter, Hortense de Beau-harnais, had been made King of Holland; while the youngest, Jerome, was now King of Westphalia.

However, two of Napoleon's sisters were in Paris: Caroline and Pauline. Caroline was the wife of the dashing cavalry leader, Joachim Murat, who had replaced Joseph on the throne of Naples. She was by far the cleverest of the family: a scheming, boundlessly ambitious woman, with pretensions to being knowledgeable about literature. She owned a unique collection of bawdy books.

Pauline, the beauty of the family, was as licentious as she was lovely. She was Napoleon's favourite sister and the only one of the brood who had a real affection for him. She had had many lovers; and, seven years earlier, Roger had had a hectic affaire with her. It had ended with her marriage to Prince Borghese and, to her fury, being ordered by Napoleon to live with her husband in Italy. For some while she had been back in Paris, and lived in a magnificent mansion, which she had furnished with great taste; but her health had been undermined by a disease she had contracted while in San Domingo, and Roger found her sadly changed.

As every member of the Bonaparte family, with the exception of Napoleon, detested Josephine on account of her superior birth, both the Princesses retailed to Roger with high delight all the rumours they had heard, which now made it as good as certain that their brother intended to divorce her.

On October 14th, the Peace of Schönbrunn was signed, by Champaguy, Duc de Cadore, who had succeeded Talleyrand as Foreign Minister, and Prince Metternich; by the 20th Napoleon was back in France and arrived at Fontainebleau. With him came the news that, while at Schönbrunn, a young fanatic named Staps had attempted to assassinate him. Before the attempt could made,

Colonel Count Rapp had taken from the youth a long knife. Staps, who was perfectly sane, had then shouted that Napoleon was the curse of his Fatherland and, when offered pardon, told the Emperor that, if freed, he would again try to kill him.

At Fontainebleau, poor Josephine's marriage received its mortal blow. When she was about to go to her husband's bedroom, she found that he had had a doorway in the passage leading to it bricked up.

Now that the peace had at last been signed, there was a whole series of official celebrations, and *Le Moniteur* gazetted a long list of honours. For their special services in the campaign, Prince of Wagram was added to Berthier's titles, and Davout, Duc d'Auerstadt was made Prince d'Eckmühl, while Masséna was raised to Prince d'Essling.

The Kings of Holland, Westphalia and Naples all came to Paris, and many other royalties who now owed allegiance to Napoleon. But for these splendid fêtes, parades and fireworks the ordinary people no longer showed their old enthusiasm. Even the double celebration on November 25th of the anniversary of the Emperor's coronation and the victory of Austerlitz failed to draw from the crowds the frantic cheering with which the Emperor had been greeted in former years.

Roger's position as a friend of numerous people close to the Emperor enabled him to keep abreast with the moves in the matter that was now uppermost in everybody's mind. On November 30th, Napoleon and Josephine parted. Their leave-taking was prolonged, and heart-rending on both sides.

She had married him only because she had been persuaded to do so by her former lover, the then powerful Barras. After only a single night with her, Napoleon had been compelled to set out to take over the command of the Army of Italy, and she had promptly been unfaithful

to him. Again, during the many months he had spent in Egypt, she had carried on openly an affair with a handsome army contractor, named Hippolyte Charles. Yet, later she had come to love her husband deeply, and was caused great distress by his infidelities.

He, on the other hand, during the early years of their marriage had loved her to distraction and, although he had arrogated to himself the right to take as a mistress any woman who temporarily appealed to him, he had never ceased to sleep with her frequently, and often she read him to sleep.

He had elevated her to the position of the First Lady in Europe, grudged her nothing and smothered her with jewels. For her part, she had been an immense help to him because, as an ex-aristocrat, she had been capable of reigning over his Court with dignity, graciousness and charm.

At their parting he had not disguised the fact that he was desperately loath to put her from him, and did so only because he could not bring himself to forgo his ambition to form a dynasty. She was to receive a huge pension and live at Malmaison, the beautiful private home that she had nearly ruined him by buying while he was abroad and still only young General Bonaparte.

Even so, Roger wondered how she would manage to maintain it, for she was boundlessly extravagant. It had been estimated that, during the five years she had been Empress, she had spent the equivalent of a quarter of a million pounds on clothes alone.

On December 16th, the Senate formally decreed the divorce.

That night Roger again asked his master for leave to go to the South of France, and it was granted; so having spent the following day tidying up the work on which he had been employed, and drawing a considerable sum from

the Paymaster's office, he drove out to Passy in a high good humour.

During the past seven weeks, his attendance on the Emperor at State functions, gala nights at the Opera and balls given by numerous Ambassadors, had prevented him from being with Georgina as frequently as he would have wished. But he had managed to spend two or three nights a week with her. Realising his situation, she had not complained, but resigned herself to the quiet life, made pleasant by every comfort the good Velots could devise for her, and amused herself by again taking up her hobby of painting.

Now, on hearing Roger's news, she joyfully embraced him and cried happily, 'At last, then, we shall be able to spend all our days together, and soon get back to England!'

Kissing her fondly, he replied, 'Yes, my love. We'll be together; but I have other plans for our immediate future, should you approve them. 'Tis now much too late for us to get home for Christmas and, much as you long to see your Charles, within a few weeks he will be returning to Eton. At this time of year England, with its cold, rain and mud, is a dreary place. Why, therefore, should we hurry to it when, instead, we could enjoy the sunshine at my little château near St. Maxime?'

After considering for a moment, she said, 'Dear Roger, you are right. 'Twill be a splendid opportunity to enjoy a honeymoon before, instead of after we are married.'

Next day in Paris he paid farewell visits to Talleyrand and a number of his other friends. He also called on an ex-brother A.D.C., the Comte de Lavelette, who had been made Minister of Posts, and asked him to expedite a letter he had written the previous night. It was to a couple named Dufour who, although he went to his little château very infrequently, he had arranged to have paid a good salary regularly, to keep the place in order for

57

him. In the letter he said that he would shortly be arriving with his wife, and that everything must be made ready for their reception.

On the 18th they said good-bye to the Velots and set off in a comfortable travelling coach that Roger had bought the day before. Their route lay through Fontainebleau, Auxerre, Châlons, Lyons, Valence, Avignon and Aix, then by the inland road that ran parallel to the coast in the direction of Nice. The distance was something over five hundred miles, but they travelled by easy stages, so that they had time to visit the buildings of historic interest in the cities through which they passed. The inns at which they stayed were comfortable and, as since the days of Louis XIV the French had been famed for their cooking, Georgina enjoyed for the first time many of the excellent local dishes.

But there were several occasions on which she was saddened by what was happening in the towns and villages. Moncey's *gendarmes*, assisted by troops who cordoned off inhabited areas, were ruthlessly hunting down deserters. Youngsters and quite elderly men alike were being dragged from houses and farms, and hauled off to the nearest barracks, regardless of the tears and pathetic pleading of their women folk. Even a game leg from an old wound received in battle, or the loss of one eye, did not save them from enforced re-enlistment as cannon fodder for the Emperor.

When they reached their destination, the Dufours greeted them cheerfully, and they had proved good stewards during Roger's long absence. The house was clean and orderly, the furniture had been kept polished and they had filled every available vase with carnations. With appreciation, but furtively, they eyed the beautiful Georgina; for the last time Roger had brought a lady to the house as his 'wife', she had been, although they had remained ignorant of her true identity, the equally lovely

Princess Pauline, not long since the widow of her first husband, General Leclerc.

They had arrived on the last day of December, so were able to celebrate the coming in of the year 1810 with a dish of freshly-caught lobsters, forced asparagus and peaches, washed down with a magnum of champagne. Both of them were in excellent health and took such joy of each other that they remained in bed together for the whole of New Year's Day.

Next morning, when Roger took his beloved round his small domain, she was delighted with it. There was no garden in the English sense, but masses of flowers, a hot-house in which an old gardener grew peaches and pine-apples, orange, lemon and mandarin trees on which the fruit was already ripening, and a little vineyard. A still greater attraction was the blue sea dappled with sunshine, and the long beach of golden sand which, as the house lay some distance from the town, was nearly always deserted.

Roger had always sent generous contributions to the local charities, and the church. Moreover, as one of the Emperor's A.D.C.s and a hero of the Army, the people of the district accounted it an honour that, at times, he should reside among them. In consequence, he was informed by Dufour that the citizens of St. Maxime intended to come out to the château and welcome his new wife. The same thing had happened when he had brought Pauline there, and he had awaited the demonstration with considerable anxiety; but fortunately no-one had realised that she was Napoleon's sister. Preparations were hastily put in hand : a large supply of food got in, a cask of good wine from the vineyard broached, and tables set up on the terrace, which had a fine view of the bay.

In due course the crowd, headed by the Mayor and the Curé, arrived. Addresses of welcome were read by both, and a little girl presented to Georgina a huge bou-

quet. Roger replied, and took the occasion to announce that he and his wife were on their honeymoon, so wished to be excused from offering or accepting any invitations. This in no way damped the cheerfulness of his self-invited guests. A good time was had by all, and it was not until late in the evening that the last of them, a little unsteady after the amount of wine they had consumed, happily took their departure.

The lovers then entered on a halcyon existence. For over eight weeks they lazed in the sunshine, strolled hand in hand among the vineyards and olive groves, rode up into the hills, or picnicked on the beach. Long ago, as a boy at Lymington, Roger had mastered the art of sailing, so he bought a small yacht and they went in her on expeditions to towns and villages along the coast. Both of them were well read, and had travelled widely, so they never lacked things to talk about, or episodes in their past to laugh over. During those long weeks in which, night and day, they had only each other for company, Georgina became convinced that Roger had proved his contention that, now they were older, they would never tire of each other; and she looked forward happily to their being married when they got back to England.

It was early in March that an event occurred which caused Roger considerable perturbation. A courier arrived from the Emperor. Such a thing had never happened before and, had it done so while he was supposed to be at St. Maxime but was actually away on one of his secret trips to England, his absence could have proved far from easy to explain.

The contents of the despatch also gave him much food for thought. It was in Napoleon's own almost illegible scrawl, and briefly conveyed that he was worried about Josephine. Apparently the officer whom he had appointed to act as the Comptroller of her Household at Malmaison had proved far from satisfactory, and she had asked if

Roger could replace him. Anxious to please her, Napoleon had granted her request, with the proviso that he could spare Roger for only a few months, until she was more satisfactorily settled. He then ordered Roger to return to Paris, in order to take up his new post as speedily as possible.

This summons placed Roger in a nasty quandary. He had intended, later in the month, to take Georgina across to Bordeaux and, in a village somewhere along the coast there, find a smuggler who would run them across the Channel. But could he, with any decency, deny the consolation of his friendship to the unhappy Josephine?

That night he discussed the situation fully with Georgina. Being of a most generous nature, she said that, as the appointment was to be only for a few months, he must do as he had been asked, and that she would remain on at St. Maxime until he could rejoin her.

He accepted her view that he must leave her for a while; but was worried that her return home would be so long delayed. After some thought he hit upon an idea that would enable her to leave France more speedily. The British Navy, being dominant in the Mediterranean, constantly patrolled the coast from Gibraltar to Genoa, and hardly a day passed without one of the patrolling frigates passing within sight of St. Maxime. If he could put her aboard one of them, when it next put in to Gibraltar for supplies it could land her there and, as the one-time Countess of St. Ermins, he had little doubt that the Admiral in command would give her passage in another ship to carry her to England.

Three days elapsed before a ship came close enough in for her to be reached without undue risk and, fortunately, at midday the wind dropped to hardly a breeze; so for the afternoon she lay about three miles offshore, almost becalmed.

As Roger was anxious that no-one in the town should

see him put Georgina aboard, they waited until an hour or so before twilight was due to fall before leaving the house. Early in the afternoon he had made certain through his telescope that the frigate was British; Georgina had then packed most of the clothes he had bought for her while she was living at Passy and, having told the Dufours that they were going for a trip in the yacht, they had carried the bags down to her.

With the approach of evening, the usual breeze from the land caused the sails of the ship to fill a little, and she began to put on way. But Roger was not displeased as, without the breeze, he could not have sailed his yacht, and he felt confident that he could overhaul the frigate. Before they hoisted the anchor they took a long, tender farewell of one another, but Georgina put a brave face on their parting, and the yacht was soon churning up a ripple at her bow.

It took them over two hours to come up within hailing distance of the frigate, but that suited Roger well, as he did not want to run even the slight risk of one of the officers on board recognising him as Mr. Brook. To reduce the possibility to a minimum, he had put on his oldest sailing clothes, and it was now nearly dark.

The watch answered Roger's hail; then a lengthy exchange took place, during which the Captain came on deck. At first he was most reluctant to take a female aboard; but, on being assured that she was the Countess of St. Ermins, a well-known beauty who had many influential friends, he decided that it was better not to risk a reprimand from his superiors for having refused to assist her to escape from enemy territory.

At length a breeches buoy was let down, Roger lashed Georgina firmly into it, then she was hauled up. He had lowered the sails of his yacht and now sat down in the stern while she gently rocked. After waving Georgina away, he sadly watched the ship until she had dis-

appeared into the darkness. He then hoisted sail and turned the yacht in the direction of St. Tropez, where he intended to sleep that night.

The following afternoon he told the Dufours that their mistress had received news that a member of her family was dangerously ill; so she had had to leave for Marseilles at a moment's notice. Next morning, with a heavy heart, he took the road to Paris.

CHAPTER VI

A NEW MISSION

WHEN, on the 12th March, Roger reached the capital, he found it agog with excitement over the Emperor's approaching marriage, and was glad to learn that the bride was to be the Archduchess Marie Louise of Austria, the nineteen-year-old daughter of the Emperor Francis.

The Russian alliance, entered into with such enthusiasm by the Czar in the summer of 1808, when the two Emperors had met on a raft in the middle of the river Niemen at Tilsit to agree an armistice, had never been popular with a great part of the Russian nobility; and later, when the two Emperors had met again at Erfurt, Alexander—a mental as well as a born autocrat—had baulked at the suggestion of giving his sister to a Corsican upstart. Finally, to avoid offending Napoleon, his formal proposal had been rejected by the Dowager Czarina on the excuse that her daughter was still too young to marry.

The result must be a further weakening of the Franco-Russian alliance, which gave Napoleon security in the north and could lead to his becoming still more powerful through the conquest and partition of Turkey; so Talleyrand, Fouché, Roger and everyone else who was secretly hoping for Napoleon's downfall were very pleased that the new Empress was to be the Austrian.

Having made his service to the Emperor, Roger rode

out to Malmaison. Josephine received him with delight, had the best guest suite in the house prepared for him and said that he must order anything he desired, at her expense. During the next few days he took over from her Comptroller and found that there was nothing basically wrong with the running of the household. It was simply that the official had endeavoured to check Josephine's extravagance, and had shown no tact in doing so. Feeling confident that he could always persuade the Emperor to give her more money, Roger made few changes and soon settled down to his new life.

As spring was now well on the way, much of his time was spent with Josephine in her beautiful garden. Flowers were her chief delight. Tens of thousands of bulbs were blooming in the glades, and in the hot-houses there were many rare tropical plants that she had had sent from her native Martinique. But, although she no longer drove into Paris, she was far from leading the life of a recluse. Apart from the enmity of members of the Bonaparte family, she had been universally popular and her old friends flocked out to Malmaison to visit her; so Roger was kept up-to-date with all that was going on at Court.

Berthier had been sent to escort Marie Louise from Vienna, and the Emperor was to receive her at St. Cloud. But, with his usual impatience, instead of adhering to the arrangement, as soon as he learned that she had crossed the frontier, he drove at full speed to meet her. To the surprise and dismay of her attendants, he dashed into a house where she had broken her journey to rest and, although soaked to the skin from having been exposed to the pouring rain, fervidly embraced her. He then hustled her out to his carriage and carried the frightened girl off to his palace at Compiègne. Then he declared his intention of sleeping with her that night. Vigorous protests were made, because the marriage had not yet taken place; but she had been married by proxy to her uncle before

65

leaving Vienna. Declaring that to be good enough for him, Napoleon whisked her up to bed.

She was quite an attractive girl, with light brown hair, blue eyes and a very fresh complexion, and had a good, somewhat buxom figure; but she was very shy and, not unnaturally, she had been greatly distressed at having to leave her family. When waiting on her one morning in her apartments, Berthier had found her weeping bitterly. She had pointed out to him that everything there was dear to her. There were a tapestry that had been worked by her mother, pictures painted by her uncle Charles, drawings by her sister; and, above all, she was heartbroken at having to leave behind her little pet dog.

In spite of her sadness and timidity, Napoleon was enchanted with her. He could not do enough to reconcile her to exile and, a few days after they reached Paris—thanks to Berthier's having hatched a little plot with her father before leaving Vienna—he was able to give her a delightful surprise. Unlocking a door, he pushed her into a room—and there were her tapestry, her paintings, all the other things she treasured, and her little dog.

To begin with, her shyness caused her to be haughty with the French ladies who formed her Court; but soon she made some good friends, and entertained those with whom she became intimate with the strange trick of being able to wiggle her ears.

The marriage was celebrated in Notre Dame on April 2nd, with almost unbelievable splendour. Not only were there a galaxy of subject Kings and Princes with their consorts, row upon row of High Dignitaries, Ambassadors, Marshals and Generals, but nearly every family of the old French nobility: de Rohan, de Richelieu, de Chevreuse, de Nemours, de Brissac, de Coigny, de Poligniac, de la Tour d'Auvergne, de Chalais and the rest were represented. For the past six years these émigrés had been welcomed back by Napoleon to add lustre to his

Court. They were not permitted to use their old titles, but to many of them he had given new ones when he had created thirty-one Dukes, three hundred and eighty-eight Counts and one thousand and ninety Barons.

Now, on this festive occasion he made a new distribution of honours, and Roger found himself elevated to the rank of Count, with which went a pension of thirty thousand francs per annum, as it was Napoleon's practice to ensure that his nobility had ample funds with which to support their dignity. All the Marshals had been endowed with great estates and a few, like Berthier, had revenues of over a million francs a year.

In April, a matter that had been giving Napoleon considerable concern for some time boiled up into a major issue. His fat, neurotic brother Louis, whom he had made King of Holland, far from acknowledging to whom he owed his crown, declared that he had been sent to rule over the Dutch by God's will. On the one hand he taxed his subjects unmercifully to pay for every sort of extravagance; on the other he pleaded their interests as an excuse to thwart Napoleon at every opportunity.

But, in the present instance, he undoubtedly had a case. After Nelson's victory at Trafalgar, it had become clear that for a number of years to come the French Fleet would not again have the strength to challenge the Royal Navy. The invasion of England no longer being a possibility, Napoleon had conceived another means by which he hoped to force Britain into suing for peace.

This was his Continental System, initiated by him in a decree published at Berlin in the summer of 1806. By it every country in which the Emperor's writ ran was ordered to cease importing goods from England. Commerce was Britain's strength, as by it she acquired the great sums with which she had financed France's neighbours to make war on him. Through his System, he expected not only to prevent, from lack of funds, further coalitions

being formed against France, but also to reduce Britain to bankruptcy.

But the System proved easier to envisage than to carry out. Britain, having been first in the field with an Industrial Revolution, had become the emporium of Europe for manufactured goods. Moreover, it was her vast merchant fleets that brought to the Continent the products of the tropics, such as sugar, coffee, spices and innumerable other desirable items that had for long added enjoyment to the meals of Europe's millions.

As a result, smuggling had increased to enormous proportions and, while it could to some extent be suppressed in France, many other countries had proved openly recalcitrant. The Pope, for one, had refused to deprive his people of their little luxuries, so Napoleon had had him arrested and imprisoned and annexed the States of the Church. Another, and the worst leak in the blockade, had been Portugal. It was for that reason that Napoleon had sent General Junot with an army to Lisbon and was endeavouring to subdue the whole Peninsula.

Now it was Louis who refused to co-operate, and came to Paris to tell Napoleon that, the Dutch being a nation of merchants, the System was ruining his people and he would not tolerate it. Napoleon replied furiously that if Louis would not, he would remove him from his throne and annex Holland.

However, Louis was given one last chance. It was known that British commerce was suffering cruelly from the embargo, which was bankrupting many of her merchants. So, with the possibility of bringing France's inveterate enemy to heel, Louis was authorised to make overtures to the British Government on the lines that, either negotiations for a peace should be entered upon, or he would give way to the Emperor and close the mouth of the Scheldt.

Soon after the negotiations started, Louis returned to Paris and, in a flaming temper, accused Napoleon of having gone behind his back and sent his own emissary to London with proposals for a cessation of hostilities. With equal rage the Emperor denied it. But Louis produced evidence that an agent named Fagan was actually there.

It was then discovered that Fouché, Talleyrand's powerful partner in the secret endeavours to prevent Napoleon from entering upon further wars had, on his own authority begun peace talks with the British; and that the proposed agreement could have led to a *coup d'état* in which the Emperor would have been forced to abdicate.

The proofs were such that Fouché could not deny them. After years of power second only to that wielded by his Imperial Master, he was disgraced, exiled to his estate in Provence, and his Ministry of Police, with its countless thousands of spies operating all over Europe, was given to General Savary, Duc de Rovigo.

But that did not save Louis. Soon afterwards he was deprived of his Kingdom, Holland was made a part of France, and he went into exile at Toplitz in Bohemia.

By mid-May Roger had been for over two months the Comptroller of Josephine's household and, devoted to her as he was, he felt that the time had come when he could decently ask to be relieved of his appointment; then, with the happy prospect at last of marrying Georgina, return to England. But it would have been highly dangerous simply to resign overnight and leave Paris. The safe course was to return for a few weeks to Napoleon's service until a suitable opportunity arose, such as the Emperor's temporarily leaving Paris, or sending him on a mission, when he could disappear without his absence becoming at once remarked upon.

Accordingly he told Josephine that he was now anxious to seek some form of more active service, and she

reluctantly agreed to let him go, assured him that she would always value his friendship, and gave him a diamond-encrusted sword-belt as a mark of her appreciation of his companionship at this distressing time in her life.

Two days later he waited on Napoleon, who was in a good mood and glad to have him back. For a week, he again assisted Berthier in organising the stream of troops and supplies that continued to pour south into Spain. The Emperor then sent for him.

The now paunchy, bullet-headed master of Europe was pacing angrily up and down in front of his desk. Turning toward Roger, he thrust out his great, broad jaw and snapped in his atrocious Italian-accented French :

'Breuc, I have a mission for you. Those accursed Germans are plaguing me beyond all endurance. Neither by requests nor threats can I induce them to carry out my decrees. Hamburg has now become the worst hole in my System. Daily, American ships loaded with British goods arrive in the mouth of the Elbe, and nothing is done about it. My mind is made up. I will tolerate this no longer. I intend to take over Hanover, and make it a part of France.'

Roger raised an eyebrow and, having British mercantile interests in mind, said, 'With all due deference, Sire, might that not lead to more trouble than blocking the hole is worth? I gather that recently there have been quite a number of demonstrations against our troops in the north German lands. The measure Your Imperial Majesty proposes might well lead to open rebellion.'

In the old days Napoleon had often consulted his Marshals and other advisers on his plans, and sometimes modified them in accordance with sound suggestions; but for a long time past his arrogance had become such that, once set on a project, he would listen to no-one. Now, he snarled :

'And what if it does? Davout is there as my representative; and he is well termed "the Iron Marshal". He will put down any outbreak that occurs. He takes a pleasure in hanging traitors, spies and every kind of trouble-maker. On my behalf, he'll teach these German curs a lesson they'll not soon forget. Hanover having for so long been subject to England, the people there have treachery toward me in their blood. The more of them that Davout sets dangling at the end of a rope, the better.'

For a minute or two the Emperor resumed his pacing in silence, then he went on more quietly. 'It is to Davout, Breuc, that I wish you to go. My intentions in this matter must be kept so secret that it would be dangerous to put them on paper. But he knows that you have long been in my confidence in many matters. Tell him I wish him to alert his most trusted officers; to make certain that none of our garrisons can be surprised and no bridge or key point in communications taken by a *coup de main* should the Hanoverians elect to rise against us. Then, when I send the word, the whole country can be put in fetters overnight. Now, be off with you.'

Roger bowed himself away in an excellent humour. Nothing could have suited him better than this mission. With every month it was becoming more and more difficult to get clandestinely across from France to England; whereas from a German port it would be comparatively easy. As the Emperor's missions brooked no delay, within an hour he was in the saddle and heading north-east. By way of Soissons, Namur, Düsseldorf, Osnabrück and Bremen, in six days of hard riding he reached Hamburg.

During his journey he had had second thoughts about the interests of British commerce, and decided that it would serve his country better if the Germans did rise; since, so many French troops having been withdrawn for service in Spain, it might now prove more than even

71

Davout could do to hold Hanover down. At the worst, it would become a second running sore for France. He therefore intended to deliver the Emperor's message, but to pervert it slightly. He could give the impression that, although Napoleon meant to annex the country, he did not plan to do so in the immediate future. Meanwhile, he wished Davout to take the severest possible measures against all Hanoverians who expressed anti-French sentiments. The result might then be that this persecution would lead to a popular rising before the Marshal was ready for it.

Louis-Nicolas Davout, Duc d'Auerstadt and Prince d'Eckmühl, had taken over as his headquarters the ancient castle near Herrenhausen, just outside the free city of Hamburg. It had been, up till the end of the past century, the residence of the sovereigns of Great Britain when they visited their Kingdom of Hanover. On dismounting in the main courtyard, Roger handed over his horse and asked to be taken at once to the Marshal, only to learn that he was not in Hamburg. Further enquiry of a staff officer produced the information that he had gone to Berlin, in order to discuss with the Ministers of the King of Prussia the question of improving the conditions of the French garrisons in the principal fortresses of that country, which formed part of his command.

Normally, any officer carrying orders from the Emperor would have at once demanded a fresh horse and set off for Berlin. But the prospect of joining Georgina in England now being so close, Roger decided against doing so. Instead he would say that he was going to, but spend the night at an inn, there change into the civilian clothes he had brought with him in his valise and, the following morning, start looking for a ship's captain who, for a handful of gold, would put him across the North Sea.

It then crossed his mind that one of his oldest friends, Fauvelet de Bourrienne, was the Emperor's Minister in

Hamburg, and that it would be very pleasant to take the chance of seeing him again. So he rode back down the long avenue of lindens and into the city. At the French Embassy he enquired for the Minister and, shortly afterwards, was shown into his palatial office.

Bourrienne was of noble birth, and had been one of the very few youngsters who had shown kindness to Napoleon when they were cadets together at the military academy at Brienne. On leaving there, he had entered the diplomatic service and, when recalled during the Revolution from a post in Germany, had preferred to remain in exile rather than risk being guillotined. But when Bonaparte became an Army Commander, he had recalled his old friend's intellectual gifts, and written to him, guaranteeing him immunity if he would return and become his secretary.

Bourrienne had accepted the offer and, for the eight years that followed, served as Napoleon's *Chef de Cabinet*. He spoke several languages fluently, had a most retentive brain and could take dictation as fast as even Napoleon could speak; so he had proved invaluable, and for several lengthy periods Roger had worked as one of his assistants.

Unfortunately, in 1805 this extremely able man had made an unlucky speculation which threatened to ruin him, and had recouped his loss by helping himself to the public funds. Napoleon allowed his Marshals to loot conquered countries, rob their churches of gold plate and extort jewels from their nobility; but one thing he would not tolerate was the embezzlement of his own Government's money. So Bourrienne had been dismissed and rendered almost penniless until the Emperor had relented to the extent of giving him this post at Hamburg.

He was delighted to see Roger, who disclosed the reason why he was in Hamburg, although he naturally did not mention that he had no intention of carrying out his mis-

sion. For an hour the two friends talked gaily over old times, then Bourrienne insisted that Roger should dine with him and be his guest for the night.

Over dinner they discussed the state of things in North Germany, and Bourrienne described it as a boiling pot, off which the lid would soon be blown. The whole of Hanover, Prussia and their adjoining states were seething with discontent and hatred of the French.

In the previous year there had been several mutinies by German troops, some of which had proved difficult to put down, and two that had caused great consternation. A Prussian Major, named Frederick von Schill, had left Berlin at the head of his regiment of Hussars, crossed the Elbe and carried insurrection into Hesse and Westphalia. He had twice defeated French troops sent against him, capturing prisoners, guns and the fortress of Domitz. Several months had passed before his luck had given out and he had been killed. The Duke of Brunswick had been even more successful. With a corps of volunteers raised in Bohemia, he had invaded Saxony, occupied Dresden and driven off the Westphalian troops commanded by their King, Napoleon's brother Jerome. He had then fought his way right across Germany to the mouth of the Weser and there embarked his men on British ships. He was now commanding them under Wellington in Spain, where they were known as 'The King's German Legion'.

Bourrienne predicted even more serious mutinies to come, and probably a rising *en masse* of the people, who were becoming agitated to fever pitch by the anti-French propaganda of von Stein.

They were still sitting over some fine brandy when a footman came in and told the Minister that General Jomini had called for a document. Bourrienne had him shown in and, as he entered the room, cried, 'Welcome, *mon cher General,* welcome! You must join us in a glass of brandy. You know de Breuc, of course.'

Jomini was a Swiss. By his writings on military matters he had earned the reputation of a sound strategist. Roger had met him a year or so before, when he had been Chief of Staff to Marshal Soult. Having shaken hands, they sat down together while their host went along to his cabinet to fetch the document. When he returned, he handed it to the General and said :

'It has just occurred to me that, as you are going to Berlin, de Breuc might accompany you. He has despatches for Davout, and would be on his way there now had I not persuaded him to stay here for the night.'

The General bowed to Roger. 'It would be a pleasure. I should be most happy to have your companionship, and you would find travelling in my coach as fast as and less fatiguing than going by horse.'

Had Roger not called on Bourrienne and disappeared overnight, there would have been no hue and cry after him; but if he did so now, in the morning his host would think that he had left the Palace on some private business and had become the victim of an accident, so the police would be ordered to find him. That left no alternative but to accept Jomini's offer, which he did with no great inward annoyance, as he could easily get back to Hamburg within three or four days.

Accordingly they set off together at six o'clock the next morning, slept the following night in the coach and completed their one-hundred-and-sixty-mile journey in eighteen hours without incident.

At the French Embassy they were given an early breakfast and Roger learned that Davout, although staying there, had spent the night at Potsdam, in order to attend a review being held that morning by King Frederick William. Jomini went about his business and, an hour later, Roger presented himself to the French Ambassador, M. de Brinevillers.

Roger had not met him before, but knew that he was a

ci-devant Marquis, who had been a diplomat under the old Monarchy. It was to that, and Napoleon's policy of taking into his service noble, returned exiles, that he owed his appointment. He was a tall, gaunt man with a supercilious air and irritable manner. Roger gained the impression that, like so many of his kind, while ready enough to accept benefits from the Emperor, he despised the new regime and particularly disliked Napoleon's habit of frequently sending soldiers on diplomatic missions.

Their conversation was brief. Afterwards the Ambassador had a footman show Roger up to a bedroom where he could freshen himself up, and stay the night if he wished. Roger then went for a stroll round the city, returning at midday. In the early afternoon Davout drove up, escorted by a guard of Prussian cavalry. Half an hour later, Roger was closeted with him.

The two men had no liking for each other, owing to a passage between them that had taken place some years earlier. At that time Roger had been the Princess Pauline's lover. She had wanted him to marry her, and persuaded him to ask the Emperor for her hand. Napoleon did not wish to quarrel with his favourite sister, so he had not replied with a curt refusal. Instead, with his usual duplicity, he told Roger that if he was to become one of the family he must be given high military rank, and for that he needed special military training. He had then sent him to Davout who, at Bruges, was commanding one of the corps assembled for the invasion of England.

Roger had expected to receive instruction on the high direction of war, and the provisioning of armies. But Davout, on the Emperor's secret instructions, had put him on a course of intensive training for junior officers, which entailed great physical endurance while living on the minimum of rations. Moreover, as Davout disliked officers on the gilded staff, he had, on his own account, temporarily demoted Roger to Lieutenant.

76

Meanwhile, as Napoleon had expected, the volatile and amorous Pauline had got herself another lover and had become engaged to Prince Borghese. On learning this, Roger had been so furious that he had stolen a horse and ridden hell-for-leather back to Paris. Davout, who was the strictest disciplinarian in the Army, had promptly demanded that Roger should be arrested as a deserter; but the Emperor, having had his little joke, only laughed as he felt that Roger had already been punished quite enough for his temerity.

The affair still rankled, so the interview between the two men was far from cordial. Roger said his piece, declared his intention of starting back for Paris on the following morning, and took an unsmiling leave of the Marshal Prince d'Eckmühl.

By then dinner was due to be served in half an hour. The Ambassador was already receiving guests in the big salon. Soon after Roger joined them, the usher announced, 'His Excellency Count von Haugwitz, Chief Minister to His Majesty.'

Roger was standing near the door. He had been presented to the Count at the Conference of Erfurt. Their eyes met. Recognition was instant and mutual. The Prussian gave a gasp, pointed at Roger, turned to the Ambassador and cried:

'This . . . this officer is the man who murdered my brother! I must ask Your Excellency to hand him over to my police, so that he can be tried and executed.'

FOR a moment Roger stared in utter consternation at
von Haugwitz; but only for a second. Next moment he
had regained his composure. Swinging round on the
French Ambassador, he declared indignantly :

'Your Excellency, this charge is false! I have never
murdered anyone!'

'You are *M. le Colonel de Breuc*?' his accusor shot at
him angrily.

In such company Roger could not possibly deny his
identity. Fighting down his apprehension, he bowed and
replied courteously, 'I am Colonel le Comte de Breuc, at
Your Excellency's service.'

'Then you are the man!' The Minister's arm shot out,
pointing at him again. 'You murdered my brother! Yes,
and your own wife. At Schloss Langenstein, last September, you did them both to death most foully.'

Davout had entered the room immediately on the
heels of the Prussian Chief Minister. His eyes and those
of everyone else present were riveted on Roger as he
sought desperately to make up his mind what line to take.
To speak of the forged von Stein letter would not help
him here. Von Hardenberg, the Minister's predecessor,
had been pro-British. That had been why the Emperor
had insisted that King Frederick William should dismiss
him and replace him with the pro-French von Haugwitz.

And while his younger brother, the Baron, had served as a diplomat his pro-French attitude had also been widely known. It would not for a moment be credited that he was in communication with von Stein and preparing to lead a rebellion in the Rhineland against the French.

Suddenly Davout said sharply, 'Well, Breuc; have you lost your tongue? Were you at Schloss Langenstein last September? You must answer His Excellency's accusation. Come now, speak up.'

'I was, Your Highness,' Roger replied. 'But I was there on the orders of His Majesty the Emperor.'

'For what purpose?'

'You must excuse me if I refuse to answer that, without first obtaining the Emperor's permission.'

'I see. And what of the charge? Did you bring about the death of the Baron and your wife?'

'Their deaths were, Your Highness, an accident. I swear to that.'

'It is a lie,' stormed the Prussian. 'This man was having an affaire with my brother's wife, and made off with her. That very afternoon his own wife and my brother were found dead in the bottom of a wine press. He, and no-one else, had both the motive and opportunity to murder them.'

Roger realised that if he admitted to having, with Georgina's aid, carried them from their rooms and lowered them into the press, his case would be hopeless; so he said quickly, 'Anyone who was living in the Schloss had the opportunity, and how do you know that no-one other than myself had a motive? The Baron was a hard master. He may have behaved brutally to one of his servants, and the man resolved to be revenged upon him.'

'Had that been the case, the man would not also have killed your wife,' von Haugwitz snapped.

'He might have. All four of us had separate rooms, and the Baron and my wife were lovers. On going to the

Baron's room in the middle of the night, the murderer would probably have found her with him. If so, he would have killed her to prevent her raising the alarm. I had no hand in the matter. I swear it.'

The Minister's face was white with rage and hatred. 'I do not believe that for one second,' he snarled, 'and I demand that you be handed over to the Prussian authorities to stand your trial.'

Roger turned swiftly to de Brinevillers. 'In Your Excellency's Embassy I am on French soil. As a Frenchman I claim sanctuary.'

The Ambassador looked uncomfortably, first at von Haugwitz then at Roger and said, '*Monsieur le Colonel Comte*, if this were a political charge, I should, of course, be in a position to protect you. But this is a criminal charge.'

'Even so,' Roger insisted, 'I claim your protection. And I do so in the name of His Majesty the Emperor. As I have told you, I went to Schloss Langenstein on his business. I am told that, after my departure, a warrant was issued for my arrest. On arriving back in Paris, I gave His Majesty an account of this whole affair. Realising that it would not be safe for me to re-enter Prussia, I asked him to take steps to quash the charge. He willingly agreed, and said he would inform the Prussian Ambassador, the Baron von Brockenhausen, that he desired the warrant to be withdrawn. Of this there must be a record at your Ministry of Justice.'

'This is another lie,' declared von Haugwitz. 'Were that the case, as this affair concerns me so closely, it is certain that I should have been informed of it.'

Again de Brinevillers looked uneasily at Davout. 'Your Highness will, I am sure, agree that this is a very delicate matter, so I should like to discuss it with you in private.'

The Marshal nodded. 'Very well. I suggest that *Colonel*

le Comte de Breuc should retire to a room where he can be placed under guard. When we have dined, you and I will decide on what is to be done.' Turning to his A.D.C., he added, 'Marchand, take de Breuc to the small library. I make you responsible for his safe keeping.'

As Roger, his head held high, was escorted from the room, he heard the Ambassador apologising to his guests that the recent scene should have taken place in their presence. There followed a burst of excited conversation, which faded as he walked through the big hall and accompanied the A.D.C. into a small library at the far end.

The room had two tall windows looking out on to a large garden. For a moment he contemplated escaping by one of them. But, to do so, he would have to kill, or render unconscious the A.D.C. Such a desperate act could be taken as an admission of guilt. In any case, it would set Davout and de Brinevillers irrevocably against him, and his only hope lay in their protection.

The A.D.C. was a pleasant man and expressed his sympathy. Roger thanked him, then turned away, as he had no desire to talk and a great need to think.

It could be that the Emperor had forgotten to make his wishes known to von Brockenhausen; but that seemed unlikely as Napoleon's memory was phenomenally good. Again the Prussian Ambassador might have failed to pass on the wish to the proper quarter in Berlin. Yet again it was possible that the memo did lie in a file at the Ministry of Justice and that von Haugwitz had not been told about it. Still again, his ardent desire to avenge the death of his brother might have led him to lie deliberately when he had asserted that he knew nothing about the document.

Whichever was the case, Roger would never have dreamed of entering Prussia had he not felt confident that the whole matter had been cleared up and no charge

would be made against him. But it was pointless to think of that now. He could only curse himself for having taken the matter for granted, and wonder with no little fear what the outcome would be.

Only too well he realised how unlucky he was that his fate should lie in the hands of two such men as de Brinevillers and Davout. The *ci-devant* aristocrat, who could no longer call himself a Marquis, obviously had an antipathy for Napoleon's people, and would be particularly unsympathetic toward one who had been made a Count; while the dour Marshal would not lift a finger to save a man whom he regarded as having once been a deserter.

Over three hours elapsed while Roger endured this terrible suspense. During that time no food was brought to him or his companion and, at length, he asked the A.D.C. if he could have a glass of wine. The officer shook his head, and replied :

'I regret, *Monsieur le Colonel,* but I dare not leave the room. His Highness the Marshal is extraordinarily strict; even more so with his officers than with his men, and particularly so with those in positions of responsibility. He visits any dereliction of duty with the most condign punishments, and my duty is to see that you do not escape.'

'Then, damn it, man,' Roger replied angrily, 'use your head. Put it out of the door and shout for a bottle.'

Apologetically the A.D.C. did as he was bid and, soon afterwards, they were silently drinking hock together. Some twenty minutes later, Davout and de Brinevillers came in.

Addressing Roger, the Ambassador said, '*Monsieur le Colonel Comte*, His Highness and I have discussed your affair, and I regret that, the charge being a criminal one, I cannot see my way to give you sanctuary here in the Embassy.'

'But, Your Excellency,' Roger pleaded, 'you do not seem to realise that, should you hand me over to the Prussians, it may cost me my life.'

'You maintain that you are innocent,' Davout remarked coldly. 'If that is so, you will be acquitted.'

'Not necessarily, Prince. Unfortunately, the circumstances in which these deaths took place are very strongly against me. And, against the possibility of an unjust verdict being given, as a French officer it is your duty to give me your protection.'

Davout's eyes narrowed, and his brows·drew down in an icy frown, as he asked, 'Do you presume to teach me my duty?'

'Yes,' replied Roger firmly. 'Not to myself, but to the Emperor. As I have told you, it was his wish that the charge against me should be withdrawn. If, through some error, his request—which to these damned Prussians is tantamount to an order—has not reached them, I insist that I be given asylum in the Embassy until a courier has been despatched to His Majesty and returned with his decision.'

'Very well,' the Marshal agreed. 'Your request is not unreasonable. A courier shall be sent to the Emperor. But in the meantime the decision does not rest with me. It is for His Excellency to say.'

De Brinevillers shuffled uncomfortably and, with his eyes avoiding Roger's, muttered, 'Prussia is our ally, *Monsieur le Colonel*. It is my responsibility to maintain harmonious relations with King Frederick William's government, and his Chief Minister has made a personal issue of this. As you are charged with a criminal offence of the first order, he has right on his side. I cannot afford to quarrel with him over a matter that has no bearing on the sovereign rights of France. He has already sent here an escort for you, and a formal demand that you should be handed over. I fear that I must comply with it.'

83

For several minutes longer Roger argued and pleaded in turn, but without avail. The only concession he could secure was a promise that de Brinevillers would use his influence to ensure that no trial took place until there had been ample time for a courier to go to Paris and return. Five minutes later he was under arrest, sitting beside a Lieutenant of Police in a closed carriage that drove off accompanied by a mounted escort.

The carriage halted in the courtyard of a large, bleak building that was obviously a prison. Roger was taken inside and put in a narrow but clean cell. He asked for food and a quarter of an hour later a warder brought him a *brodchen,* in which had been inserted a thick slice of veal, and a mug holding what looked like coffee. Setting down the mug, the man said with a malicious grin :

'No doubt you'll enjoy this. It's a true Frenchie brew made of acorns, as prescribed for us all now by your pig of an Emperor.'

Roger made no reply, and he knew it would be futile to report the man, as it was quite certain no action would be taken against him for insulting the sovereign of France. He thought it probable that the warder's attitude indicated the way in which most Germans now regarded Napoleon; and it boded no good for him as a Frenchman in one of their prisons.

Next morning he was taken to an office and formally charged with the wilful murder of his wife and *Herr Baron* Ulrich von Haugwitz. Afterwards he was searched. He had already surrendered his sword; now a small dagger he always carried, his money belt and the jewels he was wearing were taken from him. Back in his cell, he congratulated himself on having had the forethought the previous night to conceal between his stockings and the soles of his feet six gold pieces; but, in the worst event, they were nowhere near the sum needed to bribe anyone to help him to escape.

The twelve days that followed seemed interminable to him. The food was edible, but of poor quality. The malicious warder evidently put a little salt into the water he brought, which rendered it impossible to drink, so Roger was reduced to falling back on the filthy acorn coffee; which caused him in turn to curse the Emperor and his Continental System. He asked for books and news sheets and was brought a few, but found the German script so difficult to read that he soon gave up the attempt. In vain he tried to persuade himself that Napoleon could not fail to bring about his release. But Paris was a long way off and the Emperor might have suddenly set off on one of his long journeys to Spain, Italy or Austria. Again, some accident might befall the courier who had been sent to Paris, or von Haugwitz be so set on vengeance as to risk his own future by refusing the Emperor's request for the warrant to be withdrawn.

His fears proved only too well founded. On June 13th, a young man named Menou, who was on the staff of the French Embassy, came to see him. Having expressed the Ambassador's regrets, he reported that no message regarding Roger had been received from the Emperor, although ample time had now elapsed for one to do so; and that Roger's trial had been fixed for two days hence.

To outward appearances, Roger took this bad news calmly, but, although he had been endeavouring to prepare himself for such a blow, his heart lurched and seemed to sink to his boots. Having thanked the young man, he asked that a good lawyer should be provided to defend him; to which Menou replied that one had already been instructed and would come to see him on the following day. There being no more to be said, he then bowed himself away.

Next morning the lawyer arrived. He proved to be a tired-faced, elderly man, named Johan Peffer. The fact that he was a German filled Roger with fury and further

dismay. As a distinguished French officer he felt that he was entitled to some consideration. He had expected de Brinevillers to enquire after his well-being while in prison, perhaps send him a gift of books and wine; and, at the very least, come in person to break the bad news of the Emperor's failure to respond. But the Ambassador had done none of thse things. And now, by failing to send a French advocate to undertake the defence, he had shown a callous indifference to Roger's fate that was hard to credit.

But time was short, for the trial was to take place the next day, so there was no longer time left to secure another lawyer. All Roger could do was to repeat to the crop-headed Prussian what he had said about the tragedy at Schloss Langenstein when he had declared his innocence at the French Embassy. Herr Peffer made copious notes, asked a few pointless questions, gloomily advised pleading 'guilty'—which Roger flatly refused to do—then glumly took his departure.

At the trial the next day, no senior representative of the French Embassy was present, only young *Monsieur* Menou. But the trial having been postponed for a fortnight, in order that a courier could be sent to Paris, had cut two ways. It had given ample time for the prosecution to bring a number of witnesses from the Rhineland; so there were several other faces that Roger recognised—among them the Baron's steward, Big Karl, and the coachman whom Roger had forced into driving himself and Georgina to Coblenz.

The evidence by the servants that Roger had been the lover of their mistress and, despite their attempts to prevent him, carried her off, was incontestible. And it would have been useless for him to defend his action by stating that he had learned of a plot to murder them both, which was being hatched by his own wife and the Baron, since he had not a tittle of evidence to support it.

But worse was to come. It emerged that, on the discovery of the bodies, the Baron's doctor had been sent for. He now gave evidence that, having examined them, he was of the opinion that they had both had a powerful drug administered to them. That, Roger needed no telling, was a fact. His object in going to Schloss Langenstein had been to save Georgina from the threat of being murdered by her husband. Knowing that it would prove difficult to get her away, he had bought the drug before leaving Vienna, against the possibility that he might have to drug a powerful watch-dog.

The Baron's valet followed the doctor and testified to having found the empty bottle that had contained the drug, on the floor of his master's room. The bottle was then produced.

Next, a quietly-dressed, elderly man, whose face Roger vaguely recognised, went into the box. When he gave his name before taking the oath, he also stated that he was an Austrian subject. To Roger's utter consternation, he suddenly realised that the man was the apothecary from whom he had bought the drug. Evidence was then given that, the name of the apothecary being on the bottle, he had been questioned in Vienna. Now he identified Roger as the man to whom he had sold it.

That proved the *coup de grâce*. No-one in the court any longer had the least doubt about Roger's guilt. He was sentenced to be executed one week from that day.

CHAPTER VIII

RESURGENT GERMANY

BACK in his cell, Roger endeavoured to accept calmly the evil fate that had befallen him. Rack his brains as he would, he could think of no way by which he might attempt to save himself. The factor which rendered him so helpless was his complete isolation. Had he been in a similar situation in Paris or London there would have been a score of influential friends on whom he could have called for aid. By belatedly admitting the truth—that he had drugged his wife and the Baron, but had expected them to regain consciousness within a few hours—he might have secured a revision of sentence to a term of imprisonment for culpable homicide. But here, in Berlin, he had not a single friend he could call upon to have his case reviewed by a high legal authority. On the contrary, as a Frenchman, every hand was against him.

Yet a lifetime in which he had many times feared his death to be imminent had conditioned Roger never to leave any step untaken that, however slender the chance, might place him in a more favourable situation. So that evening, he asked for paper, ink, a pen, and sand and wrote letters to both de Brinevillers and Davout.

In both letters he confessed that he had been responsible for the deaths of which he had been accused, but maintained that the thought of murder had never even

entered his head. He then swallowed his pride, wrote of his many years' service to the Emperor, which His Imperial Majesty had recognised by making him a Colonel, one of his A.D.C.s, a Count and a Commander of the Legion of Honour, and pleaded that, as fellow Frenchmen, they should exert themselves at least to save his life.

But, having secured a promise from one of the senior warders that the letters would reach their destinations, he had little hope that his desperate appeal would move either the haughty, *ci-devant* Marquis, who had already displayed his indifference, or the hard-hearted Marshal, who had long resented having failed to have Roger brought to book as a deserter.

He could assume that his letters would reach de Brinevillers within a few hours, and Davout in Hamburg in two days' time. So an acknowledgment of that to the Ambassador might reach him the next day, and that to the Marshal well before the end of the week. But the terrible days dragged slowly by without his receiving a reply from either.

On June 21st, his week would be up. On the morning of the 20th he was taken from the cell he had occupied for three weeks to the condemned cell. At midday, the prison chaplain, a Lutheran pastor, came to see him, and asked if he could assist him to make his peace with God. Roger politely declined the offer, upon which the German, assuming Roger to be a Roman Catholic, said that he would endeavour to get for him the services of a priest. That offer Roger also declined, so, after expressing his sympathy for the prisoner and urging him to face death with fortitude, the chaplain withdrew.

In the afternoon Roger again asked for writing materials and wrote a letter to Georgina, in which he declared their lifelong love to be the greatest blessing ever granted to him. He went on to say how distressed he was that, now she had at long last promised to marry him,

that could not come to pass. But that since, from their youth onward, such a close bond had been established between their spirits and as they had always agreed when talking of reincarnation, in which they both believed, he had no shadow of doubt that, in future lives, they would again become devoted lovers.

Before ending his letter with blessings upon her, her son Charles and his daughter Susan, whom he knew she would continue to mother as though she were her own child, he inserted a paragraph which ran :

I pray you do not again ever have doubts about the occult powers with which you have been endowed. You will recall that in Paris, when you gazed into your crystal, we decided that the vision you saw was a step back in time, and that you were seeing me during the months I was a prisoner at Guildford. But that was not so. You saw me here in this cell for the condemned, talking with the Lutheran pastor, who came to see me at midday.

When he had finished his letter to Georgina, he wrote another to his oldest friend, Lord Edward Fitz-Deverel, who was known to his friends as 'Droopy Ned'. Having recounted to Droopy how he had at last come to the end of his tether, he asked that, should anything befall Georgina, he would take care of Susan, and gave him a power of attorney to administer the estate she would inherit.

He addressed the two letters, then enclosed them in an outer envelope that contained a note to Bourrienne. Feeling sure that his old friend must know a great deal about the smuggling activities that took place in Hamburg, he asked that his letters to Georgina and Droopy should be sent to England by a safe hand; and he had no doubt that his request would be granted.

When the warder came with Roger's evening meal, he took the letters and, now showing some compassion for a man who was about to die, readily agreed to pass them on to the Governor of the prison for despatch.

To occupy his mind during this last evening of his life, Roger, lying in his narrow bed, set about recalling many of the perils he had survived and the enjoyment he had derived from the love of a number of beautiful women of most diverse character.

At length his thoughts diverted from the grim fact that at dawn he was to be led out and shot, he dozed off. But soon after midnight he was roused by the opening of his cell door and the light from a lantern carried by his warder.

Behind the warder was the prison Governor. Smiling at Roger he said, '*Monsieur le Comte,* it is my pleasant duty to inform you that you have been reprieved. Here is a letter that, I understand, will inform you of the reason for your good fortune.'

Thunderstruck, and hardly able to believe that he was not dreaming, Roger stammered his thanks, took the letter and, when the Governor had withdrawn, opened and read it. It was from Davout; a hasty note scrawled without prefix, and ran :

> *On my return from an inspection, I received your letter, and was greatly surprised to learn that His Imperial Majesty had not responded to your appeal which, I understood, de Brinevillers was sending to him. As a Frenchman dedicated to the service of our great Emperor, and knowing that you once, when in Venice, saved his life, I could not find it in me to allow matters to take their course. I therefore took it upon myself to exert great pressure upon King Frederick William. In consequence, His Majesty has agreed to commute your sentence to ten years' imprisonment.*

Ten years! From sudden wild elation, Roger's spirits swiftly sank. Such a sentence was appalling to contemplate. He would be over fifty before he was released and by then such zest for life as remained to him would be for ever gone. The thought of the discomfort and poor prison fare were bad enough, but the prospect of month after month dragging by, without change of scene or activity, was even worse.

From his boyhood on he had led a fuller life than any of his contemporaries he could think of. He had travelled in nearly every country in Europe, visited Egypt, Persia, the West Indies, Zanzibar, India and Brazil; crossed the Channel clandestinely a score of times, ridden many thousands of miles, been present at the battles of the Nile, Marengo, Eylau, Austerlitz and numerous other conflicts, and had personally transacted affairs of state with Kings and Ministers. Moreover, while he was too fastidious to be promiscuous, several of the most beautiful women he had ever set eyes on had become his mistresses.

A future in which he was confined by the grey walls of a prison would, he knew, be for him a living death; and he almost wished that instead he was to face a firing squad within a few hours. But, after a while, his old resilience to misfortune returned. He had escaped from prison on several previous occasions; so, given patience, he might succeed in doing so again.

On re-reading Davout's letter, he saw that it provided a possible explanation for a thing that had greatly puzzled him. He had never for one moment believed that, if informed of his situation, the Emperor would abandon him to his enemies; particularly to the Prussians, whom he loathed and had often contemptuously referred to as 'a miserable, semi-barbarian people'. It was evident that Davout had expected de Brinevillers to send a courier to Napoleon and, indeed, it was the Ambassador's, not the Marshal's business, to have done so. It now looked as

though, either from spite or idleness, de Brinevillers had failed to carry out his promise; and Roger determined, if he could regain his freedom, to call the haughty, *ci-devant* Marquis to account.

Next morning he was required to part with his uniform and put on a suit of convict's clothes. He was then taken in a prison van to another prison on the outskirts of Berlin. There, after being entered on the register, he was given a somewhat better cell than that he had been occupying, and his dreary round as a long-term prisoner began.

The food was sufficient, but monotonous and unpalatable. As a noble, he was not made to work, and allowed paper, writing materials and a limited number of books, with which to while away the hours. Twice a day he was taken down to an inner courtyard for exercise with a number of the prisoners. While they marched round and round in single file, they talked to one another in whispers; but they had soon learned through the prison 'grapevine' that Roger was a Frenchman, so they promply sent him to Coventry, condemning him to an isolation that he found hard to bear.

Even so, by overhearing their low-voiced exchanges, he was able to pick up a certain amount of information; and in July was saddened by a piece of news that distressed them all. Queen Louisa of Prussia had died.

She had been a beautiful and gallant lady, and the idol of her nation, filling the need of her subjects for a truly patriotic figurehead, in which her cowardly husband had so lamentably failed. Roger had been presented to her at the Conference of Erfurt, and recalled how bravely, but vainly, she had striven to persuade Napoleon to return the great fortress of Magdeburg to Prussia, and lighten the terrible burden of taxation under which her people groaned.

Early in August he heard of another event, that filled

his German fellow prisoners with fury and apprehension. In a brilliantly-executed *coup,* Davout had taken over Hanover without a shot being fired, and that country had become part of the French Empire. As Davout commanded not only in Hanover, but also the French garrisons in all the major fortresses in north Germany, the Prussians naturally feared that Napoleon's next move would be to dethrone their King, and that they, too, would be deprived of even the shadow of independence.

During these weeks, Roger had studied with the utmost care the prison routine and the precautions taken to prevent prisoners from escaping. To his great disappointment he found that in this respect the Prussians were much more thorough than the people of most other nations, so that, apart from the remote possibility of some unexpected happening, there seemed no likelihood of his regaining his freedom. He was still further depressed by his belief that, given the co-operation of a group of his fellow prisoners, he might possibly have organised a mass break-out; but their antagonism toward him put that out of the question.

However, Hanover having become a French province overnight had resulted in a new wave of unrest in Prussia. In every town, crowds singing patriotic songs marched through the streets and demonstrated outside the town halls. In several places troops mutinied and manifestos were reaching the King and his Ministers daily, urging them to throw off the French yoke.

Although Frederick William was the most unwarlike of Kings, he was an intelligent and liberal-minded man. Before the French invasion, the common people had groaned under a serfdom similar to that in Russia; but defeat had brought to the nations benefits previously undreamed of. Stein, Scharnhorst, Gneisenau, Shon, von Hardenberg and others of the King's advisers had urged

upon him that the only way to put fresh heart into the nation was by sweeping reforms; and he had agreed.

Serfdom had been abolished, the ownership of land— previously restricted to the upper classes—was made available to all, centralisation was replaced by local government, and a great programme for increasing education entered upon.

For the first time a university was established in Berlin, and others were given large grants which enabled them to increase their student bodies greatly. And now it was the students who were the mainspring of the anti-French agitation. Incited by the writings of Stein, Fichte, Steffens, von Humboldt and many more, they were demanding with patriotic frenzy that their country should no longer remain subservient to the hated Emperor. Since his victory he had milked Prussia of over six hundred million francs, and his Continental System was leading to the bankruptcy of hundreds of merchants. A secret society for the liberation of Prussia, named the *Tugenbund,* had been formed, and was joined enthusiastically by members of all classes.

With October there came a fresh wave of riots aimed at forcing the Government to act and break off the alliance with France. Many of the leaders of these demonstrations were arrested and several score of them were brought to Roger's prison. It soon became so crowded that another truckle bed was put into his cell, and he was given for a companion a long-haired youth who was one of the agitators.

The young man's name was Hans Grotten. On learning that Roger was a Frenchman, he abused him and his master until he was out of breath. Roger took it quietly, then told him that the majority of Frenchmen, and even more their women, now hated the Emperor as much as the Germans did. This greatly surprised Grotten, and when Roger explained how Napoleon was bleeding

France white, and that the greater part of his soldiers had not seen their homes for half a dozen years, the fiery student became less antagonistic.

Even so, his bitterness was not against the tyrant Emperor only, but the French as a nation. He said that wherever their garrisons were stationed, they regarded themselves as a superior race, and behaved like ravening beasts. In the daytime they pushed people out of their way and, at night, waylaid and robbed them. They made constant requisitions of horses, carts, cattle and poultry, for which they did not pay, and no woman was safe from being dragged off into the bushes by them. Complaints against them were useless, as their officers treated the Prussian authorities with contempt.

With the introduction of the students and liberal intellectuals into the prison, a new excitement began to seethe among the older inmates. This was caused by daily demonstrations outside the prison by mobs demanding the release of the newcomers. Bets of clothing and small personal possessions were being freely made on whether the Government would or would not give way. The demonstrations developed into riots and, on two evenings in succession, shots were fired. It then leaked out that the authorities had become frightened that the mob would break into the prison and forcibly release the captive agitators; so the prison was to be evacuated and the prisoners transferred to the fortress of Spandau.

On October 10th, the prisoners were roused in the early hours of the morning, hustled downstairs by the warders, now reinforced by troops, and herded into a long line of prison vans. While this measure was being carried out, Roger looked eagerly about him, hoping for a chance to escape. But one of the soldiers had a bayonet pointed at his back, so he dared not make a dash for it. Within a few minutes of having reached the main courtyard, he was compelled to enter one of the vans,

into which were already crowded a dozen other prisoners.

The doors were slammed and locked. The van moved off at a walking pace. It traversed about a mile; then faintly, its occupants heard shouts. They increased to a roar. The van came to a halt. Pressed against one another inside, the prisoners were seized with a fever of excitement.

It was evident that the plan to transfer them to Spandau in the middle of the night had become known to the insurgents, who had laid an ambush with the intention of rescuing them. Shots were fired. Their hearts sank, as it seemed very doubtful if the mob would be able to overcome the armed escort. The hubbub increased. The captives hammered with their fists on the sides of the van and threw their weight against the doors in an endeavour to burst them open. They yielded a little, but the lock and bolts were too strong to be forced. With cries of desperation, they renewed their efforts, but still the doors could not be opened.

Suddenly there came the crash of steel on iron. The whole van shook. Blow after blow followed. Someone outside was making a mighty effort to smash the doors in with a big axe or crowbar. The wooden panels splintered. Eager hands tore aside jagged pieces regardless of splinters and laceration. Another minute and the captives were tumbling pellmell out of the van into the cheering crowd that milled about it.

Roger scrambled to his feet. There was a quarter moon, which gave enough light for him to take in the wild scene. Not a soldier was in sight; neither were there any dead or dying students lying in the roadway. Evidently the troops were in sympathy with the would-be liberators of their country. They must have fired over the heads of the crowd, then made off to avoid having to use their bayonets. Without waiting to thank his deliverers,

97

Roger pushed his way through the mob and ran down a side road as fast as his legs could carry him.

He did not pause until he was breathless, then he continued on at a fast walk till he had put well over a mile between himself and the spot where the prison vans had been ambushed. The shouting had died away in the distance. Feeling himself safe now from immediate recapture, he sat down on a grassy bank at the roadside to bless his luck and consider how best he could retain his freedom.

He still had the six gold pieces that he had kept concealed under the soles of his feet during the seventeen miserable weeks he had spent as a prisoner. That would be enough to get him to Hamburg, but nothing like sufficient to bribe a smuggler to run him across the North Sea. Moreover, he felt an overwhelming urge to settle accounts with de Brinevillers before leaving Berlin.

Having rested for a time, he began to walk again, now heading towards the eastern end of the city. When he reached it, dawn was coming up and people were already stirring in the tumbledown shacks and tenements. For an hour he loitered in a deserted alley, then when the shops began to open he furtively made his way along the street until he came to a second-hand-clothes dealer. Peering cautiously in, he saw that the proprietor was an elderly Jew. Well aware that this downtrodden race was always sympathetic toward those in conflict with the authorities, Roger went in.

The suit he was wearing gave away the fact that he was an escaped convict, and he did not seek to conceal the fact. Instead he said that he was a journalist who had been imprisoned for writing an article abusing the Government for its subservient attitude to the hated French, and was desperately anxious to obtain clothes that would enable him to make his way back to his home in Hesse-

Kassel. He could not have posed as a Berliner, but his *hoch-deutch* was quite good enough for him to be accepted as a south German; and when he produced one of his pieces of gold, the Jew, displaying his yellowed fangs in a smile, showed that he was quite willing to bargain with him.

The bargain driven was a hard one, as Roger had to part with two of his pieces of gold. But in exchange he got a patched pair of trousers, a padded cotton jacket, a dark cloak ragged at the seams and a felt hat with a floppy brim that would partly conceal his face.

Now confident of avoiding trouble should he run into a patrolling policeman, his next visit was to a shop that, among other things, sold aids for the war wounded. Many poor wretches had lost an eye in the fighting, so a black eyeshade would help to make him more difficult to recognise without making him conspicuous. Having purchased one, in the same shop he bought a long, sharp knife, which he concealed in the upper part of his trousers, and several lengths of thin, but strong cord.

Now hungry, he went to a small general store, at which he obtained a loaf of bread, a pound of ham, some slices of *apfel strudel*, a slab of chocolate and a bottle of wine. His mouth watering at the thought of consuming these delicacies after several months of prison fare, he hurriedly sought a place where he could lie up for the day. After twenty minutes spent exploring noisome alleys, he came upon a big timber yard. The place seemed to be deserted, so he decided that it would serve and, further exploration having brought him to a shed, he settled himself comfortably in it on a pile of sacks. After gorging himself on the good things he had bought, he stretched himself out and was soon fast asleep.

He did not wake until well on in the afternoon. Hungry again, he had another enjoyable meal, then whiled away the evening hours as well as he could, thinking of Geor-

gina, the joy of being back in England and how he could best get de Brinevillers on his own.

Patiently he waited until he judged it to have been dark for well over two hours; then he started on his long trudge to the other end of the city. When he reached it a clock in a tower told him that it was still much too early to carry out the plan he had formed, so he went into the *Tiergarten* and sat on a bench there for a long spell. At last the hour of ten chimed from a nearby steeple. Getting up, he stretched himself and, after taking several wrong turnings, found his way to the French Embassy.

As he had spent the best part of a day at the Embassy, he knew the general layout of the big mansion and that it had a fine garden. An ill-lit alley ran along the wall at the end and, after carefully reconnoitring the wall, he found a place where he could scale it. On the spikes at the top he tore his cloak, but it was already so ragged that the additional tear made little difference. He was only apprehensive now that there might be a watch-dog loose in the garden. But as he scrambled to the ground, only the crunch of his feet on dead twigs disturbed the stillness.

Advancing cautiously, he surveyed the back of the house. There were lights in the uncurtained windows of two of the ground-floor rooms. Above them was a terrace, from which a broad flight of stone steps led down to the garden. Along the terrace ran the reception rooms. To Roger's relief they were all in darkness, showing that de Brinevillers was not entertaining that night. From all but one room on the second floor, the gentle glow of candles showed through drawn curtains. In all such mansions they were the best bedrooms, and the people who occupied them would be getting ready for bed. He had little doubt which was de Brinevillers' room, because the central room was much larger than the others and had a big bay window. It could be taken as certain that the

Ambassador would have chosen this principal bedroom for himself and, as he was unmarried, sleep alone there.

The moonlight was sufficient for Roger to see that one window of the room was open. Had it not been, he would either have had to take a far greater risk to reach the room by some other means, or abandon his project altogether. There were also lights in several of the lesser bedrooms on the two upper floors.

Withdrawing, Roger went in search of the gardener's domain. It proved to be a good-sized outhouse with a loft. On the ground floor, with spades, scythes and other implements, there were two ladders. The longer would easily reach from the terrace to de Brinevillers' bedroom windows. On trying its weight, Roger found that, although it would need all his strength, he should be able to haul it upright.

Not far from the back of the house there were several lofty trees. Gliding over to one of them, Roger climbed up into a fork. From there he could see down into the uncurtained ground-floor rooms. In one, a secretary was still at work, in the other a footman in his shirt-sleeves was belatedly cleaning silver. The light in one bedroom had now gone out, but one showed in that which had previously been unlit. As it was next to the principal bedroom, Roger guessed that it was probably the Ambassador's clothes closet.

One by one during the next hour the lights went out, until the great building was in darkness. Coming down from his perch, Roger went again to the gardener's outhouse. Going up to the loft he found some sacking and a ball of stout twine. Descending, he bound thick pads of sacking round both ends of the ladder, so that when he dragged it up the stone steps to the terrace, it would make no noise. He then partly lugged and partly carried it to the foot of the steps and laid it down there. He had more than halved the effort needed to bring it into use,

but it was still much too early to make his attempt on de Brinevillers.

Another hour or more went by. When he heard one o'clock chime from a nearby steeple, he decided that the time had come to act.

CHAPTER IX

DEATH STALKS AT MIDNIGHT

By that time, unless there was someone ill or wakeful in the house, all the inmates should be in their first deep sleep. Lifting one end of the ladder, Roger drew it slowly up the steps until he had it on the terrace. Next came the critical stage. Could he get it up against the windowsill? To raise it needed every ounce of his strength. For one awful moment he feared that it was going to overbalance and fall backwards on him; but a final effort was just sufficient to sway it in the right direction.

Standing back, he closed his eyes and mopped the sweat from his forehead, then remained quite still until his heart had ceased pounding and his breathing had returned to normal. Testing every rung of the ladder before putting his full weight on it, he made his way up to the window. As he opened it further, it creaked a little. For a full minute he held his breath, but no sound came from inside the room. Putting a leg over the sill he slipped inside. He was now behind the heavy curtain. Gently he drew it a little aside, so that the moonlight should filter in and, by it, he could see the position of the bed. It was a big four-poster, half-way along the room and sideways on to the window. The mound of bedclothes showed that someone was sleeping there. For a second it occurred to Roger what a fool he would have made of himself if, after all, it was not the Ambassador.

Having edged round the curtain, he drew the long knife from his trouser belt and, putting his feet down flat as he took each step, advanced to the bedside. Laying a hand on the sleeper's shoulder, he gave it a gentle shake. As the shoulder moved with a jerk, he said in a low, clear voice :

'Attempt to call for help and I will drive my knife straight down into your heart.'

A man's head came up and a voice gasped, 'Who . . . who are you?'

The voice was that of de Brinevillers. His mind now at rest, Roger whispered, 'My name is Death, and I have come to claim you.'

'No, no! This cannot be!' the Ambassador exclaimed. Struggling up into a sitting position, he stared in terror at the dark, cloaked figure wearing a hat with a floppy brim.

'If I am not Death, at least I carry it,' Roger said quickly. 'Reach for your tinder box and light your bed-side candle. Then you will know me. But one cry and you will never speak again.'

With trembling hands, de Brinevillers lit the candle, then jerked round his head to look at Roger's face. As he recognised him, he whispered hoarsely, 'De Breuc . . . I thought . . .'

'No matter what you thought,' Roger cut him short. 'I am here to ask you only one question. Why did you not send a courier to the Emperor?'

'I . . . I assumed that the Prince d'Eckmühl was doing so,' the terrified Ambassador stammered.

'Ha!' Roger exclaimed. 'I guessed as much; but, in fairness to you, had to make certain. Had you had the sense to lie and maintain that you had sent the courier, I could not have proved otherwise. As it is, you have con-demned yourself out of your own mouth. It is you who are Ambassador to the Court of Prussia, not Davout. It was your responsibility to do your utmost to protect a French officer from the malice of Prussia's Chief Minister.

By your callous indifference, you left me to die. Tell me now, can you give me any good reason why I should not make you pay for that with your life?'

Tears started to de Brinevillers' eyes and began to run down his cheeks. Clasping his hands, he broke into desperate pleading:

'*Colonel! Monsieur le Comte!* I beg of you to spare me. At the thought of my negligence I now grovel for pardon. But clearly God did not intend you to die—for your sentence was commuted. And now you must have escaped from prison. You are far from safe yet though. Without help the chances are you will be caught before you can get out of Prussia. I offer myself now as your life line. I will provide money, horses, a good disguise—everything —and make certain that you get safely across the border.'

'Yes, you will provide me with money, horses, everything,' Roger sneered, 'then betray me within five minutes of my leaving you. Is it likely that I'd trust you? Do you take me for a fool? Now lie down and turn over on your stomach.'

'No, no!' wailed the wretched man. 'Have mercy! Spare me, I implore you.'

Roger gave him a swift prick in the arm with his long knife and said harshly, 'Do as you are bid. I do not mean to kill you; at least, not yet.'

At this partial reassurance de Brinevillers squirmed over, so that he lay face downwards. Roger put down his knife near the lower end of the bed, where he could snatch it up again in a moment, produced one of the pieces of thin cord from his pocket; pulled down the bedclothes and said:

'Now put your hands behind your back.' With a groan, the Ambassador obeyed. When Roger had lashed his prisoner's hands firmly together, he told him to sit up and asked where he kept his money.

De Brinevillers shook his head, 'I have none up here.

The Embassy funds are kept locked up down in the basement. But let me ring for my valet. I'll shout to him through the door to rouse our Chancellor. He has the key and will bring up any sum for which you like to ask.'

Roger laughed. 'And have him raise the house about my ears? No, thank you. But if you've no money here, I'll vow it's in this room you keep your jewels. They will do instead.'

As he spoke, he gave a quick glance round the room, and his eye fell on a small, brass-bound chest. Nodding toward it, he added, 'I doubt not they are in there, and I see your keys are here beside your bed. Now, hold up your head and open your mouth. I've no mind to let you shout for help while my back is turned.'

Sweat and tears streaming down his face, de Brinevillers obeyed. Taking another piece of cord from his pocket, Roger thrust the middle of it into his victim's mouth and tied the two ends firmly behind his head; so that he could still gurgle but not cry out.

Moving over to the door, Roger locked it then picked up the keys and went over to the little treasure chest. When he had unlocked it he saw that it had in it a considerable quantity of jewels and a small bag of gold *thalers*. As he pocketed several fine rings, brooches and diamond shoe and hat buckles, he smiled over his shoulder, ' 'Tis only fair that you should pay for my journey back to France, and such of these pretty trinkets as are over I'll keep as souvenirs of this merry meeting. Now for some more suitable clothes. Get out of bed and walk to the door of your closet.'

Again de Brinevillers did as he was told. Roger came up behind him, loosened the gag and said, 'It may be that your man sleeps in the closet. If so, as I open the door you'll immediately order him to remain silent. Should he not, I'll have to kill you both. And you will be the first, for I'll drive my knife through your back.' He

then thrust his hand past the Ambassador's waist, gripped the door-knob, turned it and pushed the door open.

The room was in darkness and there was no sound. Roger tightened the gag again and retied the knot.

Turning away, he lit a second candle from the first, kneed de Brinevillers in the backside, which made him stagger forward, and followed him into the closet.

The window was at one end of the long, narrow room; at the other there was a mahogany commode with, on one side of it, a washstand carrying a basin and ewer and, on the other, a small table on which there were a writing pad and a crayon for making notes. Both sides of the room were lined with hanging cupboards and presses. One after the other Roger opened them and took out undergarments, a coat and waistcoat of fine blue cloth, a pair of white buckskin breeches, silk stockings, a frilled lawn shirt, a gold-laced hat, leather riding gloves, a pair of tall boots, spurs and a grey, triple-collared cloak. Stripping to the buff, he threw the dirty, ragged garments he had been wearing on to the floor.

Having dressed himself in his purloined finery, he took a good look at the row of various shaped bottles on a shelf above the washstand. He had no intention of harming de Brinevillers unless it proved necessary, but was determined to humiliate him, and decided that the commode and the items on the shelf provided an adequate means of doing so.

The Ambassador had continued to stand near the door in resigned misery. Roger gave him a push towards the commode then pulled off the pointed nightcap he was wearing, opened it up and put it point downwards in the china receptacle. Tipping only a little water from the ewer into the basin he proceeded to lather his hands well with soap. Having rinsed them he poured the soapy water into a large tooth glass. Swallowing it would, he felt sure, cause anyone to be sick, but he had a mind to make a

thorough job of his project; so from various bottles on the shelf he added spoonfuls or a dash of Macassar hair-oil, eau-de-Cologne, hand lotion, bath essence, laxative and insect repellent, until the tumbler was full. Setting the glass down, he made de Brinevillers kneel in front of the commode, then undid his gag and said to him harshly:

'You will now drink this concoction. Should you refuse or attempt to spit it out, I'll slice your ears off.' As he spoke, he picked up the tumbler and held it to the Ambassador's lips.

The wretched man's hands were still bound behind his back, so he could put up no effective resistance. Muttering a curse, he took a sip of the repulsive mixture, screwed up his face and shied away.

With a swift flick of his wrist Roger drew the point of his knife across his victim's right cheek, and snapped, 'Come now! No nonsense! Drink it down or it will be the worse for you.'

The cut was barely skin deep but blood began to ooze from it and it had been painful enough for renewed terror to cause sweat again to break out on de Brinevillers' forehead. Leaning forward he took a gulp from the glass. As he swallowed he made a hideous grimace and his eyes bulged.

Roger grinned. 'That's better, now another.' But the kneeling man violently shook his head and spat out what little of the filthy mixture there remained in his mouth.

'So little Brinne means to be naughty eh?' Roger was frowning now. 'Then nannie must help him take his meddie.' Having laid his knife down on the washstand, he suddenly shot out his free hand and seized the Ambassador by the nose. As he opened his mouth to gasp for breath, Roger lifted the glass against his lower lip and poured half its contents down his gullet.

Still held firmly by the nose, he writhed in agony. His eyes started from his head and sweat, mingling with the

blood on his cheek, poured down his face. After a good, long minute, Roger let go of him. His stomach heaved, he gave a great belch and jerking forward his head was violently sick into the nightcap-lined commode.

For several minutes he remained there vomiting and retching. When he lifted his head he was gasping desperately for breath and tears were streaming from his eyes. But Roger still had no mercy on him. Seizing his nose again tightly between finger and thumb, he poured the remaining contents of the glass down de Brinevillers' throat. There followed an agonised gurgle, another great belch and, a moment later, the callous diplomat who had left Roger to die was again being as sick as a poisoned dog.

For minutes on end, with only brief intervals between, violent internal explosions caused the contents of the Ambassador's stomach to spurt up out of his mouth and down his nostrils, while pressure on his bowels caused their muscles to give way. When his stomach had become as empty as a drum his tormented retching still continued and, from breathlessness and agony, he was near fainting.

Roger, meanwhile, had not been idle. With some more lengths of cord he lashed his victim firmly to the commode, so that his head was held down immediately above the china receptacle that held his vomit. The closet now stank to high heaven and, knowing that it would continue to do so until it was opened and aired, Roger fired his parting shot. Turning to the small table on the far side of the commode, he wrote in clear letters on the note-pad.

Perfume suited to the character of M. de Brine-villers with the compliments of M. le Colonel Comte de Breuc.

109

As it was now some twenty-four hours since Roger had escaped, the hunt for him would already be up; so having left his 'card' at the Embassy would not increase his danger of being recaptured. But de Brinevillers' valet would find his master in the morning, and it was most unlikely that the man could refrain from telling his fellow servants such a juicy story; so all the odds were that before nightfall half of Berlin would learn who had inflicted this terrible indignity on the hated French Ambassador, and be laughing their heads off about it.

Without another word to his victim, Roger left him, snuffed the candles and descended the ladder into the garden. Ten minutes later, he was over the wall and walking gaily down a still-silent street, as though he were a gallant who had just spent a few hours with his mistress.

For the remainder of the night he again sat on a bench in the deserted *Tiergarten*. Soon after dawn he left it and walked out into the street. Swaggering into a nearby inn that had just opened, he enjoyed a hearty breakfast. As he paid his score, he asked the whereabouts of the nearest horse-dealer. De Brinevillers would not yet have been found; but even so time was now precious, as he could describe the clothes Roger had taken. At the horse-dealer's, he bought with the Ambassador's *thalers* the best mare available and saddlery for her. By eight o'clock he was riding out of Berlin in the direction of Stettin, which lay to the north. Having laid this false trail for ten miles, he turned west and, by byroads, got on to the main road for Hamburg. Stopping only to snatch four meals at wayside inns and to doze in the parlours of two of them for a couple of hours, he reached Hamburg in the afternoon on the 12th.

During his long ride he had had ample time to think out what would be best for him to do when he got there. It was certain that von Haugwitz would have been informed of his escape and do his utmost to have

him recaptured. The Minister's writ ran only in Prussia, but he could request the authorities in neighbouring States to have Roger looked for and, if found, apply for his extradition; so to get out of north Germany as speedily as possible was imperative.

Even in such a large port, to find a smuggler to put him across the North Sea might take several days, so he had decided to risk a big gamble. There was little Bourrienne did not know about the illicit trade carried on with England, and he had frankly told Roger that he was making a fortune by winking his eye at it. Roger had, therefore, made up his mind to throw himself on the mercy of his old friend.

On arriving at the Palace, he did not dare send up his own name. However, apart from the private apartments, such places were open to anyone who cared to walk into them. So, having handed over his horse, he walked boldly upstairs to the ante-room beyond which Bourrienne's office was situated. As Bourrienne was not a military commander, there was no sentry on the door, but several people were standing about there. Mingling with them, Roger waited his chance. Then, as a portly German came out, he thrust aside a footman, stepped through the door and slammed it behind him.

Bourrienne was seated at a big desk near the window. Beside him a secretary was standing taking dictation. As Roger entered, they both looked across at him. Bourrienne's mouth dropped open in amazement. Before he could speak, Roger put his finger to his lips, enjoining silence. With a little nod of understanding, Bourrienne told the secretary to leave the room. Immediately the door had closed behind him, Roger's old friend exclaimed:

'*Mon Dieu!* Can it really be you? I thought you dead these three months gone.'

Roger shook his head. 'No Davout succeeded in get-

ting my sentence reduced to ten years' imprisonment. Did he not tell you?'

'No. He said not a word of it. But both of us are fully occupied by our duties, so we see very little of each other. *Mon vieux,* I am delighted. Yes, delighted.'

With a feeble smile, Roger said, 'Alas, I am far from out of the wood yet. A student riot when I was being transferred from one prison to another enabled me to escape. But I stole the clothes I wear, so could be identified by them if my enemy, von Haugwitz, asks the assistance of the Hanoverian police.'

Bourrienne laughed. 'My dear fellow, perhaps in prison you did not learn of it, but Hanover is now part of France. I am no longer Ambassador here, but Civil Administrator. No-one dare touch you, and whenever you wish I can send you back to Paris.'

Roger had not realised that this would be one of the effects of the changed state of Hanover; and, while he had been confident that his old friend would not give him up, he had felt that for him, as an Ambassador, to agree to compromise himself by getting a wanted criminal out of north Germany was quite another matter. After a moment, he said :

'Of course, I should have known that. But 'tis not to France though that I wish to go. You have yourself experienced the Emperor's ingratitude to those who have served him. In my case he could not be bothered to save me from a firing squad, and in any event I am sickened unto death of his eternal wars; so I do not mean to return to him. As you know, I was born in Strasbourg; but my mother was English and I have numerous English relations. When I have been over there secretly on the Emperor's business, little suspecting my perfidy, they have treated me most kindly. If I can possibly get there I have decided to forswear war for the future and make England my home.' In making that statement he knew that

he was maligning Napoleon but it was essential for him to win Bourrienne's sympathy.

His friend considered for a moment, then smiled. 'To get you across should not be difficult. I have many contacts with merchant Captains who keep me supplied with coffee and other luxuries. I am certain that, in the course of a few days, I can arrange matters. But, my poor friend, you look sadly worn.'

Fingering the stubble on his chin, Roger replied, 'I am indeed. I rode desperate hard from Berlin and am in great need of sleep. If you can, as you think, get me to England, I'll be for ever grateful, but at the moment I'd bless you for a bed.'

One side of the room was lined with book-shelves. Bourrienne pressed a secret spring and a section of them swung forward, revealing a narrow passage. Beckoning to Roger, he led the way along it, up a flight of stairs to his private apartments. Showing Roger into a bedroom, he said :

'No-one will disturb you here. Later I will call you in time to shave and wash before we sup together. I have a dinner engagement that I cannot break; but I shall be back by nine o'clock.'

With a nod of thanks, Roger began to pull his clothes off. In no time he had tumbled into bed and was sound asleep. Five hours later he was still sleeping when Bourrienne's valet woke him. The man had already brushed his clothes and lit a fire in the room. In front of it Roger was soon lathering himself in a hip bath. Greatly refreshed, and infinitely relieved to know that he had nothing more to fear, he joined Bourrienne in a room along the corridor where, before setting out for Berlin, he had dined with him.

Over the meal Roger gave an account of his trial, the miserable months he had spent in prison, his escape and how he had avenged himself on de Brinevillers. At the

thought of the haughty, *ci-devant* Marquis in the position in which Roger had left him, Bourrienne laughed uproariously; then he said:

'And all this while I believed you dead. No doubt about that crossed my mind, because I saw an account of your execution in a Berlin news sheet. At least, one which appeared on the day it should have taken place. The affair had created such a stir that three whole columns were devoted to it, and the article ended with the gleeful statement that the fiendish French murderer, Breuc, had met a death too good for him in front of a firing squad that morning.'

Roger nodded. 'The article must have been written the previous day and printed during my night in the condemned cell. But tell me, did you receive the two letters I sent you, and forward them to England?'

'Yes; and by a safe hand. The captain who took them has since returned and reported to me having despatched them in Harwich. They reached me on the same morning as the article, so I enclosed it in the letter for the Lord Edward Fitz-Deverel.'

Bourrienne then gave Roger an interesting piece of news. Toward the end of August, Marshal Jean Baptiste Bernadotte had been invited by the Swedish Diet to become their Crown Prince.

Roger had at one time been sent by Mr. Pitt on a mission to Sweden, so he knew the history of its royal dynasty. The Vasas had, at one time, ruled over a great part of the Baltic lands, including Finland in the north and German Pomerania to the east. The able and warlike King, Gustavus III, had fought Catherine the Great of Russia and, being fanatically opposed to the French Revolution, had enthusiastically joined the First Coalition, in the hope of crushing this new People's State. But, in March '92, he had been assassinated by masked in-

114

truders at a ball, and that had brought to an end Sweden's era as a great power.

He had been succeeded by young Gustavus Adolphus IV, another fanatical champion of legitimacy, but having an unbalanced mind. After launching a disastrous assault on Bernadotte, who was then commanding in northern Germany, he had, against the advice of his generals and nobility, sent his army against that of Russia in Finland, whilst himself remaining in Stockholm and directing it in such a crazy fashion that it had been defeated piecemeal. By March 1809, his people had become so angered that they had supported his leading men in deposing him.

The autocratic powers of the Crown had then been greatly reduced, so that Sweden had become a constitutional Monarchy, with a Diet to be re-elected every five years, and Gustavus' uncle had ascended the throne as Charles XIII. Having no son, he had recognised as his heir a Danish connection, Prince Christian Augustus, and made peace with Russia by ceding Finland. But in the following year, which was the present one, Prince Christian had died as a result of a fit of apoplexy.

That much Roger knew, and from there Bourrienne took up the story. Charles XIII being old and feeble, and it having become apparent that inbreeding had brought madness into the Vasa strain, the Swedish magnates had decided to invite some healthy and vigorous man to become heir to the throne.

For several years past Napoleon had been gobbling up Europe, so what better insurance could there be against his deciding to swallow Sweden than to ask one of his Marshals to become their Prince Royal? Their choice had fallen upon Bernadotte for the following reasons:

He was not only a general of the first rank. When, as Napoleon's Viceroy, he had governed north Germany, he had shown himself to be a brilliant, humane and just ruler. Moreover, during the later stages of the Franco-

Prussian war, when he had driven a Swedish army from Pomerania, he had captured one of their crack cavalry regiments in Lübeck, invited its officers to dinner and given them some very sound advice on the policy that should be pursued in the best interests of their country.

When approached, Napoleon, who had always been jealous of Bernadotte, had been loath to agree to his aggrandisement, and endeavoured to fob off the Swedes with one of his lesser Marshals. But they would not have it. They had sent direct to Bernadotte a deputation consisting of their veteran Field Marshal, Count Hans Henrik von Essen, and several of the officers with whom Bernadotte had talked in Lübeck. And he had accepted.

To the Emperor's fury, when summoned by him Bernadotte had arrived in the uniform of a Swedish Field Marshal, and a most acrimonious discussion had followed. Bernadotte had asked to be relieved of his Princedom of Ponte Corvo, his rank as a Marshal of the Empire and, above all, his French citizenship. Napoleon could not believe his ears. He had made three of his brothers and his brother-in-law Kings of foreign countries; but they had all remained Frenchmen and subservient to him. He expected Bernadotte, like Murat, to remain a Marshal, govern as he, Napoleon, directed and, whenever called upon, leave his Kingdom to command an army in his wars.

But Bernadotte remained adamant. Courageously he insisted that, if he was to be Prince Royal of Sweden, he must become a Swede. At length, Napoleon gave way but demanded that Sweden should become his ally and place her army at his disposal in any future war. To that, too, Bernadotte refused to agree, maintaining that peace or war was a matter to be decided solely by the will of the Swedish people. Angry, bewildered and not knowing what to reply, the Emperor had succumbed and, in September, Bernadotte had left France to become not, like Napoleon's

116

brothers, a puppet King forced upon a hostile people, but a Royal Prince elected by the will of a nation.

Roger wondered how Bernadotte's wife, Desirée, would like being Princess Royal among a haughty, ancient aristocracy. She and her sister Julie were the daughters of a Marseilles silk merchant named Clary; and Julie, having married Napoleon's elder brother, Joseph, was now technically Queen of Spain.

He knew Desirée much better than he did her husband, as he had been acquainted with the Clarys for many years. When Bonaparte had been a down-at-heels artillery officer, the wealthy Clarys had welcomed him and Joseph into their family circle. As both the girls had large dowries, the brothers had asked for their hands in marriage. Their father was dead, and their brother had reluctantly consented. Joseph had married Julie, but Napoleon, although Desirée was his first love, had jilted her to marry the aristocratic Josephine de Beauharnais. But the Emperor had always retained a soft spot for Desirée; and it was he who, as he happened to be reading a book with a hero named Oscar at the time of her son's birth, had insisted that she should give the child that name.

As things had turned out, it could not have been more appropriate, and Roger wondered how much Napoleon's affection for his old love had contributed to his letting Bernadotte have his way, instead of having him arrested as a potential danger. But he could not think that, having been brought up in the sunshine of the South of France, pretty, retroussé-nosed, little Desirée was going to enjoy much the bitter cold of a northern Kingdom.

When he asked Bourrienne how Bernadotte had been doing during his first months as Prince Regent, his friend shook his head.

'Owing to her wars of the past seventeen years, Sweden has become a miserably poor country. Ponte Corvo was,

of course, extremely wealthy. While a Marshal of the Empire he had amassed the fortune of a multi-millionaire, and my spies tell me that he is using it all to pay Sweden's debts. But his position is very precarious. The Emperor has demanded that he should subscribe to the Continental System and prohibit all commerce with England. If he does so, Sweden will face final ruin. If he does not, his old enemy, Davoust, has orders to use his army here to invade Sweden. From Denmark that could be done with ease. Our allies, the Danes, would be delighted, and Sweden has no army worth the name with which to defend herself.'

Roger nodded. 'So that's how things stand. Well, Bernadotte is undoubtedly a courageous man and, by the standard of the times, an upright one; so one can only hope that he pulls through.'

Three days later Roger said good-bye to his old friend and went aboard an American ship that plied regularly between Hull and Hamburg, bringing English woollens over to the Continent. The weather proved fair and the voyage uneventful. On the evening of October 18th, he landed in England, and the following night he arrived in London; now home for good, all his adventures and perils behind him, and about to start a new life with his divine Georgina.

As was his custom, he went straight to the Earl of Amesbury's mansion in Arlington Street, as his Lordship's son, Lord Edward Fitz-Deverel lived there, and whenever Roger came to London, was delighted to have him as a guest.

When the front door was opened by a footman, it chanced that Droopy Ned was just crossing the hall. Turning to see who the visitor was, he peered at Roger with his short-sighted eyes. Suddenly, he dropped the book he was carrying and cried :

'God stap me! I'm seeing a ghost.'

Advancing, Roger laughed, 'No, dear Ned. I am no ghost, although I know you believed me dead. 'Tis my very self, home again at last, and overjoyed to see you.'

The two old friends hugged each other, then Roger asked, 'What of Georgina; is she well?'

'She was, as ever, in bounteous health when I saw her not long since.'

'Where is she, Ned? Down at Stillwaters? I cannot wait to see her.'

'Nay, she is not at Stillwaters, but down at Newbury,' Droopy replied.

Roger grinned. 'And what, pray, is she doing there? What e'er it be, I'll fetch her back within twenty-four hours. For, know you, before we parted seven months ago, she at last promised to marry me.'

A look of consternation suddenly appeared on Droopy's face and he blurted out, 'Oh, Roger, my dear! How can I tell you? But she married again, only a se'nnight since. She is now Her Grace the Duchess of Kew.'

CHAPTER X

A LIMITED COMPENSATION

DURING the long years since Roger had run away from home to escape having to become a midshipman, Fate had dealt him many savage blows; but never one so shattering as this. His eyes wide with surprise and shock, he stared at his friend and whispered:

'It can't be true!'

Droopy Ned shook his head. 'Alas, dear Roger, it is. Like myself, she believed you dead. We both received your letters written in a cell for the condemned, and with mine there was a cutting from a Berlin news sheet. It stated that you had been executed that morning.'

'The article had been printed overnight, before it was known that Marshal Davout had succeeded in getting my sentence commuted to ten years' imprisonment.'

'Thank God for that. But we never learned of it. Georgina and I both mourned you as dead. She was so stricken that she shut herself up for ten days and refused to see anyone. Then she wore black for you for three months, as though you had been her husband.'

'But, dam'me Ned, to marry again! Before she wed von Haugwitz she had remained a widow for years. Why, in God's name, should she again rush into matrimony so swiftly?'

With a shrug of his narrow shoulders, Droopy replied, 'Several factors I think contributed to that. She told me

that with your death all that was best in her life had ended. Her youth was over, and all zest for pleasure gone. She must resign herself to middle age. Her father's death, coming shortly after we received news of yours, was also a big blow to her.'

'What! Colonel Thursby dead?'

'Yes, of a heart seizure in mid-July.'

'Oh, poor Georgina!' Roger exclaimed. ' 'Twas he who furnished her fine mind with a thousand matters that are closed books to most women, and so enabled her to enchant her friends with intellect as well as beauty. He came second only to myself in her affections; and spent a great part of each year with her. I, too, shall miss him sadly, for he was more a father to me than my own. But why, Ned, why if she sought distraction from her sorrows, must she marry, of all people, old K? He must be near twice her age, and has a most unsavoury reputation.'

'Old K', as the Duke of Kew was popularly known, was indeed a far from pleasant character. He was immensely rich and a great patron of the Turf. He had a big house at Newmarket and, when younger, had often backed himself to win a sackful of guineas by competing either in horse races or driving a tandem. But he was a slovenly man who took no care for his appearance, often going about in awful old clothes and a battered hat. This, and other eccentricities, together with his well-known lewdness and lechery, had long made him notorious.

Again Droopy shrugged. 'I think she was in so sad a state that she cared not what became of her. He had pursued her all through last season; and, you may recall, she had oft boasted that she would become a Duchess before her hair turned grey. It may be that in accepting him she felt she was bowing to a decree of Fate.'

'Well, she's got her full coronet of strawberry leaves,' Roger said bitterly, 'and left me to moan the loveliest dream of my life.'

Taking him by the arm, Droopy said, 'Come, Roger, let us go upstairs. A glass of wine will at least make you feel no worse.'

'A glass!' Roger gave a harsh laugh. ' 'Tis a bottle I need; nay, a dozen.'

And he meant what he said. When, on returning to the West Indies at the end of 1795, he had learned that his wife, Amanda, had recently died in giving birth to their daughter, Susan, he had made himself drunk for a week. Now he followed that precedent and, for days, never left his bedroom while emptying bottle after bottle of Madeira. In vain Droopy begged him to moderate his potations, fearing that he would do himself an injury; but he remained maudlin and almost silent day after day while nursing his grief.

Lord Edward Fitz-Deverel was an unusual character for the age in which he lived. He abhorred all blood sports, horses, and any form of exercise. His interests lay in ancient religions, collecting antique jewellery and experimenting on himself with Eastern drugs. On the eighth morning after Roger had become his guest, he was amusing himself by translating a Greek papyrus that had come from Egypt. To his surprise, Roger came into his room, freshly shaven and dressed with his usual, almost foppish, elegance. The only signs of his long debauch were a slight watering of his eyes and the redness of his face. Sitting down, he crossed his silk-stockinged legs and said:

'Well, Ned. I fear I've behaved like a very sot this past week; but, at least I've got the plaguey bile out of my system. I'm now as resigned as ever I am like to be to Georgina's having married.'

'Zeus be praised for that,' Droopy replied, rubbing his high-bridged nose with a long, slender finger. 'And what now are your plans? You know that, as ever, you are welcome to stay here as long as you wish.'

'Thanks, Ned. I'll gladly accept your hospitality until

I can settle on how to occupy myself in the future. But tomorrow I'd like to go down to Stillwaters and spend a night or two there. That is, if Georgina has left my little Susan in her Great-Aunt Marsham's care.'

'She has, at least for the present, while she is—er—during these first weeks of her marriage.'

Roger gave a cynical laugh. 'You would have said, "while she is on her honeymoon", eh? Though how she can bring herself to pleasure that old roué passes my comprehension. But we'll not dwell on that. I'll take a stroll round the town now, and buy some gee-gaws for my daughter.'

On her return to England in the spring, Georgina had given Droopy a true account of the events at Schloss Langenstein, so that evening Roger had only to relate the story of his imprisonment and escape.

Next morning he rode the twenty miles to Stillwaters, near Ripley in Surrey, which had long been Georgina's home. The day following his arrival, Droopy Ned had sent a messenger down to let Mrs. Marsham and Susan know that Roger was not dead; so they received no shock when he entered the house and greeted them. As for the greater part of his manhood he had lived abroad, his daughter was almost a stranger to him; so he was most agreeably surprised when she cried out with delight and threw herself into his arms.

Susan was now nearly fifteen and well developed for her age. She had her mother's auburn hair, freckles and blue eyes, with a feminine version of Roger's finely-chiselled features. There could be no doubt that, within a few years, she would be one of the toasts of the town. He felt justly proud of her, and her joy in seeing him again greatly added to his pleasure in giving her the costly furs and jewels suitable to her age that he had brought with him.

But before he had been in the house for long he was

overcome by the same depression he had felt during his last visit, when Georgina had been in Germany and married to von Haugwitz. The stately mansion, with its lovely garden, woods and lake, gave him little pleasure now that they were no longer animated by her gay spirit. As he wandered about the splendid, lofty, now-empty salons, he was filled with nostalgia as he recalled the days when they had been crowded with statesmen, poets, ambassadors, painters and lovely women. A visit to the suite so often occupied by Colonel Thursby caused him new grief at the loss of that gentle, clever and dear friend; while Georgina's rooms, their fine furniture now under covers, brought home to him more strongly than ever the bitter disappointment he had suffered on learning that it was now no longer possible for him to make her his wife. Sitting down on the side of her big bed he thought of the way in which they had often frolicked in it, and was near to bursting into tears.

On the morning after his arrival he felt that he could bear to remain there no longer; yet was plagued by the thought of his duty to Susan. Often enough he had reproached himself for having been such a bad father; and, now that he had the opportunity of repairing his neglect of the girl, he was contemplating leaving her again within a matter of hours.

Then he hit upon a plan that greatly revived his spirits. He meant, in any case, shortly to live again at Thatched House Lodge in Richmond Park, a 'Grace and Favour' residence of which Mr. Pitt had given him the life tenancy for his services to the Crown. He would have Aunt Marsham and Susan to live with him there for a while.

That afternoon he told them of his plan. Mrs. Marsham said that such a change would be pleasant, and Susan jumped for joy. Then, struck by a thought, she said, 'But, Papa, we must be back here by mid-December, for Charles will be returning from Eton.'

124

She had been brought up with Georgina's boy, and knowing their devotion to each other Roger replied, 'Unless his mother has other plans for him, we'll have him, too, at Richmond, and make it a truly merry Christmas.' Half an hour later he had mounted his horse and was on his way back to London.

After riding a few miles it suddenly occurred to him that if the report of his death had reached the Prime Minister, the tenancy of Thatched House Lodge might, by now, have been given to somebody else; so he made a slight detour in order to go there. To his considerable relief he found Dan Izzard, the ex-smuggler who acted as caretaker for him, up on the roof replacing a broken tile. As had always been the case after Roger's long absences, the house and garden had been well cared for and Dan, although now ageing, was still hale and hearty. Since Amanda's death Roger had occupied the house only for brief periods at long intervals, so it had not even occurred to Dan that his master might be dead, and, giving a cheerful hail, the old salt came nimbly down the ladder to welcome him.

Roger stayed only long enough to knock back a noggin of rum with his bearded retainer, and tell him to engage an adequate staff during the coming week; then he rode on in the gathering twilight to Arlington Street.

For the next ten days he took up again the life he normally led while in the capital. It was the dead season, so many of the big mansions in the West End were closed and shuttered, while their owners took toll of pheasants and partridges in the country. But Parliament was in session, the leading clubs: White's, Brook's, Boodle's and Almack's, still had their quotas of gamblers every night, a play at Drury Lane was nightly drawing crowds, there were several other good pieces on and a number of exhibitions.

As Roger and Droopy were both members of White's,

they went there frequently, and Roger was soon brought up-to-date with the political scene. Early in 1806, after over fourteen years of unremitting effort by Pitt to check the destruction by the French of the old order in Europe, Napoleon's victory at Austerlitz had broken the Third Coalition and, with it, Pitt's heart. Exhausted and in despair, the great champion of true liberty had turned his face to the wall and died.

His Ministry had shortly been followed by one led by his lifelong rival, James Fox. It had been composed mainly of Whigs and been termed, 'The Ministry of All the Talents'. But it had turned out to be a coalition of weak, discordant men who lacked all initiative in prosecuting the war. Fox's death, that September, had heralded the end of its short life and, for two decades, rule by the Whigs.

In December the Duke of Portland had brought together a Cabinet with Spencer Perceval as Prime Minister. Perceval was a very skilful politician, and a fluent orator, but not a very forceful personality. However, he had George Canning as Foreign Secretary, and Lord Castlereagh as his Secretary of State for War.

At Oxford Canning had been one of a circle of brilliant young Whigs, but his admiration for Pitt brought him over to the Tories. In 1800 he married Portland's sister-in-law, who was a great heiress. He was made Postmaster General, then in 1807 Perceval had given him the Foreign Office.

Castlereagh had made his name as Lord Lieutenant of Ireland. He had fought hard for Union and Catholic emancipation; but George III had rejected these measures so stubbornly that, in 1801, Pitt had resigned and Castlereagh with him. In 1805, on Pitt's return to office, Castlereagh had been made Secretary of State for War and, later, under Perceval, again filled that office.

Both Canning and Castlereagh had striven hard to re-

arouse the determination of the war-weary British people to defeat Napoleon, and had prosecuted hostilities with renewed vigour. The former had been responsible for the cutting out by the British Navy of the Danish Fleet at Copenhagen, thus preventing it from falling into the hands of the French and again giving them near-parity at sea after their defeat at Trafalgar. The latter had initiated the use of fire ships, in an attempt to destroy the great French flotilla at Boulogne, which was being assembled for the invasion of England.

Unfortunately, early in Perceval's ministry, the two had quarrelled. On the withdrawal of the British Army from Corunna, after Sir John Moore's death there, Canning had pressed for a renewal of the war in the Peninsula and had sent the able Marquis Wellesley as Ambassador to the Spanish Junta of Insurrection. It was he, too, who had secured the appointment of the Marquess' younger brother, Sir Arthur Wellesley, as Commander of the new British Army sent out to aid the Spaniards. An undertaking had then been given that all the support of which Britain was capable should be used for this campaign. Castlereagh had agreed but, after the British had withdrawn from Copenhagen, sent the troops there to Gothenburg instead, in order to close the Baltic to the Russians. Then, without Canning's knowledge, he had sent a British expedition to the fever-ridden island of Walcheren, at the mouth of the Scheldt, where it had failed dismally in its objective of capturing Antwerp.

Angered by this dispersal of troops which he had expected to be sent to reinforce the Army in the Peninsula, Canning had demanded Castlereagh's dismissal, with the threat that otherwise he would himself resign. Neither Perceval nor Portland had had the courage to inform Castlereagh of this situation, so he had not been made aware of it for several months. When at length it came to his knowledge, the two Ministers had quarrelled

furiously and fought a duel. The first shots of both had gone wide. Canning's second shot had glanced off a button on Castlereagh's coat, and Castlereagh's had slightly wounded Canning in the thigh. Both had then resigned.

The Marquis Wellesley replaced Canning as Foreign Secretary. He had spent a number of years as Governor General of India and proved a most able administrator. It was there, too, that his brother Arthur had made his name, as Commander-in-Chief during several victorious campaigns. Having long ruled over vast territories, when the Marquis returned to England in 1806 his associates found him extremely haughty and self-willed. At the Foreign Office he proved the same, rarely bothering to attend Cabinet meetings, and holding the Prime Minister in contempt.

Lord Liverpool had taken over the War Office from Castlereagh, and had followed his policy of greatly increasing the army establishment; so that, including reserves, it now stood at over half a million men. Between them, he and Wellesley had overcome the former considerable opposition to continuing the war in the Peninsula, and were now the strongest men in the Government.

However, the burning question of the hour was a recurrence of the King's malady. Some twenty years earlier his mind had become unstable, which had resulted in George, Prince of Wales, becoming temporary Regent. The King had recovered but, in recent years, had become increasingly feeble both in mind and body. A cataract had made him totally blind in one eye, and another in the other eye had so restricted his sight that he could not recognise anyone at a distance of more than four feet. He had, moreover, recently become quite mad, imagining that he was still King of Hanover, and that the Countess of Pembroke, for whom in his youth he had nurtured a secret passion, was his wife.

He was a simple man and very pig-headed. His

disastrous refusal to give his colonies in America a measure of self-government had led to their total loss; and his deeply religious scruples made him adamant in resisting all measures that would give equal rights to his Catholic and Nonconformist subjects. But he had gained the love of his people by his intense patriotism and the fact that he grew the biggest turnips in England—which had earned him the nickname of 'Farmer George'.

On the other hand, the Prince, now long known as 'The First Gentleman in Europe', was disliked and distrusted by both the nobility and a large section of the people. He was dissolute, a liar and a spendthrift of the first order. Again and again his mountainous debts had had to be paid, and his earlier morganatic marriage to Mrs. Fitzherbert—a Catholic—had been far from gaining him popularity.

As he loathed his father, he had done all he could to annoy him and, with that in view, made himself the patron of the Whigs. It was this, now that a Regency would again have to be proclaimed, that was causing great concern to the Tory peers; and, to protect their government, they were endeavouring to render the Prince almost powerless by hedging the Regency about with many restrictions.

It was not until towards the end of November that Roger saw Georgina again. By then Mrs. Marsham and Susan had been installed in Thatched House Lodge, and he was greatly enjoying having his pretty and cheerful young daughter in the house. But fairly frequently, when he accepted invitations to social functions in London, he spent a night or two with Droopy Ned.

On this occasion they had both been present at a dinner given by the Earl of Malmesbury at the Beefsteak Club, which he had taken over for the evening. The great diplomat, now retired, had been one of Roger's earliest patrons. He had become very deaf but, nevertheless, it

had been an hilarious evening. Next morning Roger had decided to ride in Rotten Row. It was a pleasant autumn day, so quite a number of ladies were taking the air in their carriages. Among them was Georgina, looking as lovely as ever, her dark curls falling on the collar of an ermine cloak, and wearing an enormous picture hat crowned with white ostrich feathers. Catching sight of Roger, she jerked the string tied to her coachman's little finger, and her carriage pulled up.

CHAPTER XI

THE TRAP

ROGER's heart began to pound. He could not make up his mind whether he was glad or sorry to see her. But he could not ignore her beckoning hand. Dismounting, and with his horse's reins over his arm, he made a leg, then put one foot on the step of the carriage and, with a smile, asked :

'Well, how does it feel to be a Duchess?'

Georgina hesitated nervously for a moment before breaking into hurried speech, 'No different. But Roger, my dear, let's not talk of that. Oh, I pray you not to hold it against me, for I believed you dead. It seems that we are fated never to marry. I can only thank God that you are still alive.'

'I, too,' he agreed. 'Although for a while after I got back to England I wished myself dead. But does our meeting here not remind you of another occasion when we met by accident?'

'Why, yes!' she exclaimed, with a quick smile. ' 'Twas on this very spot that, in '89, we encountered each other after your return from four years on the Continent. How strange a coincidence.'

'It is indeed. What would I not give that we might roll back the years and again enjoy what followed our meeting.'

Her big eyes suddenly lighting up, she leaned forward

and whispered. 'Roger, why should we not? I have always retained the little house on the height above Kensington village, for the sake of its studio. Let us meet there this evening.'

'There's nothing I'd like better,' Roger whispered back. 'But what of your Duke?'

She shrugged. 'The old fellow is still down at Newmarket. He no longer cares for London, and I made it a condition of our marriage that I should come here when I wished. I've been lying these past few nights at Kew House, his mansion in Piccadilly. It has a glorious view over St. James' Park, but for tonight I'll forgo that vista. Join me at our old haunt, dear Roger, no later than eight o'clock.'

Feeling a dozen years younger, Roger drove out that evening to Georgina's *petite maison*. In the old days she had used it not only to have painting lessons from Sir Joshua Reynolds and Mr. Gainsborough, whom she had incited to a jealous rivalry as her teachers; she had also secretly received there the beaux she had decided to pleasure.

Roger thought it unlikely that she would fail to bring from Kew House a supper of some sort; but, against the chance that she had found it awkward to explain a sudden demand for a picnic basket on a November evening, he had brought as a contribution two bottles of champagne, a cold roast duck and a Strasbourg pâté that had recently been smuggled over.

Now dear Jenny, who for so many years had served Georgina as a personal maid and confidant, was happily married to an ex-bosun and living in a cottage she had been given on the Stillwaters estate; so it was another buxom young woman named, as he soon learned, Harriet, who opened the door to him, took the valise he had brought and smilingly showed him in to her mistress.

Clad only in a silk chamber robe, Georgina was lying

on a comfortable sofa before a roaring fire. Jumping up, she threw her arms about him and he drew her soft, yielding form into a tight embrace. When they had temporarily taken their fill of kisses, she bade him go into the bedroom and get out of his heavy clothes. When he returned he had on only his chamber robe. Taking her in his arms again, he pushed her back on the sofa, buried his face in her neck and let his hand caress her opulent thighs. She opened them to him, but only for a minute, then pulled his hand away. Her eyes were closed and her breath was coming fast, as she panted :

'Roger, you devil, desist. I vow you would seduce a saint, and I'm mightily tempted to let you have me here and now. But I'll not. Young Harriet will soon be bringing us our supper. She would be hard to shock, for I know my coachman to be her lover. Even so, I've no wish to let her see me half-naked, my legs entwined with yours, and you up to the hilt in me. 'Tis not as though we had not the whole night before us.'

Roger laughed. 'Then, sweet, you'd best send for some cold water, so that I may reduce my manhood to more normal proportions.' But he let her go and rearranged his robe more decorously.

They supped beside the fire. Georgina was much amused by Roger's idea that she would even dream of giving an explanation to her chef on requiring him to produce food for her to take out of the house at any hour of the day or night. She had brought oysters, a hen lobster, a game pie and a pineapple, as well as ample wine. Both of them had always had hearty appetites, so they tucked into this fine selection of good things until they were both belching between their bouts of laughter.

Over the meal Roger told her all that had befallen him since he had put her on to the frigate off St. Maxime. At his description of de Brinevillers lashed to the commode,

with his nose only six inches above its pot, tears of mirth came to Georgina's eyes and she cried:

'Oh, the poor wretch, how I should have loved to see him; but he deserved worse. Had I been there I would have rubbed his face in it.'

Her voyage home had been without incident. Before she had been an hour aboard the surly Captain had given up his cabin to her and was eating out of her hand. At Gibraltar, the Admiral commanding there had been an old friend and made no difficulty about securing her a passage in the first ship bound for England. In the Bay of Biscay it had been rough; but she was a good sailor, so had ridden out the three-day storm and been landed safely at Portsmouth in mid-April.

When Roger asked her about her marriage, she said, ' 'Tis well enough. The news of your death and, following closely on it, that of my beloved Papa, reduced me to a state that I have never before experienced. I felt so low that I no longer cared what happened to me. By summer, soon after I returned to town, a dozen men were, as usual, after me. I could not stomach the thought of going to bed with any of them. But I'll confess that I was tempted by the thought of becoming a Duchess and wearing the famous Kew emeralds; so, in the autumn, I accepted the old goat.'

' "Goat" is a fitting description of him,' Roger remarked a shade acidly. 'I well remember how, to the amusement of passers-by, he used to lean over his balcony in Piccadilly and beckon up the whores to rut upon. Since you say that you had no desire left to bed with even a handsome man, it amazes me that you could find it in you to give yourself to an ugly, elderly roué.'

Her eyes widened, and she cried, 'Do you then suppose that I let him make love to me? Lud, no! He's long past that; as impotent as a new-born child. He now gets his pleasure by seeing me naked. But that means nothing

to me. A cat may look at a king. So, when I feel well disposed toward him, I let him gaze his fill.'

The clock on the mantel chimed ten. As though at a signal, they smiled at each other and stood up. Georgina led the way to the bedroom, Roger followed her, carrying a bottle of champagne. Two minutes later, they were between the black silk sheets of her bed.

During the night, between bouts of love-making, they dozed or talked and made plans for the future. Before consenting to marry her Duke, Georgina had wisely discussed with him their marital relations. Since, as she had supposed, age had rendered him impotent, she had told him that she would not marry him unless he left her free to satisfy the urges natural to a woman of her years. As his main reason for wanting to marry her was the right to show her off in public as his, to the envy of other men, he had agreed, provided she took care that her amours should not become generally known.

In consequence, however much the servants at Kew House might prattle, she did not have to account to her husband for her comings and goings. Overjoyed that they would be able to spend two or three nights a week together as long as she remained in London, Roger raised the question of Christmas.

Naturally, they wanted to spend it together, if possible; but either for her to have him to stay at Newmarket or for him to have her at Richmond they felt to be too blatant. It then occurred to her that the answer to the problem was for them all to spend Christmas at Stillwaters. It had been the children's home for the greater part of their lives and, as Susan's father, Roger was accounted one of the family. It might even make a pleasant change for the old Duke and, provided they were discreet, he would give them no trouble.

The three months that followed turned out to be one of the happiest periods of Roger's whole life. Although

his hope of settling down for good with Georgina had been dashed, the fact that she had a complaisant husband enabled them to see a great deal of each other both in private and public, since both the Duke and all society were aware of their lifelong friendship and that whenever Roger was for a while in London he had escorted her everywhere.

Susan's stay at Thatched House Lodge had at last enabled him to get to know his daughter well, and he experienced a hitherto unknown joy in the affection shown him by this gay, pretty young creature who called him Papa.

When she and Mrs. Marsham returned to Stillwaters, he followed them a few days later. Georgina and her Duke were already installed, and Roger found the old man more congenial company than he had expected. His Grace was no fool, had a cynical wit and an excellent taste for claret, old Madeira and vintage port. From a few sly remarks he made, it soon became apparent that he had tumbled to it that Roger was his wife's lover; but, as their long friendship provided them with excellent cover, it suited him much better to be cuckolded by Roger than for her to start a new affaire which might have provoked a scandal.

As, from the beginning, Georgina had insisted that she and her husband should occupy separate rooms, having seen her to bed he always left her round about midnight; so Roger, to whom she had given his old room on the far side of her boudoir, was able to sleep with her for the greater part of the night.

Young Charles came down from Eton the day after Roger arrived, and the children enjoyed the happiest Christmas they had known for years. Roger and Georgina rode with them every morning and, anxious that the young Earl should become a good swordsman, Roger spent an hour or two every day teaching him to fence.

On Christmas Day there were dozens of presents for everybody, golden guineas in the Christmas pudding and, at the end of the meal, the candles having been put out, a blazing snapdragon was brought in, from which they snatched the raisins at the risk of burning their fingers. Then, in the evening, they sat in semi-darkness round the Yule log, telling ghost stories.

On Boxing Day, they had the traditional servants' dinner and dance; then, for the 27th Georgina had invited a hundred of her neighbours to a ball and, for the first time, the children were allowed to take part in such a festivity. In the days that followed there were a special party for them to entertain their contemporaries, visits to neighbours and entertainments given by them. The church bells of Ripley rang in 1811 and the inmates of Stillwaters celebrated the New Year with all the time-honoured games and songs.

On January 3rd, for appearances' sake, Roger returned to Thatched House Lodge, but it had been agreed that, as soon as Charles went back to Eton, Mrs. Marsham and Susan should again join him there, and that later in the year Roger should pay a visit to Georgina's new home at Newmarket. Meanwhile the 'little season' was about to open in London, so she would be living for a while in Piccadilly and they would be able to see each other as often as they wished.

A fortnight later, at a diplomatic reception, Roger ran into an old acquaintance. This was a tall, dark man with beetling eyebrows, named Alfonso de Queircoz, who had been First Secretary at the Portuguese Embassy at Isfahan when Roger had been there in the summer of 1807.

There had been no friendship between them there, because de Queircoz had been madly in love with the Ambassador's beautiful daughter, Lisala, and Roger had cut him out; but it was for another reason that the meeting was far from welcome. In Isfahan the Portuguese had

known him as *M. le Colonel de Breuc*, a member of the French mission.

However, on previous occasions he had surmounted such awkward situations arising from his dual identity; so, having returned de Queircoz's bow, he waited with a half-smile on his lips to hear how the diplomat would address him.

As it turned out, he was not called on to resort to his well-established catalogue of plausible lies, for de Queircoz said, 'Sir, you must pardon me for accosting you, but you bear so strong a resemblance to *M. le Colonel de Breuc* that I feel sure you must be his English cousin.'

'Indeed, Sir, I am,' Roger replied. 'In appearance we are near-twins and have oft been mistaken for each other. I take it then that you know him?'

'Yes, we met in Persia, and to my cost. I was then paying court to the lovely Lisala de Pombal; but, after your handsome cousin's arrival on the scene, she had no eyes for anyone but him.'

Roger nodded. 'It seems, then, *Senhor*, that you have been twice fated to be thwarted by my family. For you may have heard that later, in Lisbon, I met Lisala, accompanied her to Brazil and married her.'

'Yes, I did hear that. Also that, eighteen months or so ago, she died in mysterious circumstances in Germany. Please accept my sincere condolences.'

'Alas, it was so.' Roger's face took on a suitable expression of grief. 'As you no doubt know, her death was caused by a strange accident which has never been accounted for.'

'So I gathered, although my informant could give me no details of the tragedy. I can only again condole with you, Sir, on your great loss.'

'I thank you, *Senhor*.' Roger bowed, and was about to move away, when de Queircoz said:

'While I naturally resented your cousin ruining my

chances with the *Senhorita* in Isfahan, having lost any hope of her returning my affection I bear no ill will toward you, Sir, in that later she became your wife. Two nights hence we are giving a reception at the Portuguese Embassy, and I should be honoured if you would attend it as my guest.'

It happened that Roger was free for that evening so, out of politeness, he accepted.

When he arrived at the reception, the dark-browed Portuguese received him most courteously, presented him to the Ambassador, and then to several agreeable ladies. Later in the evening he rejoined Roger, refilled his glass with wine and led him over to a small table; then said:

'It is not for me, Sir, to enquire into your circumstances; but, unless you are immensely rich, it surprises me that you have not yet claimed the great fortune that awaits you in Lisbon.'

Since Lisala's death Roger had had so many other things to occupy his mind that his being his wife's natural heir had never occurred to him.

De Queircoz was going on: 'The late Marquis' sister, Dona Arahna, returned from Brazil last summer. When she learned that Lisala was dead and had left no will, she applied for permission to administer her late niece's estate on behalf of her son, Captain Don Carlos, who is serving with the Anglo-Portuguese contingent under General Graham, which is bottled up with the Spanish in Cadiz. But the court ruled that the Marquis' nephew had no title to inherit unless it was proved that you, too, were dead or, for a period of seven years, had failed to make your claim. So you have only to go to Lisbon and complete the formalities, then the whole of the de Pombal millions will be yours.'

Roger thanked the Portuguese for having given him this valuable information, talked on with him for a while,

then left the party deep in thought. The following night he discussed the matter with Georgina.

There seemed no reason to believe that de Queircoz knew that Roger had been accused of his wife's murder and sentenced to death on that account; nor, as that had taken place at the other end of Europe, that anyone in Lisbon should be aware of it. Even if they were, in Portugal there was no likelihood whatever of his being apprehended for having escaped from a Prussian prison. And, although during the past twenty years he had amassed a quite considerable fortune, the prospect of becoming immensely rich was not a thing to be lightly thrown away.

He was, however, somewhat troubled by the ethics of the matter. Lisala would not willingly have left him a button, and it seemed unfair to deprive the *Senhora* de Arahna's son, who had come into his uncle's title, of the means with which to support it, and also of the family estates.

Georgina then suggested a compromise. Why should not Roger go to Portugal, establish his claim in the courts and afterwards divide his inheritance? He could hand over to the young man the estates, with sufficient money to maintain them, but keep for himself a good part of Lisala's fortune. Having made this suggestion she added :

'During the past two months there has been hardly a day that we have not spent part of together; but we must not go on like this indefinitely, otherwise old K will say that our affaire is becoming too obvious and will start making trouble. To honour my bargain with him I ought now to spend a month or so at his seat near Newmarket. Meanwhile, you could go to Lisbon and, at least, put in your claim. Then, on your return, I'd come back to London and we would renew the happy life we have been leading.'

Roger agreed that if he went abroad for a while that would be a good way of retaining the Duke's passive

140

acceptance of him as Georgina's lover; so, the following morning, he went to the Foreign Office and sent up his name to the Marquis Wellesley, whom he had met several times in society.

Three-quarters of an hour later, the Marquis received him and listened politely to his request for a passage to Lisbon; then he said, 'So you are going abroad again, Mr. Brook? I am delighted to hear it, as I have no doubt your secret activities will prove of great value to my brother.'

Staring at him in surprise, Roger replied, 'I do not understand Your Lordship. To what secret activities do you refer?'

'Don't fence with me, man,' the haughty Marquis said with a frown. 'Having been Foreign Secretary for near eighteen months, I have had ample time to go through the secret files. From them I learned that for many years Mr. Pitt accounted you his most resourceful secret agent, and more recently you sent from Vienna valuable information to my predecessor, George Canning.'

Roger relaxed. 'Then, my lord, I'll not deny it. But I have no intention of resuming my dual identity when I am in Portugal. My object in going to Lisbon is solely to claim an inheritance that is my due.'

'That is to be regretted. I had supposed that you had become weary of leading an aimless life in London and intended again to serve your country by securing for us particulars of the intentions of the French. However, since you have a matter requiring your presence in Lisbon, I will willingly secure you a passage in one of His Majesty's ships.'

Having thanked the Marquis, Roger left his address and took his leave.

He did not have long to wait as, now that a considerable part of Portugal was in British hands, warships and transports were constantly leaving for Lisbon. Moreover,

there would be no necessity for him to land secretly on a deserted shore at night, as he had three years earlier, when the country was occupied by the French.

The following morning a sealed packet was delivered to him at Thatched House Lodge. It contained instructions that, two days hence, he should report to Captain Hurst of H.M.S. *Swiftsure*, lying off Greenwich; also a letter addressed to General the Viscount Wellington and a note from the Marquess asking him to deliver it personally to his brother.

Roger had already told Susan that he would be going abroad for a few weeks, so she and Mrs. Marsham were to return to Stillwaters. After packing the things he was likely to need, he took a fond farewell of his daughter and went up to London. That night and the next he spent with Georgina out at her little house above Kensington village. She was now loath to let him go, but resigned herself to it after he had promised to take care of himself. Next morning he said good-bye to Droopy Ned, then went down to Greenwich and presented his credentials to Captain Hurst, who allotted him a little cabin and said he was happy to have his company.

The *Swiftsure* was one of the newest frigates and she had, for the time of year, a good passage. Roger suffered only one day of really bad seasickness, and landed at Lisbon on the 31st January.

Within a couple of hours he was installed at the *Leao d'Ouro,* a comfortable inn at which he had stayed previously. While he was unpacking his bags, he ran over in his mind the course that the war in the Peninsula had taken.

It had been started by Napoleon in October 1807, with the object of forcing Portugal to accept his Continental System and cease importing British goods. Without warning he had despatched an army, under General Junot, to capture Lisbon and coerce the Prince Regent into agree-

142

ing to his demands. Only just in time the Royal Family had escaped by sea and fled to Brazil. But Napoleon had a mind to be master of Spain also. As his reluctant ally, Spain had been bullied by him into sending her best troops to garrison fortresses in Germany, while he deployed his French troops against Austria. Then, when Spain was almost defenceless, on the excuse that the British might invade Portugal he had sent large forces, theoretically to resist such an invasion, but actually to seize, by guile and treachery, the principal fortresses in Spain.

In March, King Carlos IV had been forced to abdicate by his son Ferdinand. Napoleon had lured both of them across the frontier to Bayonne, on the pretext of adjudicating between them; but had made them prisoners. This had roused the Spanish people to such fury that, on May 2nd, the citizens of Madrid had revolted against Murat who, a few months earlier, had occupied the capital and been nominated the Emperor's Lieutenant-General.

Napoleon's next move had been to bring his brother, Joseph, from Naples and make him King of Spain, replacing him on the throne of Naples by Murat. By then it was high summer, the whole of Spain in revolt and a Junta had been formed of Spanish notables. They had little control over their scattered forces, but entered into an alliance with Britain. In an attempt to suppress the risings, Marshal Moncey had been despatched to Valencia and General Dupont down to Seville, but Moncey was forced to retire on Madrid and, to the grievous humiliation of the French who, under Napoleon, had never before suffered such a defeat, Dupont had been compelled to surrender at Baylen. Joseph had then panicked, evacuated his new capital and retired behind the Ebro.

Meanwhile, the Spaniards were putting up a fanatical resistance. Saragossa was held by Palafox until the city

was reduced to ruins by Lannes, and the French under General Duhesme were besieged in Barcelona. On August 3rd, a British army under Sir Arthur Wellesley landed in Mondego Bay. Junot went out from Lisbon to meet it and, at Vimiero, was so heavily defeated that he had to surrender. Most unfortunately, within hours of having won the battle, two Generals senior to Wellesley arrived from England and superseded him. Instead of making the whole French Army prisoner, they had entered into a Convention with Junot at Cintra to send his whole force back to France in British ships. For this incredible piece of folly, all three Generals were recalled to England and court-martialled. Only Wellesley was exonerated.

Meanwhile, Napoleon had ordered the corps of Ney, Mortier and Victor to Spain and, in October, arrived himself on the frontier to direct operations. The Spanish armies, though large, lacked all co-ordination; so the forces confronting the Emperor were strong only on the wings. Smashing through their weak centre, he routed them utterly and retook Madrid.

The year 1809 had opened by Sir John Moore landing in northern Spain. Unaware of Napoleon's great strength and believing that Madrid was still holding out, he sought to create a diversion in Old Castile and cut the Emperor's line of communication. But Napoleon learned of his whereabouts and concentrated a much larger army against him. His hasty retreat had ended with the battle of Corunna and his death. The bulk of the British army had been evacuated, leaving only a small force under General Baird, which had retired on Lisbon.

At this juncture Napoleon received information that Talleyrand and Fouché were conspiring against him, so he returned to Paris at full speed, after leaving directions as to how the campaign was to be brought to a successful conclusion. Ney was to hold down Galicia, while

Soult took Oporto, then Lisbon. Victor was to take Badajoz, then Seville. Sebastiani was to crush the Spanish resistance in the south.

In March, after an appalling slaughter of men, women and even children who, under their Bishop, had striven to defend the city, Soult had taken Oporto; but, hemmed in on all sides by guerrillas, he had not felt himself strong enough to advance any further. The following month Wellesley landed at Lisbon with a considerable army. Victor cut a large Spanish force to pieces at Medellin but, like Soult, isolated and without reinforcements, became stuck there.

In May Wellesley decided to move fast against Soult and, if successful, rapidly turn about and attack Victor. By a daring crossing of the Douro where the banks of the river were so precipitous that they had been left unguarded, he heavily defeated Soult and chased him out of Oporto; but he just failed to catch Victor, whose army had been reduced to such a state of starvation that he had withdrawn to the valley of the Tagus.

Wellesley then formed a plan with the Spanish generals that they should make a demonstration against Madrid, while he attempted to crush Victor. On June 27th, the British and French met at Talavera. Sebastiani's army had by then joined Victor, and King Joseph had brought up the last reserves from Madrid, so the French now greatly outnumbered the British. The battle was a most bloody one. It lasted two days, and there were over twelve thousand killed and wounded. Victor refused to believe that the British line could not be broken and sent his columns against it again and again. The line held, and Wellesley won a resounding victory, but he was robbed of its fruits by the hopeless incompetence of his allies, so he swore that never again would he operate with Spanish troops unless they were under his command.

Madrid might still possibly have fallen to the British

had not Wellesley learned that Soult, reinforced by Mortier's corps, was moving up from Galicia with the intention of cutting his communications. His army was so exhausted that it could not fight another battle; so he was compelled to beat a hasty retreat into Portugal.

In the late summer and autumn, Spanish forces continued, in widely-separated areas, to engage the French, but Wellesley—who in September was, for his victories, created Baron Douro and Viscount Wellington—flatly refused to commit British troops with them; so their gallant efforts were defeated again and again.

Although the French were being harried everywhere, Napoleon's war with Austria being as good as over, he was pouring more and more troops into the Peninsula; so Wellington, fearing that his much smaller army would be driven into the sea, retired on Lisbon and began to construct across the neck of the isthmus on which it stood the afterwards famous lines of Torres Vedras. These were not mere entrenchments, but solid earthworks, strengthened by palisades. The first line was twenty-nine and the second twenty-two miles in length. They included one hundred and twenty-six redoubts and were defended by four hundred and twenty-seven pieces of artillery.

Meanwhile, in the south Soult had taken Seville and Napoleon sent Masséna, who had the reputation of being the most able of all his Marshals, to command the army in Portugal. Fortunately for Wellington, the Emperor decreed that the assault on Lisbon should not begin until every man he could spare had crossed the Pyrenees. This gave the British a seven-month respite to prepare their great defensive wall. Moreover, during these months, Wellington was able to take other valuable measures. These included the embodiment and training of many regiments of Portuguese, and securing the consent of the Portuguese Government to render central Portugal a desolate wilderness. Its towns and villages were all evacu-

Soult took Oporto, then Lisbon. Victor was to take Bada-joz, then Seville. Sebastiani was to crush the Spanish re-sistance in the south.

In March, after an appalling slaughter of men, women and even children who, under their Bishop, had striven to defend the city, Soult had taken Oporto; but, hemmed in on all sides by guerrillas, he had not felt himself strong enough to advance any further. The following month Wellesley landed at Lisbon with a considerable army. Victor cut a large Spanish force to pieces at Medellin but, like Soult, isolated and without reinforcements, be-came stuck there.

In May Wellesley decided to move fast against Soult and, if successful, rapidly turn about and attack Victor. By a daring crossing of the Douro where the banks of the river were so precipitous that they had been left un-guarded, he heavily defeated Soult and chased him out of Oporto; but he just failed to catch Victor, whose army had been reduced to such a state of starvation that he had withdrawn to the valley of the Tagus.

Wellesley then formed a plan with the Spanish generals that they should make a demonstration against Madrid, while he attempted to crush Victor. On June 27th, the British and French met at Talavera. Sebastiani's army had by then joined Victor, and King Joseph had brought up the last reserves from Madrid, so the French now greatly outnumbered the British. The battle was a most bloody one. It lasted two days, and there were over twelve thousand killed and wounded. Victor refused to believe that the British line could not be broken and sent his columns against it again and again. The line held, and Wellesley won a resounding victory, but he was robbed of its fruits by the hopeless incompetence of his allies, so he swore that never again would he operate with Spanish troops unless they were under his command.

Madrid might still possibly have fallen to the British

had not Wellesley learned that Soult, reinforced by Mortier's corps, was moving up from Galicia with the intention of cutting his communications. His army was so exhausted that it could not fight another battle; so he was compelled to beat a hasty retreat into Portugal.

In the late summer and autumn, Spanish forces continued, in widely-separated areas, to engage the French, but Wellesley—who in September was, for his victories, created Baron Douro and Viscount Wellington—flatly refused to commit British troops with them; so their gallant efforts were defeated again and again.

Although the French were being harried everywhere, Napoleon's war with Austria being as good as over, he was pouring more and more troops into the Peninsula; so Wellington, fearing that his much smaller army would be driven into the sea, retired on Lisbon and began to construct across the neck of the isthmus on which it stood the afterwards famous lines of Torres Vedras. These were not mere entrenchments, but solid earthworks, strengthened by palisades. The first line was twenty-nine and the second twenty-two miles in length. They included one hundred and twenty-six redoubts and were defended by four hundred and twenty-seven pieces of artillery.

Meanwhile, in the south Soult had taken Seville and Napoleon sent Masséna, who had the reputation of being the most able of all his Marshals, to command the army in Portugal. Fortunately for Wellington, the Emperor decreed that the assault on Lisbon should not begin until every man he could spare had crossed the Pyrenees. This gave the British a seven-month respite to prepare their great defensive wall. Moreover, during these months, Wellington was able to take other valuable measures. These included the embodiment and training of many regiments of Portuguese, and securing the consent of the Portuguese Government to render central Portugal a desolate wilderness. Its towns and villages were all evacu-

ated, the peasants taking to the mountains and the towns-
folk brought into Lisbon.

By the summer of 1810 there were three hundred and
seventy thousand French troops in the Peninsula, and in
August Masséna invaded Portugal with one hundred
thousand of them. But, before advancing on Lisbon, he
delayed to besiege and capture several fortresses. When
he at length approached the capital, he found the British
deployed in a strong position outside it at Busaco, for
Wellington had decided that if he could fight a successful action it would greatly strengthen the morale of his
own men and the Portuguese people. Masséna, who had
never before encountered the British, imagined he would
have an easy victory but, to his amazement, in a short,
sharp battle, his assault columns were driven back with
heavy losses. Well satisfied, on October 11th, Wellington
withdrew his army behind the lines of Torres Vedras.

Masséna, having reconnoitred these tremendous defences, reluctantly decided that they were too strong to
be forced; so he withdrew his men and settled down to
besiege Lisbon. But he soon had cause to become extremely worried. For scores of miles round, there was not
a head of cattle or a bale of hay, and only a trickle of supplies could reach him, because every convoy was attacked
by the Spanish insurgents. During those winter months
he was losing hundreds of men a day through harassing
raids and snipers, and his men were becoming weak from
near-starvation.

Such was the situation when Roger arrived in Lisbon.

That afternoon he called at the British Legation and
was received by the Minister, the Rt. Hon. Sir Charles
Stuart. Roger was surprised to find in so important a post
such a youngish man, for the Minister was only a little
over thirty; but he proved very pleasant and, when Roger
had told him his reason for coming to Lisbon, at once
promised to put him in touch with the Legation lawyer.

Then, after Roger had given him the latest news from London, he invited him to dine the following evening.

Next day, Roger waited on Lord Wellington, whom he had met several years before in India. When he handed Wellington the letter from his brother, the General read it, then gave him an appraising look and said :

'The Marquis informs me that you have a dual identity, that you have spent many years on the Continent as one of Bonaparte's A.D.C.s and have supplied our Government with much valuable information. I recall now that when I went out to India I was charged to deliver a confidential letter to you from Mr. Pitt, and at the time I registered the fact that you must be a man of some importance. I would be greatly interested if you would care to tell me something of your activities while with the French.'

For over half an hour Roger spoke of the strange career that had led to his becoming a Commander of the Legion of Honour, a Count and known throughout the French Army as *'le brave Breuc'*.

Wellington listened fascinated and when Roger had done said, 'Mr. Brook, it is evident that your facilities for obtaining information of the highest order are unique. I take it that you have met Marshal Masséna ?'

'Yes, my lord, on numerous occasions. Davout apart, I regard him as the cleverest of all Napoleon's Generals, and his record makes him even more outstanding.'

'As you know, he is at present laying siege to us here in Lisbon; or, rather, he thinks he is. But in fact it is we who are besieging him. Our defences are secure and to us the seas are open, so we'll never lack for reinforcements or supplies. Whereas he, poor devil, is encamped in open country and surrounded by a sea of enemies. The number of his troops is dwindling daily, few convoys get through to him so he must be becoming desperate. Soon now he must take a decision. Either he must throw everything he

148

has got into a forlorn hope by an attack on our lines, or retire into country where he can secure supplies for his famished troops. My information about enemy troop movements could not be bettered, because every Portuguese man, woman and child is for us and against him. Daily I receive reports of every foray he sends out, even down to a troop of horse. But what I have no means of discovering is what course of action he contemplates taking when he no longer dare remain inactive, watching his army disintegrate. In his letter my brother says that you have no wish to resume your old activities. But, by going to Masséna, you could obtain this invaluable information for me. Will you not place me greatly in your debt by doing so?'

Roger smiled. 'My lord, I pray you to excuse me. 'Tis a highly dangerous game, and I have been monstrous lucky to survive for so long. I am here only to lay claim to an estate that I have inherited. Once that is settled, I am determined to return to England.'

'Very well, Mr. Brook.' Wellington stood up to indicate that the interview was over. 'I appreciate your point of view. But in Portugal, as in most other countries, decisions by the courts are apt to be long delayed. You do not strike me as a man who takes kindly to idleness. So, should you become bored here, perhaps you will reconsider my request. In the meantime, if there is any way in which I can be of service to you, you have only to let me know.'

Having thanked him, Roger took his leave and went out to renew his acquaintance with the city.

That evening at the Legation, the Minister presented him to his wife and niece. Lady Stuart was a large, imposing lady who, at first sight appeared formidable, but Roger found her to be a most kindly soul. Her niece, Deborah, lived with them because her own mother was dead. She was a tall, thin, dark girl and by no means a

beauty which, no doubt, accounted for her shy, retiring manner.

At dinner eighteen people sat down at the long table. On one side Roger had a fat, much bejewelled lady who was the wife of a Portuguese General, on the other a girl whom he judged to be about nineteen. When he had been presented to her, he had learned that she was Lady Mary Ware. After they had exchanged a few remarks, she told him that she was a friend of Deborah Stuart's, and she had been invited out to spend the winter at the Legation.

She had a very small, but shapely figure. Her hair was brown and her eyes green. Above them, well-marked eyebrows that turned up slightly at the ends gave her a somewhat perky, quizzical expression, and this was strengthened by a slightly retroussé nose. What she lacked in size she made up for in vivacity, and Roger soon found her a most entertaining companion. When he had told her what had brought him to Lisbon and that he expected to be there for several weeks with nothing to do, she said:

'Then, Mr. Brook, if you do not find the society of young females too boring, you must accompany Deborah and myself on some of our drives, for all our officers are always occupied with their duties, and the company of a gentleman would be very pleasant for us.'

He politely accepted her offer, although at the time he was not greatly attracted by the idea of acting as escort to two young women who could not long ago have left school.

Next morning he went to see the Legation lawyer, a Mr. Herbert Lessor, and put the matter of the de Pombal estate in his hands. In the afternoon he went for a stroll and, by chance, saw Lady Mary and Deborah Stuart in their carriage. Lady Mary waved to him, had the carriage pull up and invited him to join them. Having nothing to do, he assented and spent a pleasant hour in their company.

Deborah proved as shy and tongue-tied as she had in company, so it was Mary who did most of the talking. In fact, she was a born chatterbox and Roger found her chatter amusing. In consequence, when she asked him to come for another drive with them the next day, he readily agreed. From then on, except when it rained, it became a regular thing for him to accompany them on their drives through the deep enclave of pleasant country that lay inland from Lisbon, but inside the lines, or take them shopping; and, being completely at a loose end, he found it both a pleasant and novel occupation to squire two young girls. Sometimes they were accompanied by the buxom and sanguine Lady Stuart, but on most afternoons she was busy with her many charities: comforts for the wounded, assistance to widows of soldiers killed in the war, Anglo-Portuguese friendship and so on.

Naturally he told them nothing of his past secret activities, but he was able to regale them with tales of his early days in France, as a lawyer's apprentice, and of his travels in Egypt, India, Brazil and the West Indies, to which they listened wide-eyed, and they were greatly flattered to have secured such a handsome and interesting man of his years as their cavalier.

He soon learned Lady Mary's history. Her family was an old one, having first been ennobled during the Wars of the Roses, and later elevated to an earldom by Charles II. But her great-grandfather had been ruined in 1720 by the South Sea Bubble. For the past ninety years the family had lived very simply on a small property near Maidenhead. Mary herself was an only child and an orphan. Her mother had died in giving birth to her, and her father the previous year. On his death, the Maidenhead property had passed, with the title, to a distant cousin: a Canon of Peterborough Cathedral, who was a man of no fortune and had a large family of his own, so could do little for her. In consequence, she was very

badly off, with only a small income, which she was now ekeing out by staying for long periods with friends such as Deborah, whom she had known at the Seminary for Young Ladies at which she had been educated. But, in spite of her straitened circumstances and inability to afford expensive clothes, she was always cheerful and faced her uncertain future with courage.

During the fortnight after he first met the girls, as well as seeing them in the daytime, he twice dined at the Legation and saw them several times at receptions and dances in other houses.

It was on the 13th February that, after a drive on a pleasant sunny afternoon, he was handing them from the carriage outside the Legation, when he suddenly caught sight of de Queircoz. With him at the foot of the Legation steps were two Portuguese *guardas*. Suddenly pointing at Roger, de Queircoz cried :

'That is he ! Seize him and he shall answer for the death of the Marquis de Pombal.'

CHAPTER XII

'HE WHO LAUGHS LAST'

DUMBFOUNDED, Roger stared at the dark-browed diplomat. After a moment his brain again began to function. The Marquis had died in distant Brazil, but evidently on the return of his sister, the *Senhora* de Arahna, particulars of his death had become known in Lisbon, and de Queircoz knew, or thought he knew, who had killed him. But why should he be the person to accuse Roger? And why had he left his post in London to return to Lisbon?

That could be explained by his having come to the conclusion that *Colonel de Breuc* and Roger Brook were the same person. The strong resemblance of the two, together with the fact that it was the Colonel who had captured Lisala's affections in Teheran, and Mr. Brook who had later married her, were ample grounds for such a belief.

Within seconds Roger had solved the riddle. On meeting him in London de Queircoz had seen an opportunity to be avenged. He had dangled the de Pombal inheritance as bait, Roger had swallowed it, and his enemy had obtained leave so that he could follow Roger to Lisbon and denounce him. Yet Roger had a feeling that, behind the jealous malice of the Portuguese lay the still greater malevolence of Lisala's evil spirit seeking his destruction.

To have been tried and condemned for murder in

153

Prussia had been ordeal enough. His life had been saved by Davout only at the eleventh hour, and his rescue from a prison van by rioting students had been a piece of unforeseeable good fortune. To be tried again, only eight months later, for another murder he had not committed, seemed an outrageous injustice. And this time he would not be so lucky. The de Pombal family had great influence and the sympathies in a law court would be with them. Knowing how black a case could be made against him, he felt that once in the hands of the Portuguese his fate would be as good as sealed.

There was only one course open to him. It was to fight his way into the British Legation and seek sanctuary there.

His resolution was taken within half a minute of de Queircoz having called on the *guardas* to seize him. The taller *guarda* produced a warrant, stepped up to him and laid a hand on his shoulder. Roger gave him a violent shove that sent him reeling back, then darted toward the steps leading up to the door of the Legation. Before he could reach them the other *guarda* had flung his arms round his waist and had him in a bear-like hug. Exerting all his strength, Roger strove to free himself, and bashed with his fists at the man's head, but he buried his face in Roger's chest and gamely clung on. In desperation, Roger kneed him in the groin. His eyes popped, he gave a yelp of agony and relaxed his hold. But, only an instant after he had pushed the man away, his arms were seized from behind. The taller *guarda* had come to his companion's assistance. In vain Roger kicked out backward, his heels failed to find a mark and his arms were forced behind his back.

Even as his heart sank at the realisation that his bid to escape capture had failed, help came from an unexpected quarter. Little Mary ran forward, shouting,

'Desist, fellow! How dare you lay hands on a English-

man!' Then, lifting her parasol, she jabbed it over Roger's shoulder at the *guarda*'s face.

The iron ferrule caught him on the cheek, ripping the skin up toward the side of his left eye. With an oath, he let Roger go and clapped his hand to the wound, from which blood was flowing freely.

Roger lost not an instant and again dashed for the steps. The man he had kneed in the groin was crouching in the gutter, retching, and incapable of making any attempt to stop him. But de Queircoz swiftly stepped into his path. Drawing back his fists, Roger feinted with his right, then with his left hit the Portuguese a terrific blow on the side of the jaw. His head jerked back, his knees gave way, and he collapsed in a heap on the lowest step. Next moment Roger had jumped over him, mounted the rest of the flight and come to a halt, panting, just inside the Legation doorway.

The two girls ran up and joined him. Mary, her green eyes bright with excitement, asked, 'Is it really true that you killed the Marquis de Pombal?'

'No,' he panted. 'No, but it might prove devilish hard for me to prove that I did not. And . . . bless you . . . Mary, for your courage. Had you not come so bravely to my rescue I . . . would shortly have found myself in a Portuguese prison, and heaven only knows if I'd ever have got out of it, except to be marched to a scaffold. If His Excellency is in, I must see him at once and explain to him my situation.'

Five minutes later, the three of them were with the Minister in his study. When he had been told of the scene that had just occurred outside the Legation, Roger said:

'This is a very different legacy left to me by my late wife. As Your Excellency knows, she was the Marquis de Pombal's daughter. I accompanied her family when the Prince Regent fled to Brazil and, for a short while, shared

a house with them in Rio. For some time past, Lisala had been my mistress. I had asked the Marquis for permission to marry her, but he refused it and desired me to find some other lodging, because he felt that my constantly being in Lisala's company would prejudice his securing for her a husband from among the Portuguese nobility.

'I moved to an inn. After that it became impossible for Lisala and me to continue our affair. As there seemed no hope of our situation improving, and life in Rio was more uncongenial than I can possibly describe, at length I decided to return to England in a British frigate which had arrived in the harbour. I received, at that juncture, a message from Lisala, saying that she was *enceinte* and that unless I came to her assistance, she would be condemned to spend the remainder of her life in a convent.

'Since I believed her to be carrying my child, I could not possibly abandon her; so I decided to carry her off and made use of the Marquis' head Negro slave, one Baob, as a go-between, to arrange our elopement. At night I went out to the house where the de Pombals were living. With Baob's help I got a tall ladder up to the window of Lisala's room. Just as I reached the sill the Negro betrayed me and roused the house by shouting, "Thieves! Thieves!"

'Lisala was ready dressed and waiting for me. The slave's outcry awakened her duenna, the *Senhora* Cristina de Jahlo, who slept in the next room. She came running in to us. Lisala was subject to the most violent fits of temper and was completely unscrupulous in getting her own way. She had long hated the old woman, so sprang upon her and, when she fell to the ground, began to batter in her face. I pulled her off and out into the corridor. The Marquis then appeared upon the scene, sword in hand, with his sister, the *Senhora* de Arahna, behind him. Furiously Lisala shouted at them, revealing that I

had long been her lover and that she was carrying my child.

'Horrified, the *Senhora* fainted and the Marquis made a savage lunge at me. I parried the thrust, and we fought silently for maybe two minutes. Suddenly my ankle was gripped and pulled from under me. It was the old duenna who had crawled from Lisala's room, and thrust an arm past her feet without her being aware of it. I lost my balance and fell to the ground. Next moment the Marquis was towering over me, his sword pointing downward, about to drive it through my heart. I squirmed aside. The point of the blade buried itself in the floor. He then flung himself down on me and endeavoured to strangle me. For a few moments I struggled desperately with him. Then suddenly he went limp. I thought he had had a seizure of the heart. But, as I staggered to my feet, I saw the hilt of a dagger protruding from his back. With her stiletto, *Lisala* had stabbed her father to death.'

'Merciful God, how awful!' Mary exclaimed.

Sir Charles nodded. ' 'Twas parricide, the most terrible of all crimes. Do you give us your word, Mr. Brook, that this is the absolute truth about how de Pombal died?'

'I do, Your Excellency. 'Tis the truth, the whole truth and nothing but the truth. To that I swear. Lisala's face was a living lie. A beautiful mask behind which lay the most evil mind I have ever encountered. I am convinced now that her act was inspired only by her determination not to allow herself to be incarcerated in a nunnery. But, at the time, I was very conscious that by her deed she had saved my life. So, having got her safely aboard the frigate, next morning, though with reluctance, rather than cast aside a woman carrying, as I thought, my child, I had the captain of the frigate marry us. As I feel sure I told you early in our acquaintance, she died some sixteen months ago.'

'In view of her nature as you describe it, I cannot feel

that is a matter for condolence,' the Minister remarked gravely. 'But this other business troubles me, and we must discuss it with our lawyer. I will send for Mr. Lessor and also send a lackey to collect your belongings from the inn where you have been lying. Meanwhile you will, of course, dine with us and I will order a bedroom to be prepared for you.'

Roger stood up and bowed. 'I am indeed grateful to Your Excellency for your kindness, and deeply regret that I should have become a cause of trouble to you.'

Dinner, to which fewer than a dozen people sat down an hour later, proved a far from gay meal, as everyone present had heard some version of the attempt to arrest Roger for murder.

Soon after they had finished, Mr. Lessor arrived and went into conference with Roger and the Minister. When Roger had again given an account of the Marquis' death, the lawyer said, 'Mr. Brook, you have my sympathy for it seems that a case very difficult to disprove could be made against you. And, should you be indicted on a capital charge, I should have to advise His Excellency that, under international law, he would not be within his rights to continue to give you sanctuary here. However, as de Queircoz played no part in the affair, you could be convicted only on the evidence of the *Senhora* de Arahna and the duenna. I am already in touch with the de Pombal family's lawyers with regard to the inheritance. They are a firm of high repute and fortunately well known to me. Tomorrow morning I will see them and find out if they have received instructions from the *Senhora* to take proceedings against you.'

Roger spent an uneasy night, then waited with impatience until Mr. Lessor arrived the following midday, to report to him and the Minister the result of his interview with the de Pombals' lawyers.

The *Senhora* de Arahna had sent for the head of the

firm three days before. De Queircoz had just arrived from London with the news that Roger had left there for Lisbon, and was with her. Holding Roger responsible for her brother's death, the *Senhora* naturally wished to be avenged. She had admitted, however, that she had not actually seen him deliver the fatal stroke, but said that the duenna, Dona Christina, had done so and would give evidence to that effect.

At that point Roger broke in to say, 'Then the old woman will be committing perjury. And the reason she has agreed to do so is not far to seek. I gathered that she had dissipated any fortune she ever had, and is entirely dependent on the de Pombals. 'Tis clear that she is being bribed to bear false witness.'

'You may well be right,' Mr. Lessor agreed. 'But, in view of the extremely strong circumstantial evidence against you, Mr. Brook, should that be supported by her testimony I greatly fear we can have little hope of securing a verdict of "not guilty".'

'Think you it would be possible to get hold of the duenna,' Roger suggested, 'and offer her a much larger bribe to tell the truth?'

'I could not undertake to do so personally, but I might arrange for her to be approached by a third party. I doubt not, too, that money lies at the root of this affair. The *Senhora* de Arahna stands to gain much more than revenge by your death. Her application made on her return from Brazil for her son, the present Marquis, to inherit, was disallowed by the courts; but with yourself out of the way he would come into the whole of the de Pombal patrimony.'

'Then I pray you, Sir, engage a go-between to approach Dona Cristina. When the killing took place I was lying on the ground with the Marquis on top of me; so she could not possibly have failed to see my late wife drive the stiletto into her father's back. Promise the old

159

woman anything in reason to withdraw the statement they say she is prepared to make.'

'Ahem!' the lawyer coughed. 'I—er—hesitate to raise the question, Mr. Brook, but I count it improbable that she could be induced to earn the opprobrium of the de Pombal family unless she was assured of receiving a very substantial sum, and the odds are that she would require to be paid in cash. Have you large funds readily available here in Lisbon?'

'No,' Roger replied, 'but I am possessed of a moderate fortune, and could have the money required transferred from London.'

Looking decidedly uncomfortable, Mr. Lessor said, 'For any ordinary transaction that would serve. But in this we are circumscribed by time, and I doubt if I could get your draft discounted before the end of the week. Then the negotiations with the duenna might take another week or more. Meanwhile, if the authorities request His Excellency to surrender your person, he can hardly refuse to do so.'

'They have already made that request,' Sir Charles put in. 'I received it at eight o'clock this morning. To gain a few hours for Mr. Brook, I replied that I could not comply until I had consulted our lawyers. But the Portuguese are our allies. They have the law on their side, and it is my duty to maintain good relations with them. I feel, therefore, that unless the matter can be settled within the next twenty-four hours, I shall have no alternative but to hand Mr. Brook over.'

'I am grateful to Your Excellency for having secured me that much grace,' Roger said, 'but in so short a time I see little hope of our buying over the duenna. Once I have been arrested, the case will go forward and our chance of persuading her to retract become very much more slender. It seems the only course open to me is to

160

leave the Legation tonight and endeavour to get aboard a ship that will carry me to England.'

The Minister shook his head. 'I fear you will not find that possible. The Legation is under observation by *guardas*. And, as your enemies are people of influence, they will no doubt have pressed the authorities to have others watching for you on the docks.'

Roger remained silent for a moment, then he said, 'May I impose on Your Excellency's good nature by asking you to send a note to General Lord Wellington informing him of my situation? As it is impossible for me to go to him, I pray you request him to come here sometime this evening; so that, before I am arrested, I may confide to him a matter of considerable importance.'

Sir Charles having readily agreed to oblige Roger, the conference broke up.

Somehow Roger got through the rest of the day, spending most of it in the company of the two girls. Both showed great concern for him. Deborah, who was deeply religious, said she would pray for him several times each day while he was in prison. Mary, who was of a more practical turn of mind, urged him to attempt to escape arrest, and proposed that they should smuggle him out of the back of the Legation in a large hamper. But, even had the Minister consented to risk becoming compromised by lending himself to such a plan, to take the hamper down to a ship would be certain to arouse the suspicions of the *guarda,* who would insist on having it opened.

Neither of the girls could suggest anywhere else to which it could profitably be taken. Roger, however, had his own ideas about that, although he was not prepared to disclose them for the moment.

Lord Wellington did not arrive until after dinner. In the Minister's study, over a decanter of port, he was in-

formed more fully of Roger's situation, then Sir Charles tactfully left them alone together.

When the door had closed, the tall General ran a finger down his big, high-bridged nose, smiled and said, 'So, Mr. Brook, you are, after all, going to make an expedition into enemy-held territory.'

Roger smiled back. 'I might have known, my lord, that you would have guessed why I should have taken the liberty of requesting you to come here. Although I am innocent of the deed of which I am accused, I see no hope of proving that. Since to save my life I must leave Lisbon and tonight, the only sure method of doing so that presents itself is for me to ask your aid to cross the lines, and there resume my French identity.'

'And then?'

'I could make my way to any of a dozen places on the French-held coast and thence have a smuggler run me across to England. But if I do that, I'll still have this charge hanging over my head should I ever return to Portugal, and a time may come when I'll wish to do so. Moreover I am loath to leave the field to these people who have sought to entrap me. There is a possibility that, given a month or so, Mr. Lessor may be able to secure me a clean bill. If so, I could return to Lisbon and claim my inheritance.'

'And during this month or so?'

'Doubtless I could make my way into Spain and there lie low. But since I must spend it in enemy-held territory, 'twould be unpatriotic of me not to take the opportunity of serving your lordship; so I'll go to Masséna's headquarters.'

'Ah! There speaks the man I had supposed you to be.' Wellington stood up and patted Roger on the shoulder. 'It remains then only for us to decide how you can be removed from here.'

'This afternoon, Lady Mary Ware suggested that I

162

should be smuggled out in a big hamper; although, of course, knowing nothing of my secret activities, she could think of no place to which I could then be taken.'

After a moment's thought Wellington said, 'I like it not. The agents watching the house might suspect you to be in the hamper. You are tall to pass as a woman, but could do so in darkness. And, if you left the Embassy on my arm, no policeman would dare challenge you.'

Roger laughed. 'I'll count it an honour, my lord, to have you as my cavalier.'

Within an hour, final arrangements had been made. Roger signed a draft on Hoare's Bank for five thousand pounds which Mr. Lessor would discount, then do his best to win over the duenna. Next day the Minister was to inform the Portuguese authorities that, during the night, Roger had left the Legation without anyone being aware of how he had done so, and send a sum of money as compensation to the *guarda* whom Mary had wounded with her parasol. Lady Stuart who, fortunately, was a tall woman, provided Roger with female attire and un-earthed from the attic a long-discarded wig. Tittering, the girls helped him to pad out his chest. At nine o'clock, he took an affectionate leave of them and expressed his gratitude to the Stuarts. Lord Wellington's carriage was driven up, his mounted escort called to attention and Roger, stooping to disguise his height, left the Legation on the General's arm.

Twenty minutes later, Roger's clothes and belongings were sent after him to Wellington's headquarters. After he had changed, he spent two hours in conference with the General. Masséna, having remained for a month before the lines of Torres Vedras and decided that they were too strong to justify an assault, had retired to the town of Santarém, some twenty miles north-east of Lisbon, and his army was encamped about it. The country between had then become a no-man's-land, on which

163

vedettes of British cavalry occasionally had brief encounters with troops of French, seeking, generally in vain, for hidden supplies left behind by the peasantry. Owing to Wellington's scorched-earth policy, it was almost uninhabited; but, here and there, Portuguese continued to live secretly in caves and barns, as postboxes through which news of enemy movements could swiftly be transmitted to the British. On a large-scale map, the General pointed out to Roger half a dozen of these hide-outs, and gave him the password by which their occupants would know him to be a friend.

Then he said:

'Masséna will be certain to question you about the state of things in Lisbon. Without going into details, tell him the truth. That not only has my own army been greatly reinforced during the winter months but I have also embodied, trained and armed, many thousands of Portuguese, and I am very pleased with them. The first regiments I formed participated in our clash with Masséna at Busaco. They stood up well to the assault and had good reason to be proud of themselves.

'It will then be for Masséna to take the decision to which the starving condition of his army is driving him nearer every day. Should he decide to gamble everything on an all-out attack, I'll let him come right up to our lines, then tear him to pieces with my artillery. If, on the other hand, he elects to fall back into Spain, I want to be ready to follow him with all possible speed and hope to trounce him thoroughly in the open field.'

Having promised to do his utmost to obtain this information, Roger was provided with a horse and one of the General's A.D.C.s who would see him through the lines and accompany him for the first few miles of his journey.

Well before dawn they were outside the lines. In a village not far distant the A.D.C. took him to a half-

ruined church, in the crypt of which the priest, Father Joao, had concealed himself to act as one of the intelligence post-boxes. Two miles further on, they stopped at a small wood, in the centre of which a farmer named Leandro had dug himself a hide-out for the same purpose. After a third visit, this time to a cave occupied by several men, the A.D.C. left him.

For what remained of the morning Roger rode on through the desolate countryside, and it was not until he was nearing Santarém that he encountered a troop of French Chasseurs. On his hailing them in French, they galloped up to him and he asked their officer to be taken to the Marshal Prince d'Essling. His accent being perfect, the officer had no doubts about his nationality, and sent him with a sergeant and two troopers to Masséna's headquarters.

When he arrived it was getting on well into the afternoon. In a mansion in the centre of the town, he found the Marshal and his staff about to sit down to dinner. Masséna was then fifty-five; but evidently the strain of conducting his present campaign had aged him considerably, as Roger thought he looked very much older than when he had last seen him some two years earlier. His appearance was not improved by a black eye-patch he had to wear owing to an accident while on a shoot at Fontainbleau, in which Napoleon had shot him in one eye.

He was greatly surprised to see Roger and the more so because he was in civilian clothes, as he had assumed that Roger had brought him a despatch from the Emperor; but he at once invited him to join them at dinner and, sitting next to him while eating a meagre meal, Roger gave a slightly edited account of how he came to be in Santarém.

He described how the Emperor had sent him on a mission to Davoust in north Germany, how he had been

accused of a murder that he had not committed, and his only means of getting away had been to board an American vessel that was sailing for England. He then reverted to his old story, already known to several of the officers present, about his mother having been English, although he had been born in Strasbourg; how, on her death, he had been sent to be brought up by an aunt in Hampshire until, fired by the news of the Revolution, he had returned to France to enlist and how he had since revisited England several times on Napoleon's secret business, without anyone there realising that he had become a Colonel in the French Army. His English relatives believed that he spent a great part of his time travelling in the East, so had welcomed his recent return, but to maintain that fiction he had had to spend several months there. Then, when he felt that no-one would be surprised at his going abroad again, he had secured a passage to Lisbon as the easiest way of getting back to the Continent and his master.

Told with all Roger's flair as a raconteur, the story was highly plausible, so accepted by all those present without question.

After the meal, Masséna carried him off to his office and, as soon as they were seated, asked:

'How long were you in Lisbon?'

'It was the best part of a month,' Roger replied, 'before I felt that I had been there long enough for my stay to be accounted an ordinary visit; and, before leaving, I laid a false trail by taking passage in a Portuguese ship bound for Madeira.'

'Then you had ample time to assess the present strength there of the English?'

'I did indeed, *mon Prince*. You may be sure I kept my eyes well open.'

'Tell me, then, all you can about them.'

Roger obliged and spent the next half-hour giving par-

ticulars of the very considerable army Wellington had under him.

When he had done, the Marshal said, 'Tell me now about milord Wellington. What sort of a man is he, and how do his troops regard him?'

'He is a tall man with blue eyes and a thin, very high-bridged nose. When he speaks it is with a very slight lisp. But he is not a great talker, although he can be convivial at times. At least, he used to be. When I first met him in India, we had a mutual friend—one William Hickey—and at his house, with several others, we were wont to punish the Bordeaux pretty heavily.

'Milord Wellington, the Emperor and myself are of the same age: all born in '69. He comes of an Irish family, or rather an English one that has long been settled in Ireland. Such families form the aristocracy there. Not one such as we had in France before the Revolution, but, I am told, similar to that in the Southern States of America. They have big houses and are boundlessly hospitable, but lack elegance, being greatly given to country pursuits. They regard the native Irish much as the Americans do their Negro slaves; and, indeed, the poor wretches are little better off.

'The Irish milords are also, by English standards, poor. The General was the sixth child of the Earl of Mornington. The Earl's passion was music, and he squandered his small fortune giving and financing concerts. His whole family thought of little else. Milord Wellington was devoted to his violin; but not long after he entered the Army he decided that his love of playing absorbed much too much of his time, so he burned his fiddle.

'The eldest son, Richard, now the Marquess Wellesley, was the bright child of the family. Their father died when Arthur, that is the General, was twelve, and left his widow very badly off. Richard scraped enough money

together to send Arthur to Eton, but only for about two years.'

'Eton? What is that?' Masséna enquired.

'It is England's most famous public school, and for many generations a large part of the nobility have been educated there. On leaving Eton, Arthur's mother took him with her to Brussels. While there, I gather, the tutoring he received was patchy and indifferent. He was then sent on his own to an academy at Angers, where little was taught except riding, fencing and dancing. But the young nobles who studied there were made free of the great houses, such as those of the Ducs de Brissac and de Praslin. It was in such society that he acquired his polish and unfailing good manners.'

'Bah!' Masséna exclaimed, and turned to spit into a spittoon. 'And that while youngsters like myself were leading a dog's life, half-starved and beaten, as cabin boys. But proceed.'

Roger smiled. 'Your Highness will have even more cause to disapprove of the next few years in milord's career. At eighteen, his brother bought him a commission in the 73rd; a Highland regiment. But he did not remain in it for long. Through influence he got himself transferred from regiment to regiment, with a step up each time. He rose from Ensign to Lieutenant-Colonel in seven years, and during the whole of this time neither saw active service nor spent more than a week or two on a barrack square. He lived in Dublin, as an A.D.C. to the Lord Lieutenant and sat in the Irish Parliament.'

The frown on Masséna's sallow face deepened. 'Such a system is iniquitous. But how, after such a poor education and those years of idleness did he ever become a successful General?'

'It was, I think, the campaign of '94 that made him. You will recall that the English invaded the Low Countries. Milord took his regiment on that expedition.

168

I've no need to remind Your Highness how hopelessly incompetent as a General is their Duke of York. Ill-directed, administered by idle nitwits, constantly short of supplies and with the troops totally uncared for, the army floundered about for a while, then retreated into Holland. The winter there that year was terrible. The troops were in rags, starving and dying from intense cold.'

'Enough! Enough! We have been suffering similar hardships here. My men are dying daily by the hundred. But not from lack of thought for them. 'Tis this accursed country and the myriad of brigands who prevent all but a trickle of supplies from reaching me. Ah, well. Go on now.'

'It was, I am told, this disastrous campaign that led to milord Wellington's becoming what he is today. He real-ised that success in war depended on healthy, well-fed troops. A great part of his time is spent in ensuring that his men lack for nothing. In consequence they adore him, are always in a condition to fight well, and when called on to make an extra effort never fail him.

'All through his youth his income was insufficient for him to support his position. In '96 his debts became so burdensome that, to escape his creditors, he went to India. There fortune favoured him. In the meantime his clever brother, Richard, had risen to a high position in the Government. In '98 he arrived in Calcutta as Governor General. It was he who fought the Mysore war against Tippoo Sahib. Wellington treated his Sepoy troops with the same fatherly care as his British regiments. Although still a junior commander he was responsible for the suc-cess of the campaign and, afterwards, won high praise for his administration of the conquered territory. There followed the Mahratta war, in which he achieved strik-ing victories at Assaye and Argaou. Richard had already been rewarded by being raised in the peerage to Marquess Wellesley. In 1804 the General received his knighthood

and returned to England. In 1807 he commanded the troops in the successful operation against Copenhagen. In 1808 he was sent to Portugal and Your Highness will be aware of his activities while in the Peninsula.'

'I am. Only too well. And of the new tactics he was introduced, which have so bedevilled us. Victor was the first of our Marshals to encounter them. At Talavera he twice sent his massed columns against the British line, only to be repulsed with terrible loss. Both King Joseph and Jourdan urged him to break off the battle, but he insisted on a third assault, only to meet with a shattering defeat. The fire power of those redcoats in line is devastating, and Wellington's other innovation of having his battalions form squares when about to be attacked by cavalry would break the heart of even Murat.'

Masséna then asked what Roger intended to do, to which he replied, 'My obvious duty is to report back to the Emperor as soon as possible. But I confess, even though I speak fluent Spanish and some Portuguese, I dread the thought of attempting to make my way through the murderous brigands who infest this country.'

'You would be mad to do so. In it every hand is against us. Even those of the children.' The Marshal shuffled among the papers in his desk, drew one out and went on :

'Just listen to this. It is a translation of a catechism that the Spanish priests make the children learn by heart :

'Question. Child, what art thou?
Answer. A Spaniard, by the grace of God.
Q. What do you mean by that?
A. An honest man.
Q. Who is our enemy?
A. The Emperor of the French.
Q. What is the Emperor Napoleon?
A. A wicked being, the source of all evils and the focus
    of all vices.

170

Q. How many natures has he?
A. Two; the human and the diabolical.
Q. How many Emperors of the French are there?
A. One actually, in three deceiving persons.
Q. What are they called?
A. Napoleon, Murat and Manuel Godoy, the Prince of the Peace.
Q. Which is the most wicked?
A. They are all equally so.
Q. What are the French?
A. Apostate Christians, turned heretics.
Q. What punishment does a Spaniard deserve who fails in his duty?
A. The death and infamy of a traitor.
Q. Is it a sin to kill a Frenchman?
A. No, my father, heaven is gained by killing one of those heretical dogs.'

The Marshal laid the paper down. 'That shows you the hydra-headed monster to which we are opposed. If once it was discovered that you are a Frenchman, these fiends would roast and eat you. No, Breuc. You must stay here as one of my A.D.C.s. Since you understand their infernal tongue, you can be of use to me interrogating prisoners and translating captured documents.'

Roger agreed and thanked the Marshal. The interview being over, he then went off to find quarters and secure for himself a suitable uniform.

In the next few days he learned from his brother officers how matters had been going in other parts of Spain. There were several large Spanish armies and, whenever they joined battle with the French, they were always defeated. But the survivors faded away into the mountains where they re-formed to attack again; and they showed great courage in defending their cities, often refusing to sur-

171

render until half the citizens had been killed or wounded and a great part of the buildings reduced to rubble.

The previous autumn, Soult had invaded Andalusia. He now had his headquarters in Seville and had subdued the whole of southern Spain except for Cadiz. The red-faced, self-opinionated, ex-drummer boy Victor was besieging it. But, as the city was situated at the end of a nine-mile-long spit of land, without the assistance of a fleet there was little hope of taking it.

In the north-west Ney had earlier made a joint plan of campaign with Soult. When attacked by a large Spanish army, instead of coming to Ney's assistance, Soult had marched off to the south. Declaring that he had been betrayed and abandoned, Ney had evacuated Galicia and withdrawn his army into the plain of Leon. Thereupon the Emperor had ordered him home. A heartrending scene had followed, when Ney had had to say farewell to his famous Sixth Corps, which had been formed in 1804 at Boulogne as part of the *Grande Armée* that was to invade England, and which he had commanded ever since. But Ney was now back in Spain, commanding a corps under Masséna, as also was Roger's old friend Androche Junot, Duc d'Abrantès, who had failed so lamentably to hold Lisbon.

In the north-west, St. Cyr had been sent to subdue Catalonia. He had defeated the Spanish armies in the field, then laid siege to Gerona, the great fortress that blocked the eastern road through the Pyrenees from France to Spain. With great gallantry it had held out for six months. To take it cost the French twenty thousand men and when it did fall they were still harassed by clouds of enemies.

Angered by St. Cyr's lack of success, the Emperor had recalled him and sent Augereau to take over his command. Augerau had hung every Spaniard he could lay his hands on, in the hope of intimidating that rebellious people. His ruthless measures had proved useless. The

Catalans continued to fight on and so many of the Marshal's enterprises failed that Napoleon had recalled him in disgrace and replaced him with Macdonald. But the Marshal who had recently won his baton at Wagram fared little better.

Only further south in Aragon had the French done well. In that province General Suchet had reduced the people to obedience by initiating a policy entirely contrary to that of all the other French Generals. He cleared the country of brigands, who blackmailed the peasantry into maintaining them, paid a fair price for everything he commandeered, suppressed corruption, refused to allow King Joseph to steal works of art in that part of Spain, gave Spaniards a say in local government, began to rebuild Saragossa, restored its bullring and endowed hospitals and orphanages in the city.

But in every other part of Spain French armies were cut off, bogged down, half-starving and unceasingly harassed. Over three hundred thousand men were locked up there and only their numbers prevented their annihilation.

It was early on the morning of March 3rd that Masséna called his senior officers together and glumly informed them that they must now face the fact that their campaign had proved a failure. He said that he had appealed again and again for reinforcements, which would have given him sufficient strength to break through the lines of Torres Vedras; but the Emperor had not sent them. An alternative hope had been that Marshal Soult would bring his army up from the south, so that they might combine in an attack on Lisbon; but Soult also had failed them. Masséna then praised the extraordinary endurance his officers and men had shown all through the terrible winter months. Finally he said that, having been reduced to such straits, he could ask no further sacrifices of them, so he had decided to retreat and preparations were to be made to move in two days' time.

Roger had hoped to secure longer warning of the Marshal's intentions. Now, with less than forty-eight hours before the retreat began, it was imperative that he should get the news to Wellington with the minimum of delay. But he could not simply mount a horse and ride off toward Lisbon. He had to have a pretext for leaving the headquarters, and he had already thought of one which might serve the purpose.

After the meeting, Masséna returned to his office. Roger followed him, asked permission to make a proposal and, on receiving it, said, 'Your Highness will naturally have foreseen that, as soon as milord Wellington learns that you are withdrawing, he will come out from Lisbon and fall upon our rearguard?'

'Of course,' replied the Marshal tartly. 'The man is not a fool.'

'No, and therefore, Marshal, he would not dare to throw his whole force into the pursuit if Marshal Soult was coming up from the south to take him in the rear.'

'True. And I would to God it were so; but it is not.'

'It might be, if you sent a despatch to him, telling him of your difficult situation and asking for his help.'

Masséna shrugged. 'The Duc de Dalmatia has no love for me; otherwise he would have come to my assistance weeks ago. That apart, to ensure a despatch reaching him I'd have to detach a whole regiment of cavalry as escort for my courier; and I've no mind to do that.'

'It could be attempted in another way,' Roger suggested. 'If I put off this uniform that was found for me and instead put on the civilian clothes in which I arrived here, by passing myself off to the Portuguese as a Spaniard, I believe I could get through.'

With his one eye, Masséna stared at him. 'Then it is not without reason that people speak of you as *le brave Breuc*. Since you volunteer for this dangerous mission, I gladly accept your offer.' Dipping his feather pen in the

inkpot, the Marshal at once set about writing a despatch to Soult.

As Roger watched him, he was smiling to himself. The countryside for many miles outside Lisbon was under the observation of the British and their allies; so he had little to fear and, while he had on occasion acted with great courage, it was largely through such deceptions, when he was believed to be facing danger that did not exist, that he had earned the soubriquet of *le brave Breuc*.

Half an hour later he was on his way, riding hard through the deserted no-man's-land. By midday, when he was within five miles of the lines of Torres Vedras he saw a vedette of British Lancers. Turning his horse toward them, he hailed their Captain and two minutes later said to him :

'Sir, I have information of the highest importance for milord Wellington. Marshal Masséna is breaking camp and the day after tomorrow will begin his retreat. My horse is no longer in a state to travel fast. I pray you carry this news to Lisbon with all possible speed. Tell His Lordship that it comes from the man against whom the de Pombals threaten to bring an action. It is for that reason I do not want to enter the city. Be good enough also to tell him that I'll be found at the church of Father Joao not far from here, and that I am anxious to hear as soon as possible from Mr. Lessor, the Legation lawyer.'

The young Captain instantly realised the importance of the news. Telling his sergeant to carry on with the patrol and taking only an orderly with him, he set off at a gallop.

Now walking his horse, Roger covered the last mile to the church and, early in the afternoon, went through the ruin down into the crypt. Father Joao was there and made him welcome, producing a bottle of wine, bread and meat. Then, when Roger said that he would like to pass the

night in the crypt, the chubby little priest took from a chest a palliasse for him to sleep on.

Tired after his ride, he slept until the evening, then joined his host in another meal. Soon afterwards, the A.D.C. who had first brought Roger there arrived, and with him was Mr. Lessor. The A.D.C. conveyed Wellington's warmest thanks for the valuable service Roger had rendered. Then Mr. Lessor took him apart and told him the result of his negotiations with the de Pombal lawyers.

Dona Cristina had flatly rejected the offer of a bribe, but it was possible that an accommodation could be arrived at with the *Senhora* de Arahna. She was prepared to withdraw the accusation if Roger would forego his inheritance in favour of her son, the new Marquis.

Roger did not hesitate for long. Until de Queircoz had drawn his attention to the fact that he was the heir to Lisala's fortune, that had not even occurred to him. He had ample money for his needs, so was not being called upon to face a crippling loss and, in any case, he had meant to make over the de Pombal estates to the family.

He therefore agreed. But, wary of falling into another trap, he said he would not enter Lisbon until the transaction had been concluded, and he wished to be present himself when the *Senhora* signed the document stating that she had now received proof that it was not he who had murdered her brother; so she and her lawyer must come out to the church and sign it there.

As she would not be in any danger so close to the lines, Mr. Lessor said he saw no reason why she should not do as Roger wished. He and the A.D.C. then rode back to Lisbon.

The following afternoon he returned, accompanied by the *Senhora,* de Queircoz and her lawyer. De Queircoz, having been robbed of his revenge, only bowed stiffly and regarded Roger with silent hostility; but the *Senhora,*

having promised the duenna a handsome pension to lie, knew that Roger was innocent and she had succeeded in securing a great fortune for her son, so she greeted him very civilly.

When the terms of the documents were discussed, the *Senhora* pointed out that it was not sufficient for Roger to renounce the inheritance, since Lisala had been carrying his child. He must also do so on the child's behalf, as otherwise it would become the next heir.

Roger had already thought of that, so he agreed and had the deed drawn up to read that he renounced his claim on behalf of himself and the heirs of his body.

The papers were signed, witnessed and exchanged. Then, with a cynical little smile he bowed and said:

'Now, *Senhora*, I have some information for you which will, I fear, somewhat distress you. Lisala's child was duly born at Erfurt. It was a son. I took him and Lisala's old nurse back to Paris and made arrangements for their support and wellbeing at a farm outside the city.

'The boy was a fine, healthy infant so, no doubt, he still thrives there. As soon as it is possible to do so I will arrange for him and his nurse to come to you here in Lisbon. To spare you an unpleasant surprise at the child's appearance, I must now tell you that he is a black piccaninny. And with the best will in the world I am incapable of begetting a Negro.

'He is not my son. His father was your slave, Baob, to whom Lisala shamelessly gave herself when in Brazil. I have renounced the inheritance on behalf of myself and the heirs of my body. The boy is no heir of mine, but he is Lisala's. So he, and not your son, will now get the de Pombal fortune.'

CHAPTER XIII

THE FORWARDNESS OF
LADY MARY WARE

Furious at having been outwitted, the *Senhora* and her companions left the crypt. Shortly afterwards, having thanked Father Joao for his hospitality Roger, accompanied by Mr. Lessor, followed them back into Lisbon.

Although the village was less than two miles outside the lines, it took the best part of half an hour to reach them, because Wellington's army was at last leaving behind the great earthworks that, during the winter months, had served to protect it so well. Along the road advanced a steady stream of British and Portuguese infantry, guns, limbers, wagons and, behind each contingent, the little band of male and female camp-followers that all Generals detested, because they embarrassed troop movements, but could not get rid of without risking mutiny from their men.

As, time after time, Roger had to turn his mount aside on to the verge of the road, he noted with pleasure the greatly superior appearance of these troops to the ones he had left on the morning of the previous day. The uniforms of the French were threadbare, many of them had been wearing patched coats, broken boots and battered shakos. Their faces were thin from insufficient food and their eyes lacked lustre; whereas Wellington's men showed ample evidence of his care of them. Their uniforms were of good English cloth, with little sign of wear, their belts

were pipe-clayed and their equipment brightly polished. They were ruddy-faced and in excellent health, owing to ample and regular rations. As they marched, they were singing or bandying jests.

Arrived at last in the city, Roger parted cordially with Mr. Lessor and headed for the Legation. As he approached it he was thinking how pleasant it would be to see little Lady Mary again, and it was only then that it crossed his mind that, during many of his idle moments while at Masséna's headquarters, his thoughts had turned to her.

The Minister, his family and guests had just risen from dinner and were in the big salon. As Roger was announced, Mary was standing just inside the doorway. Her green eyes lighting up, she gave a cry of delight, impulsively ran forward, laid a hand on Roger's arm, went up on tiptoe and kissed him on the cheek.

Lady Stuart was nearby, talking to General Picton. Raising her eyebrows, she exclaimed not unkindly, 'Really, Mary! What unmaidenly behaviour.'

Mary's cheeks went scarlet. But Roger covered her confusion by crying gaily, ' 'Tis an occasion for kissing and rejoicing. I am now cleared of that false charge that was to have been brought against me.' Then he stepped up to the Minister's buxom wife and kissed her.

Next moment Sir Charles was shaking him heartily by the hand and saying, 'Mr. Lessor looked in on me this midday, to inform me that your affair was as good as settled. It must be a great relief and we are all delighted for you. But you were not in time for dinner, so must be hungry.' Looking quickly round, his eye lit on his niece and he said to her :

'Deborah, my dear, take Mr. Brook into the dining room and see that he is served with anything he fancies; then tell Smithson to have a room prepared for him for the night.'

Mary joined Deborah and Roger as they moved away. In the dining room the table had just been cleared, but the footmen were setting out a cold buffet on the sideboard for later in the evening. With a girl on either side of him, Roger tucked into a game pie and slices of York ham. It was the first good meal he had had since leaving Lisbon, and he happily contrasted it with the meagre fare at Masséna's headquarters.

Between mouthfuls he answered the girls' eager questions. They had no idea that he had been on a secret mission, but supposed he had been lying low outside the lines while Mr. Lessor did his best to prevent a charge of murder from being brought against him. When he told them how it had been settled to the discomfiture of the de Pombals, they both went into gales of laughter.

On returning to the salon they found that Lord Wellington had come to take leave of the Minister, as on the following day he was to take the field against Masséna.

On seeing Roger, he greeted him simply as an acquaintance whom he had not seen for some days. But ten minutes later, without being observed, he managed to wink at him, then turn his head in the direction of a small salon that led off the large one. Roger skilfully brought to an end a conversation he was having with a naval Captain and sauntered into the small room. As on most occasions when there was not a large party at the Legation, it was empty. Wellington joined him there, closed the door and said :

'Mr. Brook, I cannot thank you enough for the great service you have rendered us. Now I am anxious to have a long talk with you, as there must be much valuable information you can give me about the condition of Masséna's army and other matters you must have become acquainted with while at his headquarters.'

Roger bowed. 'I had had it in mind, my lord, to write

a full report tonight, and wait upon you with it in the morning.'

The General shook his fine head. 'Nay, I'd liefer have it from your own lips; for there are many questions I wish to ask you. I shall be leaving shortly. I pray you slip away soon after, and we'll drink a bottle of port in my private quarters.'

Three-quarters of an hour later, they were closeted in a small, map-lined study adjacent to Wellington's bedroom, a decanter of port between them. For half an hour Roger passed on all he had seen and heard whilst at Santarém, and another half-hour went by answering the questions the keen-eyed General shot at him. At length, refilling their glasses for the third time, Wellington said:

'The parlous condition to which Masséna's troops are reduced makes it tempting to launch an all-out attack in the hope of overwhelming them. But his regiments must still contain many hard-bitten veterans of Bonaparte's past campaigns. Even in adversity they can be counted on to put up a stiff resistance. Moreover, you tell me that Masséna has Ney and Junot with him. The first is one of the most able Marshals and the other at least a courageous leader. So, in this case, discretion may prove the better part of valour. Britain has only one army in the Peninsula, whereas the French have six. Should I be defeated and driven into the sea, we'd be back again where we were in 1807, and Bonaparte the master of the whole continent. By following Masséna up closely, we should be able to inflict heavy losses on him, with little loss to ourselves. That, I think, would be sounder than to risk facing him in a pitched battle.'

Roger smiled. 'I am no General, my lord; but in you and your army are Britain's one hope; so, had I your responsibility, that is certainly the course I would pursue.'

Nodding, Wellington said, 'And now, Mr. Brook, re-

garding yourself. You have been charged by Masséna to carry a despatch to Soult.'

'Oh, come, milord,' Roger laughed. 'Surely you do not expect me to deliver it? 'Tis an appeal for help and, if responded to, could seriously jeopardise your own plans.'

'True. But you tell me that Masséna and Soult are bitterly jealous of each other, so it is unlikely that the latter will come to his colleague's aid. In any case, if it is not delivered for a week, it would be too late for him to intervene effectively.'

'What, then, is to be gained by delivering it at all?'

'It would provide a reason for your arriving at his headquarters.'

'My lord,' Roger said with a frown. 'When we first talked of my former activities, I made it plain that I was most averse to risking my life again carrying out secret missions; so I pray you to excuse me.'

Wellington leaned forward, his bright eyes held Roger's and his voice was earnest. 'Mr. Brook, you have already rendered me a great service. You have it in your power to do me another, and no-one else enjoys the unique dual personality that enables you to talk on intimate terms with French Army Commanders. By going to Soult you could, I am certain, find out his intentions. If he means to remain in Seville, well and good. But should he march north, even belatedly, although he would be too late to aid Masséna, he could cut my communications with Lisbon. Warned in time I could still pursue Masséna, but not with my whole force. I'd detach a division under Hill or Picton to guard my rear and hold off Soult until I had been able to retire to the safety of my base here. I ask this not only for myself, but for our country.'

Roger sighed, then gave a pale smile. 'How can I refuse, my lord? So be it, then. But last time I had a very adequate reason for leaving Lisbon. What excuse can I

give to Sir Charles and others for again disappearing
beyond the lines?'

After a moment's thought, Wellington replied, 'Since
you speak French, Portuguese and Spanish fluently, you
could become a useful member of my staff. I will appoint
you one of my civilian secretaries, have you given some
work which will keep you employed for a week, and
orders that, when it is completed, you should join me in
the field. But instead, of course, you will proceed to
Seville.'

So once more the die was cast and, none too happily,
Roger made his way back to the Legation.

In the morning he told the Stuarts of his appointment.
Mary was torn between pride that her cavalier should
have elected to take an active part in the war, and disappointment that he would not be able to accompany her
and Deborah again on their afternoon drives. But she was
greatly cheered when Sir Charles insisted that Roger
should continue to occupy a room at the Legation, which
would enable her to see quite a lot of him.

Roger then reported at Wellington's headquarters.
The General had already left, but before leaving he had
briefed his chief secretary, who gave Roger a pile of Portuguese documents to translate. He found the work
laborious and dull, but as the secretary was unaware of
the secret reason for Roger's appointment, there was no
avoiding it; and he was somewhat consoled by being able
to enjoy Mary's vivacious company in the evenings.

On Sunday the Stuarts made up a party with
several friends to drive out and picnic at Cintra.
Deborah was not well, so was unable to accompany them,
with the result that, after the meal, Roger for once had
Mary on her own for well over an hour. Together they
strolled through the wood of cork trees that covered the
big hill dominating the plain. Having come upon a mossy

bank, they sat down on it. Presently she said in a low voice :

'Mr. Brook, since you lost your wife, have you ever thought of marrying again?'

For some time past he had sensed that she was falling in love with him, and instinct told him now that she had asked the question to give him an opening. Anxious to spare her feelings, he smiled at her, shook his head and lied :

'No, my dear, I am too restless a type to settle down to a domestic life. Were I a much younger man, and not set in my ways, I'd propose to you; for you will make a sweet wife for some lucky fellow. But I am old enough to be your father and, after a few months, you would find me impossible to live with. So that is entirely out of the question.'

'Perhaps you're right,' she murmured a little sadly. 'But I believe I could make you happy.'

He took her hand and pressed it. 'You could indeed, were I able to shed ten or fifteen years. But, since I cannot, we must just remain good friends.'

For a moment she was silent. Suddenly she laughed, turned her face up to him and said, 'Then that's reason enough for you to kiss me.'

Laughing in reply, he took her in his arms and put his lips to hers; but it was a very gentle kiss, quite unlike those he normally gave to women.

Her arms went round his neck and she pressed herself against him. He could feel her heart pounding and her lips began to move under his. Greatly tempted as he was to respond, he quickly controlled himself. Taking his mouth from hers, he kissed her on the ear, the hair and the nose. Then he held her away from him, shook his head and said :

'You are a wicked little baggage. Had I been a younger man, you might have led me to seduce you. Then there

184

would have been tears and a sad ending to our friendship. Come now, put your pretty bonnet straight, and we'll rejoin the others.'

For a moment she looked chastened, then she pouted and said, 'I think it horrid in you to have formed such an opinion of me.'

Laughing, he pulled her to her feet, dusted off some fallen leaves that were clinging to her dress and took her by the arm. Within a few minutes she was smiling again and chattering away as merrily as ever.

On the morning of March 11th, Roger said good-bye to her and the Stuarts and set off for Seville. For several days past, after the long months of stagnation, Lisbon had been in a fever of excitement as news from the front came in. The two armies were in close contact and Masséna was retreating; but his retreat showed no sign of becoming a rout. Under their veteran leaders, his divisions were taking advantage of every favourable piece of ground to fight rearguard actions. But they were severely hampered by having lost so many horses, and those that survived were too weak to charge; so the British cavalry were having a field day, cutting down small bodies of French, or taking them prisoner wherever they came upon them.

As Roger crossed the few miles between Lisbon and the now abandoned lines of Torres Vedras, he encountered several small batches of these tattered, woebegone captives, who had hardly the strength left to continue marching, being brought in. While in the opposite direction, a constant stream of reinforcements and supply wagons was moving up toward the front. Beyond the lines the stream flowed on north-eastward, but he turned away to the south-east and, not long afterwards, was riding through deserted country.

By road Seville was a good two hundred and fifty miles away and the greater part of the journey lay through

185

mountainous regions. As he could not hope to secure remounts, he expected it to take him the best part of a week, and the possibility of his being able to buy meals was dubious, so he had with him a good supply of food.

During the whole of the first day he was still in the great area of middle Portugal, where the earth had been scorched, so he saw only a few peasants in the distance. That night he slept in a deserted farmhouse. It was not until the evening of the second day that he entered a village which was still inhabited. There, to account for the foreign accent with which he spoke Portuguese, he said that he was a Spaniard from the Basque country in the far north. The man to whom he spoke accepted his statement without question and, in one of the few stone houses, he ate a meal of stew, then slept the night there.

For some weeks past the weather had been mainly good, with many days of spring sunshine. But when he woke next morning, he found that it had broken. Rain was teeming down, and he spent a miserable day alternately trotting and walking his horse up and down steep gradients, where the indifferent roads had become muddy rivers. Still worse, when twilight fell he was up in the mountains and, although he rode doggedly on until it was almost dark, he failed to come upon a village. Soaked to the skin, he spent a miserable night huddled in a cave.

Next morning it was still raining, but by midday he entered a small town where he was able to get a hot meal. That evening he crossed the frontier into Spain. Again the country was mountainous and so sparsely inhabited that night came down before he could hope to reach a village; so he had to doss down in a charcoal burner's hut.

On his fifth day he entered another town, and there gave himself out to be a Portuguese from the region of the Douro. A good meal at an inn partially restored his

spirits, and that night he was lucky, for he came upon a quite large country house surrounded by a sadly-neglected estate. Its owner, an old gentleman, received him courteously—accepted his statement that he was a Portuguese wine-shipper whose business had been ruined by Napoleon's embargo on trading with England and that he was on his way to his sister who had married a citizen of Seville—then said he would be happy to have his company for supper.

Roger then learned that his host had sent his family into Seville, and was living in the house with a few servants only to protect it from being looted and occupied by bandits. Over the meal they talked of the miseries brought about by the war and both drank to the eternal damnation of Napoleon. That night Roger again enjoyed the luxury of sleeping between sheets.

Late on the afternoon of the sixth day he sighted a foraging party of French Hussars. All through his journey he had feared to encounter a band of brigands who would have robbed, stripped and probably killed him. Immensely relieved, he rode up to the troop and announced himself as *Colonel le Comte de Breuc*, carrying an urgent despatch from the Prince of Essling to the Duke of Dalmatia, and asked to be at once conducted to Soult's headquarters. The officer detached his sergeant and two men as escort for him and, an hour later, Roger was riding into Seville.

There he found Soult's army in a very different state from Masséna's. Groups of well-turned-out officers and men were strolling about the city, ogling the *señoritas*—who did not appear to share the almost universal hatred of the Spanish for the French—or sitting drinking in the wine shops. Their Commander-in-Chief had taken over the splendid Alcazar Palace, and Roger was led through its courtyards, with their beautifully-carved Moorish arches, grilles and fountains, to the room of one of Soult's

adjutants. An hour later, he was ushered in to the grey-haired Marshal.

Roger explained his having arrived in Portugal by the same story he had told Masséna, adding that, after spending a few days at the Prince's headquarters, he had volunteered to carry a despatch to Seville. He then gave the news that hunger had forced Masséna to fall back on country where his troops could obtain supplies, and handed the despatch over.

Soult broke the seals, read the appeal for aid, casually tossed it on to a heap of papers and said, 'His Highness of Essling has my sympathy, but I fear there is no way in which I can assist him. Some months ago I received an order from the Emperor to co-operate with him by moving against Lisbon from the south. But His Majesty had no idea of conditions here, and his order was quite impractical. You know his temper, Breuc. He would become berserk with rage if I abandoned southern Spain, and deprive me of my command. Holding it down is no small commitment, and it was as much as I dared do to spare Mortier's corps for an advance into Estremadura. That, at least, was a valuable contribution, as we defeated a Spanish army there on February 19th, then laid siege to Badajoz, which fell a week ago today.'

Badajoz was the most important city between Seville and the Portuguese frontier, but many miles north-east of the direct route to Lisbon. Knowing Soult and Masséna's dislike of each other, Roger guessed that the former had deliberately selected this diversion as an excuse not to go to the latter's assistance; but he smoothly remarked:

'My congratulations on this fine achievement, Marshal. No doubt you felt it essential to reduce that great fortress, before permitting the Duc de Treviso to turn west and advance towards Lisbon.'

'Exactly. It would have been most rash to allow Mortier

to march direct into Portugal, leaving Badajoz untaken on his flank. The big garrison there might have made a sortie and severed his communications with my main army. And now, Breuc, I take it you will remain here with us.'

It being impossible for Roger to reply that, having found out that Soult had no intention of going to Mas-séna's aid, he himself wanted to get back to Lisbon as soon as he could, he appeared to hesitate as he said, 'I hardly know, Marshal; but I suppose that having de-livered His Highness of Essling's despatch, I ought to en-deavour to rejoin him.'

Soult put up a protesting hand. 'No, no, Breuc. I could not allow it. You have taken risk enough in making your way alone through hostile country all the way from San-tarém. To expose yourself again to the risk of being killed and eaten by our barbarous enemies would be madness. And, if you did get back to the Prince, in his present plight you could do him no earthly good. Report to my Chief of Staff, du Maurier. He will have a uniform found for you and provide you with work suited to your con-siderable abilities. I shall be glad to have you on my staff.'

Having expected that he would have to remain for some time at Soult's headquarters, Roger reconciled him-self to doing so and, after thanking the Marshal, went in search of his Chief of Staff. Du Maurier, a fat and pleasant man, took him to the Mess for a meal, then allo-cated to him a room on the upper floor of the Palace in which, tired out after his long day, he went early to bed.

Next morning a suitable uniform was brought to him, and du Maurier told him that, as he spoke Spanish, he was to sit on a tribunal that Soult had set up to hear com-plaints by the citizens of Seville against abuses by the troops.

His new work proved a revelation. Normally, all Napoleon's Marshals treated the people of conquered

cities extremely ill, looting their houses and allowing the troops the greatest licence in bullying the men and forcing the women. Soult was particularly notorious for this unscrupulous behaviour. He was known to be the greatest looter of them all, and had accumulated a collection of paintings, church ornaments and jewels said to be worth many millions. Yet, by his orders, the tribunal was heavily biased in favour of the Spaniards. Fines, imprisonment and demotions were freely inflicted on officers and men of his army.

Roger no longer wondered at having found the people of Seville so well disposed toward their French rulers, and he soon learned from his brother officers the reason for this new policy of appeasement. Unlike that of Suchet in Valencia, it was no disinterested move aimed at restoring order and justice in conquered territory. Apparently, after having butchered half the inhabitants of Oporto, and taken that city, Soult had nurtured the dream of turning northern Portugal into a kingdom for himself; but Wellington had driven him out of it. Now that he had become the overlord of southern Spain, in spite of the fact that Napoleon's brother, Joseph, was still in Madrid and, legally at least, King of Spain, the Marshal was planning to make himself King of Andalusia.

On capturing Seville, he had set about the business of confiscating works of art—particularly Old Masters, which were his special delight—with his usual gusto. But, recently, he had had second thoughts, for he had decided that the most satisfactory way of becoming a permanent ruler was to induce the people to ask him to become their King. With this in view, he had returned to the churches all the gold plate, reliquaries and chalices he had stolen, and instituted the tribunal as a means of winning popularity at no cost to himself.

Naturally, Roger derived considerable pleasure from

righting the wrongs done to unfortunate Spaniards; and, although he had been in Seville before, he enjoyed visiting again the sights of interest and strolling in the beautiful garden of the Alcazar. One afternoon, when he was walking in it with a brother officer, between the trees proceeding down a cross-path he caught sight of a surprising figure.

It was apparently a Captain of Hussars in a beautifully-tailored, sky-blue uniform; but the skin-tight smalls covered the plump bottom of a woman, the gold lace of the tunic protruded in a most suggestive curve, and beneath the busby dark ringlets fell to the epaulettes on the shoulders. Halting in his tracks, Roger exclaimed:

'*Sacré bleu!* Just look at that. Am I seeing things, or are we now giving commissions to young women?'

His companion laughed. 'Have you not seen her about the headquarters before? She is Anita, a lovely young Spaniard. Our Marshal is a great one for the women, and summons a fine variety of them to his bed. But Anita is a special case. She is his permanent mistress, and accompanies him everywhere. By putting her into uniform he has saved her the inconvenience inseparable from wearing female clothes when she rides out with him on reconnaissance.'

After a week in Seville, Roger decided that the time had come when he could disappear without arousing suspicion that he had left deliberately.

For the sake of exercise most of his brother staff officers went for a ride outside the city, either early in the morning or in the evening, and there had been one occasion when one of them had failed to return, presumably through having ridden too far afield and fallen into the hands of the enemy or marauders.

There was only one difficulty in carrying out a deception on these lines. The officers usually rode out in parties and rarely alone; but Roger had thought of a way in

which he could rid himself of a single companion.

On the afternoon of the 24th he asked a Major Theophile Simplon, with whom he had ridden out before, if he would care to go for a ride with him. Simplon accepted and it was agreed that they should meet in the stables in half an hour's time. Roger got there well in advance of the Major, taking with him, wrapped up in paper, his civilian clothes. Telling the groom on duty that he would saddle his own horse, he spread the folded coat and breeches on the animal's back and strapped the saddle over them. Then he stuffed his soft-brimmed hat into one saddle holster and into the other a packet of cold meat that he had taken from the Mess side table when no-one was in the room.

Simplon, little suspecting the trick that was to be played on him, joined him shortly afterwards and, side by side, they rode out of the city. When they were some two miles from the walls, they came to wooded country, which suited Roger's purpose. They had turned down a ride where no-one could see them even from a distance, and were walking their horses. Roger dropped half a length behind his companion, then took a stiletto from under his jacket and dug the point sharply into the rump of the Major's mount.

With a spasmodic jerk, the animal reared, gave a loud neigh and bolted with the unfortunate Simplon. Roger had estimated that, the Major having had no warning of what would befall, his horse would cover the best part of half a mile before he could bring it under control. When, with flying hooves, it had sped a hundred yards, Roger turned off into another ride and put his own horse into a gallop.

Having ridden on for an hour, he pulled up at a place where some big boulders had rolled down a mountain to the side of the road. Among them he changed into his civilian clothes and left his uniform and befeathered hat.

Then he pressed forward at the best pace he could expect from his mount, heading for the house in which he had spent his last night before reaching Seville.

Night fell long before he arrived there. The moon gave sufficient light for him to keep to the right road, but he had some difficulty in finding the house and it was close on midnight when he entered the short, overgrown drive that led to it.

The place was in darkness, but he hammered with his riding crop on the door until a flickering light appeared and a servant, opening a grille in the door, asked suspiciously what he wanted. On his giving the name he had used on his previous visit, the man remembered him and went to rouse his master.

When the old gentleman appeared, Roger told him that, on reaching Seville, he had learned that his sister and her husband had been killed by their house collapsing on them, as a result of the bombardment during the siege of the city. As he knew no-one there and had very little money, he had decided that his best course was to make his way back to his native Oporto, where he at least had other relatives and numerous friends. The old man then commiserated with him, gave him a bed for the night and saw to it that he had a good breakfast before setting off again in the morning.

He spent his second night at a wayside inn, his third in a mountain cave and his fourth in a deserted farmhouse. On the fifth day he was riding again through the scorched-earth country, with the cheerful prospect that, if his luck held, by the following night he would be back in Lisbon. But, alas for those happy thoughts, his luck did not hold.

Both on his outward journey and during his return, he had taken every possible precaution to avoid other people, however innocent-looking. A score of times, on seeing vehicles, horsemen or peasants approaching along the

193

road, he had quickly turned off into a wood or down a bridle path, where he could remain concealed until any likelihood of danger was past. But on this afternoon he was caught unawares.

The road he was on wound through a rocky gully. As he rounded a sharp bend in it, two ragged, bearded men with muskets rose from among the rocks, pointed their weapons at him and called on him to halt.

Had he been in open country, he would have set spurs to his horse and risked being hit as he galloped off. But the two men were no more than fifteen paces from him, so he did not stand a dog's chance of getting away without being seriously wounded. Cursing below his breath, he pulled up and, at a gruff order, dismounted.

As he did so, in Spanish mingled with enough Portuguese for the man to understand him, he declared himself to be a Spanish patriot carrying a message from General the Marquis de la Romana to Lord Wellington.

One of the men was a little runt, but it was he who had spoken for both, and he said, 'Maybe, comrade, maybe not. We'll soon find out. You are coming with us.'

The other man slouched forward and took Roger's horse by the bridle, while the runt cautiously took a few paces sideways until he was behind Roger and could point his musket at his back. Giving him a quick prod with the barrel, he said:

'Come on. Get moving.'

To Roger, the three-quarters of an hour that followed seemed never-ending. As he trudged along, he recalled all the accounts he had heard, both from British and French acquaintances, of the terrible fate that befell those who were captured by brigands. That they really cooked and ate people he believed to be a slander; but he had no doubt at all that their hatred for their enemies was so intense that they tortured unmercifully the French soldiers who fell into their hands, and often finished them off by

skinning them alive, burning or disembowelling them. He could only pray that his knowledge of Spanish and Portuguese, together with his long-since-perfected ability to lie convincingly would enable him to get away with his life. At the least he could expect to be robbed of his money, and would be lucky if they even left him his clothes.

The man holding the horse led the way down the steep, rocky road until the gully ended, opening out into country where there were small woods and land that had previously been cultivated. At length they turned off the road on to a track that ran alongside a coppice. Beyond the trees there lay a by-road and, on the far side, a good-sized country house. As they approached it, Roger guessed that it had been evacuated by its owner and that the brigands had moved in as squatters.

When they had walked up a short drive, they halted for a moment in front of the house. The runt muttered something that Roger did not catch to the bigger man, who led the horse away, evidently taking it to a stable at the back of the premises.

They had not bothered to take Roger's sword from him. Now that he had only one man to deal with was, he felt, the time to use it. But his hand had hardly moved toward the hilt, before the musket barrel was again pressed against the base of his spine, and the runt said:

'Go on. Into the house. You can tell your story to *O Diabo dos olhos azuis*; and we'll see what he has to say about it.'

To whip out his sword at that moment would, Roger felt, have been the last act of his life. There was nothing for it but to obey. Seething with anger and frustration, he walked up the steps that led to a door which stood half-open and, prodded by the runt, crossed a hall into a once-pleasant, but now dilapidated salon.

There were three other men and two slatternly women there. One of the men was lounging on a sofa, the fine

brocade of which was badly stained by spilt wine. Across his lap lay one of the women, with whose plump breasts he was toying. Roughly pushing her aside, he stood up and Roger saw that he was a giant. He was heavily bearded, there was an ugly gap in his front teeth where two were missing, and he had extraordinarily prominent blue eyes.

'Here we are, *Diabo*!' the runt cried to him cheerfully. 'Brought you a bird that should be worth the plucking.'

Roger promptly burst into speech, again mingling Spanish and Portuguese, but in a manner that ensured he could be understood. With lavish detail he fabricated an account of how General de la Romana had sent him to beg milord Wellington to provide his army with some additional pieces of artillery.

The giant listened patiently, uttering not a word until Roger had to stop talking after having repeated himself several times, and being unable to think of anything else to say. There followed a full minute of nerve-racking silence, then *O Diabo* gave a great bellow of laughter and cried:

'Stupid pig. You are a Frenchie, as anyone could see. There's not a doubt of it. Look at his fine boots and his sword, comrades. They are an officer's, or I'm a red-headed whore. And they're his own. The boots fit him like a pair of gloves. Get a fire lit in the coach-house, comrades. We'll have some fun with this spawn of a louse tonight.'

CHAPTER XIV

THE DEVIL WITH BLUE EYES

THE blood drained from Roger's face. His very worst fears were about to be realised. The thought of being scorched until he screamed and screamed in vain made his flesh creep and filled his mind with horror. He felt certain there was not the least possibility that the great brute they called 'the blue-eyed devil' was either joking or just trying to scare him. This was not Spain, but only owing to a divergence of dynasties. In blood and outlook the Portuguese were closer to the Madridlenos than the Catalans or the Basques. And Spain had been the home of the terrible Inquisition. On the hypocritical pretext that they were saving souls, the priests had burned Jews, Protestants and Moors—thousands of them. Those *auto-da-fes*, by which the Church had rid herself of her enemies, had been Roman holidays for the people. Great crowds of them had watched poor wretches writhing at the stake. They had obviously delighted in the spectacle, otherwise they would not have stood there enduring the horrible smell of roasting flesh. And now these monsters in human form were about to burn him !

It took only a few instants for these ghastly thoughts to race through Roger's brain. Within seconds he had taken his decision. Far better be shot in the back than burned alive; and, if he was quick enough he might kill *O Diabo*

before the ball from the runt's musket smashed through his spine and made him choke in his own blood.

Many years of handling weapons and an unusual agility had made him a most formidable swordsman. He was a good twelve feet away from *O Diabo,* but he thought the odds favoured his chance of spitting the great brute before a bullet in his back brought him crashing to the floor. With one smooth, swift motion his sword came out of its sheath like a ripple of light. As he drew it, he sprang forward, halving the distance between his enemy and himself. His right arm was drawn back behind the blade so that his lunge would have all the force he could put into it.

Next moment he was within four feet of the giant and had delivered his thrust. But the woman with whom *O Diabo* had been toying on the sofa was standing with her arm through his. From Roger's sudden change of expression she must have guessed his intention. With the agility of a ballet dancer, she pirouetted on one foot, bringing herself round in front of her tall lover. The point of Roger's blade ripped into her shoulder.

She gave a piercing scream. The impact had thrown her against *O Diabo*'s chest. Her free arm jerked upward and she flung it round his neck to prevent herself from falling. It was only then that Roger realised he had not been shot in the back. Evidently the runt felt that would be too swift a death for him, and did not want them to be robbed of their sport.

Roger gave a violent tug on his sword, but it was embedded in the muscles behind the woman's shoulder and would not come out. Instead, the force of his tug pulled the woman away from *O Diabo*. Her arm was wrenched from round his neck, and she fell to the floor. As she hit it, Roger's sword snapped off about nine inches from the point.

In any case, he would have had no chance to make

a second lunge at *O Diabo*, for the runt had dropped his
musket and seized him round the waist. Quick-witted as
ever in an affray, Roger lifted the hilt of his sword as
though to strike himself in the stomach. On it were the
clasped hands of the runt. The heavy hilt came smashing
down on them. The runt gave a howl of pain, followed
by a spate of blasphemous curses, and let go. At that moment *O Diabo* was occupied in lifting his woman from
the floor and getting her on to the sofa.

Instantly Roger swung round. The two other bandits
had been lounging at the far end of the room near a pair
of french windows. As Roger sprang forward to attack
O Diabo they had jumped to their feet and come running to the runt's assistance. On entering the salon, Roger
had registered the windows as a possible means of escape.
If he could deal with the two men who were now almost
upon him, and elude *O Diabo*, who would be certain to
pursue him, there was just a chance that he might get
away through the windows.

His sword was a slightly curved cavalry sabre, and still
had two feet of blade. The nearer of the men coming at
him was a lanky youth who still had down on his receding
jaw. Roger had no time to raise his sword, so brought it
swishing round at elbow level. It sliced into the lower
part of the youth's arm. As the blood spurted from the
savage cut, he gave a yelp, clapped his hand to the wound
and reeled sideways, lurching into his companion, who
was just about to strike at Roger's face with a pike. The
collision diverted the blow and gave Roger his chance.
He bounded toward the open window.

Seconds later he heard the crashing of heavy feet. *O
Diabo* had left his woman and was after him. But he still
had a chance. He was a very fast runner. If only he could
get through the window, he had a good hope of out-
distancing his pursuers. Alas for that hope. At that very
moment the man who had taken his horse round to the

stable appeared outside the window. Sizing up the situation in the salon at a glance, he swiftly drew a thin-bladed dagger and crouched on the threshold barring Roger's way.

Unless Roger had rushed upon the man's stiletto, he would have had to pull up in his wild career, and feint with his broken sword before striking out to cut him down. Even the pause of a moment would, he knew, bring *O Diabo* on him from behind. But there was still just one hope. The other three men were hard on *O Diabo*'s heels, so the door of the room, left half-open by the runt, was unguarded.

Roger swerved toward it. He had one foot in the air and was now sideways on to *O Diabo*. The giant's great fist shot out and caught him squarely on the cheek. The blow seemed to jolt every tooth in his head. For a second stars and circles whirled against blackness before his eyes. His sword dropped from his hand. With one foot still in the air, he heeled over and crashed to the ground.

For four or five heart-beats he lay there. Then, bemused but with the instinct of self-preservation still uppermost, he struggled to get up. Next moment the whole pack was round him. The runt gave him a vicious kick in the ribs, but he shot out a hand and grabbed the bandit's other leg by the ankle, threw himself sideways and brought the little man down on top of him. Gasping in a deep breath, he raised both hands and got them round the runt's throat.

In vain the runt beat at Roger's face with his bleeding hands. Three of his fingers had been broken by the sword hilt, so pain prevented him from putting any strength into his blows. *O Diabo,* evidently thinking the little man's plight amusing, stood back and guffawed; but the bandit's other comrades came to his assistance. Seizing Roger's arms they strove to pull them away, and to break

his grip on the runt's neck. Panting now, and with sweat pouring down his face, Roger hung on like grim death, pressing his strong thumbs firmly into the soft flesh below the other's chin. His mouth had opened and his tongue stuck out. His dark, fear-stricken eyes began to pop. Another minute and he would have been strangled into unconsciousness. But before half that minute had gone Roger felt a hand thrust up between his legs. It was that of the woman he had wounded, using her sound arm. The hand found his testicles, grabbed them and squeezed. A ghastly pain shot up from them into his stomach and seemed to pierce his heart. He gave a scream of agony, let go of the runt's neck and fainted.

When he came to, he was still lying in the same place on the floor. His breath was coming in gasps, tears were running down his cheeks and stabs of pain racked his body. His head was splitting and his jaw ached from the blow *O Diabo* had struck him on the side of the face. For several minutes he lay quite still, endeavouring to decrease the pain by taking only short, shallow breaths. After a while he turned his head, first to one side, then to the other, dimly taking in what was going on in the room.

O Diabo was again lounging on the sofa, now smoking a long clay pipe. The wounded woman was having her shoulder bound up by the other woman, who had taken no part in the fight. The runt had disappeared, presumably to nurse his injuries, so had the man who had been his companion in the ambush. There remained the two who had been with *O Diabo* when Roger had been brought into the room. One was a stout, brawny fellow with ginger hair. The other was the youngster whose arm Roger had slashed. He was darker-skinned than the others and had a flattened nose, so was probably half Negro. His wound had already been attended to and his arm was in a sling.

201

Both the door of the room and the french windows were still open; but they might have been bolted and barred as far as Roger was concerned. He was in such pain that he found it difficult to concentrate his thoughts and if he had managed to get to his feet he doubted if he would be able to walk, let alone put up a fight.

After a time *O Diabo* finished his pipe, got up and crossed the room to help himself to a mug of wine from a jug that stood on a side table. As he passed Roger he noticed that his eyes were open. Kneeling, he raised Roger's head, put the mug to his lips and said:

'Drink some of this, Frenchie. It'll put a bit of strength into you.'

The wine was coarse and sharp, but Roger sucked it in gratefully, thinking meanwhile that this giant with the bright blue eyes could not be altogether evil. But his flickering hope of mercy was short-lived, as the other added, 'If we can't get you back into fair shape, you'll kick the bucket too soon and spoil our evening's sport.'

Roger stopped drinking, let his head fall back and groaned.

'Scared a bit, Frenchie?' the big man grinned, showing the ugly gap in the centre of his upper row of teeth. 'But we can't let French pigs live. That would be a sin, according to our priests.'

For a moment he was silent, then he went on, 'Still, I've got a soft spot for a man who puts up a good fight; and you certainly did that. So I'll give you a choice of deaths. Shall we burn you, skin you alive or shove a bayonet up your arse?'

His flesh again creeping with horror, Roger did not reply, gave another groan and closed his eyes.

Passing his great arms under Roger's body, the giant lifted him as though he were a child, carried him over to a battered *chaise longue* and laid him on it. Before turning away, he said, 'You've plenty of time to think it

over. Alfonso, that's the chap you nearly strangled, wants to see you dance, so I said I'd give him an hour or two to pull himself together.'

The 'hour or two' seemed to Roger the longest he had spent in his life. He could almost have wished that his brain had not started to work again, as he could not keep his mind off the ghastly deaths of which he had been given a choice. Even being burnt seemed slightly less terrible than being flayed, and the bayonet should be quicker than either. But would it? He had known men suffering from an internal haemorrhage take several hours to die, and they always died writhing in agony.

Twilight fell and two candles stuck in bottles were lit. As darkness came, deep shadows obscured the far corners of the room. At length the door creaked. Alfonso the runt came through it. Both his hands were bandaged and there was a compress round his neck. Pausing beside Roger, he leered down at him, spat in his face, then walked over to *O Diabo* and said hoarsely :

'I'm a shade better now. Well enough, anyway, to enjoy seeing the French pig fried.'

Standing up, *O Diabo* came over to Roger and asked, 'What's it to be, Frenchie? The fire, the knife or a bloody hole in your guts?'

Roger was still in great pain, but the long lie on the *chaise longue* had recruited his strength a little. He felt that he would be able to stand up, and even walk a few steps. But he knew that he was utterly incapable of putting up another fight. Rallying his resources, he was able to reply clearly and firmly, 'You are not going to kill me in any of those ways; or in any other way. Because I am in a position to buy my life.'

O Diabo gave a bellow of laughter. 'Listen, comrades. The fool thinks he can buy his life because he has a few gold pieces on him.'

'I've more than a few,' said Roger quietly, 'but I . . .'

The other cut him short. 'That's all to the good. Let's have them.'

Roger put his hands to his waist, in order to get at his money belt, but he was still very weak and fumbled with the buttons of his suit. Seeing his intention, *O Diabo* impatiently pushed his hands aside, undid the buttons, made Roger sit up and pulled the belt from under his vest.

The others now crowded round as their leader emptied the pockets of the belt on a nearby table. There were packets of Spanish, Portuguese, English and French gold coins and the special reserve Roger always carried, a little washleather bag containing a number of small diamonds.

When the bandits had finished exclaiming on their luck at having made such an unusually rich haul, *O Diabo* turned back to Roger and grinned, 'St. Christopher himself must have sent you to us, Frenchie. Out of your money we'll buy him a score of candles. But don't fool yourself that you're going to live. When we'd stripped you, as we're about to now, we'd have come on the belt and taken it anyhow.'

'Of course.' Roger gave a slight nod. 'I'm not such a fool as to have failed to realise that; but you did not let me finish.'

'What more have you to say?'

'As you will have gathered from the contents of my money belt, I am a man of some importance. That I am a French officer, I now admit. I am *Colonel Comte de Breuc,* and a Commander of the Legion of Honour.' Roger was still in considerable pain and the effort of talking had made the sweat again break out on his forehead. As he paused to wipe it away with the back of his hand, *O Diabo* shrugged his great shoulders and said :

'Save your breath, Frenchie. You were going to tell us that your friends will pay a fine ransom for you, weren't

you? Maybe they would, but maybe they'd put the
thumbscrews on my messenger until he brought them
here to make an end of us. That is, if there was a Frenchie
General in this neighbourhood. But there isn't. Now the
English have chivvied Masséna away from Lisbon,
there's not a French army within a hundred miles. So
put that out of your mind and choose your death. Come
on now!'

Roger had thought of suggesting that he should get
himself ransomed; not by the French, whom he had
realised were much too far away, but by the British.
Knowing that he was quite a wealthy man, Sir Charles
Stuart would not have hesitated to provide the money.
But an appeal to the British Minister meant having to
declare himself an Englishman. He had no possible means
of proving that, and it was certain beyond all doubt that
O Diabo would not believe him. With a calmness that he
was far from feeling, he played his last card.

'All you say is true enough; but I was not thinking of
asking you to send a request to my General to ransom
me. I am capable of ransoming myself.'

'And how, Frenchie, would you do that?' *O Diabo*
gave him a cynical smile. ' 'Tis known that your Emperor and Satan are one, so maybe you think a prayer to
him would bring you a shower of gold. But I'll wager he
won't answer.'

Managing a smile, Roger replied, 'And I certainly
wouldn't take you. I've a far more reliable way of producing a fortune. Some two and a half years ago, when
General Junot entered Lisbon, I was with him. I need
hardly tell you that it is the custom of French officers of
high rank to collect souvenirs of the cities they capture. I
collected the jewels of the Marquis de Pombal, before he
left for Brazil. Later, you will remember, the English
landed in Portugal, our army was defeated and, by the
Convention of Cintra, we were shipped back to France.

Fearing to have the jewels taken from me, I buried them in a safe place a few miles outside Lisbon. Ever since then the English have occupied that part of the country; so I've had no chance to collect them. They must still be there.'

O Diabo's blue eyes had opened wide with interest as he listened to this story. Having roused his cupidity, Roger hurried on, 'You can have no idea of this treasure unless you see it. There are ropes of pearls, tiaras blazing with gems, crosses with rubies and emeralds, a girdle of solid gold set with turquoises, high combs studded with diamonds, rings, ear-rings, watches and breast ornaments, all fashioned from gold and jewels. Their value is fabulous. They would fetch many million *moredores*. Enough for all of you never to have to work or risk your lives as robbers again. When the war is over you could live in a town as rich people, or buy farms on which others would labour for you. Promise me my life, and all this is yours.'

There was a moment's silence, then the group broke into an excited babble. With the mentality of children they began to tell one another of the splendid figures they would cut when they had all this money. *O Diabo* slowly nodded his bearded head :

'You shall take us to it. But don't get any idea that we shall give you a chance to escape on the way. Any tricks and we'll hang you by your thumbs to the branch of a tree, then light a small fire under you that will burn your feet away.'

The effort to tell his story while still in great pain had completely exhausted Roger. Closing his eyes he lay back on the *chaise longue*. A sense of unutterable relief flooded through him at knowing that he was not now to die a ghastly death within the next hour. But he had gained no more than a reprieve. The treasure he had described so temptingly did not exist. It was only a figment of his vivid imagination; and already that vivid imagination

was beginning to conjure up the awful treatment he would receive when *O Diabo* and his gang discovered that they had been fooled.

The childish excitement of Roger's captors was coupled with a childish faith in his fairy story. He was now a being to be humoured and cherished. They put pillows under his head, gave him more wine and put to rights his clothes which had become dishevelled when his money belt had been pulled from round his waist.

The woman who had not been wounded went off to cook the evening meal. A small table was put beside the *chaise longue*, so that he could eat in comfort. The meal consisted of a rabbit stew, highly flavoured with garlic, and slabs of a coarse cake, in which there was a generous supply of the locally-dried raisins. Roger loathed garlic but, knowing how important it was to recruit his strength, he managed to get most of his portion down by swiftly adding to each mouthful a swig of wine.

When he had finished the meal, *O Diabo* asked Roger anxiously if he thought he would be sufficiently recovered to start the next morning. For a moment Roger remained silent, weighing the pros and cons. As long as his captors remained ignorant that the treasure was a myth, his life was safe, so it was very tempting to postpone setting out for Lisbon for a day or two. On the other hand, the moment of truth had to be faced sooner or later, and the suspense to which he would be subjected until it did would be harrowing. So he said that, after a night's rest, he hoped to be well enough.

The powerfully-made, red-headed man, whose name was Paolo, supported him upstairs to a bedroom, and helped him to undress; but, when he lay down on the bed, took the precaution of tying his wrists with lengths of cord to the wooden bedhead. There was sufficient slack in the cords for them not to cause him any discomfort;

but, even had he been in good shape, they would have prevented any attempt to escape.

Paolo had only just left him when the woman who had cooked their supper came in. Pulling down the blanket with which Roger was covered, she eased up his vest, exposing his private parts. As his hands were attached to the bedhead, he could not resist her, and was seized by panic. His terror that she meant to inflict further injury upon him entirely eliminated any embarrassment he might have felt. But, as he squirmed away from her and began to shout, she only laughed and held a pot of ointment up for him to see. She began gently to massage his testicles with the cream. It was a concoction of crushed poppy seeds in fat, and it soon dulled the ache from which he was still suffering. Some twenty minutes after she had blown out the solitary candle and closed his door behind her, he drifted off to sleep.

When he woke in the morning he wondered for a moment where he was; then, like a nightmare, his ordeal of the previous evening came back to him. His jaw began to ache again, but he was greatly relieved to find that the pain in his groin was now hardly noticeable. That he had not, as he had feared after the slut's attack on him, been deprived of his manhood was a matter for thanksgiving; but whether it would ever again be of any use to him seemed highly problematic. Once more a terrible dread of the *dénouement* that must take place when they came within a few miles of Lisbon drove all other thoughts from his mind.

He had been awake only a quarter of an hour when Paolo came in, untied him, helped him into his clothes and took him down to breakfast. In the salon, while they were all eating, a fine wrangle took place. All the members of the band wanted to go on the expedition, because each of them feared that, if he were left behind, the others would make off with the splendid spoil. But only four

horses, including Roger's, were available. After much argument, *O Diabo* ruled that the Negroid youth and the runt Alfonso should be left there with the women, because the arm of the one and the broken fingers of the other would prove a serious handicap on horseback. He, of course, would go himself and take Paolo and the runt's original companion, whose name was Francesco.

Lisbon was the best part of a day's ride distant, and Roger told *O Diabo* that, owing to his recent injury, he doubted if he could go that far; but the giant said that if he collapsed they would lie up somewhere for the night. When the horses were brought round, he had a blanket strapped over Roger's saddle, to make it more comfortable for him; and, on mounting, Roger found that riding would not prove as painful as he had expected.

Gradually the morning hours wore away and during that time they made good progress. At midday they halted and, among some trees at the roadside, ate some of the food they had brought with them. Afterwards Roger hoped they would take a siesta, and there might be a chance of his getting away. But *O Diabo* was anxious to press on. Roger had calculated that if they did they would probably come to within a few miles of Lisbon by late afternoon, and he was determined that they should not get there before twilight was falling. So he declared that he was in no state to ride further until after he had had a good long rest. Reluctantly the giant agreed, but tied Roger's hands, then hitched the other end of the rope to a tree, so that there should be no risk of his making off if his three captors fell asleep. Resigning himself to abandoning this faint hope of escape, he stretched out on the fallen leaves and fell into a doze.

The rest did him good, and when they set off again he was feeling no worse than he had when they had left the bandit's quarters that morning. But the nearer they came to Lisbon the more his fears for his life crowded in on his

mind. There had not been a moment during their journey when he had not scanned the roads along which they advanced for some feature which might lend itself to his chances if he set spurs to his horse and caused it to bolt. But *O Diabo* rode beside him, with Paolo and Francesco in the rear. One or other of the latter would almost certainly have shot him in the back before he could have covered fifty yards.

At length, in the far distance, the spires of Lisbon came in sight, and the lines of Torres Vedras could be seen clearly, less than a mile away. From a gateway in them there emerged a road and on it lay Roger's one remaining hope. For some minutes past he had been watching it with intense anxiety, and had seen two small groups of troops pass along it. If only he could get his captors near enough, and divert their attention for a moment when another group was passing, he meant to take his life in his hands, yell for help and endeavour to reach them.

But they were still a good way from the road when *O Diabo* said to him abruptly, 'Come now, Frenchie. You said you had buried the treasure about a mile from where the lines are now; and we're nearer to them than that already. Get your bearings, and be quick about it.'

Turning his horse a little to the left, Roger pointed to a gully about a hundred and fifty yards away, and replied, 'It's somewhere in the far bank of that stream over there.'

The party trotted toward it and looked down at the slowly-flowing, shallow water. With a shake of his head, Roger said, 'It is over two years since I hid the stuff, so it may take me a little time to find the place. It wasn't here, anyway, but further downstream I think.'

O Diabo grunted. 'Then we'd better cross the stream and walk along under the far bank. Close to, you'll stand a better chance of recognising a mound or a bit of out-

crop that will guide you to it. We'll leave our horses here.'

That was a blow to Roger, as it deprived him of the chance to gallop off, crouched low over his saddle bow. But his nerves were so strung up that he could think of no reasonable objection. As he dismounted, he ruefully accepted the fact that, if he could raise the courage to break away, he would now have to run for it.

Francesco was left to hold the horses while *O Diabo*, Roger and Paolo scrambled down the near bank and splashed through the shallow water. On the far side Roger turned left. Every step he took would bring him nearer the road. But, on looking toward it, his heart sank. It was now empty.

Moving as slowly as he dared, he pretended to examine every hollow and protruberance in the four-foot-high bank, whenever he dared taking a quick look over it in the direction of the road. The light was now fading, but it would be an hour or more before darkness fell; so he could not hope that it would swallow him up should he escape the first shots fired at him as he made his dash for life and liberty.

They had made their way about two hundred yards along the gully, when Roger saw a small convoy emerge from the gateway in the lines. It consisted only of two wagons, with two men riding in front of them and two behind, and it was moving at a walk. For another five minutes Roger continued to scrutinise every inequality in the bank. The convoy advanced with maddening slowness, and *O Diabo* was becoming impatient. Halting, he growled :

'From what you said, Frenchie, the place can't be as near the lines as this. We must have passed it. Or perhaps it's upstream from the place where we crossed. We'd better turn back.'

The convoy was still four hundred yards away. But

Roger felt that if he agreed to return upstream, he would be no better off. It was now or never. With sudden resolution he gave *O Diabo* a violent push that sent him reeling backward into the water. Then he bounded up the bank and ran for his life.

CHAPTER XV

THE SERPENT ENTERS EDEN

As Roger raced forward over the rough grass, he shouted with all the strength of his lungs, 'Help! Help! I am an Englishman! Save me from these brigands.'

He saw the four mounted men and the drivers of the two wagons all turn their heads in his direction. Next moment he was flat on his face on the ground. He had not tripped and fallen; but, after covering the first twenty yards, deliberately flung himself down. Had he not done so, he would probably have got no further as, at that range, Paolo could hardly have failed to miss him. But his timing had been good. Only seconds after he hit the earth, a musket banged and the bullet whistled overhead.

Coming to his feet, he ran on again, his brain making frantic speculations. How long would it take for Paolo to reload? A minute perhaps. But by now *O Diabo* would have picked himself up. Had his musket fallen into the water with him? If so, the powder would be damp and the weapon useless until it had been dried and reprimed. But it might have fallen on the yard wide strip of sandy earth that ran alongside the stream. In that case, seething with rage, he would be taking aim at that very moment at the 'Frenchie' who had cheated him.

The two wagons had halted. The four horsemen had left the road and were coming in Roger's direction, but

only at a cautious trot. 'Help!' Roger yelled again. 'Gallop, damn you. Gall...'

His last word ended in a choking gasp. A musket had banged behind him and the ball smashed into his right buttock. He staggered a couple of steps, then his leg gave under him and he hit the ground with a thump. At the same moment he heard *O Diabo* shout:

'Come on, Paolo! Out with your knife. We'll get the lying dog yet!' Then came the sound of swift feet thudding heavily on the grass.

Roger's wound was not as painful as he would have expected. In fact, the place where he had been hit seemed to have gone numb. But evidently the bullet had penetrated his thigh and come out there, as the right leg of his breeches was becoming saturated with blood. With an effort he forced himself up on to his feet.

For a moment he glimpsed the two brigands running toward him. They both had their knives out and their faces were convulsed with rage and hate. Apparently they were so maddened with disappointment at the loss of the great fortune they had been visualising for the past twenty-four hours that they were willing to risk an encounter with the oncoming soldiers rather than allow Roger to escape.

His terror mounting afresh, Roger jerked himself round and made to run again. But it was the bone of his leg that had deflected the bullet. As he put his weight upon it, he was seized by an agonising pain. He staggered a few steps, then again fell to the ground. Rolling over, he sent a frantic glance in the direction of the approaching horsemen.

At his second shout, they had broken into a gallop. Now they were no more than forty paces from him. One of them pulled up and fired a carbine. The bullet got Paolo squarely in the chest. With a loud grunt, he threw up his arms and collapsed. But *O Diabo* still came on.

Seconds later he reached Roger. Holding his knife high, he slashed downward with it at Roger's heart. Roger jerked himself violently away, but could not avoid the knife. Nevertheless, his movement saved him. Instead of the point piercing his chest, it struck the buckle of his belt, driving the breath out of his body, but snapping off short. By then the nearest horseman was right above *O Diabo*. The soldier's sword swished up, then down. The blade clove the giant's head from skull to jaw. Without a sound he collapsed on Roger, gushing blood and brains all over him.

Of what happened after that Roger had only a confused memory. Loss of blood had caused him to faint. When he came to, he realised vaguely that he was being carried on a stretcher and that his wounds had been roughly bound up. His next memory was of being put to bed and given a draught.

When he woke the following morning, English voices told him that he was in a ward of a military hospital. Soon becoming conscious that he had an urgent task to carry out he endeavoured to sit up, but fell back groaning. Pain flamed in his thigh and bruised stomach, causing him to gasp for breath. When he had recovered a little, he called to a passing orderly. Reluctantly the man went off in search of the surgeon-in-charge.

When the surgeon arrived, it took all the determination Roger could muster to persuade the man that his patient was not suffering from delirium, and to insist that the British Minister be fetched to receive from him a confidential message from Lord Wellington.

Late in the afternoon Sir Charles arrived. By then Roger was in a fever, but his mind was still clear enough to ask for screens to be put round the bed, then say to his visitor :

'I have no message for Your Excellency from milord Wellington; but a most urgent one for him. Before he left

Lisbon he charged me with a special task. I succeeded in carrying it out, but I am anxious that my name should not be given in connection with my message. I pray you write to him as follows :

' "The man your brother recommended to you has been in Seville. He talked with Soult. Victor has made no progress with the siege of Cadiz. Mortier took Badajoz on March 10th, but will advance no further. Soult's ambition is to make himself King of Andalusia. You may therefore be certain that he will not leave Seville." '

The Minister gave a slow smile. 'From the interest Lord Wellington displayed in you when he was here, Mr. Brook, I suspected that you must be something more than a casual traveller. I realise that this very welcome information is of the first importance, since it will enable Wellington to use all his resources in pursuit of Masséna. It shall be despatched to him under double seal, with all possible speed, and I will arrange for the courier to be escorted by a troop of horse, to ensure that he reaches our General safely.'

Weakly, Roger returned the smile. 'I thank you, Sir. That is a great weight off my mind. But I am in poor shape, so you will forgive me if I do not now talk further. You might, though, give my love to little Mary.'

Had Roger's mind been in a normal state, he would not have singled out Mary, much less used the word 'love', when referring to her. He would simply have sent his respects to 'the ladies'. But Sir Charles did not appear to notice that he had made what, in those times, could be taken as a declaration. Laying his hand lightly on Roger's shoulder, he said :

'I was happy to learn from your surgeon, Mr. Brook, that apart from a bruising of your thigh bone, you have sustained only a flesh wound. So we may hope that you will be able to get about again before long. In the mean-

216

time, it will be my pleasure to ensure that every care is taken of you.'

The strain of the interview caused Roger to have a relapse. For the greater part of the next forty-eight hours a succession of opium draughts kept him unconscious; but on his third day the fever left him and, for a short while that afternoon, he was allowed to see visitors. Enquiries had been made daily by the Legation about his progress, and now Mary and Deborah arrived with fruit, flowers and wine.

Screens had again been put round his bed and, unabashed by Deborah's presence, Mary kissed him lightly on the forehead. Sir Charles had, of course, kept to himself the fact that Roger had carried out a dangerous mission and penetrated the French headquarters in Seville, so the two girls assumed that he had been with Wellington until sent back for some reason to Lisbon.

He naturally confirmed their belief, but told them, as was only too true, how he had fallen into the hands of brigands a day's march from the city, induced them to accompany him there then, when they had come within sight of British troops, broken away from them.

Deborah told him that her uncle had asked for him to be given a private ward, but the hospital was now so full of wounded sent back from the front that this had not been possible. To his delight, she added that, as soon as he was well enough to be moved, he was to occupy his old room at the Legation.

Roger learned that Wellington's pursuit of Masséna was going well. The French were in a desperate plight, as they retreated across the mountains of central Beira. Nearly all their horses were dead, so they had had to abandon most of their wagons and many of their guns, while the men, demoralised by long privations, were deserting by the hundred or dying by the roadside.

Quite casually, as though it was of little importance,

just before the girls left, Mary gave him a piece of news that had reached Lisbon two days earlier. On the 20th, Marie Louise had presented the Emperor with a son, who was to be known as the King of Rome.

The event might be of no great significance to Napoleon's enemies, but Roger knew how much it would mean to the Bonapartes. At last the Emperor had achieved his dearest ambition—a son fathered on the daughter of an Imperial house that claimed its descent from the Emperors of Rome and Byzantium. He could imagine the fabulous jewels that Napoleon would shower on the young mother; the spate of honours poured out to friends and high officials of the Empire; the fireworks, fêtes, parades and balls that, regardless of expense, would celebrate the arrival of this little heir to territories stretching from the Baltic to the tip of Italy. He could also imagine the rage and bitter disappointment with which several members of the Bonaparte family would be filled by this royal birth. Joseph, as Napoleon's eldest brother, had always regarded himself as having the best claim to succeed him. While still believing himself incapable of begetting a child, Napoleon had as good as expressed his intention of nominating the son of Louis by Hortense as his heir. And Murat, spurred on by his ambitious wife, Caroline, had been led to believe that his immense popularity with the French Army and people would lead to their offering the crown to him rather than to any of the Bonaparte brothers.

During the next few days Roger made good progress. Except at the times when his wound was dressed, he was fairly free from pain. The healthy flesh of his buttock and thigh promised to heal well; so his badly bruised thigh bone was the only matter for concern, and his surgeon said he should be able to get about on crutches by the end of the week.

The girls came daily to see him, little Mary looking

218

quite ravishing in a simple pink dress and a new spring
bonnet. On the morning of April 5th he tried walking
with crutches and found that he could do so without
straining his injured leg; so, on the following day he was
moved in an ambulance to the Legation and there most
kindly welcomed by Lady Stuart.

That evening the Minister came up to spend an hour
with him and gave him more precise details of the progress
of the war. Wellington had led five divisions in pursuit
of Masséna and detached two under General Beresford
to guard his rear against Soult, advancing into Estremadura and, if possible, relieve Badajoz. Unfortunately,
Badajoz had fallen to Mortier much earlier than
expected; but, now it was known that the French did not
intend to move against Lisbon, a large part of Beresford's force had become available for other operations.

In the north, no pitched battle had been fought, but a
constant series of independent actions by brigades and
regiments. Marshal Ney had commanded the French rearguard with such skill that only on one occasion had he
been caught napping. This had been three days earlier
at Sabugal. The British light division had surprised the
French 2nd Corps in a fog and killed or wounded over
a thousand men. News had come in that morning that
Soult's army had been driven out of Portugal, and had
retired on to the great stronghold of Ciudad Rodrigo,
which was all the Marshal had left to show for an inglori-
ous campaign.

Next morning a footman helped Roger to dress, then
get downstairs to sit in the garden. In the afternoon he
went for a drive with the girls. But the unaccustomed
exertion tried him so much that, on their return, he asked
to be helped up to bed. By the time his dinner was brought
up to him his fatigue had passed off and, after the footman had taken away his tray, he lay back on his pillows
thinking how lucky he was to have made such good friends

219

at the Legation and be able to convalesce in such comfort.

At about eight o'clock there came a gentle knock on his door, and when he called 'Come in,' Mary entered the room, carrying half a dozen books. Smiling at him, she said :

'As usual, there were quite a number of guests for dinner, so when we'd finished I managed to slip away. I thought you might be bored; so I've brought you something to read.'

When he had thanked her, she asked, 'What were you thinking about when I came in?'

'How lucky I am to be here, and how very kind to me you all are,' he replied truthfully.

She made a little moue. 'I was hoping you would say you were thinking of me. I nearly fell through the floor with embarrassment when Sir Charles returned from the hospital that first day and said you had sent me your love. But when I got up to my room I hugged myself with delight. You do love me, don't you?'

Roger was in a quandary. He had no intention whatever of marrying Mary, and to seduce an unmarried girl whose upbringing gave him every reason to suppose that she was a virgin was against his code. The idea had never even crossed his mind. He was loath to encourage the tender feeling she obviously had for him, but at the same time, most reluctant to hurt her. She had laid the books on the bed and was standing beside him, her green eyes solemnly fixed on his.

Taking her hand, he said gently, 'Mary, my dear, of course I love you; but I'm not going to allow my affection for you to get the better of my judgment. As I told you that day when we picnicked out at Cintra, I'm too restless a man to settle down to married life. Moreover, I'm much too old for you.'

She shook her head and her ringlets danced. 'For such

an intelligent man, you are really very stupid. I'm sure I could make you happy.'

'I'm sure you could,' he smiled, 'but the trouble is that I could make you happy only for a while. I'd again get that itch to travel. Then you'd be miserable, and try to persuade me not to. The result would be tears and quarrels.'

For the best part of a minute she was silent, then she said, 'Very well. I accept that. And I promise that I won't try to prevent your leaving Lisbon when you wish to go. But while you are here, I want you to treat me as though we were secretly engaged. You see, I haven't got a very bright future. I'm just averagely pretty, but not a beauty; and I haven't got a penny of my own. So when I do marry, it is almost certain to be someone that I don't really care about, and perhaps even older than you. I'd like to have just one romance in my life to look back on. Do you understand?'

Tears were brimming in Mary's eyes and Roger felt deeply sorry for her. Had he not been a nearly helpless invalid, he would have made some excuse to get a passage in the first ship leaving for England; as he felt that the sooner she saw no more of him, the better it would be for her. But as things were he knew that he would not be fit to travel for at least two weeks. In the circumstances, to refuse her request would have been brutal, and he swiftly made up his mind that, if he was going to pretend to be her fiancé, he must give her as much joy as possible by entering into the game wholeheartedly.

'Of course I understand,' he said, 'and I am truly delighted that you should offer me such happiness. But you must not take such a poor view of your attractions nor be so pessimistic about the future. You are not only a very lovely girl, but your gaiety and charm make you a wonderful companion. I'm certain that before long a man nearer your own age, and of ample fortune, will come into your

life and beseech you to marry him. Now, I only pray that he does not come on the scene while I am in Lisbon. Come now; give me a fiancée's kiss.'

Smiling, she quickly pulled her hand from his, perched herself on the edge of the bed and flung her arms round his neck. He held her tightly to him and her soft lips melted under his.

After they had spent a very happy half-hour, she said reluctantly, 'Roger, my love, I really must leave you now. Lady Stuart might come up to see if you wish anything, and if she found me here that would be terrible. We still have to be awfully careful, too, as if the family find out that you are making love to me, Sir Charles might ask your intentions, and that would be most awkward.'

'You're right, sweet Mary. But, as things are, it's going to be plaguey difficult for us to see each other alone with any frequency.'

For a moment she remained thoughtful, then she said, 'I think I will take Deborah into my confidence; though I'll not tell her that our engagement is only make-believe. Then, when you decide to leave, I'll say that, having got to know you better, it was I who decided against your formally asking for my hand. Deborah is entirely to be trusted and, with her connivance, we'll be able to snatch meetings now and again in the summer house at the bottom of the garden.'

They embraced again and, after several long kisses, she left him to rejoin the party downstairs in the salon.

The ten days that followed were some of the most pleasant that, apart from those with Georgina, Roger had ever spent. His wounds had healed well. By the end of a week he was able to dress himself, and could get about with only a stick for support. Spring was in the air, but it was much warmer than it would have been in England, and nearly every day, with Deborah's assistance, he managed to get the best part of an hour alone with Mary.

Their meetings were usually in the summer house; but, on days when that could not be managed, she insisted on coming to his room, although he endeavoured to persuade her not to. After his fourth day at the Legation, his injuries no longer prevented him from dining downstairs and afterwards joining in conversaziones, or listening to music with the other guests; so, if Mary came to his room it had to be late at night, after everyone had gone to bed and could be presumed to be asleep.

Greatly as he enjoyed these midnight visits, his reluctance to let her make them was not alone on account of the risk she ran of being found out. That was inconsiderable, as her room was only two doors away from his in the same corridor. His main objection was that she came to him with only a dressing gown over her night robe, and from the beginning of their affair he had been highly conscious that she was a very passionate little person. When they embraced, she always pressed her body hard against his, her eyes grew moist, her breathing rapid, and she deliberately tempted him to take the sort of liberties with her that were not unusual between respectable engaged couples. Being himself passionate, he took great joy in kissing her breasts and fondling her, but he was determined to go no further and the restraint he forced himself to exercise placed a great strain upon him.

It was on April 16th that she asked him to accompany her and Deborah to the hospital, as a cousin of hers, a Brigadier, had been wounded and arrived there the previous day. They drove there with flowers, fruit and wine and were shown up to a private room on the third floor. The man in the bed was fair-haired, florid-faced and a year or two older than Roger. Having happily greeted Mary and Deborah, he looked at Roger, who was standing behind the girls, and exclaimed :

'God's boots! If it's not old Bookworm Brook! Fancy seeing you here.'

Roger had already recognised him and had gone quite white. It was George Gunston, a man whom he had heartily disliked all his life. Bowing, he said coldly, 'The surprise is mutual.'

Mary glanced curiously from one to the other and said, 'So you two are already acquainted?'

Gunston laughed. 'Indeed we are. We were at school together. Most of us were keen on sports, but Brook always had his head buried in a book. That's why we gave him his nickname.'

Roger's smile was icy. 'You may recall that I spent a good part of my time learning to fence and shoot with a pistol, and in those accomplishments I became somewhat better than yourself.'

'That I'll not deny. So I find it all the more surprising that you have not volunteered for the Army.'

'Really, George!' Mary stamped her little foot. 'It's plain to see that you dislike each other. But I'll not have you quarrel in my presence.'

Both men then refrained from making any further antagonistic remarks; but the atmosphere remained uncomfortable. So, after having enquired about George's wound, and learned that he was disabled only by water on the knee, owing to a spent shell-splinter having hit it, his visitors took their departure.

Immediately they were back in their carriage, Mary demanded to know why Roger so disliked her cousin. After a moment he replied, 'It's not only because Gunston bullied me unmercifully at school. I'd not harbour a grudge against him for all these years on that account. But we have come into collision on numerous occasions. In our early twenties, we fought a duel; later, when I was for a while Governor of Martinique, he endeavoured to seduce my wife's young cousin. Later still, in India, he was largely responsible for her death. That he happens to be

a cousin of yours is regrettable, but the fact remains that he is a cad.'

'No, you are wrong about that,' Mary protested. 'It's obvious that you have had a prejudice against him from your schooldays, and happened to come up against him later in unpropitious circumstances; so you have seen only the worst side of him. But he's not a cad. He is a gay, amusing fellow, good-natured and generous. Of course, he is a very full-blooded man, and something of a woman-chaser. I'd wager, though, that your wife's niece led him on. And that's not to be wondered at, for he's a fine, handsome man. You can't blame him if many women find him attractive.'

No more was said at the time; but, that afternoon in the summer house, Mary reopened the question by saying, 'It pains me greatly that two people whom I like should be enemies, and I want you to make it up with George. He is much too easy-going a man to bear malice against anyone, so it must be you who are keeping this old feud alive. Please, for my sake, make it up with him and agree to let bygones be bygones.'

As water on the knee was unlikely to prevent Gunston from riding a horse for much more than ten days, he would then be leaving Lisbon again for the front. It being unlikely that Roger would be called on to see much of him, albeit with some reluctance, but to please Mary, he agreed to her request. The following morning they paid another visit to the hospital. There, with commendable impartiality, Mary read both men a lecture and made them, looking a little sheepish, shake hands.

Two mornings later, Mary, who made most of her own clothes, said to Roger, 'I have a bolero that I want to finish and Deborah is helping me. But today we ought to send George some more fruit and wine. I'd like you to take it to him, if you will. It will show better than anything that you really are willing to be friends and, if you

are alone together, that will give you a chance to explain how lack of understanding each other's point of view led to your past differences.'

Roger could hardly refuse, so he took the things to the hospital and was shown into Gunston's room. The florid Brigadier's fair eyebrows went up and he said with a laugh, 'Well, this is an honour! Damned good of you, Brook, to bring me more wine. I can do with it; and I'm greatly obliged to you.'

'It's a pleasure,' Roger responded to this friendly greeting. 'I trust your knee is better.'

'Thanks, it's getting on pretty well. I was mightily disappointed at having to leave my Dragoons just after we'd pushed old Masséna out of Portugal. But what's the good of a cavalryman if he can't ride a horse? And the field hospitals are so riddled with lice that I thought it better to be carted down here in an ambulance than stay up there behind the line. I should be able to get back, though, in a week or so. Take a chair, and join me in a glass of wine.'

Feeling that it would be churlish to refuse, Roger uncorked one of the bottles he had brought, and poured out two glasses. Then the two old enemies drank each other's health. For a while they talked about the campaign and various mutual acquaintances, until they got on to Mary and her dead parents, and Gunston remarked:

'You're a damned lucky fellow, Brook. You have always had a way with the women, and it needed only half an eye to see that little Mary is quite besotted about you. What luck for you, too, that you should both be sleeping under the same roof. She's a game little filly, and as hot as mustard. I'll wager you have your work cut out to satisfy her. Don't you dare get her with child, though, or you and I will quarrel again.'

Roger's face had become dead white. His blue eyes

blazing, he came to his feet and cried, 'You filthy-minded brute! How dare you slander a virtuous girl like Mary! I'll call you out for that, and this time I'll kill you.'

Gunston's fair eyebrows shot up again. 'Hold hard!' he exclaimed, raising himself on his pillows. 'It's no slander to speak the truth, and I know of what I'm talking. Mary's no virgin. To call me out on her account would be behaving like a quixotic ass. She's been had by half a dozen fellows; and if you haven't had her, more fool you. That demure look of hers is naught but a fire-screen in front of a fire. Damn it, man! I've had her myself. It was one afternoon in a punt, up a backwater on the Thames. She made the usual maidenly protests, but once I got between her legs I only had to push a bit and, in no time, she was begging me to give it to her hard.'

To that Roger could find no adequate reply. Seething with rage, he turned about, stamped out of the room and slammed the door behind him.

By this time he could walk without a stick and had begun to exercise his game leg, so he had carried the bottles and fruit to the hospital in a basket. He made his way back to the Legation by instinct rather than by looking which way he was going, for his mind was in a turmoil.

Recalling Mary's midnight visits to his room, he again visualised all that had taken place; the unconcealed passion with which she had kissed him and, lying outside the bedclothes, pressed her little body against his; the liberties she had let him take without protest; the way she had enjoyed having him kiss her breasts. Short of actually handling his manhood, she had left nothing undone to rouse him. No girl of her upbringing could have more blatantly offered herself. What an idiot he had been not to take her. But that could soon be rectified.

That evening he broke a rule that he had so far forced himself to observe and, when they were alone together

for a moment, asked her to come to him later. With a conspiratorial lift of her slanting eyebrows, she smilingly consented.

During the hours that followed, he could hardly contain his impatience. While they were in the salon he had difficulty in keeping his eyes off her. With each glance he took in her feminine charms with new appreciation: the pretty face with its gay, humorous expression, the glossy ringlets that made such a perfect frame for it, the full, red-lipped mouth, just made for kisses, her pouting breasts that gently rose and fell beneath her lace fichu, the well-rounded little bottom, the outline of which could be seen as she stooped with her back to him when picking up a flower that had fallen from another lady's corsage.

Up in his room he paced restlessly to and fro for an hour before undressing and getting into bed. There he tried to read, but found it impossible to concentrate. Every few minutes he glanced at his big turnip watch which lay on the bedside table. The hands seemed positively to crawl. At last it was midnight, but he knew that he could not expect her for another half-hour at least. Continuing to wait through those last thirty minutes proved almost unbearable. He was even tempted to go to her. But he knew that she shared a clothes closet with Deborah, who occupied a room next to hers; so that would have been madness. At last she came to him.

Her coming was such a relief that it restored calmness to his mind. He did not mean to rush his fences. By showing more emotion than he usually displayed when she made her midnight visits, he would surprise and might disturb her. Closing the door softly, she ran over to his bed, put her arms round his neck and kissed him. He returned her kiss, but restrained himself from putting more ardour than usual into it. Happily, she climbed up on the bed, as she had done on the last two occasions and,

while he lay under the bedclothes, settled herself comfortably lying beside him on the eiderdown.

For a while they continued kissing, then talked of the
events of the day. Presently he began to play with her
breasts until her nipples hardened. She closed her eyes
and her breathing quickened. Having roused her to a
state suitable to his design, he whispered:

'My adored one, why not come into bed with me? The
bedclothes make such a horrid barrier between us. I long
to have your dear body next to mine, so that I can embrace
you more closely.'

After hesitating a moment, she replied, 'I . . . I don't
think I ought to.'

He gave a little laugh. 'Why not, since we now look on
each other as engaged? All engaged couples do so if they
get the chance.'

She drew a quick breath. 'Very well, then, but I must
keep my dressing gown on.'

'Of course,' he promptly agreed, and sat up.

As she slipped off the bed, he pushed back the bedclothes and she got in beside him. Within a minute they
were locked in a close embrace and kissing breathlessly.
But still he refrained from rushing matters. It was not
until ten minutes later that he untied the sash of her
dressing gown, pushed it aside and, kissing her again,
let his hand begin to wander.

She made no protest when he eased up her long night-
dress, as she had let him feel her on two previous occasions. Again she closed her eyes and glued her mouth to
his. He gave her another minute; then, still playing with
her, used his elbow to push her legs apart. Abruptly,
before she could protest, he threw one of his legs over
hers and came on top of her.

For several heart-beats she did not resist him; then,
as she felt his staff, she pulled her mouth from his and
gasped:

'Roger! Roger! What are you doing? Stop! Oh, stop!'

But by then his object was as good as accomplished; yet he had to thrust hard to penetrate her. It crossed his mind that, being so small a woman might account for her parts also being so small, although that was contrary to his experience. Next moment her resistance ceased. She gave a cry of pain, then let him have his way. Soon afterwards her fingernails were biting into his back and she began to move jerkily under him, until they suddenly clenched hard in a climax.

But as they ceased their passionate wrestle and lay panting, he felt no joy, only a sick distress. He knew now that Gunston had deliberately lied to him, with the malicious hope that this would happen. Mary had, after all, been a virgin.

For a few minutes she lay absolutely still. Then she pushed him roughly from her and almost fell out of bed. By the light of the solitary candle, he saw that tears were running down her cheeks and that her mouth was strangely distorted into an ugly shape.

Suddenly her eyes blazed and she cried, 'Roger! Oh, Roger, how could you do this to me? You have robbed me of the only thing I had to give a husband. I hate you! I hate you! I never wish to set eyes on you again.'

Then, sobbing as though her heart would break, she fled from the room.

CHAPTER XVI

ENGLAND, HOME AND BEAUTY

ROGER was still sitting up in bed. Bowing his head, he covered his face with his hands. There were tears in his eyes. He felt shaken, sick and, for once, utterly at a loss. He had done a terrible thing—committed an act which in his own mind amounted to a crime—and, most shattering thought of all, there was no possible way in which he could give Mary back her virginity. Even the Saints would have proved incapable of performing that kind of miracle.

Had Gunston been in the room, his life would not have been worth a moment's purchase. With malice aforethought he had told a tissue of lies. His assertion that Mary had had several lovers and about having had her himself in a punt was a fabrication from beginning to end. But was it? Perhaps not quite. Possibly there had been an episode in a punt, in which Gunston had tried to seduce Mary and she had repulsed him. She had said frankly that she liked and admired him, so she might have let him kiss, cuddle and fondle her, but then told him that she was determined to keep her virginity for a husband.

It was a normal assumption that a girl of Mary's class and upbringing would be a virgin; but, if such an episode had taken place, that would have made Gunston certain of it. Knowing that both Mary and Roger had passionate natures, if Roger was told that she was easy game it was a

foregone conclusion that he would attempt her and, as she was in love with him, there was a fair chance that she would give way. It must have been thus that, with diabolicul cunning, Gunston had hoped to bring pain and grief both to the man he hated and the girl who had refused him. And he had succeeded.

The more Roger thought about it, the more convinced he became that Gunston had made love to Mary and that, after leading him on, she had refused to go the whole way. That gave rise to another thought. How much was Mary herself to blame for what had happened? Because a girl looked demure and, when in company, behaved with becoming modesty, it did not in the least follow that she was not subject to strong sexual urges and, given the chance, could not resist indulging them in secret. Undoubtedly Mary was like that, and did not realise that such conduct was unfair to the man or that, if she played with fire too often, one day she would get burned. Such women could not change their natures. The only satisfactory solution to such cases was marriage. But that Mary had largely brought her seduction on herself was no consolation to Roger.

Thinking of marriage stirred another chord in his mind. Mary's bitter resentment at his having taken advantage of her could be overcome. He could make reparation for his act by saying that he would marry her, and she would count her virginity well lost. But almost immediately he put the thought from him. Except when they were living together, he and Georgina had never been faithful to each other. In view of the fact that for ninetenths of their adult lives he had been absent from England, to have denied themselves other loves would have been absurd; but those other loves had never loosened the bond between them. And her husband was an old man. He might die at any time, leaving her free to marry again. If so, Roger's dearest wish that he and

Georgina should spend their middle years and old age as husband and wife might yet be realised. On no account must that prospect be jeopardised. Guilty as he felt himself to be, fond as he was of Mary and desperately sorry for her, that was too high a price to pay to restore her happiness.

His bedside candle was burning low. He got out of bed to light another. As he did so he saw that there was blood on his night shirt and blood in the bed. Although he might have expected such a possibility, the sight of the crimson stains came as a shock, and presented a very worrying problem. How, in hell's name, was he to explain them away?

An even more difficult question was the course he was going to take in the morning. Could he patch things up with Mary? He might have if he could have got her for an hour on his own, but that was impossible without her connivance and, even then, he greatly doubted if he could persuade her to forgive him. She had said that she wished never to set eyes on him again; and he felt certain she had meant that.

The probability was that she would pretend illness so as to remain up in her room the next day; then, when she came downstairs the following morning, expect him to be gone. If she found him still there, she would be desperately embarrassed when they came face to face, and that might lead to a very awkward scene. But upon what possible pretext could he leave the Legation at such short notice?

He had intended to stay on for another week or two, until his complete recovery would make it an abuse of hospitality to remain there longer. A few days before it seemed proper for him to leave, he would have enquired about ships leaving for England, secured a passage in one and told his host that he had done so. He could not say next morning that he had already booked a passage, as

he would at once be asked the name of the ship, in order that his luggage could be sent on board. He thought for a moment of saying that he had received an urgent message requiring him to rejoin Lord Wellington with the minimum of delay. But how and when could he have received such a message, without anyone in the Legation knowing anything about it? Besides, they all knew that he would not yet dare to ride a horse, as that would cause his thigh wound to reopen.

His thigh wound. That was the answer. By making use of it he could kill two birds with one stone. He would open the wound himself, and say that it was due to his having had a fall. That would not only account for the blood on the sheets, but also enable him to ask to be taken back to hospital to have the wound stitched up again.

When he looked at his turnip watch, he was surprised to see that it was only a quarter past one. So much seemed to have happened in the past three-quarters of an hour that he would have expected it to be much later. To proceed with his plan at once would have meant rousing the house in the middle of the night, and putting a number of people to considerable inconvenience; so he decided to postpone it until the morning.

His long day of waiting in anticipation of a happy consummation of his affair with Mary, the awful catastrophe it had proved and his anxieties since had taken a lot out of him; so he slept much better than he had expected. He woke at his usual hour, soon after six, then spent some minutes miserably recalling the night's events and steeling himself to carry out his plan for getting away from the Legation that day.

From the marble washstand he collected his razor, then bared his thigh. The scar still showed red just below his hip, and he was most loath to inflict a fairly serious new wound on himself. Yet he knew that half-measures would

only defeat his object. A doctor would be sent for and would patch him up there in the Legation.

Gritting his teeth, he slashed with the razor hard across his thigh. Blood gushed out and ran down his leg. Quickly he cleaned the razor by dipping it in the water jug, put it back in its usual place, grabbed a towel, got back into bed and pulled the silken bell-rope beside it.

A few minutes later the footman who valeted him came into the room. Holding the towel, now covered with blood, hard against the wound, Roger explained that on getting out of bed, he had tripped and his thigh had come into violent contact with the corner of a nearby table.

Having expressed his concern, the man ran off and soon afterwards Sir Charles and his wife arrived on the scene in their chamber robes. With exclamations of dismay, the good lady went for lint and a bandage and, on her return, succeeded in reducing the flow of blood, put a cold compress on the wound and bound it up.

The Minister then said he would send for his doctor; but Roger quickly protested, 'Nay, Your Excellency, I have already trespassed too much on the kindness of yourself and Lady Stuart. I could not bring myself to do so further. Besides, the wound must again be sewn up by a qualified surgeon; so I pray you have me removed to the hospital as soon as may be.'

Reluctantly Sir Charles and his wife agreed. A quarter of an hour later, Roger was carried downstairs by two footmen who accompanied him to the hospital where a bed in a ward was found for him. Gritting his teeth he again submitted to the painful business of being stitched up, then considered the problem of what his next move should be.

His only concern now was that Mary would feel com-

pelled to accompany Deborah on visits to him. But next morning, his fears on that score were allayed. Deborah came, accompanied by her aunt, and he learned from them that Mary had been stricken with an intermittent fever, which they attributed to fish poisoning. Whether she was actually ill or shamming, he had no means of knowing, but it certainly seemed probable that the shock she had sustained had resulted in her running a temperature. However, she would not be able to maintain for long that she was ill; so he decided that he must now get away from Lisbon as soon as possible and, when his visitors had gone, he asked his surgeon to enquire for him about passages to England.

The surgeon was averse to letting him leave his bed in less than a week, but when stitching up Roger's wound he had formed the opinion that it could not have been reopened in such a manner as a fall against a table. Suspecting from this that there was something unusual about the affair, he did not protest further when Roger asserted that most urgent business required his presence in London.

A passage was secured for Roger in a returning transport that was sailing from Lisbon four days later. He felt he ought to call at the Legation to make his farewells; but decided against it in case by then Mary had found it too difficult to sham illness any longer. So, on Lady Stuart's second visit to him, he begged her forgiveness for his apparent discourtesy, giving as his reason that he would have had to be taken to the Legation in an ambulance, as he was as yet forbidden to walk.

On April 22nd, an ambulance took him down to the dock and he was put aboard. Several other empty transports were in the convoy, and they were slow-going vessels, so it was not until May 6th that he landed at Portsmouth. But the passage had been a comparatively smooth one and, by then, his wound had healed again.

The following night he was in London and giving Droopy Ned an account of his adventures during the past three months. In the interim there had occurred no political upheavals. Mr. Perceval had succeeded in weathering the storms that had beset his early tenure of the office of Prime Minister. If not a brilliant man he was devout, honest, a very skilful Parliamentarian, and much beloved by his family and friends.

His most recent troubles had been the high price of gold, which had led to a Bill being passed enforcing the acceptance of banknotes as legal tender for any sum; and the continual cry of merchants from all quarters of the kingdom that they were being ruined by the measures taken by the Government in retaliation to Napoleon's Continental System. But Wellington's successes in the Peninsula had greatly heartened the war-weary nation.

The poor, aged King showed no sign of recovering from his madness. Bearded, blind and muttering crazily, he continued to live, now confined to his apartments at Windsor. Meanwhile, 'Prinny' had got well into his stride as Regent. Although he greatly resented the way in which his powers had been restricted by the Regency Bill, he had at least made no further trouble for the Government by inciting his Whig friends to hamper it. Egotistical and disloyal by nature, it was typical that, except for Sheridan and a few minor cronies, he had abandoned his Whig friends now that it suited his interests to cultivate the Tories. He treated his unfortunate wife shamefully and continued to be grossly extravagant, both of which counts caused him to be very unpopular with the people.

But the London season was in full swing. The coverings on the furniture of the great mansions in the West End had been removed. In many of them servants, up to the number of fifty, scuttled about with brooms and

dusters, laboured in kitchens and laundries, carried end-less cans of hot water up to the bedrooms, heated curling irons, uncorked bottles of wine by the dozen, or waited at table. Scores of footmen in gaily-striped waistcoats ran through the streets carrying messages by day or *flam-beaux* by night, to light the way for their masters and mistresses. Carriages, coaches and sedan chairs frequently formed solid blocks in the narrow thoroughfares. Every night many thousand candles lit the great houses and in a dozen or more of them there were balls, concerts and routs from which the aristocratic revellers rarely came away before dawn. So, back at last in England, Roger could anticipate a gay and carefree summer.

Learning from Droopy that Georgina was in residence at Kew House in Piccadilly, the morning after he reached London he set off in high spirits to call on her.

As soon as they were alone, they embraced with their old fervour; but, having noticed his bad limp, Georgina quickly put him from her and demanded to know how he had come by it. Smiling, he told her only that he had been captured by brigands in Portugal and had been wounded when escaping from them, then asked when they could have a long session together.

'Why not today?' she replied with a laugh. 'Tonight I am bidden to the Duchess of Devonshire's ball and am to be escorted there, though 'tis only two hundred yards up the street, by my latest beau, young Lord Chalfont. But I'll send my Negro page with a message to put him off, and another to her Grace praying her to excuse me because I am plagued by a migraine. We'll take luncheon together here, then drive out to Kensington and spend the night there.'

So, to Roger's great satisfaction, the matter was arranged. Three o'clock found these lifelong lovers out at Georgina's studio and half an hour later in her big bed,

238

with no intention of leaving it except to partake of snacks until well into the following morning.

After they had made love with all their old ardour, with Georgina's head comfortably pillowed on his chest, Roger spent over an hour telling her how he had been accused of murder by the de Pombals, of his missions to Masséna and Soult, of his terrible twenty-four hours as the prisoner of *O Diabo* and, finally, of the calamitous ending of his affair with Mary.

When he had done Georgina said lazily, 'The little fool. Girls like her who deliberately excite men's passions deserve all they get. I count her monstrous lucky to have lost her maidenhead to a man as chivalrous as yourself. Most gallants would have been greatly angered, told her it served her right, and refused to spare her blushes by leaving the house at considerable inconvenience to themselves. For having opened your wound in order to accommodate her, you deserve a martyr's crown. I can think of no other man who would have done the like.'

'You are ungenerous to my sex, dear heart. In no other way could I account for the blood in the bed and get myself out of the Legation the following morning. I'm sure that any decent man would have acted as I did, had he spent many hours in Mary's company.'

'Why so? Was she then so unusual bewitching?'

'Indeed she was. I'd not rate her as a great beauty, though she had a most piquant face and enchanting figure. It was her personality that was so attractive. As I have told you, she is an orphan, has no fortune and, to maintain herself with any decency, she was almost entirely dependent on the charity of her friends; yet she faced a bleak future with unfailing gaiety. That she allowed me to fondle her was, I am convinced, not with any intent to lead me on, but because she is very passionate by nature and, since she was in love with me, could not subdue her cravings. Yet, unlike Lisala, she had not a trace of evil

239

in her, and during our games ever displayed a sweet modesty. She has, too, a high courage. Had she not attacked that *guarda* with her parasol, I'd not have escaped into the Legation but been dragged off to a Portuguese prison. Apart from yourself, dear love, and Amanda, I've never known a more joyous and delightful companion.'

Georgina sniffed. 'Since you found her such a paragon and have ample money of your own, I wonder that you did not marry her.'

'Is it likely?' he replied in quick remonstrance, giving her nearest curl a little tug. 'You wicked piece! How dare you suggest such a thing when you are married to a man near twice your age. Old K can last but a year or two. And nothing would induce me to jeopardise my prospect of making you mine for ever, once the old fellow has snuffed it.'

She sighed. 'Alas, dear Roger, I fear fate has decreed that we'll never be man and wife, at all events not for a long time to come. I've had no chance to tell you before, but early in April he had a stroke. He is now paralysed, poor wretch, and can neither rise from his bed nor talk. Yet the doctors declare him to be in all other respects as healthy as a man of fifty. His sexual activities apart, he has never indulged in any excesses. He gave up drink long ago that he might disport himself more vigorously in bed. Country pursuits and regular exercise have kept all his muscles in good trim and now he is fed only on simple, sustaining foods. With naught to age him further, the doctors say he may last another ten years.'

For some minutes Roger was silent, then he said, 'What you tell me is a sad blow to my hopes. Even so, I have no mind to marry again, and I am now home for good. Half a loaf was ever better than no bread. As long as we can be together frequently, I'll be content with that.'

Lifting her face, she kissed him. 'As a mistress, I am yours, and will be only yours as long as you remain in England. Now, my beloved, nibble my ears and make love to me again.'

For the rich it was a halcyon summer. Regardless of the eighteen long years of a war that still showed no prospect of ending, they danced, drank, gambled, duelled, gossiped and flirted. For the middle classes it was a period of increasing strain from shortage of money. More and more merchants went bankrupt and the rest were hard put to it to meet their bills. For the poor, it dragged by, in week after week of ever-greater penury and distress. The harvests had been bad or indifferent for many years in succession, so food was scarce and expensive. Owing to the decline in commerce, many thousands of workers had been laid off from the new factories. In the old days, the country folk had at least had their cottage industries to support them and, in hard times, their lords of the manor had regarded it as a duty to tide them over. But during the past five decades great numbers of workers had migrated to the towns and had become slave labour. The industrialists were hard men and felt no obligation to give money to hands for whom they could no longer find work. In consequence, the slums teemed with poor, idle, wretches, watching their children starve for lack of a crust.

For that Roger was no more to blame than others of his generation and station, few of whom were even aware of the misery being endured by their fellow men in the Midlands and northern towns.

Old Dan had, as ever, taken good care of Thatched House Lodge and, as Roger had not expected to be in Lisbon for much more than a month, he had kept on his excellent cook-housekeeper, Mrs. Muffet. A week after his arrival in London, he again took up his residence there, and sent for Mrs. Marsham and Susan to join him. Every

week he rode up to the metropolis and spent two or three nights there, sometimes escorting Georgina to big receptions and dancing the night away; at others with her in the delightful seclusion of her studio out at Kensington.

The war in the Peninsula dragged on. Masséna, having withdrawn from Portugal, had left as the fruit of his exhausting nine-month campaign and the loss of twenty-five thousand men, only the great fortresses of Ciudad Rodrigo and Almeida. Wellington proceeded to lay siege to the latter, while Masséna endeavoured to inject new life into his exhausted army in the neighbourhood of Salamanca. He had lost nearly all his cavalry and had not enough horses to pull his guns; but he had never lacked courage, and was determined not to let Wellington take Almeida without a fight. Being so heavily handicapped, he appealed to his colleague, Bessières, who was commanding in the north, for a loan of cavalry and artillery. The younger Marshal came to look on, but brought with him only fifteen hundred horse and a single battery. With some forty thousand men, Masséna marched to the relief of Almeida.

On May 5th, he found Wellington, with an army of some six thousand fewer than his own, blocking his path on the heights of Fuentes d'Oñoro. A two-day battle ensued. Twice Masséna sent his massed columns against the British line; both times the line held. But the Marshal had despatched a strong column round the southern flank of the British. This forced them to retire, but the French were too exhausted to follow them up and again fell back on Salamanca. A few days later General Brennier, the commander in Almeida, blew up the walls of the city and gallantly cut his way with his garrison through the besiegers. Thus fell the last stronghold held by the French on Portuguese soil.

Meanwhile the Emperor, furious at Masséna's having

abandoned the attempt to take Lisbon, had appointed the young and ambitious Marmont to supersede him. On the 12th May the great soldier who had held the bastion of Switzerland against the Russians in '98, while Bonaparte was in Egypt, made Napoleon's victory at Marengo possible by holding starving Genoa, played a leading part in a score of victories since and was accounted by the French people second only to the Emperor as a leader of armies, handed over his command. His career was finished.

There followed a series of marches and countermarches. General Beresford, who had been detached to protect the British lines of communication against an attack from the south, had attempted to re-take Badajoz. Soult came up and the bloodiest battle of the whole war took place. The French lost six thousand men and, of the British army which totalled only eight thousand and narrowly escaped defeat, one out of every two men was either killed or wounded.

Having left a considerable part of his army to watch the French, who were again regrouping in the neighbourhood of Salamanca, Wellington marched south, but arrived too late to assist Beresford and, soon afterward, found himself confronted with the combined armies of Soult and Mortier. By stripping Leon and Andalusia of troops, they had mustered an army of sixty-two thousand men, whereas Wellington had only fifty-two thousand. Retiring behind the river Caya, from June 22nd to the 4th July, with great anxiety, he awaited their attack. It never came. Soult learned that a Spanish army under General Blake was threatening Seville, so he marched away to defend the city that he had hoped to make his capital.

Mortier's army, covering Badajoz, was too strong for there to be any hope of taking the place, so Wellington marched north again and laid siege to Ciudad Rodrigo.

Marmont swiftly assembled his men from their cantonments about Salamanca and arrived on the scene with sixty thousand men, compelling the British to abandon the siege and retire from the frontier. The active Marmont followed them up and in September Wellington was forced to fight two rearguard actions. But the young Marshal did not feel himself strong enough to invade Portugal and, soon afterwards, both armies retired into winter quarters.

That summer, in the north and east, Macdonald was occupied with holding down Catalonia and the long siege of Figueras; while Suchet—who had been told by the Emperor that his Marshal's baton lay inside the walls of Saragossa—had taken that city and, now a Marshal, continued to dominate Valencia. From Cadiz an Anglo-Portuguese contingent had been despatched by water down the coast, with the object of taking Victor's army in the rear. It was not large enough for the task, so Victor defeated it, but remained unable to take Cadiz.

All over the Peninsula it was the same frustrating situation for the French. Wherever they were called on to fight, they had to bring up reinforcements from another area, which promptly fell into the hands of the Spaniards who had again to be ejected. It was this Spanish tenacity and gallantry that saved the British from being overwhelmed; for, although Napoleon had three hundred thousand troops in the Peninsula and had lost another one hundred thousand in killed, wounded, prisoners and death from starvation, the French were never able to concentrate a force of more than sixty thousand against Wellington's fifty thousand.

At the end of the London season Roger went to stay with Georgina down at Newmarket and spent the greater part of August there. But it did not prove a happy visit. When Georgina had gone to London earlier in the year, Old K's youngest sister, Lady Amelia, had insisted on

moving in to look after her paralysed brother. She was a dour spinster in her early sixties, and had strongly disapproved of his marriage. Despising deceit and hypocrisy, Georgina did not seek to hide the fact that Roger was her lover, and Lady Amelia regarded it as an outrageous breach of decency that the Duchess should be indifferent to the servants knowing that she received a lover in her room every night. There was nothing Lady Amelia could do about it; but they had to have her with them at every meal and most evenings. This made conversation stilted and created a frigid atmosphere that cast a blight on their happiness.

Roger spent September at Richmond, but few of his friends had returned to London, so time hung heavily on his hands. To begin with he had greatly enjoyed having Susan to live with him, but now the novelty had worn off. She was a charming young girl, and he liked to see her about the place. He often took her riding and bought her expensive presents. But she had never been abroad, took no interest in the war, knew nothing about international affairs and, as yet, had no experience of life. So she made a poor companion for a man of Roger's active, well-stocked mind.

At the end of the month Georgina came to London for ten days, and for this brief interval they had the satisfaction of being able to resume their liaison in propitious circumstances. But toward its close they had a disagreecent.

For many years past Georgina had been a shining light in high society, and she had innumerable friends. During the autumn it had long been her custom to make a round of visits to the country houses of those with whom she was most intimate, and she felt that she could not possibly break all the engagements she had made during the London season.

This meant that, except for a night or two now and

then when passing through London between visits, she would be unable to see Roger until she took up her residence again in Piccadilly shortly before Christmas. The thought of having to get through the best part of three months without her made Roger miserable, and he begged her to excuse herself from some of the invitations she had accepted. But this she refused to do, and said :

'Roger, my dear, you ask too much. Even for you I am not prepared to give up my old friends. And, after all, what is three months? In the past you have at times absented yourself from me for years at a stretch.'

'That is true enough,' he agreed. 'But during those periods I was very fully occupied in serving my country abroad, whereas now I have naught to do that interests me. My life out at Richmond has become deadly dull, and I am sick to death of mooning about, listening to the scandals of the town. Apart from being with you, I have nothing to look forward to except an occasional men's dinner, and I no longer derive much pleasure in consuming more port than is good for me.'

'There is a simple solution to your malaise,' Georgina replied. 'The two happiest years of your life were '90 and '91—between the Liberal Revolution in France and the coming of the Terror, when you had temporarily left Mr. Pitt's service and were married to Amanda. You must marry again.'

'My love, I have already told you that I'll not do that, lest your husband dies and you again become free.'

'Roger, in this case 'tis folly to wait for dead men's shoes. The condition of my poor old Duke shows not the slightest change. He may well live to be a hundred. And, did you marry again, it would make no material difference to us. Except when you were wed to Amanda and I to Charles, neither of us has ever been faithful to our spouses. Apart from maintaining happy relations with my friends, I am as free as the wind; and with your subtle

mind you'd find no difficulty in inventing plausible excuses to leave your wife now and then, in order that in secret we could be together for a time.'

Having declared that he would not even consider her suggestion, Roger was unhappily compelled to leave the matter there; and Georgina took her departure for the country.

In October Roger spent a fortnight at Normanrood in Wiltshire, the seat of Droopy's father, the Earl of Amesbury. His long talks with his best friend were one of Roger's greatest joys; but one of Droopy's was experimenting with Eastern drugs. He had recently discovered a new one which he had begun to take regularly, with the result that on several occasions he lay unconscious for as long as eighteen hours and, on coming round, was muzzy for a considerable time. It was only with difficulty and toward the end of his stay that Roger persuaded his friend to give up this dangerous habit and promise not to drug himself more than once a month in future. Meanwhile, for much of his stay he was thrown on the company of the other members of the house-party, none of whom was particularly congenial to him.

He had arranged for the end of his stay to coincide with Georgina's return to London, and they spent two nights together. She then went off to make other visits, and again he had to amuse himself as best he could while living at Richmond.

Bored by his sojourn there, in mid-November he decided to go to Brighton. For a decade or more past, owing to the Prince Regent, it had taken the place of Bath as England's most fashionable watering place. The 'Corinthians', as the young bloods were termed, frequently went down there in their spider-like phaetons, making huge wagers on their timing. 'Prinny' had built for himself an exotic palace resembling those of Indian Rajahs. Here the beaux and belles assembled nightly, to dance and

gamble. Roger, having been presented on a previous occasion, had the entrée and mingled with the gay company.

Although the Prince Regent was not popular with the masses or with the Tory nobility, he was with his own set, who cared little for their country and cheerfully overlooked the fact that he was a most undesirable character. By day Roger amused himself by going to races, cockfights, boxing matches and viewing the activities along the front at Hove, where long terraces of elegant houses were going up. The virtue of most of the ladies in the Prince's set was decidedly easy, and he entered on a brief affair with a fair-haired charmer, by name Mrs. Peggy Wardell; but cut it short to keep another assignation with Georgina in London.

After three days she left again, and once more he tried to settle down at Richmond. Now that it was December, everyone's thoughts were turning to Christmas, so he set about buying presents and preparing for the festive season. But his heart was not in it. He kept on thinking of the months ahead. He was again to spend Christmas as Georgina's guest at Stillwaters and during the 'little season' in January, he could look forward to a few weeks with her, but what then? She was a splendid horsewoman, so would go to the shires to hunt; and it seemed unlikely that he would see much of her until Kew House was reopened for her at the beginning of May.

It was on an afternoon in mid-December that, while riding in Richmond Park, he witnessed an accident from a distance. A closed carriage and pair was coming in one direction and, from the other, a cabriolet driven at great speed. The lighter vehicle took a corner too sharply and collided with the carriage, taking off one of the wheels; it then overturned in a ditch.

Setting spurs to his mare, Roger galloped over. A young

buck was climbing out of the wreckage of the cabriolet, and Roger shouted at him:

'You young fool! You deserve to be horsewhipped for your carelessness.'

The youth, who was unhurt, went red in the face and shouted back, 'Dam'me, Sir. Mind your own business. I've a mind to call you out for that.'

'By God, you'd better not!' Roger roared. 'I can pip an ace at thirty feet. And I eat striplings like you for breakfast. Look to your horse, and make yourself scarce before I trounce you.'

Dismounting, with his arm through the mare's bridle he ran to the carriage. It had heeled over on one side and one window was smashed. The coachman had succeeded in clinging to his box, so was unhurt and was now endeavouring to open the carriage door, which had jammed. With Roger's help he got it open. On the floor inside lay a young woman. Her forehead was bleeding where, when pitched forward, she had cut it on the glass of the shattered window, and she had fainted. As they lifted her out, Roger gave an exclamation of surprise. It was Mary.

Roger told the coachman that he lived nearby, so he would send someone to put the wheel back on the carriage; meanwhile he had better unharness his horse and follow him. He then hoisted the unconscious Mary on to his saddle bow and rode off with her to his house.

On arriving there, she came to when he lifted her down and, with equal surprise, recognised him. Quickly assuring her that the cut on her forehead was only skin-deep, and that after an hour or two of rest she would be able to proceed on her way, he carried her inside. There, as Mrs. Marsham and Susan were out visiting friends, he bellowed for his housekeeper, Mrs. Muffet.

Together they got Mary upstairs to a bedroom and laid her on the bed. Leaving Mrs. Muffet to bathe Mary's

cut and make her comfortable, Roger went downstairs and sent his gardener, his groom and Dan to get the wheel back on the carriage. Soon afterwards, Mrs. Muffet came down to report that the young lady's condition gave no cause for alarm; upon which Roger told her to bring tea for two in an hour and a half's time, then go up and find out if their guest felt sufficiently recovered to join him, or would prefer to have tea taken up to her.

While the time passed, Roger revived his memories of Lisbon and wondered how Mary had fared since that most distressing night when he had ravished her.

At half past four, Mrs. Muffet came in with a hearty tea; sandwiches, scones, crumpets and cake, and said that the young lady was now feeling quite herself and would shortly come downstairs. A few minutes later Mary came in, looking as pretty as ever, except that her ringlets were partly hidden by a bandage round her forehead.

Roger was far too experienced a man to show any awkwardness, and so embarrass her. Smiling, he advanced to meet her, with both hands outstretched, and said:

'My dear, I'm so glad you sustained no serious injury from your accident, and how glad I am that I was on hand to look after you.'

Returning his smile, she replied, 'It was a horrid moment when I was thrown against the window of the carriage; but I was most fortunate in your coming to my assistance.'

They sat down before the roaring fire and she poured tea for them. Then, glancing round the drawing room, with its rich carpet, graceful Adam furniture and fine china, which Roger had collected through the years, she remarked:

'What a lovely home you have here, Roger.'

Into his mind there flashed the empty months ahead, and Georgina's advice on how best to fill the long inter-

vals when they could not be together. Leaning forward, he said impulsively :

'You like it, Mary? Then why not share it with me? I would love to have you as my wife.'

Her mouth fell open. Then she sadly shook her head. 'Oh, Roger, had you only asked me when we were in Lisbon. I have been married these past three months.'

CHAPTER XVII

A CALL OF CONSCIENCE

ROGER suddenly gave a hoarse, unnatural cackle of laughter. Mary stared at him in puzzled dismay, wondering from his totally unexpected proposal followed by this weird reaction if he had gone out of his mind. But recovering quickly, he said :

'I'm sorry, Mary; but I really am beginning to believe that my late wife cursed me before she died. I have since been accused of two murders, and you are the second woman whom I should have liked to marry and who would have liked to marry me, yet could not do so because she had married someone else.'

'Then you have indeed been unfortunate,' Mary commiserated with him. 'And atop of that you were grievous wounded by that brigand. I was told, too, that your wound reopened the night that . . . that night.'

'Yes. But, as it turned out, that was a fortunate coincidence.'

'Was it?' she questioned. 'Secretly, I formed the belief that you deliberately opened your wound in order to be taken quickly from the house and so spare my feelings.'

He smiled. 'I'll admit now that it was so. I had done you a great wrong; and it was the only way I could think of to accede to your wish that you should never set eyes on me again.'

'You are a very gallant gentleman, Roger. I did not

deserve such consideration, for I realise now that I brought what happened upon myself.'

'It would not have happened had it not been for your cousin, George Gunston. Out of hatred for me, he led me to believe that you had already had several lovers, and himself among them one afternoon in a punt up the Thames. Believing that, and attracted to you as I was, I'd have been a poor sort of man had I not sought to have you pleasure me too.'

Her smooth forehead creased into a frown. 'So that is what led you to it. You were, then, right about George. What a blackguard he must be. I will admit, though, that there was a basis for his story of the punt. He is a handsome, dashing fellow and I was attracted to him; so, one afternoon, I did allow him some liberties and repulsed him only when he attempted to go too far. I fear I have been given an over-passionate nature.'

'Nay, Mary, I'd not subscribe to that. There is a big difference between passion and lust, and you are no victim of the latter. A natural warmth in a woman is a gift of the gods, enabling her to make happy the men she cares for, and in doing so derive much happiness herself. Do you know what has happened to Gunston?'

'As far as I am aware, he is still in Portugal.'

'In that case, as the war there shows no sign of ending, it may be several years before I run across him again. When I do, he'll find himself faced with a heavy bill to pay for what he did to us.'

'No, Roger, please. No good could come of your calling him out, and you might be injured yourself did fortune not favour you. Let bygones be bygones. Instead, let us rejoice that, owing to this chance meeting, we are again friends.'

While they were talking, they had begun their tea. Roger buttered a crumpet for her, put it on her plate and

253

said, 'Tell me now about your husband. What manner of man is he?'

She shrugged. 'He's well enough. 'Tis an irony that you should have declined to marry me because you considered yourself too old, for he is a year or two older than yourself and, both in mind and body, gives the impression of being still older. But he is kind, considerate and has ample money. He is a Mr. Jeremiah Wicklow, a merchant in the City and trades mainly with cities in the Baltic.'

Roger raised an eyebrow. 'So you married into trade? That distresses me for you, as I fear it unlikely that many of your acquaintances will have proved willing to receive your husband.'

She sighed. 'In that, alas, you are right. One could not expect them to. 'Tis a sad come-down for the daughter of an Earl, but beggars cannot be choosers. Since I left Mrs. Hoitot's Academy, friends I made there, like Deborah, have been most kind to me. But one could not expect them to continue having me to stay indefinitely. The only alternative to marriage was to become the companion of some old woman, and be at her beck and call day and night. I preferred to stomach a man, providing he was of a pleasant and upright character, even if I had no love for him. And, that being so, it behoved me to keep an eye out for one while I still had my youth as an attraction. I was seated next to Mr. Wicklow at a dinner in the City, given for charity. I have never concealed my circumstances and when he questioned me about myself, I told him of them freely. He had recently been widowed and, no doubt, the thought of having a woman of title for his second wife appealed to him. Before the evening was out, he proposed to me. I said I'd take a week to think on it, then joined him one afternoon for a dish of tea at his house in Trinity Square, hard by the Tower of London. Finding it commodious and furnished with good, solid

pieces that indicated him to be a man of some fortune, I accepted him.'

'If I may, I'd like to call upon you there,' Roger said after a moment.

Smiling, she shook her head. 'No, Roger; I'd liefer you did not. I know where that would end. We would again go to bed together. And City merchants are very different from the people of our class. There are few complaisant husbands among them, or others who, feeling themselves outraged if their wives take lovers, cover their own mortification by fighting a duel on some pretext such as a quarrel over cards. Did Mr. Wicklow discover that I was unfaithful to him he would put me out into the gutter. Besides, I feel I owe it to him to be an honest wife.'

For a moment Roger had contemplated resuming his affaire with her; but he was quick to see the soundness of her objection and felt respect for her principles. Realising that it would be a wicked thing to jeopardise the security she had achieved, he refrained from endeavouring to persuade her to alter her mind, and changed the conversation by asking :

'Whither were you bound when that young fool wrecked your carriage?'

'To spend the night with cousins of Mr. Wicklow at Surbiton; and, if it be possible, I should soon now be on my way again.'

Roger stood up. 'I am loath to let you go. But by this time my people should have repaired the wheel. I'll go and find out.'

A few minutes later he returned to say that her carriage was at the door, her coachman had been given a meal, her horse watered and fed and was now being put between the shafts. Before leaving the room, he kissed her lightly on the cheek and wished her good fortune. Leading her out with the propriety he would have observed

had they been strangers, he handed her into the carriage and watched her being driven away.

Two days later Roger received a letter from the Marquess Wellesley, saying that he wished to see him; so he rode up to London and called at the Foreign Office. In view of the Marquess' haughty nature and retiring manner, he received Roger with unusual affability. After waving him to a seat, he said:

'Mr. Brook, having been a member of Bonaparte's personal entourage for so long, I take it you are well acquainted with Marshal Bernadotte, who a little above a year ago became Prince Royal of Sweden?'

'I have, of course, met him casually many times at receptions and so forth, my lord,' Roger replied. 'But I could not say I know him well.'

'But you do know him?' the Marquess insisted. 'I mean, should you meet him again, he would at once recognise you as one of Bonaparte's people?'

'Oh certainly, my lord; and I have known his wife since she was a young girl. She was daughter to a wealthy silk merchant of Marseilles, and is an old friend of mine.'

'Good! Good! Now tell me, how well are you informed of affairs in Sweden?'

'I know little about them, as for a long time past I have not been the confidant of anyone having access to secret intelligence.'

'In that case I must bring you up-to-date. On the Marshal's becoming, for all practical purposes, the ruler of Sweden, Bonaparte demanded that he should close all Swedish ports to British shipping, threatening, should he refuse, to invade Sweden. Bernadotte was most averse to doing so, because wars have reduced Sweden to a very poor country, and her only hope of recovery lies in a continuation of her commerce. But he has some reputation for duplicity, and in this matter resorted to it. He told Bonaparte that he would comply with his wishes, then

secretly informed our merchant captains that while he could not any longer countenance their bringing cargoes to Sweden, he was anxious to receive British goods conveyed in American bottoms.'

Roger smiled. 'There has never been any love lost between Bernadotte and Bonaparte. I felt certain that he would not allow the Emperor to make a puppet of him.'

'He is far from becoming that, as is clearly demonstrated by a more recent matter. In June last Bonaparte demanded that Sweden should join him in his war against Britain. Again the Prince Royal complied and, as you may know, Sweden and Britain have since been officially at war. But before giving our Chargé d'Affaires, Mr. Augustus Foster, his *congé*, Bernadotte informed him that we should pay no regard to the declaration, as he did not intend to take any hostile action against us.'

The Marquess took snuff, then went on, 'Now let us consider the situation in Russia. The friendship entered on at Tilsit between His Imperial Majesty the Czar and Bonaparte, is long since over. It cooled at Erfurt and is now moribund. You are doubtless aware that under the great Catherine, the Russian nobility adopted French culture, but ever since the reign of our Queen Elizabeth they have had commercial relations with us. During the past two centuries, our trade with Russia has increased a thousand-fold. They have no industry and have become almost entirely dependent on us for manufactured goods of every description. Thus, did they cease to receive them, it would cause almost unbearable hardship among all classes of their people. Bonaparte has brought all possible pressure on his ally to subscribe to his Continental System; but the welfare of his subjects being uppermost in the Czar's mind, he has constantly refused to do so. This has angered the Corsican to such a degree that, I am now informed, he contemplates invading Russia.'

Roger smiled again. 'That is indeed good news, my

lord. The Russians are most redoubtable fighters. Their armies alone, among the Continental nations, have successfully stood up to Napoleon. At Eylau they brought his advance to a halt, and although he defeated them at Friedland, they made him pay most dearly for his victory. 'Tis a mighty long march from the Niemen to Moscow, and only by taking that city can he hope to crush them. Such a campaign could, at long last, prove his ruin.'

'That, Mr. Brook, is also my view, and we must spare no effort to bring it about. I therefore have it in mind to follow in the footsteps of our great master, Billy Pitt, and endeavour to form a new Coalition. Sweden could play a most valuable part if she could be persuaded to become Russia's ally and ours. Do you not agree?'

'I do, my lord. But 'twould be no easy matter to bring that about. Sweden is still smarting from defeat in her recent war, as a result of which she was compelled to cede the Grand Duchy of Finland to the Czar; so I do not see the Swedes taking kindly to the thought of entering into an alliance with him.'

'True; but he will require all the aid he can secure if he is to defeat Bonaparte. So, for Sweden's help he might be willing to return Finland or, at least, make the Swedes valuable concessions. As I am dubious about the wisdom of approaching the Czar direct, I propose to send an envoy to the Swedes with the object of persuading them to become the link between ourselves and Russia. And I very much hope, Mr. Brook, that you will agree to become that envoy.'

For some while, Roger had been expecting this, so he replied at once, 'I must beg your Lordship to excuse me. I have spent half my life on the Continent, and am resolved not to return there on further missions.'

The Marquess looked down his high-bridged nose for a moment, then raised his eyes and held Roger's intently.

258

'Mr. Brook, you said that to me before you left for Portugal. My brother, Wellington, informed me later that you said much the same to him; yet you changed your mind and, on two occasions, rendered him most important services. I pray you change your mind again.'

Roger put up a protesting hand. 'My lord, the circumstances were different. On the first occasion a private matter made it necessary for me to leave Lisbon overnight. And on the second, it near as could be cost me my life. I am determined not to risk it again.'

'In this case you would not have to. You would present yourself to the Prince Royal as an old comrade-in-arms who, like himself, has decided to leave Bonaparte's service and only later, at a propitious moment, reveal yourself to be an emissary of Britain.'

'To harbour under my French identity for long might not prove possible. I have been in Stockholm before. Admittedly that was many years ago, in the time of Gustavus III; but there must still be people there who might recognise me, and I went there as an Englishman.'

'Come, Mr. Brook. Having lived as two persons for the whole of your adult life, there must have been many previous occasions when such contretemps occurred; yet those quick wits of yours enabled you to bluff your way out of them. It must be that, having been home for eight months or so, you have developed new interests here and are set against giving them up. Or, perhaps, you are contemplating matrimony?'

'No,' Roger admitted. 'Neither is the case.'

'All the more reason then that you should go on this mission. This invasion of Russia that Bonaparte is preparing to launch may well be his last throw. Having watched his rise, and seen him turn Europe into a bloodbath, surely you would like to be in at the death and take a hand in bringing about his fall?'

'You have something there, my lord,' Roger smiled,

'but I'd be fully content to read about his downfall in *The Times*.'

The Marquess sighed. 'You are plaguey difficult to persuade, Mr. Brook; but I'll not give up. I pray you to consider one fact which cannot be contested. In London —nay, in all Britain—there is not a single man other than yourself who is qualified to carry out this mission by presenting himself at the Swedish Court as a distinguished French officer who is no longer willing to serve Bonaparte. You are unique in that respect. Did I send even the most accomplished diplomat at my disposal, he could hope only for one, or at the most two, interviews with the Prince Royal; whereas you would be made welcome by him and have ample time to inform yourself of the lie of the land and his present attitude toward France, Britain and Russia, before making your proposal.

'And, think you upon the mighty issue that is at stake. This brigand Corsican has convulsed all Europe, brought death, starvation and misery to a million homes, and is now intent on bringing about yet further wholesale slaughter. 'Tis you who have a better chance than any other man of making this coming war the last for many years to come. God may have put it into your hands to restore peace to an unhappy world.'

To this moving plea Roger could find no answer. He simply said, 'I shall require a *lettre de marque*, my lord, to prove to the Prince Royal that I am an accredited envoy of the British Government, and it should be in such terms that, if taken from me, will give no clue to the purpose of my mission. May I suggest it should be like one with which Mr. Pitt furnished me long ago, which read, "The bearer knows my views upon this matter and speaks with my authority." '

'It shall be as you wish,' the Marquess nodded. 'And I can find no words to thank you adequately. When would you be ready to start?'

'I shall need a few days to make my preparations. Shall we say one day next week?'

'By all means. I will arrange a passage for you. I will also order my cashier to furnish you with ample funds. Ask him for any sum in reason and do not stint yourself. You may need money for bribes.'

On reaching the street, Roger turned into St. James's Park, and walked there for a while, considering the possible hazards that he might encounter on his new mission. Reluctant as he had at first been to accept it, now that he was committed he felt a pleasurable excitement. At least it would terminate his present frustrating existence, and again enable him to employ his active brain.

As it was still early in the afternoon, on leaving the Park he hailed a sedan chair and had himself carried to his jeweller's in Jermyn Street. There he had an assistant produce for him a book illustrating all the European Orders of Chivalry, pointed out the Swedish Order of Crossed Swords and ordered the decoration to be made for him, stipulating that it must be ready within four days. Strolling round the corner, he went into White's and wrote a note to Georgina, telling her that he was shortly going abroad again and urging her to come up to London as soon as she possibly could. He then took it to the coach office in Piccadilly and despatched it so that she should receive it the following morning.

That evening he broke to Susan the news that he would soon be leaving her for a while, and said that business connected with the de Pombal estate again required his presence in Lisbon. Next day he again rode up to London and completed the purchase of his Christmas presents. That evening, as he had hoped, Georgina returned to Kew House. Later, out at her studio, he told her about his new commitment.

She had had to say good-bye to him so many times in the past that she showed no special distress, particularly

as on this mission it did not appear as though he was going into any great danger and he would not be away for more than a few weeks.

Looking back on the past eight months, they agreed that they had been disappointing. Things would have been very different had they been able to marry. But that had been out of the question and there seemed no prospect of their being able to do so for a long time to come. When he gave her an account of Mary's accident and his subsequent talk with her, Georgina said :

'She seems a much more pleasant young woman than the first impression I formed of her. What a pity she married this man Wicklow. Poor girl; she is, I fear, condemned to lead a most dreary life and she would have made just the wife for you.'

Roger shrugged. 'Yes, I think she would; and with your dear self to bear me company at every suitable opportunity, in this our paradise, I'd have been as happy as a sand boy. But fate has decreed otherwise and, although little Mary is gone out of my life for good, still having you to cherish me I've no grounds for complaint.'

Of the next five nights he spent only one—the last—out at Richmond, completing his packing and handing out presents labelled 'not to be opened until Christmas Day'. Early on the morning of December 22nd he left for Tilbury. With a new money belt round his waist, containing gold pieces in several currencies, a few small diamonds and the *lettre de marque,* he went aboard an American freighter. The ship sailed on the evening tide.

During the short December day it had rained on and off but, as the barque dropped down the Thames, a wind got up and the sky cleared except for scudding clouds that, every few minutes, blacked out the moon. In the estuary the sea was choppy and, by the time they cleared the Nore, the ship was pitching unpleasantly as she fought her way forward. When she altered course to nor' east-

262

ward, Roger was awakened by a heavy wave slopping against the side of his cabin and thought unhappily that, as it was mid-winter, they were probably in for a bad voyage.

His fears proved only too well founded. During the days that followed, the North Sea was at its most horrible. The ship was tossed about like the plaything of a giant. She rolled and wallowed in the troughs of the great waves, then was carried sky-high to hover on their summits before cascading down another slope. The timbers creaked, clothes hanging from pegs in the cabins swung slowly to and fro like pendulums, alternately flapping against the bulkheads and standing away from them at an acute angle. Occasionally there came a loud crash as some object fell to the deck, then slithered across it.

For three days the ship ran bare-masted before the storm. Roger had always been a bad sailor, and throughout this time was as sick as a dog. He vomited until he was as empty as a drum, yet continued to retch in agony. His eyes watered, saliva ran hot in his mouth, a child could have pushed him over. He became incapable of coherent thought and would not have minded had the ship gone down.

On the fourth day the fury of the storm lessened sufficiently for her topsails and jib to be set, and Roger staggered up on deck. His clothes uncared for, his hair awry, his cheeks and chin dark with a three-day growth of bristles, he stood clutching a stanchion as he stared out across the grey-green waste. For as far as he could see, an endless succession of white-caps broke the surface, tossing up little jets of spray. No other vessel was in sight, no smudge of land was to be seen on the horizon, no indication of whether the ship was on her course or had been driven off it.

It was bitterly cold and began to rain. Soon it was coming down in torrents. Soaked to the skin, Roger staggered down to the saloon. The Captain of the barque

happened to be there. He was a hardbitten Yankee from Nantucket, who disliked the British; but when, white-faced and ill, Roger had staggered to a settee and collapsed upon it, the lean American brought over a tot of rum, lifted Roger's head and forced him to swallow the liquid.

The fiery spirit burned its way into his vitals and made him cough until he feared he was going to choke; but after a while he began to feel a little bit better, and managed to get down two ships' biscuits. As the early darkness closed in, it began to blow great guns again. By then, Roger had crawled back to his cabin. As he lay down on the still rolling bunk, he was overcome by another fit of nausea and spewed up the little he had eaten.

Next day the weather improved sufficiently for more sail to be set, but a blustering wind continued, accompanied by gusts of driving rain. Roger's bouts of actual vomiting had ceased, but he still felt queasy and his stomach was sore from the strain that had been put on its muscles. It was not until the barque had turned east, passed the Skaw of Denmark and was buffeting her way through the Skagerrak that he managed to pull himself together enough to make the effort required to shave and dress himself properly.

Christmas Day had passed unnoticed and it was New Year's Eve when the barque dropped anchor in Gothenburg harbour. Although it was already dark, Roger had himself rowed ashore. The town lay under a pall of snow, and enough light was reflected from it by a waning moon to see the old, timbered houses almost as clearly as in daytime. The glow of their lighted windows spoke of warmth and comfort within, but outside the temperature was far below zero and Roger was thankful when the coach he had hired at the dock pulled up in the yard of a big inn.

On going inside he saw that the Christmas decorations were still up and the place was crowded with people

drinking beer and schnapps. They were starting to celebrate the New Year, but he felt too weak and ill to mingle
later with them and join in the revelry. He ordered hot
punch, bread and honey to be sent up to his room, ate
while he undressed; then, with a sigh of thankfulness,
climbed into a bed that had on it a feather eiderdown a
foot thick. As he lay there, he still felt the motion of the
ship and seemed to be rocking gently from side to side,
but the hot posset and the honey had soothed his raw
stomach and he fell into a deep sleep. Even the bells of
Gothenburg, clamorously ringing in the year 1812, failed
to wake him.

He spent the whole of the next day in bed, slowly recovering from his ghastly voyage, and took the opportunity to have his suit well brushed and pressed. On
purpose he had brought only the one with him, and very
few things, for to have done otherwise could have given
away the story he meant to tell of how he had happened
to arrive in Gothenburg. He had lost over a stone in
weight, and when he looked in the mirror, decided that
the patches of grey hair above his ears had perceptibly
increased during the past year; but that had been partly
due to what he had been through while in the hands of
O Diabo. However, there were as yet no wrinkles on his
face, except for the laughter lines at the corners of his
mouth, and his bright blue eyes were as keen as ever.

The following day he felt much more like his old self.
Going out into the town he bought himself a pair of
roomy, wool-lined boots, a bearskin coat, a sea-otter
papenka, a sheepskin rug, warm stockings and under-
clothes, returned to the inn to pack, then took the seat
he had booked in the diligence leaving for Stockholm.

He had dreaded the two-hundred-and-fifty-mile journey, but need not have done so. Unlike Britain, in which
occasional periods of very cold weather cause the people
much suffering and inconvenience, the Swedes had long

265

since learned how to protect themselves during their long, bitter winters. For the whole way the roadsides were piled high with packed snow, so that the diligence seemed to be travelling through a long, winding gully, but there were no hold-ups, because the centre of the road was kept clear by relays of men from the towns and villages. Every ten miles or so fresh, flat, metal hot water containers were put in to warm the passengers' feet, and the meals at the inns on the way were passably good. Roger's only complaint would have been that, not long after each halt, the interior of the vehicle became abominably stuffy, because the windows were kept hermetically sealed.

On the evening of January 5th, he arrived in Stockholm and put up at the Reindeer's Head. Next morning he had himself driven out to the Castle. The scenery on the way there was enchanting. Snowflakes sparkled in the winter sunshine on the feathery branches of the pines and larches. Between the clusters of trees there were frozen lakes with colourfully-dressed people skating or being pushed in sleighs on them, while groups of laughing children attacked or defended snow forts and pelted one another with snowballs. But the Castle proved a grim, grey pile and Roger wondered, a shade apprehensively, how Bernadotte would receive him.

Having been passed from the sergeant of the guard to an adjutant, he sent up his name as Colonel Count de Breuc. He was kept waiting only ten minutes, then taken up a broad flight of stone stairs and along a gloomy corridor to which the light scarcely penetrated. There was no sentry on the door of the Prince Royal's cabinet and Roger was shown straight into it. The room was quite small, and filled with maps and books, some of which were even piled on the floor. The tall, handsome ex-Marshal of the Empire was now wearing the much less decorative plain blue uniform of a Swedish Field Marshal. On his broad chest there was not a single decoration.

As Roger entered, Bernadotte rose from his littered desk, smiled, held out his hand and said, '*Mon cher Colonel*. What a pleasant surprise. How do you come to be here?'

Roger returned the smile and replied, 'I come from England, Your Royal Highness. I was taken prisoner in the Peninsula while with the Marshal Duke of Dalmatia's army. From Lisbon I was sent to the Isle of Wight; but, as I speak English fluently, I managed to escape and stowed away in an American freighter that was lying in Southampton Roads. At the time I had no idea whither she was bound, and she landed me at Gothenburg six days since. Finding myself in Sweden, I felt it only proper to pay my respects to Your Royal Highness.'

There was only one other chair in the room, and it was occupied by a young Military Secretary. Bernadotte signed to him to leave the room and said to Roger, 'Sit down and tell me all you can of how things are going both with Soult and in England.'

Spreading his coat-tails, Roger took the chair. 'Of the Marshal I can tell Your Royal Highness little, as it is some ten months since I was captured. Then he had repelled Wellington from Badajoz and was again lording it in Seville as the uncrowned King of Andalusia.'

'And what, pray, were you doing serving in his army? I thought you to be a permanent member of the Emperor's staff. Had you fallen into disgrace with him?'

'No. He sent me with verbal orders for the Marshal Duke, that he did not care to trust to an ordinary courier in a written despatch,' Roger stated, knowing that Bernadotte had no means of checking up the lie. 'But Your Royal Highness can have no idea how terrible are conditions in Spain. The Spanish Generals are hopelessly incompetent, but their troops are fanatically brave. By their constant attacks they keep our forces penned into a number of comparatively small areas. Outside them the country

267

swarms with irregulars and bandits. Any Frenchman who falls into their hands would be better off had he a passport straight to hell. The tortures they employ are positively fiendish. It was my proper duty to report back as soon as possible to the Emperor. But the Marshal Duke could not spare an escort of sufficient strength to ensure me a safe passage through hostile territory; so bade me remain with him as one of his staff, which I did until I was taken prisoner.'

'And what of England?'

'Of that I had little opportunity to find out; but, from the gossip of camp guards, I gathered that the pig-headed British are determined to fight on, whatever the cost, until they finally best His Imperial Majesty, although they are suffering much hardship from bad harvests and the effect of the Continental System.'

Bernadotte nodded. 'I judge you right in that. And now, I take it, you wish me to send you back to France?'

'May it please Your Royal Highness, I would liefer that you did not,' Roger replied with a shake of the head. 'Like yourself, having followed the Eagles through so many campaigns, I am monstrous lucky still to have my life and limbs. But I am now sickened by the state of things. With England continuing to raise new armies for milord Wellington, Spain a bloody cockpit and north Germany seething with unrest, I see no prospect of peace for years to come. And for what are such miseries being inflicted on the people of many nations? Solely for the Emperor's personal glory. I have made up my mind to serve him no longer. And, chance having brought me to Sweden, I am wondering if Your Royal Highness could find a use for me?'

Bernadotte's fine eyes lit up. 'I could, indeed. But are you prepared to forgo your French citizenship and accept Swedish nationality, as I have done?'

268

'Perhaps.' Roger appeared to hesitate. 'But I pray you give me time to consider the matter.'

'That I will do. In the meantime, I could not give you a commission in the Swedish Army. But I can attach you to my person and make good use of your knowledge and experience. As you are probably aware, owing to the folly, nay madness, of King Gustavus IV, the Swedish Army suffered most grievously when it fought against Russia in an attempt to retain Finland. I found it in a most shocking state; its morale at the lowest ebb, the men ill-disciplined, their uniforms in rags and seriously lacking equipment lost in battle. Since I assumed command I have spared no effort to weld it again into a force capable of defending this country. One by one I am summoning regiments to Stockholm and here give them a week's training myself. You could assist me in that.'

'I would willingly do so, Your Royal Highness; but, alas, doubt my capabilities for such work. Having never served with a regiment in peace or war, my knowledge of the barrack square and tactics in the field is very limited.'

'No matter,' Bernadotte replied quickly. 'I've thought of a way in which you can serve me still better. You have accompanied the Emperor on many of his campaigns, have had every opportunity of observing his methods of waging war, and must be highly competent in the matter of staff duties. I will make you an instructor. In a series of lectures to my senior officers you shall describe the battles you have participated in, and the means by which the Emperor has achieved his victories.'

Roger readily agreed, then enquired after Her Royal Highness the Princess Desirée.

Bernadotte's face clouded. 'Alas, my wife found life here most uncongenial. She is the sweetest person in the world, but from you I'll make no secret of it. She was not brought up to be a great lady at a Court, and her natural-ness was ill-regarded at times by Queen Charlotte and

many of the narrow-minded nobility here; so she made few friends. Moreover, as a woman of warm southern blood, she found the freezing winter here near-insupportable, so I allowed her to go back to Paris. In due course she will rejoin me and meanwhile I am consoled for her absence by the presence here of my son, now Duke of Södermanland.'

'I recall him as a handsome boy with charming manners,' Roger volunteered.

'Yes, I am very proud of him. By instinct he always seems to do or say the right thing. He is most intelligent and progressing admirably with his studies. He loves it here, and is very popular with his new countrymen. But now I have much to do, so you must excuse me. Accommodation will, of course, be provided for you in the Castle; you will dine with us tonight and I will present you to Their Majesties.'

Roger warmly thanked his new master, who then rang for his secretary and gave him his instructions. The secretary handed his charge over to an adjutant, who took Roger to a Mess, introduced him to several other officers there and furnished him with a drink. An hour later his single valise had been fetched from the inn and he was settling into his new quarters, delighted with this propitious opening to his mission.

In the evening he was duly presented to the Royal Family. Old King Charles looked very feeble, his hands shook and he mumbled so that it was difficult to understand what he was saying. Queen Charlotte appeared to be a vigorous, determined woman. She received Roger coldly, no doubt when told that he was to join them, expecting one of Napoleon's ill-bred, jumped-up Revolutionaries; but later, when she found him to have charming manners and be accustomed to Court etiquette, she thawed out considerably. The aged Dowager Queen,

Sophia Magdalena, spoke little and gave the impression that she rarely roused herself from memories of the unhappy life she had led. There was also an ugly, elderly sister of the King, Princess Sophia Albertina. She looked half-mad, which recalled to Roger the fate of other members of the family. Queen Sophia Magdalena's husband and her son had practically ruined their kingdom, the latter had been placed under restraint as a lunatic, and the old woman's grandson was in exile in Switzerland, having been passed over by the magnates for the succession because they believed him to have inherited the family strain of madness.

In the circumstances, Roger was not surprised that they should all resent Bernadotte—a man they considered to have been a nobody—being forced upon the King as his adopted son. Or that poor little Desirée—the silk merchant's daughter—should have been so ill-received by them.

Apart from these Royalties, only ladies- and gentlemen-in-waiting were present and, although Roger endeavoured to enliven the conversation by giving fictitious accounts of his doings in Spain and of how, as a prisoner of war in England, he had succeeded in escaping, dinner proved a gloomy meal.

He soon settled down to his new role. Even the most haughty and hidebound among the Swedish aristocracy had by this time succumbed to the handsome Gascon who, in all but name, was their new ruler. The manner in which he had sacrificed his great personal fortune to pay Sweden's debts had greatly impressed them. The members of the Diet praised him for the sound reforms he proposed to them and for working from fifteen to eighteen hours a day on the nation's problems, and both officers and men admired him as a hero and General.

In consequence, far from resenting a foreigner being sent to instruct them, the senior officers of the Army

welcomed their Prince Royal's friend, Colonel Count Breuc, and listened eagerly to his descriptions of the campaigns which had carried Napoleon on waves of victory from one end of Europe to the other.

Stockholm, so aptly termed the 'Venice of the North', is one of the loveliest cities in the world, and in his off-duty hours Roger greatly enjoyed parties that were made up to go on excursions to the islands, or to skate and toboggan. A few elderly people remarked that his face was vaguely familiar, and said they thought they had met him before, but it was over twenty years since he had been in Stockholm, so he had no difficulty in persuading them that they were mistaken.

But he found the atmosphere of the huge Castle very depressing. At night it was so cold that he had to pile all his furs on top of his eiderdown to keep warm. Its long, uncarpeted corridors were tunnels of unceasing draughts, the narrow windows in the thick, stone walls barely lit them even at midday, and the furniture was mediaeval. In addition the winter days were so short that one seemed almost to be living in perpetual night. He did not wonder that little Desirée Clary had hated it.

He saw Bernadotte every day and, at times, was even consulted by him on various problems and asked his opinion of the fitness of officers he was instructing to hold their commands. Every week or so he was invited to dine with the Royal Family, and became quite a favourite of the wilful Queen.

But, as time went on, he became more and more dubious of his chances of succeeding in his mission. The late war with Russia was still very much in everyone's mind. Many of his new acquaintances had lost husbands, sons or brothers in it, and the loss of Finland had struck at the very heart of the Swedish nation. Nearly everyone was hoping that a time would come when Russia was heavily

engaged elsewhere, so that there would be a chance of winning back the Grand Duchy.

Unlikely as it now seemed that he would be able to persuade Bernadotte to enter into an alliance with the hated Russians, Roger felt that he could not possibly abandon the task he had been given without at least attempting to carry it out. And time was creeping on. Toward the end of February he decided that he must risk disclosing his true identity; so, on the next occasion when he was invited to an intimate family dinner, he pinned on his chest the Star of the Swedish Order of Crossed Swords, which he had had made in London.

Immediately he entered the salon, Bernadotte noticed it. Frowning, he marched up to Roger and demanded angrily, 'Colonel, what right have you to wear that Order?'

Roger bowed and replied, 'I wear it because I am en-titled to do so, Your Royal Highness. And if you will do me the honour to grant me a private audience later this evening, I shall be happy to inform you of the reason why I was decorated with it.'

CHAPTER XVIII

CAUGHT IN THE TOILS
ONCE MORE

CONVERSATION at the royal dinner table was always stilted. The palsied old King sat between the two Queens. Sometimes his food had to be cut up for him, he slobbered as he ate and occasionally mumbled something. The Queen Dowager never made a remark to anyone and, for most of the time, kept her sunken, black-rimmed eyes on her plate. Next to her, the half-witted Princess Sophia Albertina now and then gabbled out a few sentences or cackled with laughter. On the other side of Queen Charlotte, Bernadotte ate quickly, evidently anxious to get back to his work and thinking of it. The Queen alone kept the conversation going, as it was not etiquette for anyone to speak to the Royals unless spoken to.

The five Royals sat at a raised table on a low dais. Each of them had a lord- or lady-in-waiting and these, with such guests as had been invited, sat at two tables at right angles to the royal board. They talked together in low voices, but there were rarely more than three or four guests and those mainly regular ones, so the subjects discussed tended to lack variety.

Roger had always found these dinners boring and that night he wished more than ever that he had been in livelier company which would have distracted his thoughts with jokes and laughter. As he ploughed through his salmon, reindeer steak and portion of goose, he won-

dered if he had really been wise to make use of the Order of Crossed Swords when asking for this all-important private interview with Bernadotte.

The idea had occurred to him when he had first thought over his mission; because, as was not surprising, after eighteen years of war the great majority of Frenchmen had a rooted dislike of the English and Roger had felt that his Swedish decoration would help to offset any prejudice against his nationality that Bernadotte might have. But now he was not so certain. By wearing a decoration to which it could be assumed he was not entitled, he had obviously put the Prince Royal in a bad temper. That would make for a far from propitious opening to a difficult interview, which might have most unpleasant consequences.

His danger, as he had realised from the beginning, lay in the fact that, although Bernadotte had recently become a Swede and was doing everything possible to make his new compatriots regard him as one, he must at heart still be a Frenchman. The fact that, as a staunch Republican he had always distrusted Napoleon and was now refusing to aid in furthering his schemes, made no difference. The Emperor was only a person who symbolised a certain form of government; he was not France. And Roger must shortly confess that he had been constantly betraying the interests of France for many years. That might quite possibly lead to his being clapped in a dungeon for an indefinite period, so he was now contemplating the coming interview with some trepidation.

At last the dinner was over. On the arm of the Queen, the old King tottered into the adjacent salon, followed in strict order of precedence by all the others. With the exception of Bernadotte and Roger, the company seated itself round a fire which, although large, warmed only a segment of the large, lofty room. Bernadotte then bowed to the King and Queen and said:

'Your Majesties, I beg you to excuse me and Colonel Count Breuc from further attendance on you. There is a matter upon which I am anxious to speak to him without delay.'

The bleary-eyed King nodded. The Queen replied graciously, 'As you wish, dear son. The loss of your company is the price we have to pay for the wonderful work you are doing for us.' Then she held up her head and turned it slightly, to receive his kiss on her painted cheek.

Roger gave thanks for his dinner, wished the company good night and bowed himself out backward after Bernadotte. In the ante-room they took from a rack the voluminous fur cloaks that they always put on to protect themselves from the icy chill when making their way along the passages. With a quick, firm step Bernadotte led the way to his Cabinet and sat down behind his littered desk. He did not ask Roger to be seated, but staring at him fixedly, said in a harsh voice:

'Now, explain if you can. I find it impossible to believe that you are entitled to wear that Order, and to do so is one of the grossest pieces of impertinence I have ever encountered.'

With an air of self-confidence that he was far from feeling, Roger laughed. 'Were it not to wager on a certainty, I'd deprive Your Royal Highness of a tidy sum, if you were willing to back your conviction. King Gustavus III honoured me with this decoration for services I rendered His Majesty during the war he fought against Catherine of Russia.'

'But that was twenty years ago! You can have been but a boy.'

'True. It was in '88 and I was scarce out of my teens. I pray you, though, consult the records of the Order. There Your Royal Highness will find my name, not as de Breuc, but as Mr. Roger Brook.'

Bernadotte frowned. 'What means this mystery?'

'It is generally believed in France that I was born in Strasbourg of an English lady married to a Frenchman, and sent after her death to her sister, Lady Marie Brook, to be educated in England. The truth is that Lady Marie was my mother and my father was Admiral Sir Christopher Brook.'

'You astound me. In fact then, you are an Englishman, although long a confidant of the Emperor. To which country did you play the traitor?'

'To neither in the fullest sense. I served England whenever her interests were involved, but I have never fought against British troops. I have, as you well know, fought against France's other enemies, and rendered her many valuable services, including having once saved the Emperor's life—though I now regret it.'

'The tale you told me of having been a prisoner in the Isle of Wight was, then, untrue. What was your real purpose in coming to Sweden?'

Smiling, Roger produced the *lettre de marque* and placed it on the desk. 'I come as an Envoy Extraordinary, to confer with Your Royal Highness, and with authority to enter into negotiations with you on behalf of my country.'

Having read the document, Bernadotte said, 'This is not signed by your Prime Minister.'

'No. The signature is that of the Marquess Wellesley. As Secretary of State for Foreign Affairs and brother to our foremost General, milord Wellington, he has a greater say in our relations with other countries than Mr. Perceval, who is an amiable but not particularly forceful man.'

'Even so, as Sweden is at war with England, your mission cannot be regarded as official. I should be within my rights if I made you a prisoner.'

'I am aware of that. But Your Royal Highness will not do so, because it is not in Sweden's interest. The Emperor has more than once threatened to invade Sweden. I am

empowered to offer you an alliance with England. Do you accept it a British fleet could enter the Baltic and thwart Napoleon's intentions.'

For a moment Bernadotte considered, then said a trifle grudgingly, 'You may be seated. Tell me now, what price does England require Sweden to pay for such protection?'

Roger bowed and sat down. 'That she should put an end to her animosity toward Russia and form an alliance with her for the purpose of assisting in Napoleon's defeat. In return, England would also furnish arms for the Swedish Army, which is still so ill-equipped, and pay a large subsidy which would enable Your Royal Highness to raise further regiments.'

'The Czar might not agree. As is the case with Sweden, he is still formally allied to France.'

'Yes, formally. But the alliance now hangs only by a thread that will soon be snapped. As Your Royal Highness must be aware, for many months past the Emperor has been mustering his legions for the invasion of Russia.'

'Certainly I know it. My intelligence service would be poor indeed did I not.'

'Then it is evident to Your Royal Highness that, when the crisis comes, the Czar will need all the help he can get.'

'True. But to antagonise the Emperor and risk all on his being defeated is no light matter. What return, think you, would the Czar be willing to make if Sweden took this gamble?'

Roger shrugged. 'That, Your Royal Highness, I cannot say, but it should be considerable. Perhaps he might agree to return Finland.'

'I greatly doubt that; and, although my compatriots would give much to get the Grand Duchy back, I have no mind to press for it.' Turning in his chair, Bernadotte pointed to a map on the wall and went on, 'Regard the configuration of the northern countries, Count—er—Mr. Brook, I should say. Nature intended this great peninsula

278

to be the country of one people, and the Norwegians differ no more in language and customs from the Swedes than in France do Basques from Bretons or the people of Marseilles from those of Flanders. 'Tis not Finland but Norway that I desire.'

Leaning forward eagerly, Roger said, 'That greatly simplifies our problem. I see no ground why Alexander should object to your annexing Norway. He is a liberal-minded man, and readily accepts proposals when they make sound sense.'

'You speak as though you know him.'

'I do, Your Royal Highness. I was presented to him before his father's assassination in which I was concerned with Count Pahlen, General Bennigsen and others; although it was our intention only to depose the Czar Paul, not murder him. 'Twas the Zuboff brothers who committed that crime. I have since had confidential talks with the present Czar at both Tilsit and Erfurt, so I have come to know him quite well.'

'He has Danish connections, so do you not think he might side with Denmark on such a question?'

'Not as things are. How could he, if Sweden and Britain both gave him their support against Napoleon? Since the Royal Navy cut out the Danish Fleet from Copenhagen and milord Wellington, having landed there, spiked all the guns in their forts before leaving, the Danes have become the inveterate enemies of Britain. The Czar cannot have it both ways. Either he fights alone, or joins this new Coalition. If he does the latter, since the Danes are France's allies, he must count them, too, among his enemies.'

For the first time during their interview, Bernadotte smiled. 'I congratulate you, Mr. Brook. I knew you had a high reputation as a soldier, but had no idea you were so able a negotiator. I do not wonder that your Government gives you such far-reaching powers.'

Roger returned the smile. 'I thank Your Royal Highness for the compliment. May I take it that you are favourably disposed to my Government's proposals?'

'You may; provided that England is willing to give me a free hand in Norway.'

'Since that could not conflict with England's interests, I consider myself empowered to promise that.'

'Good.' Bernadotte handed back the *lettre de marque*. 'You will need this for presentation when you secure your audience with the Czar.'

Roger jerked upright in his chair. 'No, no, Your Royal Highness. It is no part of my mission to proceed to St. Petersburg. I was instructed only to approach you. It was naturally assumed that, should you agree to become England's ally, you would become our bridge with the Czar, and choose a suitable representative to lay your views before him.'

Bernadotte smiled again. 'I have chosen one, Mr. Brook—yourself. Who could undertake this business with a better hope of success? My Swedish diplomats are prejudiced against the Russians; you are not.'

'Your Royal Highness, I beg you . . .' Roger began.

But Bernadotte waved his protest aside and said firmly, 'I'll not take "no" for an answer, Mr. Brook. You have made it plain to me yourself that you have been deeply involved in Russian affairs, and are on intimate terms with leading members of their nobility, whose influence you can seek to aid our design. I have no-one with such assets whom I could send. I will give you a *lettre de marque* similar to the one you have; then you can speak on behalf of my Government here as well as your own. Yes, I insist on it.'

'Then Your Royal Highness leaves me no alternative,' Roger sighed. 'When do you wish me to start?'

'At once. Our ex-master at least showed us that, having taken a decision, speed in executing it is the secret of

success. I will give orders for a frigate to sail with you tomorrow morning. At this season of the year the greater part of the Gulf of Finland is frozen over, but she could take you across to Revel and from there it is not much above two hundred miles to St. Petersburg. I will, of course, furnish you with money for the part of your journey you must make by sleigh, and for other expenses. I will also make your *adieux* to Their Majesties, on the pretext that I have sent you to report on the state of our garrisons upcountry, and forgot to tell them of my intention. For the few hours that you remain here, and when you return to inform me of the Czar's reactions, you will continue to be known as *M. le Colonel Comte de Breuc*. Wait upon me here, please, at seven o'clock in the morning. I will then give you the *lettre de marque* and instructions to the captain of the frigate.' Standing up to show that the interview was over, he smiled, shook Roger warmly by the hand and added:

'This has been a most interesting conversation, Mr. Brook. It is my earnest hope that it will bear fruit. And you may rest assured that your secret is safe with me.'

As Roger undressed in his icy, stone-walled chamber, he felt no elation that he had succeeded in his mission. He gloomily reflected that, through talking too much about his past, he had hung himself with his own petard, and landed himself with another long winter journey from which there was no saying when he would return.

When he reported to Bernadotte the next morning, the Prince Royal told him that he was sending sealed orders to the captain of the frigate. These, giving Roger's destination, would not be opened until the ship had left port. In the meantime, it would be given out that he was being conveyed on the first stage of his tour of inspection, up to Osthammar. From the Prince he received the *lettre de marque* and a not very large purse of gold; then

he was taken by an adjutant down to the harbour and aboard the frigate.

It was still dark when they left the Castle, but soon afterwards a wintry sun came up to light the innumerable islands lying off the Swedish capital. After his last experience of sea travel, Roger hated more than ever the thought of going aboard a ship; but this time, in the comparatively sheltered waters of the Baltic, he was more fortunate. The sea was no more than choppy and, two days later, he was landed at Revel without having succumbed to seasickness.

After a night spent at the best inn, he hired a *troika*, had a good stock of provisions packed into it and set off along the road that crossed northern Estonia. In places, it ran near enough to the Gulf of Finland for him to catch glimpses of fishing boats threading their way among the ice floes, where the gulf was not completely frozen over. As the road was a main highway it was in fair condition and kept open, but fifty miles a day was as much as he could average; so he spent nights at Rakvere, Narva and Gatchina.

At the last place he looked at a small palace with interest. It was there that Catherine the Great had made her son Paul, whom she greatly disliked, reside. Eccentric to a point that later developed into madness, he had spent his entire time drilling his own regiment of troops. As a great admirer of Frederick the Great, he had dressed his men in Prussian uniforms, but he carried discipline to a point when it became sadistic torture, making his men stand to attenton for hours on end and having them flogged if they so much as eased a limb.

On March 3rd, his fourth day out from Revel, long after dark he entered St. Petersburg. Being familiar with the city he had himself driven to the Laughing Tartar, a big inn at which young Guards officers often gathered for drinking bouts. There he did not have to resort to any

subterfuge, as he had many friends in the Russian capital, and was known to them all as Mr. Roger Brook.

To his relief he learned that the Czar was not, as he had feared might be the case, in Moscow supervising the mobilisation of his army, but in residence at the Hermitage. By half past eight on the morning after his arrival, Roger had had himself driven out to the magnificent Palace, given his name to a Chamberlain and requested an audience.

He spent the next five hours in a vast waiting room, but it was comfortably furnished and had a number of large, porcelain stoves which kept it warm. Having nothing to do and there being nothing to read, he whiled away the time thinking about a variety of people, among them Bernadotte, Georgina, Napoleon, Droopy and the Czar Alexander.

The last was a most unusual monarch, for he was at the same time a revolutionary and an autocrat. His grandmother, the beautiful, licentious, cultured and intelligent Catherine, had given him as a tutor a Swisss named La Harpe, who was a disciple of Rousseau's. La Harpe had instilled into the young Prince the liberal ideas formulated in the Rights of Man, which were then agitating France and brought about the French Revolution. Alexander had imbibed them with enthusiasm and, on coming to the throne, had ardently desired to better the lot of his subjects in every way, even to the point of liberating all the serfs.

For this purpose he surrounded himself with young men who shared his ideas, in particular Counts Stroganoff and Novssiltzoff, and the charming Polish Prince Czartoryski. He also took into his favour Michael Speranskii, a brilliant bureaucrat. Among them they drafted plans for a Bill of Rights, based on the English Habeas Corpus Act, and to revolutionise the Government

by turning it into a constitutional Monarchy, with an elected Diet.

But, in the event, only a few minor reforms were actually carried out. An endeavour to force the nobility to free their serfs would have brought about Alexander's assassination. Theoretically, he would have liked everyone to have rights; but, if put into practice, that would have undermined the god-like authority long vested in the 'Little Father' of the Russian people and, with regard to establishing a Parliament, that was well enough for prominent citizens to air their views in, but if it came to their telling him what to do and what not to do, that was utterly unthinkable.

His enthusiasm for the French Revolution had cooled when the leaders of the people had abused their authority and initiated the Terror. Horrified by the blood bath engulfing the nobility and bourgeoisie that followed, he had belatedly joined the other monarchs in their attempt to destroy the young Republic and restore law and order.

The Russian Army had fought better than those of any of her allies; but, after several bloody battles in which they had held their own, Napoleon's genius as a general had inflicted so severe a defeat on Alexander's forces at Friedland that he had been forced to ask for an armistice.

Although at war with France, Alexander had already conceived an admiration for Napoleon, owing to the way in which he had brought order out of the chaos of the Revolution. So when in July 1807 the two Emperors met at Tilsit, on an elaborate raft in the middle of the river Niemen, he had completely succumbed to the Corsican's forcefulness and charm. In a matter of days they had agreed to carve up a good part of the world between them.

By then, after reigning for ten years, the Czar toyed with his idealistic ideas about reforms only occasionally. Instead, he had become something of a mystic and much

addicted to reading the Bible. Also, like his grandmother, he had ambitions to expand his Empire. The gentle Czartoryski was no longer his principal adviser, but Arakcheieff, his Minister of War: a rough and brutal, although devoted man.

Russia was already at war with Turkey along the lower Danube, and the two Emperors happily made a plan to divide the Sultan's vast Empire between them. Alexander was to have Turkey in Europe, which then included Serbia, Bulgaria and Greece; while Napoleon was to have Egypt, Palestine and Turkey in Asia, which would open the road for him to Persia and India. Meanwhile, he made no objection to Alexander's depriving the Swedes of Finland.

But things had not turned out in accordance with their grandiose plans. Alexander had conquered Finland, but by committing his best troops there, he was unable to make any appreciable headway against the Turks, which was the one thing that Napoleon wanted of him. Then they could not see eye to eye about Constantinople. The Czar claimed it, when the city had been taken, as part of Turkey in Europe. Napoleon would not agree to that, because it would have enabled Russia, should she become hostile, to cut his main line of communication with India. There was also, to Napoleon's intense annoyance, the Czar's passive refusal to carry out his promise of adopting the Continental System. Napoleon intended only to make use of him, and had become an egomaniac whose lust for conquest would never be satiated. Both now were arming for a mighty conflict, in which one of them must destroy the other. Thus matters stood when, shortly after one o'clock, Roger was ushered into the Imperial presence.

Alexander Paulovitch was then thirty-five years old, a fine, upstanding, handsome man with a roundish face and fair, curly hair. Extending his hand for Roger to kiss, he greeted him pleasantly:

'Welcome again to our capital, Mr. Brook. Whence have you come?'

There being no necessity to beat about the bush, Roger replied, 'From Sweden, may it please Your Imperial Majesty. I have spent some two months there, as the guest of the Prince Royal.'

'That must have been an interesting experience,' the monarch commented. 'We hear great things of our new neighbour. He proved himself an excellent administrator when acting as Napoleon's Viceroy in northern Germany, and his talents in that direction should greatly benefit his subjects. However, we are not so sanguine about his activities in his old capacity as a General. We are told that he is both reorganising and increasing the Swedish Army.'

Alexander's statement favoured Roger's design, but he had long since learned not to rush his fences; so he raised his eyebrows and said, 'May I ask Your Imperial Majesty why you should be averse to his doing that?'

The Czar shrugged. 'To a man of your intelligence, Mr. Brook, surely the reason for our concern is obvious? It is no secret that the Emperor is preparing to repudiate our alliance and wage war on us. The Swedes still bitterly resent our having taken Finland from them. Given favourable conditions they might attempt to win it back. Engaged in a death-struggle with the French, it would be most embarrassing for us to be attacked by a hostile army on our flank.'

Now that Alexander had openly acknowledged the dangers of his situation, Roger smiled, produced the *lettre de marque* from Bernadotte, and said, 'Then I hope that I am the bearer of welcome tidings to Your Imperial Majesty. The Prince Royal has never had any love for the Emperor. Moreover, he has now become at heart, as well as by naturalisation, a patriotic Swede. He, too, is still allied to France, albeit unwillingly. Under certain cir-

cumstances he would be prepared to face the Emperor's wrath by breaking that alliance and, given certain conditions, enter into a pact with Your Imperial Majesty.'

Alexander nodded thoughtfully. 'This proposal is of obvious interest to us, Mr. Brook. But what are the Prince Royal's conditions? I fear he would require the return of Finland, and we should regard that as too high a price to pay.'

'The Swedish Diet would naturally clamour for that, but the Prince Royal has already displayed so much wisdom in governing Sweden that I feel certain they would not seek to thwart any arrangements he entered into. Regarding Finland, he is prepared to let matters remain as they are. But he has ambitions in another direction. If he breaks his alliance with France, his alliance with Denmark will also lapse; and he has no love for the Danes. Would Your Imperial Majesty agree not to oppose his annexing Norway?'

'This makes your proposals even more interesting, Mr. Brook. We will ask the views of our Ministers upon them. Meanwhile, you will become our guest. We will give orders for accommodation in the Palace to be allotted to you.'

Roger bowed. 'I thank you, Sire. There is, however, another matter upon which I crave your gracious consideration.' Producing his other *lettre de marque*, he went on, 'I arrived in Sweden from England, having been sent to the Prince Royal by my Government. The object of my mission was to endeavour to bring about a new Coalition consisting of Russia, England and Sweden. As I have had the honour to inform Your Imperial Majesty, subject to your agreeing Sweden's terms, she is willing to break with the French. She would then enjoy the protection of a British fleet which would be sent to the Baltic. That could also be of use to you, Sire, for it would ensure

supplies, and probably consignments of arms, reaching your ports.'

The Czar had glanced at the *lettre de marque* and now remarked, 'This is signed by the Marquess Wellesley. He is no longer Secretary of State for Foreign Affairs, and has been superseded by Lord Castlereagh. We had this news only two days since. We are informed that seven years as a virtually autocratic monarch in India had rendered the Marquess so intolerably dictatorial that his colleagues in the Cabinet welcomed his resignation.'

This information was a blow to Roger, as it tended to undermine the authority vested in him by the *lettre de marque*; but he said quickly, ' 'Tis true, Sire, that the Marquess is a man of most haughty mien, but I have no doubt whatever that in this matter the Cabinet will endorse his policy, because it is in the interests of England to do so. Although for long periods Britain has sustained the war against France alone, she is as determined as ever to bring about the Emperor's downfall. Yet she needs peace as badly as does the rest of Europe, and the sooner it can be brought about the better for all concerned. It follows that, rather than allow further Continental nations to be defeated piecemeal, she is most anxious to give them her support; and so more swiftly bring about final victory.'

'Your premises are sound, Mr. Brook, so we will also give our consideration to entering on an alliance with England.'

The audience being over, Roger bowed himself away. An hour later his belongings had been fetched from the Laughing Tartar and he was installed in a pleasant room in the Palace. The Hermitage was a magnificent building, and he delighted in visiting again the vast, heated conservatory erected by Catherine the Great, in which semi-tropical flowers flourished even in mid-winter.

He had also always enjoyed his visits to St. Petersburg, as it was no ancient city with narrow, smelly streets. It

had been built as a new capital only a little over a hundred years earlier, by Peter the Great. Instead of wood, all the principal buildings were of stone, and it was criss-crossed with splendid, wide boulevards, having on either side raised walkways of wood, so that the citizens should not have to trudge through slush in springtime, or be splashed with mud from passing vehicles.

During the next few days Roger called upon many of the friends he had made on previous visits: the Vorontzoffs, the Pahlens, the Panins, the Dolgourskis, the Galitzins and others, including a special friend he had made—a Captain Muriavieff of the Samenourki Guards. They all welcomed his return to St. Petersburg and he was soon enjoying a round of dances and receptions. Muriavieff was a member of the gayest younger set, and Roger accompanied him with his brother officers and numerous attractive young women, on skating and sleighing parties—the last of the season as the thaw was now setting in—and was his guest at several gala dinners in the Guards' Club.

The life he was leading was a most pleasant change after the two months he had spent in the puritanical society that inhabited the draughty Royal Castle at Stockholm. But, by the end of March, he was considerably worried about having made no progress with his mission. A week after his arrival in St. Petersburg, the Czar had left his capital, to carry out a series of reviews of his troops, which were concentrating in the neighbourhood of Moscow, and had not since returned. He did so on the 1st April, but only for one night and, to Roger's chagrin, refused him the audience he requested.

The Czar did not get back until the 12th April. Again Roger persistently applied for an audience, but in vain; and he had, for another eight days, to distract his mind as well as he could with amusements. This further delay increased his concern, although he had now even better

reason to hope that when he did see the Czar his reply would be favourable; for, soon after Roger had left Stockholm, Napoleon had overrun Swedish Pomerania, and Bernadotte had already broken with him.

It was not until the evening of April 20th that Alexander sent for Roger. Having politely hoped that he had been enjoying his stay in St. Petersburg, he said with a smile:

'Well, Mr. Brook, the affair on which you came here has been satisfactorily settled, at least as far as Sweden is concerned.'

Roger bowed. 'I am delighted to hear that, Sire. But I confess myself somewhat surprised that you did not send me back to the Prince Royal with your answer.'

'We preferred to settle the matter ourselves. At our request the Prince Royal crossed the Baltic to Abo. A fortnight since, we had a most amicable discussion there. The recent failure of the Swedish Army to hold Pomerania has convinced him that, although his troops displayed bravery, they are not yet qualified to face Napoleon's veterans; and a campaign against Norway will prove excellent training for them. In return for our agreement to make no objection to his annexing that country, he has signed a pact of friendship with us. Later, when his army has become more reliable, he will enter into a full alliance with us, and personally bring his troops to aid us in defeating Napoleon.'

'Then permit me to congratulate Your Imperial Majesty. The acquisition of the Prince Royal as a commander in the field should prove most valuable. When he was Marshal Bernadotte, he was accounted one of Napoleon's most able generals, and one cannot suppose that he has lost his flair for winning victories. And now, Sire, if I may enquire, what are your intentions toward England?'

'There, too, we have acted. We decided to send one of

our most able diplomats secretly to London. He has our authority to enter into negotiations for an alliance.'

Roger looked distinctly aggrieved. 'Again, Sire, I am delighted. But you must forgive me if I take it a little hard that you did not allow me to carry this good news to London.'

Alexander shook his curly head and smiled. 'For that you must forgive us, Mr. Brook. Our reason for not doing so is that we have another use for you.'

CHAPTER XIX

CAESAR VERSUS CAESAR

ROGER was seized with awful apprehension. What now? His conscience had driven him into going to Sweden as the Marquess Wellesley's secret envoy. Bernadotte had made it next to impossible for him to leave his task half done, by refusing to go on to Russia. He should have been back in England long since. Spring was already here. In a little over a fortnight it would be May; the great mansions of London open again and teeming with gaily-dressed, laughing people. Georgina would be among them, and it was the one time in the year when, for ten weeks, he could definitely count on being constantly with her. And here was the Czar, who had obviously deliberately detained him in St. Petersburg, now affably stating that he had a use for him.

Continuing to smile, Alexander said, 'No doubt you will recall our meeting in Tilsit, Mr. Brook, in the spring of 1807. Anticipating a possible further advance by Napoleon, we were then removing our prisoners into the interior of Russia. You were among them, and still lame from a wound you had received. It was your good fortune that we elected to review the prisoners as they were marched out of the town. You seized the opportunity to throw yourself at our feet, and begged to be spared from the long march which, in your condition, would almost

certainly have brought about your death. Do you remember that occasion?'

'Yes, Your Imperial Majesty,' Roger admitted huskily.

'You will also then remember that we and our then Minister, Prince Adam Czartoryski, had several talks with you. Some years earlier, in St. Petersburg, you had been presented to me as an Englishman; so it was clear to us that "*Colonel Breuc*", as you called yourself at Tilsit, had penetrated Napoleon's entourage as a spy. Realising the great value you could be to us in that capacity, we agreed that instead of detaining you indefinitely as a prisoner we would arrange for your exchange with an officer of equivalent rank. In return you agreed to find out Napoleon's intentions for us, then allow yourself to be recaptured or, in some other way, inform us of them. Are we correct?'

Roger's mouth was dry. He swallowed hard. 'Yes, Your Imperial Majesty.'

'But you failed to carry out your promise.'

'That I admit,' Roger replied quickly. 'But only because it proved impossible for me to do so. No sooner had I rejoined the Emperor at Finckenstein than he despatched me with a military mission he was sending to Turkey and Persia. From Persia I made my way back to Lisbon and there became so involved with the flight of the Portuguese Royal Family to Brazil that I was forced to accompany them.'

'We are aware of that, Mr. Brook. You informed us of it when we met again later, at the Conference of Erfurt. May we remind you that, on that occasion, you expressed the hope that at some future time you might be of service to us?'

'Yes, Your Imperial Majesty,' Roger murmured, feeling slightly sick, for he now realised what was coming.

'Well; now is that time. We would here remark that yours is a case unique in our experience. Spies are or-

dinarily regarded as despicable people, and quite outside the pale, yet you give the impression of being a gentleman.'

Roger bridled. 'That, Sire, at least I can claim. My father was an Admiral, and while I do not suggest that I am the equal of a Romanoff, the McElfics have an ancestry as old as theirs. My grandfather was the last but one of a long line of Earls of Kildonan. As for spies, I find nothing despicable in a man who serves his country by obtaining information about the intentions of his country's enemies.'

Alexander sat back and laughed. 'Mr. Brook, you are fallen completely into our little trap. You could not more clearly have declared yourself to be a man of honour. Of course, we have no means of compelling you to it, but we are convinced that you will now honour your given word. Nay, more. I pray you, in the interests of your own country, which are now identical with ours, to rejoin Napoleon and transmit to us such knowledge of his plans as you are able.'

Seeing no alternative, Roger endeavoured to resign himself to this commitment with as good a grace as possible. Giving a wry smile, he said, 'So be it, Sire. When do you wish me to set out?'

'Tomorrow we leave St. Petersburg ourselves, and we desire you to accompany us.'

That quashed a niggling question that had entered Roger's mind. A man of honour he might be, in that he did not cheat at cards or seek to trick anyone other than his country's enemies, but simply because the Czar had had him, when a prisoner of war, exchanged for a Russian officer, was he really bound again to risk his life for an indefinite period; or should he slip away across the Baltic? It was now clear that he was not to be given the option. Alexander evidently did not trust him enough, but meant to take him to the front and push him over it.

Next day the great cavalcade of coaches, escorted by the Chasseurs of the Imperial Guard, set out. Now that spring had come, only remnants of the snow, where it had formed big drifts, remained. The flat country was a greenish brown, the roads rivers of mud, and every rivulet now swollen to a river in spate. But there were constant relays of good horses and the Imperial party reached Vilna, the capital of the province of Lithuania, and the last city on the Russian side of the Polish frontier, on April 26th.

During the weeks that followed, had Roger been acting as a secret agent for Napoleon, he could not have been better placed, as everyone at Alexander's headquarters talked freely in his presence of their hopes and fears, and of the preparations going forward to resist invasion.

The Count de Narbonne had been sent by Napoleon to Alexander with lying messages of continued goodwill; but obviously he was to find out all he could of the Russian dispositions. Tactfully, but firmly, the Czar sent the Count back with a message to the effect that he was anxious to avoid war, so had no intention of sending his troops across the Polish frontier, and he had so far not entered into an alliance with England; but would do so once the first shot was fired. Both sides now knew that war was inevitable, but were manœuvring to gain time.

Napoleon had arrived in Dresden and was holding Court there. Never before had there been such an assembly of Royalties and Great Captains: his father-in-law the Emperor of Austria, his two reliable allies the Kings of Saxony and Bavaria, the brow-beaten King of Prussia, Murat, King of Naples, Prince Poniatowski, the leader of the Poles, a score of Princes, Grand Dukes, Margraves and Landgraves, a dozen of the most famous Marshals, sullen but obedient Generals commanding troops from Denmark, Switzerland, Holland and even Spain.

Surrounded by this brilliant throng of fawning syco-
phants, the majority of whom wished him dead but dared
not refuse his demands that they should raise ever more
troops from the conquered territories, the Master of
Europe built up the most mighty army that had ever
existed, while Berthier worked night and day, despatching division after division, until six hundred and fifty
thousand troops were concentrated in east Prussia and
Poland.

Meanwhile the Russians were making their dispositions
with the far smaller forces at their disposal. Before leaving St. Petersburg, the Czar had dismissed his pacific-
minded Minister, Speranskii, and his War Minister,
Arakeheyev, had become his principal adviser. But this
brutal sadist, who delighted to have soldiers knouted to
death before him for quite trivial offences, although a
bulwark of the throne, was no strategist; so Alexander
placed himself in the hands of a German General named
von Phull.

This man had gained for himself a reputation as a master of the art of war. He was a marvellous theoretician
and had made the plan by which Prussia was to over-
whelm Napoleon in 1806. The result had been catas-
trophic for the Prussians. Nevertheless, he had, immediately afterwards, been received at St. Petersburg as
an infallible pundit, and was listened to there with awe,
in spite of the fact that he was irritable, stubborn, openly
regarded the Russian Generals with contempt and, in six
years at the Czar's Court, had not bothered to learn a
word of Russian.

The plan he produced was that the main Russian army
should be divided into two unequal halves, with a considerable gap between them. The larger, under Barclay
de Tolly, a Lithuanian of Scottish ancestry, and a cautious
man, on the left front with one hundred and eighteen
thousand troops; the smaller, under Prince Bagration,

one of Russia's best generals, who believed in attacking the enemy at every opportunity, on the right front with thirty-five thousand.

There were, in addition, two smaller armies: that of General Wittgenstein, consisting of twenty-five thousand men, which was to be stationed further in the rear, guarding the road to St. Petersburg, and another under Admiral Tormasov, which also lay far to the rear, in the east.

However, von Phull's great inspiration was to turn the little town of Drissa, on the Dvina, some two hundred miles behind the frontier, into a huge, fortified area where, if forced back, both armies could make a stand and equally well bar the road either to St. Petersburg or Moscow.

Early in June news reached the Czar that greatly cheered him. For six years past he had been at war with Turkey. On May 22nd, by a clever piece of trickery, the veteran General Kutuzov had induced the Turks to sign a peace treaty. This meant that Russia was now safe from attack on both her flanks, and could bring her army from the Danube to assist in repelling the French.

On the night of June 24th a ball was given for the Czar in Vilna. While he was at it, news was brought to him that Napoleon's army had begun to cross the Niemen by the bridge at Kovno and three others not far from it, built by his sappers. Next day Alexander sent for Balashov, his Minister of Police, and said to him:

'The mission on which we are about to send you will not stop the war; but we wish to prove to the world that we did not start it.' He then handed Balashov a letter for Napoleon, which said in effect that if the Emperor was willing to enter on negotiations, they could begin at once. But only on condition that his troops retired beyond the frontier, otherwise the Czar gave his word of honour that, as long as a single armed French soldier remained on

Russian soil, he would neither utter nor listen to a single word about peace.

Owing to obstruction by, first Murat, then Davoust and several subordinate officers, it was not until the 29th that Balashov was interviewed by Napoleon, and then it was in the same room in Vilna in which he had received his instructions; for Alexander had withdrawn and the Emperor occupied the city on the previous day.

Napoleon read the Minister of Police a long lecture about the shortcomings of his master, and even insulted him; but Balashov cleverly got his own back. When the Emperor remarked that the Russians were barbarians and irreligious, he replied, 'The piety of nations varies; but in Russia, *as in Spain*, the masses are fanatically religious.' The Emperor then facetiously asked him the way to Moscow, to which he promptly answered, 'There are several. Charles XII took that via Polotsk.' A neat crack, for the Swedish King's army had been thoroughly routed and he had narrowly escaped with his life. Balashov had then tried to persuade Napoleon that he was making a terrible mistake by invading Russia, because the Russians would never surrender, but fight on to the last man.

Berthier, Bessières and Caulaincourt, Duke of Vicenza, were present at the interview. The last-named had not long since been French Ambassador at St. Petersburg. He had got on well with the Russians and had done everything he could to strengthen the Franco-Russian alliance. With the spiteful playfulness to which he was prone at times, Napoleon struck him lightly on the cheek and said, 'Why don't you say something, you old pro-Russian?'

Deeply insulted, the ex-Ambassador said to the Emperor when Balashov had been dismissed, 'I will now prove myself to be a good Frenchman, by telling Your Majesty that this war is foolish and dangerous. It will destroy the Army, France and yourself.'

Many of Napoleon's Marshals and Ministers were of the same opinion, but it was the first time that anyone had plucked up the courage to say so to his face.

He laughed the matter off, remarking that it might take two or three summers to conquer Russia, but conquer her he would.

All this was related to Roger that same evening, as he had rejoined the French army without difficulty twenty-four hours earlier. After the Russians left, he had simply gone down into the cellar, remained there during the bombardment, and emerged on the arrival of the French. As he spoke the language perfectly and declared himself to be a Frenchman, he had been in no danger of coming to any harm, and had had only to wait there another hour or so before an advance party of the Emperor's staff arrived to take over the Czar's evacuated headquarters.

As usual, Roger's old friend, Duroc, *Maréchal de Camp* and Duc de Friuli, was in charge. His astonishment at coming on Roger there in civilian clothes was soon allayed by the account that Roger gave of his doings during the past two years. He said he had been falsely imprisoned in Berlin, escaped and stowed away in an American ship which had unfortunately carried him to England, where he had been made a prisoner of war, escaped again and managed to get to Portugal, been wounded and captured again, then sent back as a prisoner to England, escaped from there a second time and secured a passage in a ship that had brought him into the Baltic and landed him at Riga. As everyone there knew that the Emperor was about to invade Russia, he had hurried to Vilna a week ago, feeling certain that it must soon fall to the French. He then produced a stack of documents and maps that, in their haste to be gone, the Russians had left behind. None of them was of any particular value, but the gesture was good evidence that he was still a keen and useful officer.

That evening he repeated his story in more detail to the Emperor and a number of his officers. It happened that Davoust, Ney and Junot were all present. The first knew of his imprisonment in Berlin while both the latter had been at Masséna's headquarters when he was there and knew of the mission on which he had been sent to Soult; so they were not surprised that he had been captured and did not for a moment doubt that it was by the English. Napoleon and everyone else present congratulated him upon his three escapes.

Next day the uniform of a Colonel of Hussars, who had been killed during the taking of the city, was produced for him, and he took up his old duties as one of Napoleon's A.D.C.s under General Count Rapp, who was now Napoleon's A.D.C.-in-Chief.

Rapp was a blunt-spoken Alsatian and an old friend of Roger's. In fact, Roger owed his life to Rapp and General Savary. They had both been A.D.C.s to the gallant Desaix and had, together with Roger, climbed the Great Pyramid when in Egypt. Later, Desaix and his two A.D.C.s had succeeded in getting back to Europe just in time to rejoin Napoleon before the battle of Marengo. In this battle Desaix had been killed and Roger seriously wounded. Both had been left on the field among the dead and dying. The two A.D.C.s had gone out with lanterns to search for their dead General, and chanced upon Roger, thus saving him from either dying there from loss of blood, or being murdered by the human hyenas who prowled the battlefields by night, robbing the dead and dying alike.

Savary had become Napoleon's Minister of Police. It was he who had lured the unfortunate young Duc d'Enghien back over the French frontier and then been responsible for his murder. He had also lured the King of Spain and his son over the frontier, to Bayonne, so that Napoleon could force them to abdicate. Roger loathed the

crafty, unscrupulous Minister of Police; but he was very fond of Rapp and it was from him that he obtained most of the information about the strength and dispositions of the Grand Army.

The force that had crossed the Niemen consisted of one hundred and forty-five thousand French, forty-five thousand Italians, thirty thousand Austrians, thirty thousand Prussians, twenty-five thousand other Germans and seventy thousand troops of other nations. In addition to these there was an immense cavalry reserve and the Old and Young Guards; so they totalled something over four hundred thousand troops, besides which there were estimated to be roughly one hundred thousand camp-followers.

The vast cavalry screen was commanded by Murat, the central corps by Davout, Ney, Eugene de Beauharnais and Prince Poniatowski, with a corps under Reynier in reserve and Victor's corps, also in reserve, back on the Polish frontier. In the rear centre, too, were the Old Guard commanded by Bessières and the Young Guard by Mortier. Upon the left were Oudinot and St. Cyr's corps with, beyond them, Macdonald's corps and, still nearer the coast, the Prussians. Upon the right, slightly back, there was a corps under King Jerome of West-phalia and far out the Austrians under Prince Schwar-zenberg. Another one hundred and fifty thousand men under Augereau, who had taken over from Davout, were still occupying Poland and north Germany.

But, as Roger well knew, in spite of Napoleon's famous doctrine that 'God is on the side of the big battalions', in war numbers are not everything. If Talleyrand and his friend Metternich had had anything to do with it, the Austrians would be under orders not to fire a shot except in their own defence. The Prussians were there under duress and, if things went badly for the Emperor, might even go over to their old allies, the Russians. That, too,

was the case with many of the other foreign contingents. Only the Poles, Saxons, Bavarians, Danes and some of the troops from the Rhineland and Italy could be fully relied on.

As for the French, apart from the Guards' Corps, Oudinot's Grenadiers and Murat's cavalry, in Roger's view to have had to lead them into battle would have turned any General's hair grey. They bore no resemblance whatever to the magnificent Army of the Coasts of the Ocean, which had been assembled in 1804 to invade England, and which later covered itself with glory at Austerlitz and Wagram. Over half the men were little more than boys, or bitterly resentful deserters who had been dragged from their homes and forced to march again.

The huge army's only asset was that it was led by the most able, experienced and courageous warriors in the world. In addition to many of his foremost Corps Commanders, the Emperor had brought from Spain Junot, Lauriston, Montbrun, Vandamme, Hulin, Latour-Maubourg, Jomini, the younger Caulaincourt, Grouchy, Sebastiani and a score of other paladins.

Yet against that had to be set off a consideration of great importance. Not only were Napoleon's troops much inferior to those of his early days, but he, too, was by no means the man he had been. It was over two years since Roger had seen him, and he was shocked by his appearance. The bulging forehead and prognathous jaw stood out more than ever, but his hair had thinned, his shoulders were hunched and he was now pot-bellied.

Yet more important, he had deteriorated mentally as well as physically. Every day he still got through as much work as would have exhausted six other men: reading dozens of reports, dictating scores of despatches, dealing with innumerable problems that were sent to him from all parts of his vast Empire; but he was much more irritable than of old, showed contempt for all opinions which

did not coincide with his own, appeared to reach decisions without giving matters due thought and—a weakness he had never displayed before—he was at times subject to periods of lassitude during which he could not be brought to make up his mind.

As the days went by, it was more and more borne in on Roger's mind that the French High Command had great cause for worry. The heat was almost unbearable and even the march to Vilna had proved so great a strain on the troops that the size of the army had shrunk. Dysentery from drinking stagnant water, heat-stroke and partial suffocation after breathing in for hours on end the clouds of dust kicked up by endless columns of marching men, had caused hundreds a day to drop by the wayside. Still more serious was the loss from desertion and this was only the opening of the campaign.

In the blazing heat the men could march only a few miles without becoming exhausted. Water was so scarce that they fought for it, and the supply trains were so far behind schedule in coming up that both men and horses were on half-rations.

It was presumably for this reason—to rest his troops and better their condition—that Napoleon lingered for seventeen days at Vilna. In the old days he would have pushed on regardless, caught up with the Russians and probably inflicted a defeat on them that would have ended the war; but now he allowed the days to slip away as though time was of no importance.

Meanwhile, Barclay de Tolly, and Alexander with him, had retired on to the great redoubt at Drissa. Within twenty-four hours they realised the folly of von Phull's brilliant conception. Although Napoleon kept his main forces dallying in the neighbourhood of Vilna, he had allowed the corps forming his left wing to follow up the Russians. Oudinot bypassed the Drissa redoubt on one side, and St. Cyr on the other. On July 18th Barclay's

army fled from it. Narrowly escaping encirclement, it retreated along the north bank of the River Dvina to Polotsk.

In the third week in July intelligence came in that the Czar had left the army and was on his way back to St. Petersburg. Having spent two months at his headquarters, Roger could guess the reason. As an autocrat who fancied himself as a strategist, he was a menace to his Generals. During his first campaign against Napoleon in Austria, he had shown himself to be a hopeless blunderer. Evidently all his people had combined to persuade him, with tactful flattery, that to govern his vast realms it was necessary for him to return to his capital in the north.

Although the Grand Army remained comparatively inactive up to mid-July, the corps on the left flank continued to fight a series of bloody engagements. Oudinot had been ordered to link up with Macdonald, who was besieging Riga, but failed to do so and was attacked with the greatest ferocity by Wittgenstein's army. His subordinate, General Kulnev, not only inflicted a severe defeat on the French, but captured their entire baggage train and nine hundred prisoners.

Bagration, too, unlike Barclay, stood to fight when the main army did advance from Vilna. Greatly outnumbered, he soon found himself in serious difficulties. The brilliant Davout very nearly encircled him and would have annihilated his whole army had the lazy Jerome done what was expected of him. But he failed to bring up his Westphalians in time, so Bagration succeeded in fighting his way out of the trap. Davout complained bitterly to the Emperor who, furious with his useless brother, placed him under the Marshal. Jerome took such umbrage at this that he threw his hand in and, without even asking leave, rode away to his German kingdom.

The advance to Vitebsk proved a terrible ordeal. Alternately the blazing sunshine drove the men frantic

with thirst, or pouring rain turned the roads into rivers of mud. This delayed further the coming up of the transports, so the army began to suffer from semi-starvation. The country was almost featureless, half covered with thickets of birch and elder, and the few villages consisted only of a score or so of small huts. Inside, as they had only slits for windows, they were almost pitch-dark and they stank to high heaven. Cartridges had to be burned in them to sweeten the atmosphere. Horse flies and cockroaches abounded in them, making sleep impossible.

Few prisoners were taken, but from the interrogation of some of them it was learned that conditions in the Russian Army were still worse. Army contractors all over Europe had for years been making fortunes by giving short measure and supplying goods of inferior quality; but the Russians exceeded all others and the officers of their Commissariat were no better than criminals. It was common practice for them to sell a large percentage of the food for the troops and fodder for the horses; often they simply pocketed the money and did not bother to deliver any goods at all. Semi-starvation was therefore the lot of the troops but, being tougher than southern Europeans, their survival rate was much higher.

On July 26th Napoleon arrived outside Vitebsk. It was strongly garrisoned and Barclay's army lay behind it. Napoleon radiated optimism. Here, he was convinced, the Russians would make their big stand. He would storm the town, then inflict a crushing defeat on Barclay. His Grenadiers attacked, but not with the *élan* they had displayed in the old days when led by the great Lannes. It was the Russians who displayed the real fighting spirit. Wild with joy to have at last a chance to get at the hated French, their officers could not restrain them from dashing out from their defences and throwing away their lives for the pleasure of bayoneting an enemy.

The bloody conflict went on all day, in clouds of chok-

ing dust and a stifling heat, the like of which the older French troops had previously endured only in their Egyptian campaign. Again and again the attackers were repulsed. When night fell, the French had failed to penetrate the city. But in spite of the terrible losses during the the past month, caused by sickness, desertion and casualties, Napoleon still had great masses of troops at his disposal. That night he declared gleefully that next day the tired garrison would be overwhelmed, and the strong, flanking columns he had sent out would encircle Barclay.

When, at dawn, the first attack was launched, there was no opposition. Vitebsk was a city of the dead and dying. Beyond it, Barclay's camp-fires were still burning; but he had slipped away in the night.

This gave Roger much food for thought. Before the invasion and while in Vilna, the Czar's advisers had been at sixes and sevens. The Generals had argued endlessly; but no plan, other than the creation of von Phull's redoubt at Drissa, had been decided on. It was simply assumed that, if the Czar's troops failed to hold the French, they would fall back on Drissa and make a stand there; but several of the more cautious commanders had urged the Czar to take the advice that Bernadotte had given him.

This was to refrain from giving battle to Napoleon as long as he had superior numbers. To fight only a series of rearguard actions, while falling back all the time and rendering the ground over which Napoleon advanced incapable of supporting an army; just as Wellington had done in mid-Portugal before retiring behind the lines of Torres Vedras. Thus, Bernadotte had argued, Napoleon's army could be reduced by wastage and starvation until he could be attacked with a good hope of victory, or forced to retreat without even fighting a battle.

Barclay having got away, the general opinion was that no time should be lost in following him up and forcing

him to give battle. But for miles round, the reddish, sandy soil had been so churned up by horses, wagons and men that it had formed a fog of dust, greatly limiting visibility and thus preventing Murat's cavalry from determining in which direction the main Russian army had withdrawn. However, the Emperor appeared to be in no hurry, because he was convinced that, rather than allow the French to penetrate further into Russia, the Czar would again send Balashov to him—this time to ask for terms. But the days passed and the Minister of Police did not appear. Napoleon then began to talk of a three-year campaign and of spending the first winter in Vitebsk.

Bad news then came in from the eastern front. Admiral Tormasov had inflicted a severe defeat on General Regnier's corps, and three French regiments had been cut to pieces. Schwarzenberg had apparently been unable to come to his assistance and his Austrians were now the main bulwark against the army being outflanked from the right. Napoleon had intended to bring Schwarzenberg's thirty thousand men into his main striking force, but decided that he must now leave them far out on the wing.

By this time the sufferings of the army had caused it to become almost completely out of hand. The great herds of cattle collected in Prussia and Poland and supplies of flour and fodder were still many days' march behind. In desperation the troops took to indiscriminate looting. Both in Vitebsk and ranging far over the countryside around, they tortured the unfortunate citizens and peasants, in the hope of inducing them to reveal hidden stores of food. Thousands of Russian men, women and children were murdered and their dwellings set on fire. Desertion continued at an alarming rate and, as the French troops were given priority in every way, there were furious quarrels between them and their allies. In one case, far behind the front, a French troop of horse was amazed to find itself being fired on by a body of infantry a hundred and

thirty strong. It transpired that the attackers were Spaniards.

The argument at headquarters, whether to remain in Vitebsk or to advance, continued to rage fiercely. Not for years had the Marshals and the Emperor's entourage dared express their opinions to him so frankly. Murat and other firebrands were all for continuing the campaign, but the majority were against it, including Berthier, Bessières, Duroc and the outspoken Rapp who, having on one occasion been asked, 'How far is it back to Paris?' bluntly replied, 'Too far.'

Most impressive of all in advising against a further advance, was Count Daru, the Intendant General of the Army. Being responsible for supplies, he knew the position better than anyone else and chilled his hearers with the statement that, in the advance from Vilna to Vitebsk alone, out of the twenty-two thousand horses that had crossed the Niemen, eight thousand were dead. Nevertheless in the end, no offer to negotiate having come from the Czar, on August 12th Napoleon decided to march on Smolensk.

The Russian 27th Division, under General Neverovsky, had been detached from their main forces to act as a rearguard. It behaved magnificently, turning again and again to attack the far superior numbers of the French. It was only with great difficulty that Ney fought his way into Krasnoye and opened the way to Smolensk, in front of which Napoleon arrived on the 16th.

Early that morning the bombardment of the city began, and was shortly followed by the first assault. Again the Russian defence was heroic, and the French were beaten back. On the 17th the battle was resumed and for thirteen hours without a single pause the Emperor's cannon hurled their shells into the city and its suburbs. By evening a score of big fires were blazing, and later their red glow lit up the country for miles round. In the middle

of the night, the Russian guns suddenly ceased to reply, but a series of tremendous explosions were heard. Barclay had ordered the evacuation of the city, and was blowing up his magazines.

Davout entered Smolensk at four o'clock in the morning. The chaos was indescribable. The Russian dead lay everywhere, often in piles. Groans and cries came from the wounded; blinded and legless men begged to be put out of their agony by a bullet. A few thousand civilians had fled with the army, but thousands remained. Driven from their houses by the flames, they ran about the streets, seeking relatives and friends, or wandered aimlessly, imploring God and the Holy Virgin to succour them.

In earlier actions the Russians had sent all their wounded to Smolensk. Thousands of them had been concentrated in a group of warehouses in the oldest quarter of the city. There the few doctors available had done what they could for them, but the great majority had been unable to rise from the boards on which they lay. When the troops had evacuated the city, it had been impossible to take the wounded with them, and a fire had already been raging for hours in the old wooden buildings. Only a few score, scorched and blistered, had managed to stagger out alive. The roaring flames devoured all the rest.

The stench from these many hundred charred bodies was abominable. That, and the pools of blood and excrement from the dead on the streets, together with the sight of grotesquely-twisted bodies and faces distorted by agony, made many of the French sick. But it did not prevent them, with the Germans, Italians, Poles and Dutch, from beginning to loot the still unburned houses, from garret to cellar. In this it was recognised that the Prussians were the worst offenders; for, in addition to robbing their victims, they delighted in inflicting every form of brutality upon them.

With the fall of Smolensk, Napoleon had again expected to be able to launch his legions against Barclay in the open field. On the previous day he had despatched flying columns to encircle the Russians, and had joyfully exclaimed, 'At last I have them in my hands!' But again he suffered bitter disappointment. Barclay succeeded in getting his army away. A week earlier he had been joined by Bagration and the whole force retreated toward Vyazma.

Meanwhile, on the left Wittgenstein had attacked the corps of Oudinot and St. Cyr with sixty thousand men, handled them very roughly and driven them back. Oudinot being a Marshal was in command of both corps. Leading his famous Grenadiers into battle, after the death of Lannes, he had no equal as an infantry General; but he was no strategist, so things were going very badly for the French. While the Marshal was riding out on a reconnaissance, a sniper put a bullet through his arm—it was the thirty-fourth wound he had received—and he was forced to leave the field.

Gouvion St. Cyr, moody, taciturn, secretive, loathed by all his colleagues, but a man of high intelligence, took over the command. Swiftly he altered all the dispositions, heavily defeated Wittgenstein and took Polotsk. The Emperor sent him his Marshal's baton.

A change was now to take place in the Russian High Command. For weeks past, Barclay and Bagration had been engaged in a most acrimonious dispute. The latter, supported by most of the Russian nobility, was unshakeably convinced that they ought to stand and fight and, as far as he was able, without risking the loss of his entire army, he was doing so. But it was much the smaller of the two and, even with the aid of Wittgenstein, he could not repel the overwhelming hordes of French, Prussians, Rhinelanders and Italians. Barclay, on the other hand, although he dared not say so openly, was equally determ-

310

ined not to give battle. Bagration sent complaint after complaint to the Czar about Barclay doing no more than fight rearguard actions. At length Alexander appointed as Supreme Commander over both of them Mikhil Illarionavich Golenisch-Kutuzov.

The Czar was very far from liking Kutuzov because before Austerlitz he had done his utmost, as the senior Russian General present, to dissuade him from risking a pitched battle with Napoleon. The headstrong young autocrat had flatly refused to accept this advice. In consequence, he suffered a crushing defeat and had been ignominiously chased from the field.

But Kutuzov, having skilfully fooled the Turks into signing a peace, had returned from the Danube with a reputation second to none in the Russian Army. He and Bagration had been the principal lieutenants of the redoubtable Suvoroff—now almost a legendary figure as Catherine the Great's most brilliant General—and, of the two, Kutuzov was accounted the greater. He was now sixty-seven, so corpulent that he had to be driven about battlefields in a one-man carriage, and he had had one of his eyes shot out by a Turk; but he was clever, courageous and so wily that he was known as 'the old fox of the north'. His men adored him, and the great Russian nobles had such faith in him that they continued to exert so much pressure on the Czar that, autocrat though he was, he felt himself compelled to give Kutuzov the Supreme Command.

For a week after entering Smolensk the Emperor's refusal to make up his mind about the future, which had caused so much delay in Vilna and Vitebsk, again bedevilled operations. Under Murat and Davout the vanguard pushed forward toward Vyazma, but Napoleon held back the bulk of the army. Once more he felt convinced that he need go no further, as Balashov would be sent to ask for terms; but the Minister of Police did not

come. In desperation, Napoleon sent a captured Russian General with a letter to Alexander, pointing out the folly of continuing the war, but received no reply. Again he told his staff that he thought it best to postpone crushing the Russians till next year. They would winter in Smolensk, then take Moscow in the spring.

But Smolensk was a shambles and the greater part of it in ruins. They had found no large stores of food there, and supplies of all kinds had become scarcer than ever. Far and wide the troops ravaged the countryside, but with little reward for their exertions. They no longer burned the hovels in the miserable villages, because they found them burned already. The Russians were now applying the scorched-earth policy, with the utmost rigour. They were leaving nothing behind which could be of any use to their enemies. Meanwhile, from lack of fodder, more horses were dying every day and more men from wounds they had received, lack of nourishment and dysentery. A constant stream of deserters, now become bandits, trickled back the way they had come. The supply trains and field hospitals still failed to arrive in sufficient numbers.

At last Napoleon reluctantly decided that, if he wintered in Smolensk, he would risk his army falling to pieces, and that to take Moscow was the only way to compel the Czar to sue for peace. Having summoned up Victor's reserve corps of twenty-five thousand men from Poland to hold Smolensk and guard his lines of communications, on August 25th Napoleon and his Guards marched out of Smolensk by the road to Moscow. The die was cast.

CHAPTER XX

ADVANCE TO DESOLATION

THE great host trudged forward; far out on the left the Prussians, far out on the right the Austrians, both in fair trim because they were advancing through unspoiled country. In the centre, Napoleon's masses swarmed across the seemingly-endless plain, with its empty barns and burned-out villages.

One great body of twenty thousand men, at least, never lacked for food—the Imperial Guard—for it was given first call on every supply column that did come up. With bands playing and the Tricolour beneath its Eagles fluttering bravely, it marched out of Smolensk. The Emperor, riding his grey horse, wearing his plain Guides uniform, the undecorated black tricorne hat set squarely on his big head, took the road between the Old Guard and the Young Guard. Behind him rode his staff : Berthier, Duroc, Caulaincourt, his chief secretary Baron Meneval, Rapp and a score of others, with Roger among them.

Their blue and white uniforms were now dull from dust and stains of travel, but the plumes still waved from their hats, the well-polished scabbards of their swords, their stirrups and the bits of their horses shone in the sunshine. The gold of their belts, epaulettes and embroidery on their coats remained untarnished, the jewels in the Orders on their breasts glittered and scintillated. Whichever way they had been heading they would have been thankful to

leave behind the terrible charnel-house that had once been the fine city of Smolensk.

In the wake of the army there followed another army —the great motley horde of sutlers, vivandières, cobblers, sweet-sellers, tobacco pedlars, whores and ragamuffins of all descriptions. Their losses had been nothing compared to those of the armed forces, because they were not dependant on the Commissariat. In times of plenty the soldiers often gave them a share of their rations, but they always took their own supplies in small carts that they drove or pulled themselves.

One of the Army's most famous paladins had recently been overtaken by disaster. The Emperor had sent Murat and Ney ahead from Smolensk to endeavour to pin down the enemy, and they had very nearly succeeded. A most bloody encounter had taken place east of Valutina. The plan had been that, while Ney engaged the enemy hotly, Junot with the Eighth Corps, which he had taken over from King Jerome, should outflank them from the north; but he had failed to appear. Murat had galloped off in search of him, and found him with his men halted. Angrily, Murat urged him to attack at once, but Junot said his poor Westphalians were too exhausted. With a part of Junot's force, the tireless Murat then led an attack himself, but it was too weak and too late. The Russians fought him off and escaped from the trap.

Junot's failure to exert himself was, no doubt, due to the head wound he had received in Portugal affecting his brain; for, not long afterwards, he went mad. He had been with Napoleon at the siege of Toulon and served him faithfully for eighteen years. Why the Emperor should have passed over this old friend when first distributing Marshals' batons, no-one could understand. All through the seven years that had since elapsed, Junot had been hoping to receive his. Now he had lost his last chance of becoming a Marshal.

314

Behind Murat's cavalry screen, many thousands strong, Ney and Davout led the van. The main body followed, reaching Vyazma on August 29th and Gjatsk on September 1st. Four days later they were confronted with a one-hundred-and-fifty-foot-high hill, rising out of the level plain near Shevardino. Kutuzov had made the hill into a big redoubt that had to be stormed before the French could advance further. After severe fighting and at considerable loss, they took it; but it checked them for a day, which was of great value to Kutuzov whose army was working desperately hard to complete a great system of earthworks a few miles further on, either side of the village of Borodino.

Old Kutuzov was strongly in favour of the strategy advised by Bernadotte and adopted by Barclay, of letting his enemies advance further and further into the illimitable Russian steppe until they were exhausted; but he knew that he could not allow them to enter Moscow without fighting a battle. Had he done so he would over-night have become the most-hated man in Russia, and promptly been deprived of his command.

For making a stand, the Borodino position left much to be desired, but it was the best available. He disposed his army along it in a shallow, convex curve. The right followed the line of the little Kalotcha river, near the centre rose a steep ridge and to the left the ground sloped away to the valley of Utitza. Crowning the ridge was a great redoubt, in which were massed the Russian guns. Barclay commanded the right and centre, Bagration the left, where lesser earthworks had been thrown up. Having made his dispositions, Kutuzov retired to a farm two miles behind the line, and left his subordinates to fight the battle.

The Grand Army arrayed itself opposite: Beauharnais' Italians on the extreme left, Murat's, Ney's and Davout's corps, supported by other formations, in the

centre, the Guard on high ground at right centre, in reserve, and on the extreme right, Poniatowski's Poles.

For some days Napoleon had been far from well. He was suffering from his old complaint, dysuria, and could pass water only painfully, in driblets. In addition, the dust and damp bivouacs had given him a nasty dry cough, causing him loss of voice and making it difficult to dictate orders.

His anxieties were many, not least how matters were going on in Spain, where he still had two hundred thousand men tied up. Every few days couriers from the Peninsula reached him with news, and it was rarely good. Now, on the eve of the most important battle of his career, Captain Favrier arrived, having ridden from central Spain in thirty-two days. The despatch he brought reported that Marshal Marmont, one of Napoleon's oldest friends who, like Junot, had been with him at the siege of Toulon, had been seriously wounded, and that Soult had suffered a crushing defeat by Wellington at Salamanca.

When the Grand Army had crossed the Niemen, the odds against the Russians had been three to one in its favour. But ten weeks of campaigning had enormously reduced those odds. The Russians had been reinforced by General Miloradovitch's bringing up fifteen thousand men from the Danube, and Count Markov had reached the front with ten thousand militiamen. Napoleon, on the other hand, had received no reinforcements at all, and his losses in killed, wounded, by disease and starvation and in deserters had been at the least one hundred thousand men. Thus the odds now favoured him only by five to four.

On the morning of the battle, September 7th, when the two armies faced each other, the Grand Army numbered approximately one hundred and twenty-five thousand, and the Russians one hundred and four thousand.

The Russians had nearly six hundred and fifty guns and the Grand Army fewer than six hundred.

The battle opened by de Beauharnais attacking the Russian right. Soon afterwards Ney and Davout launched their massed infantry against the centre, while Poniatowski endeavoured to outflank the Russian left. The great redoubt was taken, retaken and taken again. For over ten hours the lines swayed back and forth, while two hundred thousand men were locked in conflict and unceasing carnage raged. Murat led his hordes of cavalry in charge after charge, only to have his temporary triumphs wrested from him by charge after charge of Platov's Cossacks.

All day the Emperor lay on a bearskin, only occasionally getting up to observe that part of the battle he could see through his spy glass. He gave no orders of importance, only nominating junior Generals to replace senior Generals when A.D.C.s galloped up to report that their commanders had been killed or grievously wounded. About him, covering acres of the grassy slope, sat or lay his grand reserve—the twenty thousand men of the Imperial Guard.

Late in the afternoon Ney believed that if he received reinforcements he was in a position to break right through the Russian centre. He sent an urgent appeal to the Emperor, begging him to launch the Guard. Roger was standing nearby. He had had one horse shot under him and had the bridle of his second horse over his arm. He had been slightly wounded by a small fragment of cannon ball in the left shoulder, a bullet had carried away his hat and grazed his scalp. His face was blackened by powder and his coat had been ripped down the side by the lance of a Cossack. More than half his fellow A.D.C.s had been killed or laid low, and of the few remaining he was the next for duty. He strained his ears to catch Napoleon's reply, dreading that he would be despatched back once

more through the fog of blinding smoke stabbed by the flashes of bursting cannon shells, over the heaps of wounded and between the overturned guns and limbers, to carry to Ney the longed-for message that the Guard was on its way.

The Emperor hesitated. Bessières was beside him. Leaning forward, he said, 'Sire, we are eighteen hundred miles from Paris.' Feebly, Napoleon nodded. Ney's plea remained unanswered. The Guard sat on where they were, dozing, smoking their long pipes or playing cards.

As evening fell, the battle petered out, both armies having become utterly exhausted. The Russians still held most of their positions, what was left of the Grand Army withdrew. It had been the most bloody battle in history, and the carnage was almost incredible. The Russians had lost fifty-eight thousand men and the Grand Army over fifty thousand, including fifty-seven Generals. Over one hundred thousand troops lay dead or dying on the field, and the gallant General Prince Bagration was among the dead.

Both Napoleon and Kutuzov had intended to renew the battle on the following day; but the latter considered his losses to be so serious that he would not risk it, and withdrew his army during the night. Thus, although in fact the armies had fought each other to a standstill, the Emperor was able to claim a victory. As usual, in his bulletin he greatly increased the Russian losses and minimised his own. Next day, when walking over the battlefield, he remarked that there were five Russian dead for every one of his. The cynical Rapp said, in an aside to Roger, 'He is mistaking Germans and Poles for Russians.'

The number of the dead was so enormous that no attempt was made to bury them, but the still-living were gradually collected and the overworked surgeons did what they could for them. In the next few days, by cannabilising units, the Grand Army reassumed the appearance of

a well-organised, formidable force of approximately seventy-five thousand men. The advance was then continued and, on the 14th, the main body marched up the western slopes of the Mont du Salut. Spread out below was Russia's old capital, 'the Holy City'. It was a lovely day, the spires and domes of Moscow's three hundred and seventy churches glinted in the sunshine and had the appearance of an array of fairy palaces. The Emperor was still far from well, but greatly relieved to have Moscow in his grasp at last, as he felt certain that Alexander would now sue for peace.

Murat had been sent on ahead. Kutuzov had withdrawn his main force to Fili, but left General Miloradovitch behind with a strong rearguard. When Murat reached the gates of the city, a Russian officer came out to present what almost amounted to an ultimatum. Miloradovitch requested a temporary armistice while he evacuated Moscow, or he would fight to the last man defending it. Murat agreed his terms and then an extraordinary scene of fraternisation took place.

The Cossacks had never seen such a resplendent leader of cavalry as the King of Naples. He was wearing a green, fur-trimmed jacket, pink riding breeches and bright yellow boots. His hat sprouted not only ostrich plumes but also a heron's feather aigret rising from a diamond clasp the size of a pigeon's egg. His belt and spurs were gold, and in his hand he carried a golden wand with which, instead of a sword, he directed his troops in battle. The hilt of his sabre was encrusted with jewels, and a dozen decorations blazed on his chest. While he gracefully cavorted on his splendid mount, the Cossacks cheered him to the echo, then danced the *czardas* for him.

In due course, the Emperor arrived before the gates. In his time he had accepted the surrender of a score of great cities. The Governor had come out with a depressed-looking staff, surrendered his sword, offered the keys of

the city on a velvet cushion and begged that mercy should be shown to the inhabitants. Naturally, Napoleon expected this ritual to be performed. Having fumed for a while at the rude Russians for keeping him waiting, he sent Murat in to find out why they delayed. Murat returned with the disconcerting news that the Governor, General Rostopchin had, even more rudely, ridden off with Miloradovitch and that the greater part of the population had gone with them.

Grumpily, Napoleon allowed himself to be installed in the Kremlin; but he was by no means depressed. He had remarked that a capital that is occupied by an enemy is like a woman who has been taken prisoner and is being dishonoured. Surely Alexander would not submit to Moscow continuing to suffer such an indignity? Balashov would undoubtedly soon be turning up and this time be ready to accept practically any terms as the price of peace. It was now only a matter of waiting a week or so, then the Czar would have become as much of a puppet monarch as the King of Prussia. French garrisons would occupy all his principal fortresses and the Grand Army would march home in triumph.

On the evening that the French entered Moscow, a few fires started. No-one was surprised at that, as the troops had lost no time in starting to loot the city and many of them were already drunk; so such accidents were to be expected.

After their many weeks of privation, Moscow was a bonanza. Not only were there big stores of flour and grain, but all the palaces and four-fifths of the houses had been abandoned by their owners. The cellars of many of them were well stocked with wine and brandy, there were frozen meat, fish and game in the ice pits, cakes, sweets and preserved fruit in the larders. There was hardly a soldier in Moscow that night not glutted with food, and drunk.

Next day there were many more fires and, under the pretext of saving things from the flames, the troops got down to looting on a grand scale. They ransacked every building, carrying off fine clothes, weapons, jewelled icons, brocade curtains, furniture and even chandeliers. To show their contempt for religion, they stalled their horses in the churches, chopped up for firewood the beautifully-carved panels and stalls and used the altars as dinner tables. The sacred vessels of gold and silver were melted down and the relics of saints thrown out into the street.

But the fires soon became a serious menace, and it was realised that few of them were the result of accident. Among the people left in the city there was a considerable number of shaggy, bearded men dressed in a sort of uniform that consisted of a dirty, belted sheep-skin kaftan. It transpired that they were convicts, who had been released from prison by Count Rostopchin before he left the city. Whether he had given them their freedom on condition that they became incendiaries, or whether they were inspired by a fanatical patriotism, was never satisfactorily determined. But they were setting fire to houses all over the place, and not even bothering to conceal what they were doing from the French.

Mortier, whom the Emperor had made Governor of the city, set about rounding them up. But by then it was too late. By the night of the 15th, three-quarters of Moscow was blazing, and the lurid glare of the flames was such that, three miles outside the city, one could read a book by their light.

Next day fire threatened the Kremlin. Berthier went up one of the towers to assess the danger of the situation, and nearly fell off the battlements which, had he done so, would have caused many of his compatriots to rejoice. His report was so alarming that Napoleon was persuaded to leave and move to the Petrovsky Palace outside the walls. It was too small to accommodate all his staff in com-

fort, so they suffered much inconvenience. On the fourth day they were able to return to the Kremlin. It had been saved and, by then, most of the fires had been put out; but the greater part of Moscow was a smoking ruin.

The looting and carousing continued. Some fifteen thousand of the poorer people had remained in the city, so there was a considerable number of girls and not too elderly women who, willing or unwilling, were available to the troops, who then settled down to enjoy themselves. But the Emperor's staff were far from enjoying themselves in the Kremlin, for daily he became more ill-tempered and difficult to please.

No plenipotentiary had arrived from the Czar to beg him to state the terms on which he would go home. Greatly worried, he decided to write to Alexander and point out to him that he was very wrong to inflict such misery on his people when all he had to do was to enter into a mutually satisfactory arrangement, and their sufferings would cease. Two letters were despatched by Russian officers who had been taken prisoner. Whether either of them reached his destination he never knew, but he received no answer.

His next move was to send one of his own officers, General Lauriston, to Kutuzov who by then had moved his main force down to Tula, with the object of attempting to cut the Grand Army's communications. Lauriston returned to report that all Kutuzov would say was that his master had declared that he 'would sooner grow a beard and live off potatoes than make peace as long as a single French soldier remained on Russian soil'.

It now seemed that there was no alternative for the Grand Army but to winter in Moscow, call up all the reinforcements possible and launch a new campaign in the spring to take St. Petersburg. Berthier was ordered to produce his 'Bible', as the staff called the roster of the strength of every unit in the Army that he kept with such

322

meticulous care. Together they went into the figures. It emerged that if the Emperor called up Macdonald's corps and the Prussians from the Baltic coast, that of St. Cyr, which had been left in the neighbourhood of Vitebsk, and Victor's from Smolensk, both employed in guarding the army's line of communications, Schwarzenberg's thirty thousand Austrians who had so far fired hardly a shot, and drew on the garrisons of the fortresses in Poland, Prussia and Germany, he could again have at his disposal an army of half a million troops. But how was he to feed them?

Murat's cavalry had already been despatched far and wide to seize every head of cattle, bag of flour and bale of hay they could lay their hands on, but it seemed to the French, who were used to the highly-populated areas of western and southern Europe that Moscow had been set down in a vast, almost uninhabited plain. Still worse, Murat reported that the Cossacks were becoming more daring. Only a few days before they had encountered one of his regiments, killed its Colonel and cut a great part of it to pieces. They appeared to be closing in on every side.

So, all through September and into October the scene darkened for Napoleon.

It was on the morning of the 7th that Roger, as A.D.C. on first duty, reported to him and, after an abrupt nod, the Emperor snapped:

'Breuc, you are a friend of the Czar?'

Roger hesitated only a moment. He could not guess what was coming, but knew the Emperor's fabulous memory too well to lie about such a matter. He could only pray that it had not somehow come to Napoleon's ears that he had spent a good part of the spring in St. Petersburg. Bowing, he replied:

'I have the honour to be acquainted with His Imperial Majesty, Sire.' Then he held his breath.

Napoleon regarded him glumly. 'Yes, I recall that after

you were taken prisoner at Eylau he arranged for you to be exchanged; and one day at Erfurt I noticed in my police report that you had had a private audience with him.'

'That is so, Sire.'

'Then you must go to him for me. Either he fails to receive my letters or he ignores them. I am convinced the former is the case. He is eccentric and at times has idiotic dreams of bringing in dangerous reforms which would hamstring his own authority; but he is by no means a fool. He must be made to realise that things cannot continue like this. Our people have already cut a great swathe a hundred miles wide, from Kovno to Moscow, through his country, and brought ruin to Vilna, Vitebsk and Smolensk, not to mention scores of smaller places. And Moscow! Just think what has befallen this once splendid city! Does he want me to winter here, then march on St. Petersburg in the spring and cause it also to be destroyed? Surely not!

'Tell him that I will not be unreasonable. I will withdraw my support from the Poles, so that he can do what he likes in Poland. He can have eastern Prussia too, as compensation for the damage done to Russia. You can even promise that he can have Constantinople when, together, we have defeated the Turk. Later I can think again about that. But peace we must make, and soon. He cannot know it, but our situation here is becoming desperate. Get us out of it and that will be as great a service to me as winning a major battle. I cannot give you a Marshal's baton, but I will make you a Duke. You will, of course, go under a flag of truce. Take any escort you require. Go now, Breuc, and for God's sake persuade him to see reason.'

Using the sort of *Gasconerie* that Napoleon liked about him Roger, instead of bowing himself out, sprang

to attention, threw up his head, cried, 'To hear is to obey, Sire!' turned on his heel and strode out of the room.

He could not have been more pleased at being chosen for this mission, as to find a means of communicating with the Czar had been on his conscience for some time. He could, as Alexander had suggested, have let himself be taken prisoner; but in this campaign, that would have entailed a very considerable risk. Few Russians were allowing themselves to be captured. They seemed to prefer fighting to the death, and this disregard for life frequently led them to kill off any prisoners they took. Roger would have liked to honour his bond, but was not prepared to make what might prove a futile attempt, and possibly throw away his life for nothing. As there seemed no other way in which he could convey information about the state to which the Grand Army had been reduced, he had let matters slide. Now he could report to Alexander with little risk; but he decided against taking an escort, as when he did reach St. Petersburg it would have proved a great embarrassment. Three-quarters of an hour later, he was on his way to the northern capital.

For the first twenty miles, while passing through the zone strongly held by Murat's cavalry, he wore his uniform; then, when he judged himself to be well into no-man's-land, he rode into a wood, unpacked his valise, and changed into the civilian suit he had been wearing when the French arrived in Vilna. Back on the road again, he kept a sharp look-out for patrols of Cossacks. He felt fairly confident that, if challenged, he could satisfy anyone who questioned him, as three months among the Russians in the spring had enabled him to become fluent in that language. But junior officers and N.C.O.s could, at times, prove stupid and dangerous, so he was anxious to avoid having to give an account of himself.

In the next two hours he saw three groups of horsemen in the distance, but managed to keep well away from

them, and none of them gave chase. That evening he halted at Tver, and at the hostelry there gave himself out to be a Lithuanian timber merchant. The following night he spent at Volochek, then got up very early the next morning to cover the long stretch to Chudova. From there it was not, for him, a hard day's ride to St. Petersburg, and he entered the capital late on the afternoon of October 10th.

Having handed his horse over to an ostler at the Laughing Tartar, he went into the hostelry to refresh himself, and learned that the Czar was in residence at the Winter Palace. An hour later he was there and had sent up his name. He had to wait until past eight o'clock, then a Chamberlain summoned him to the presence.

Alexander gave him a smiling greeting, extended his hand to be kissed and said, 'Mr. Brook, we congratulate you; and upon two counts. Firstly on having survived the appalling slaughter of the past five months. Secondly, on having succeeded in returning to us. We hoped you would, but feared you might find it too dangerous an enterprise.'

Roger returned the smile. 'Sire, I have been awaiting a favourable opportunity; for there would have been no sense in my setting out with a good prospect of being killed. But fortune has been most kind to me. I come to Your Imperial Majesty now as the envoy of the Emperor.'

'Well, well!' The Czar gave a hearty laugh. 'You are the cleverest fellow that ever we did meet.'

Roger did not deny it, but said, 'I think, Sire, the Emperor was influenced in his choice of me because he knows that Your Imperial Majesty has done me the honour to receive me on previous occasions.'

'And in what way can we be of service to your . . . er . . . master?'

With equal irony, Roger replied, 'Merely by acknowledging that he has fought a victorious campaign, and

again entering into an alliance with him; but this time agreeing to accept him as your overlord.'

They both laughed, then Alexander's blue eyes grew serious and he said firmly, 'We stand by the declaration we made to our people. We would sooner grow a beard and live on potatoes than make peace as long as a single French soldier remains on Russian soil. Now tell us how things are in Moscow.'

For the next quarter of an hour Roger described the state of the city and gave the approximate strength of the enemy forces based on it. He concluded by saying :

'During the past weeks the supply trains that were intended to support the Grand Army during its advance have come up. There were also considerable stores left behind in the city. These have restored to health both men and horses. But they cannot last indefinitely. Within a few weeks now the Emperor will be driven into taking a decision. His army has been so reduced that he could not order another advance with any hope of success. Therefore he must do one of two things : either winter in Moscow and risk his army starving until it is so weak that it could easily be overwhelmed, or endeavour to fight his way back to Poland.'

The Czar nodded. 'Yes, we have him. Whichever course he adopts his defeat is now certain. How right the Prince Royal of Sweden was in advising us to adopt the scorched-earth policy. He is also convinced that, should Napoleon decide to abandon Moscow, we shall have him at our mercy. We will harass him every step of the way, and ice and snow will do the rest.'

Roger agreed, then said, 'It is, Sire, now several months since I have heard any news out of England. Would Your Imperial Majesty be gracious enough to inform me if any events of importance have taken place ?'

'Indeed, yes. There has been a change of government. In May Mr. Perceval had the misfortune to be assas-

sinated. We have no details, but gather that it was by the hand of a madman who had some private grudge against him. He has been succeeded as Prime Minister by Lord Liverpool, who has retained Lord Castlereagh as Foreign Secretary.'

Giving a slight shrug, Roger commented, 'A sad business, Sire. But the change should be all to the good. Mr. Perceval was an upright and kindly man, but not very forceful. I think that Lord Liverpool, particularly with Castlereagh to aid him, will press the war more vigorously. How stands the prospect of Your Imperial Majesty entering into an alliance with England?'

'We signed a peace in July, so are now allies.'

'That is good news indeed, Sire.'

Getting up from his desk, the Czar walked over to a buhl cabinet, unlocked it and took from it a ribbon to which was attached an enamel star set with small brilliants. Turning, he said :

'We would not have you think us ungrateful, Mr. Brook, for bringing us such good tidings. This is the Order of St. Anne and we make you a Chevalier of it.' He then passed the ribbon over Roger's head and round his neck.

Greatly delighted, Roger went down on one knee, kissed the Czar's hand and expressed his gratitude. Receiving such a decoration could hardly be compared to being made a Duke, but he had not even considered attempting to earn the reward offered by Napoleon. Next moment his happiness was abruptly doused, as Alexander spoke again :

'And now, Mr. Brook, return as speedily as you can to Moscow. Give Napoleon our reply to his request that we should enter into negotiations, then endeavour to find out the line of retreat that he intends his army to take should he decide to evacuate Moscow. This could be of great importance to us. We do not ask you to risk yourself by

endeavouring to come again to St. Petersburg. But you could easily hide yourself when the French leave Moscow, then give such information as you have obtained to the first of our Generals to enter the city.'

Having got safely away from the Grand Army, Roger was most averse to returning to it. He had left England the previous December, expecting to be away in Sweden for only a few weeks; but between them Bernadotte and the Czar had already prevented him from going home for ten months. He would have protested and pleaded to be spared this new task; but by decorating him Alexander had skilfully entrapped him and made him feel that he could not decently refuse to be of further service. Stifling his annoyance as best he could, he again kissed the Czar's hand and bowed himself backward out of the room.

Roger would have liked to remain in St. Petersburg for a few days. But he knew that all his younger friends would have gone to the war, and that if he called on the older ones it would soon get to the ears of the Czar that he had disobeyed the Imperial injunction to return to Moscow as speedily as possible; so he reluctantly decided to take the road again the following morning.

He had no means of knowing whether Napoleon would elect to submit his army to semi-starvation by remaining in Moscow throughout the winter, or if he would decide on a withdrawal, at least to Smolensk; but he thought the latter more probable, as it would greatly shorten the distance supply trains from Poland would have to cover.

In either case food was going to be extremely short, and even the Emperor's entourage would have to make do on meagre rations. Concerned as ever about his own material well-being—which more than once had saved his life—Roger debated with himself what foodstuff he could buy in St. Petersburg that was easily portable and had a high quality for sustaining vigour. Eventually he decided on marzipan, as it was composed solely of sugar

and almonds, a compound hardly to be bettered for stimulating energy.

Leaving his hostelry he walked to the great, covered bazaar. Under the scores of small domes, an incredible variety of things could be bought there : food of all kinds, weapons, clothes, furs, jewels and a multitude of other items. Easing his way through the crowds of haggling people, he found a sweet-seller who had a number of large slabs of marzipan from which he cut off pieces according to the quantity required.

Having tasted a sample and judged the quality to be satisfactory, Roger asked the vendor to weigh his whole stock. Much surprised, the man complied. It came to eleven and a quarter kilos. Being of the opinion that during the coming months such a reserve of food might be of more value than pistols, Roger had it in mind to store the marzipan in his pistol holsters, even if he had to sacrifice one pistol and stick the other through his sash; so he enquired the price of the marzipan. The man did a quick calculation on his abacus and gave it him. After several minutes of bargaining, Roger got it reduced by a third, produced the money and had the sweetmeat packed up.

As it was being handed to him he distinctly heard Georgina's voice. That had happened on a few previous occasions when he had been in great danger. Although she was unconscious of it, the strange psychic link between them had enabled her to warn him and inspire him as to how best to escape the peril he was in. Now she was saying :

'Look to your right ! Roger, be quick ! Look to your right !'

Amazed as he was that in his present harmless occupation any danger should be threatening him, his hand nevertheless flew to his sword hilt, and he swivelled round as she had directed him.

No villainous figure was about to come at him with a

knife, or was aiming a pistol at him. The only person at the next stall was a short woman, wearing the clothes of a Russian bourgeoise and a scarf that partially hid her brown hair. She had just completed the purchase of a pair of soft leather boots. As she handed the money across the stall to pay for them she was only ten feet away from him. He gave a gasp. It seemed incredible, but he could not possibly be mistaken. She was the girl who, before her marriage, had been Lady Mary Ware.

CHAPTER XXI

A NEW PROBLEM

NEXT moment, the girl had taken her parcel and turned away. Roger sprang after her, grabbed her by the arm and cried:

'Mary! What in heaven's name are you doing here?'

Swinging round she stared at him. Her green eyes opened wide and she dropped her parcel. Both of them stooped to pick it up and bumped their heads together. Laughing, they drew back, and Mary exclaimed:

'But you! How come you to be in St. Petersburg?'

He shook his head and put a finger to his lips. 'I'll tell you later. But by what extraordinary coincidences we meet. Last summer in Richmond Park when I did not even know that you were back in England, and now here, of all places.'

'There was nothing extraordinary about our happening upon each other outside your home, but to do so here is, I agree, passing strange.' Suddenly Mary's pretty face became very grave and she went on, 'Oh, Roger, I cannot say how pleased I am to see you. I am in trouble; most grievous trouble.'

He smiled. 'Then you must tell me of it. I doubt not that I can find a remedy and would be most pleased to do so.'

'Not here. We can't talk here, and I'd prefer not to take you to the place where I am dwelling.'

332

'We'll go to the hostelry where I am lying, then, the Laughing Tartar. 'Tis one of the best in St. Petersburg.'

Roger collected his twenty-four pounds of marzipan, gave his free arm to Mary and they walked to his inn. In those times no hotelier ever dreamed of questioning the use a gentleman made of the chamber he had hired; so Roger took Mary straight upstairs to his bedroom.

Throwing his heavy parcel on the bed, he settled Mary in an elbow chair, poured for them both glasses of *rabinowka*—a liqueur made from blackberries, to which he was partial—and said, 'Now, tell me the worst, and we'll see in what way I can help you.'

She gave a heavy sigh. 'Roger, I am in desperate straits. I am marooned here, and cannot get home because I have no money.'

He raised his eyebrows. 'I thought your husband was a rich merchant. But let that wait, and start at the beginning. How in the world do you come to be in Russia at all?'

'I, too, believed Mr. Wicklow to be a rich man,' she replied sadly. 'And, until a few years ago, he was. But, as is the case with many other merchants, Bonaparte's Continental System brought about his ruin. When I married him he was already heavily in debt. It was not until later that I learned that. At the time he had hopes of mending his fortune; but, alas, they did not mature. His principal trade had always been with Russia. This spring his creditors were pressing him so hard that he feared to be made bankrupt and thrown into the Debtors' Prison. He then decided on one last, desperate venture. Secretly, he sold our house and all its contents to a Jew, on condition that the man should not take possession until we were gone from London.

'With the money Mr. Wicklow bought a cargo of such goods as are always easily saleable on the Russian market. He told me nothing of all this, but said I must accompany

him on the voyage. As I have ever delighted in sea voyages, and seeing foreign parts, I made no objection. All went well until we entered the Gulf of Finland. There was still much ice about. In the night a storm blew up, and our ship was driven into an iceberg. It was not a large berg, but must have had a big, jagged point below the water. It holed the ship. The sea gushed into the hold and she listed dangerously. The men worked desperately at the pumps; but it was of no avail. Within an hour the ship, with all our cargo, went down.'

'Oh, my dear,' Roger shook his head. 'What evil fortune for you.'

'Alas, I have not told you the worst. Half-frozen from the icy water, we succeeded in getting ashore. Some fisherfolk succoured us most generously and did what they could for us in their poor huts. We were no great distance from St. Petersburg, and when we were somewhat recovered made our way here. The people at the English Factory—that is the great, enclosed area with many warehouses in which our merchants store their goods—took us in.'

'I know the place. When I first came to St. Petersburg, I lived there for a while with the chaplain, a delightful and most erudite man, the Reverend William Tooke. But he is long since returned to England.'

'Well, they allotted us a lodging and Mr. Wicklow made a last attempt to restore his shattered fortunes. He had saved his bag of guineas and added to the sum by requesting me to let him sell the few small trinkets I possessed; which, by then knowing his circumstances, I willingly agreed to do. But he went about this last endeavour in a most ill-advised manner. He began to frequent a gaming house.'

'The fool! Any merchant should have known better.'

'There I agree, and I became greatly worried. 'Tis not, though, a wife's place to tell her husband how he should

endeavour to increase his capital; and, to begin with, he was very lucky. When I learned that he had amassed quite a considerable sum, I endeavoured to persuade him to take me back to England. But he could not, for he owed so much money there that he would have been lodged in Newgate. Then his luck turned. For three nights in succession he lost heavily. On the fourth morning he confessed to me that he had not a *kopek* left. We were reduced to beggary.'

'Oh, my poor Mary! When I come face to face with this criminal oaf, I'll horsewhip the hide off him for having landed you in such an awful situation.'

'No, Roger, you will not. Though he deserves it for having abandoned me.'

'What! Do you mean the villain has made off and left you penniless in a foreign city?'

'He has, indeed, if "made off" is the right expression. But he has gone to a place from which there is no return. Having borrowed from his cronies and in particular an elderly, pockmarked Russian merchant named Suslov, until they would lend him no more, six weeks ago he put a pistol to his head and blew out his brains.'

'Mary! Mary!' Roger exclaimed in distress. 'This is the end. No woman could have been cursed with more dire misfortune.'

'But it is not the end.' Mary was almost weeping. 'When Mr. Wicklow died, he owed the equivalent of a hundred and sixty pounds to Mr. Suslov. Believing him to be a good friend, in my desperation I have since borrowed from him a further sum upon my note of hand. To do so I must have been out of my wits, but I had not a penny and knew not which way to turn. And now . . . now, this Mr. Suslov . . . oh, Roger, he has turned out to be a horrid man, and is physically most repulsive. He has recently demanded that I pay all that is owed to him, or he'll

have me sent to prison. That . . . that is, if I continue to refuse to marry him.'

'God's death!' Roger roared. 'I'll cut his ears off! I'll skin the bastard!'

Mary was dabbing at her eyes with a handkerchief. After a moment she murmured, ' 'Twould serve him right, but that would not get me home.'

Roger leaned forward and patted her hand. 'Mary, my dear, I beg you, do not cry. Now I am here your troubles are over. I have ample money and will see to it that you lack for nothing.'

She sniffed and gave him a pathetic smile. 'Oh, Roger, 'tis wonderful. I had believed God deaf to my prayers, but He must have sent you to me. I can scarce believe it true. 'Tis little short of a miracle that you should be living in St. Petersburg.'

Her words suddenly reminded him that, within a few hours, he should be on his way to Moscow. Gravely he said, 'I can pay your passage home, but would be loath to let you make the voyage without a woman companion, or some honest man known to you who would act as your protector. Do you know anyone at the Factory who is shortly leaving for England, and could act in such a role?'

She shook her head. 'No, and you are right, of course. Women are infrequent passengers in ships that ply the Baltic trade, and I'd be frightened to travel unaccompanied. Without conceit, I'd be surprised if the Captain or some other man aboard did not fancy me; and, maybe, tamper with the lock on my cabin door. But if you will pay my debts and make me a small allowance, I'd be happy to stay on here until you are ready to go home yourself.'

'My dear, I am not going home. I have to go to Moscow.'

'Moscow! Can you really mean that? 'Tis in the hands of the French.'

'Nevertheless, I have to go there, and must set out not later than tonight.'

Her eyes grew wide and her face crumpled. 'Oh, Roger, no! Please! Only a moment since, I thought myself saved and safe. I implore you, do not desert me.'

'I'll not do that,' he reassured her quickly. 'I mean, I'll not leave you stranded. I can give you ample money to pay off this brute Suslov, and to stay on here for some weeks, until you can find someone suitable with whom to return to England.'

'But, Roger dear, old Mr. Suslov is not the only one from whom Mr. Wicklow borrowed money. And they hold me responsible for his debts. Hardly a day passes but one or other of them pesters me. Recently, several of them have hinted that I am cheating them by refusing to marry; for Mr. Suslov has told them that, if I'll have him, he'll pay them off. If you must go to Moscow, cannot I come with you?'

'No, Mary. That is out of the question. When we were in Lisbon I concealed it from you; but I have lived for so many years in France that I can pass as a Frenchman, and have often done so in the service of our country. I'll come to no harm in Moscow, but how could I possibly take an Englishwoman with me?'

Round-eyed, she stared at him. 'Do you . . . do you mean that you are a spy?'

He nodded. 'Yes. Do you find such an activity despicable?'

'No. Oh, no. To risk his life in such a fashion a man must be very brave. But I've always known you to be that.'

'Thank you, my dear. The fact is that I am here only on a visit. I have been in Moscow ever since the French captured the city, and am expected back there. But you can see for yourself that, if I returned accompanied by an

English lady, I should seriously jeopardise my position.'

'I think you wrong in that. I have a gift for languages and my best friend at my seminary was a French girl who, as a small child, had arrived in England as a refugee from the Revolution. To please her, we always talked together in French and, although I could not pass as a Frenchwoman, I feel sure no-one would suspect me of lying if I said that I was Flemish, or from the Netherlands.'

Roger smiled. A sudden memory of Georgina had come into his mind. She had passed herself off in that way on their journey with Augereau from the Moselle to Paris. He then remained thoughtful for some moments.

Many women had accompanied the Grand Army on its march to Moscow; in a few cases even officers' wives, who refused to be parted from their husbands. That was also the case in the English and other armies. All Generals were most averse to the practice, but it was a custom that had come down through the centuries, so they could do no more than set a limit to the number of women that the troops should be allowed to take with them on a campaign.

He could say that he had met Mary in Brussels two years ago. That she had married a Russian who had taken her to St. Petersburg, but her husband had turned out to be a brute; that she loathed the Russians, was French at heart and worshipped the Emperor, so had begged him to take her to Moscow.

Everyone there would assume she was his mistress. That would not matter; but what did matter was the sort of life she would be forced to lead. Staff officers, such as himself, never took women to war with them. In fact, the only officers who did were men of junior rank who came from the poorer classes. When following the army she would find no companions with a similar upbringing to hers, and would have to live rough. Knowing her to be

his property, no other man would dare lay a finger on her, but he thought it certain that the other women, realising that she was an 'aristo', would boycott her; and that he could not prevent.

He told her all this, adding that for the greater part of the time, his duties would prevent him from being with her, and that when the army marched, the women would follow far in the rear; so they might not even see each other for weeks at a stretch.

Tears starting to her eyes, she pleaded with him. It might be months before she could get a passage back to England, even if she could find an English couple who would act as her protectors; because Captains did not like to have unattached women on board, as the presence of an eligible female often led to trouble with the crew. Even if she could be with Roger only occasionally, and however hard the life, she was prepared to face it. She was also afraid of Mr. Suslov. Even if Roger gave her the money to pay her debt, she would not be rid of him. He was well-off and many people were under obligations to him. She would hardly dare leave her lodging, lest some of them helped him to lay a trap for her. In Russia rich men and nobles often had girls carried off for them. That Suslov had not already attempted something of the kind was, she felt sure, only because he was hoping that she would marry him.

For once, Roger could not make up his mind what to do. He felt that he could not possibly leave her. On the other hand, he knew far better than she could even imagine the hardships and misery that she would have to endure if he took her with him.

Then an idea came to him. It was due to his recalling the lovely little 'Captain of Hussars' who had been living with Soult at his headquarters in Seville. No-one would have taken her for a young man. She had not even attempted to disguise her sex, but still wore her dark hair

long, and rouged her face. But if Mary cut her hair short she could, with her piquant eyebrows and slightly retroussé nose, pass for an impudent lad. She had such small breasts that, if bound flat, they would not give her away, and breeches that were too large for her would disguise her plump little bottom.

Standing up, he took her by the hand and, with a laugh, pulled her to her feet. 'Come along, Mary. We're going shopping. That will cheer you up.'

Mystified, she accompanied him downstairs and out into the street. Returning to the covered bazaar, they went to the stalls where every kind of clothes was on sale. There he bought her an outfit resembling those worn by the footmen of the Russian nobility. Next, they went to a horse dealer, where she tried out several mounts and settled on a sturdy little chestnut. He also bought suitable saddlery and two large panniers to hold Mary's belongings, then told the man to send his purchases round to the Laughing Tartar.

By then it was time for the midday meal. Afterwards they drove down to the docks in a *drosky*. Having been told that she must take only things she could not do without, Mary went into the English Factory to collect her bits and pieces. She was a long time doing so, and Roger became a little impatient; but when she came out, she told him that she had been giving away to needy people the clothes she could not take, and had had to talk to each of them for a while, giving as her reason for leaving that she was going to marry a rich Finnish gentleman who intended to buy her an entire new outfit, then take her to Helsinki. She had also had to say good-bye to the Factor who, since her husband's death, had let her have their lodging free of rent, and had made her a small allowance from a fund to succour stranded British seamen.

By the time they got back to the Laughing Tartar, dusk was falling. Having decided that it was too late to start for

Moscow that night, Roger said, 'I'll see the landlord and get him to have a room prepared for you.'

With a little laugh, Mary replied, 'I don't think that's necessary. In Russia it is customary for footmen to sleep outside their master's door. Although I'd prefer to sleep inside.'

He gave her a quick look. 'My dear, you must not think you owe me anything for what I am doing. I've not forgotten that I took from you something which I can never repay. And, anyway, I'd do the same for any English girl who was in your wretched position.' Then he added, on a lighter note, 'The leopard does not change his spots, you know; and if you do sleep in my room, it will be at your peril.'

She laughed again. 'I can't say you did not warn me, but I'm agreeable to risk it.'

The dining room of the hostelry was not crowded, and he secured for them a corner table. Over a meal of grey caviar, *borsch,* bear steaks and jam omelette, washed down with Caucasian sparkling wine and old, hay-scented vodka, they reminisced about their time in Portugal and mutual friends. Toward the end of their dinner, they fell silent and, after a few minutes, Mary said, 'I think I will go up to our room.'

Roger ordered himself another vodka and gave her twenty minutes, then he too went upstairs, his heart beating decidedly faster than usual. He had expected to find her in his bed, and felt much disgruntled when he saw that she had collected the cushions from two easy chairs and one of the pillows from the bed, then wrapped herself in the eiderdown and was curled up, apparently already asleep, beside the porcelain stove.

Frowning and greatly disappointed, he undressed, got into bed and blew out the candle. For a few minutes he lay there, unhappily considering this new development. As Mary had been married since their affair in Lisbon,

and had refused his offer of a separate room, he thought it mean of her to deny herself to him. Contemplating the future made him still more unhappy, for with Mary in the role of his personal servant he would see a great deal of her, and she would prove a constant temptation to him.

Suddenly there was a rustle that came from near the stove. Fumbling hands grasped his bedclothes and pulled them aside. Next moment Mary had slipped into bed with him, her arms went round his neck and she kissed him hard on the mouth. When she lifted her head to draw breath, she gave a low laugh and whispered:

'Darling Roger, were you very angry with me? I fooled you beautifully, didn't I?'

'You little devil,' he retorted. 'You don't deserve to be made love to. Now get out of my bed. Go on, and be quick about it.'

'Oh, no!' she cried in protest. 'I want you, Roger, I really do. You warned me that I'd be in peril. I've got all my courage up ready to face it. You promised, so you can't disappoint me.'

'Ah, well, as I'm a man of my word, I suppose I must,' he conceded. Then, as she pressed herself to him, he exclaimed, 'Oh, Mary, what a beautiful little body you have! But damn it, girl, stop tickling me, or you'll spoil everything.'

When he woke in the morning, he found her snuggled up against him, warm and sweet-smelling, like an overgrown child. Looking down at her dark eyelashes, spread like fans on her rosy cheeks, he thought her still asleep. But she was already awake. As he moved, she opened her eyes and asked:

'Roger, do you know something?'

'Yes, dearest,' he murmured. 'Believe it or not, this is Christmas Day. You were made in heaven and Father Christmas brought you to me in the dark from out of the porcelain stove.'

'Dear, foolish one; what a lovely thought. But I was thinking about Mr. Wicklow. He must have been a very poor lover. I found that out only a few hours ago. Most times with him it was all over before it had hardly started. I much prefer horrid, brutal men like you, who take advantage of trusting young girls and rape them. This is going to be my real honeymoon. Now rape me again, darling; gently and beautifully and going on for ages and ages, just as you did last night.'

When they got up, Roger cut Mary's hair to within an inch of her scalp. As it was naturally curly, it only changed her appearance, without lessening her attractions. After she had dressed she looked, as he had hoped, like an impudent young boy. Having packed their things in his valise and the two panniers he had bought to go on her horse, they went downstairs and ate an exceptionally hearty breakfast.

By half past nine they were on the road to Moscow. To Moscow, which they could only hope would be the first stage on the far longer road home.

CHAPTER XXII

NAPOLEON SIGNS HIS ARMY'S
DEATH WARRANT

ROGER had long been accustomed to riding fast and for long distances, so it had taken him only four days to get from Moscow to St. Petersburg. But with Mary he had to amend his pace, and it was six days before they came in sight of such spires and gilded domes as had survived the fires in Moscow.

While in St. Petersburg, Roger had given Mary no details of his secret activities, but on the first morning of their journey he divulged the fact that, for many years, he had led a double life. Later he whiled away many hours telling her what he had really done during the two periods he had been absent from Lisbon, and enthralling her with accounts of his earlier adventures.

They decided that henceforth she was to be known as Hippolyte Abrail, and he would call her Hipé for short. She was to have been born in a suburb of Antwerp, the bastard son of a washerwoman, gone to St. Petersburg as a cabin boy, run away from her ship because she had been very ill-treated by her drunken captain, and got a job as a potboy at the Laughing Tartar, from which Roger had taken her. It was agreed that, in no circumstances, even when alone, should they talk in anything but French.

They had, by exercising great care, escaped molestation by the *sotnias* of Cossacks and foraging parties of the

French which clashed daily in the deep belt of no-man's-land that formed a semi-circle to the north of the city. Clad again in his uniform, and now with his young servant riding sedately behind him, late on the evening of October 17th Roger dismounted in one of the great courtyards of the Kremlin that was overlooked by the Imperial apartments.

Throwing Mary the reins of his horse, Roger pointed to an archway that led into another courtyard and, as there were several people within earshot, said curtly:

'The stables are through there. Take our mounts to them, ask for the A.D.C.s' head groom and hand them over to him to be rubbed down, watered and fed. Then return here and wait until I come out of the Palace. If anyone asks who you are, just tell them that you belong to me. I don't expect to be much more than three-quarters of an hour.'

As he expected, within a few minutes of sending in his name, a Chamberlain told him that the Emperor would receive him. He found Napoleon holding a conference in his map room; but, on Roger being announced, he abruptly cut short an officer who was speaking, and beckoned Roger to follow him into the next room. The moment they were inside it, he slammed the door and asked harshly:

'Well! What news do you bring?'

Roger bowed deeply, then sadly shook his head. 'Alas, Sire, my mission was a failure. I cannot sufficiently express my regret, but the Czar proved adamant. He will not talk of peace, at any price. That is unless and until Your Imperial Majesty withdraws the whole of the Grand Army from his territories.'

Napoleon burst into a spate of curses, using, as he did at times, expressions as filthy as any that could have been heard from a party of drunken troopers who had been robbed of their money in a whore-house. As his pallid face

became purple, Roger, who had once had to revive him from an epileptic fit, thought he was going to have another. But after some minutes, he quietened down and, his fine eyes still bulging, angrily blurted out:

'Why were you so long away? You left here on the 7th. It does not take eleven days to get to St. Petersburg and back.'

'At first the Czar refused to see me, Sire,' Roger promptly lied.

'Then you should have stopped him and spoken to him when he was out for a walk.'

Staggered at this piece of evidence of how far the Emperor's mind had deteriorated when assessing plausibilities, Roger hid his surprise and replied, 'I had no opportunity to accost His Imperial Majesty. Fearing that if I took an escort, Cossacks might not respect a flag of truce, but murder the men and myself, I travelled alone and in civilian clothes. In consequence no-one but the Czar would have believed me had I said I was your envoy. Being apparently a person of little account, it took me three days to find a Chamberlain who could be bribed to secure me an audience. I am lucky to have got back alive.'

Pacing up and down, Napoleon began to mutter to himself. When he stopped and again looked at Roger, his shoulders were bowed and there were tears in his eyes. Giving Roger's ear a tweak, he said with a sigh:

'Well, Breuc; no doubt you did your best. But I fear that stinking Romanoff has won this round. I'll make him crawl yet, of course, and burn St. Petersburg about his ears next year. Meanwhile, we must face it that our lines of communication are too long and vulnerable. Find Rapp. Tell him to summon the Marshals and other Corps Commanders for a conference at nine o'clock tomorrow morning. You may go.'

As Roger went off to find the A.D.C.-in-Chief, he al-

most felt sorry for Napoleon; but quickly put the thought from him. It was absurd to waste one iota of pity on a man who had brought such wholesale misery on the world.

Rapp was in the A.D.C.s' Mess. There had been very little for them to do since entering Moscow; so, after the fires had been put out and a day or two spent in exploring the city, they had been reduced to whiling away several hours a day at cards. On seeing Roger come through the door, Rapp got up from a table of *vingt-et-un*, walked over to him and said in a low voice:

'Welcome back, Breuc. I'm glad those *verdamter* Cossacks didn't get you. The King of Naples says they come charging out from every coppice, even against numbers superior to their own. He's losing scores of his men that way every day.'

'Our master told you, then, where he'd sent me?' Roger asked.

'Yes. He no longer troubles to hide it from those close to him that he's as jumpy as a cat on hot bricks, and he's been expecting you back these past three days. When you had still failed to appear yesterday, I told him I feared he might have to go on expecting, but he seemed convinced that as you speak some Russian you'd manage to look after yourself. Did you succeed in seeing the Czar?'

'I did, though it wasn't easy. That's why I was away for so long.'

'Have you brought us good news or bad? I'd wager ten to one in napoleons that it's bad.'

'Then you'd be ten gold pieces better off. The Czar has got the bit between his teeth. He's sworn to drive every one of us out of his kingdom.'

'I felt sure of it and, if the wits of you-know-who hadn't become addled, we'd have been out of this accursed city a month ago. *Teufel-nochmal!* What a mess he's made of

this campaign! First he kicks his heels in Vilna for eighteen days, then for sixteen at Vitebsk, then for fourteen at Smolensk; and we've been here for over five weeks. What a way to fight a war! We could easily have got here by the first week in August instead of mid-September. It was crazy to come on here so late in the year. We ought to have wintered at Smolensk.'

'It was crazy to invade Russia anyhow,' Roger replied. 'Even if we'd won and forced a peace on the Czar, he wouldn't have carried out its terms, and we couldn't have made him. Russia's not like Holland or one of the German States. It's too vast for any army to hold down, and with our old commitments we are over-extended already.'

The Alsatian nodded. 'That's what everyone is saying. From the Marshals down to the drummer boys, everyone is asking the same question. "What the devil are we doing here? There's naught to be gained, so why the hell can't the so-and-so let us march home?" Now you've brought him this final fart in the face from the Czar, I take it we'll be packing up tomorrow.'

'We will, unless he qualifies for a strait-jacket. He ordered me to tell you to summon all our military Dukes who are available, for a conference at nine o'clock in the morning.'

'Good. I'll do that. Did you have a good time in St. Petersburg?'

Roger grinned. 'It meant a pleasant change of fare, anyhow. For dinner on my last night there I had caviar, *borsch,* a bear steak and a jam omelette.'

Donnerwetter! And with several nights there, I'll wager you found one or more pretty bottoms to smack after you'd got all that good food inside you.'

Roger gave a slight wink. 'As a matter of fact, I've brought one back with me, but not the kind of whom you're thinking. He's a young Flemish lad, and on the

way home, when the cold sets in, he'll serve as a fine hot-water bottle.'

'I didn't know you were one of those,' Rapp remarked in mild surprise.

'Not habitually,' Roger laughed. 'But variety is the spice of life. The sort of women I care for are not to be had on this kind of campaign. And if I'd brought a girl she would soon have become an annoying liability; whereas this youngster will make himself useful as my servant.'

Roger had been very loath to let his friends believe him to be a homosexual, but he had decided that it was the only way that he could give Mary maximum protection. When it got round that Hipé was his 'girl', no-one would dare bully her. And few people would think the worse of him; for on long campaigns in which few women were available, homosexual relationships, although officially frowned upon, were by no means unusual. By this device, too, his companions would not think it strange if he spent much more time with Mary than he would have with an ordinary soldier servant.

Giving a little shrug, Rapp said, 'There's a lot in what you say, if one cares for that sort of fun. How about a drink?'

'Not for the moment, thanks. I have to see Sergeant Loriel about putting my young protégé on the strength for rations.'

A few minutes later he was saying to the Mess Sergeant, 'This youth I have taken on is a pleasant lad, but I don't think he is the sort who could stand up for himself very well, and I won't have him bullied. In fact, I've ordered him to let me know if anyone makes things unpleasant for him, and if anyone does I'll come down like a ton of bricks on them. But I'm sure I can leave it to you, Sergeant, to keep a fatherly eye on him.'

Roger had always treated his inferiors with an easy

politeness, so he was popular with the N.C.O.s with whom he had to deal. The Sergeant replied at once, 'Aye, Colonel; you leave it to me. Tell him to come to me and make his number, and I'll take good care of him.'

Leaving the Mess, Roger walked down several long corridors to the Camp Commandant's office. There he told one of the soldier-clerks that he had taken on a civilian servant whom he desired to sleep in his room, and said that a palliasse was to be sent there at once for the youth to doss down on.

Retracing his steps, he went down the magnificent grand staircase and ran into Duroc, who was on his way up. The Marshal of the Palace hailed him with evident pleasure, then said, *'Mon vieux,* I am delighted to see you. The Emperor told me of the mission on which he sent you, and I feared you lost to us. I only pray that you were successful.'

Roger shook his head. 'Nay, the Czar proved adamant. There's to be a conference tomorrow at nine, and my bet is that afterwards we'll be ordered to pack up and go.'

Glumly Duroc observed, 'If that is so, 'twill be none too soon. The days are shortening and, unless we make good speed, winter will be upon us. But we should have time to get back to Smolensk before the blizzards.'

'With luck, we should. But what then? We left the city in ruins, so will be little better off there than we are here.'

'At least we will be the best part of four hundred kilometres nearer the Polish frontier, so supplies will reach us with greater ease.'

'If Kutuzov lets them. I gather that he now has an army that in numbers exceeds ours.'

'Ah! That's the rub. But as we retreat we'll pick up reinforcements. The corps of Oudinot and Macdonald and Schwarzenberg's Austrians could be called in. That would again give us parity with the Russians.'

'Should we do that, how are we to feed such a host all through the winter months?'

'God knows, *mon ami*! God knows! We can only hope that Victor and St. Cyr will succeed in keeping our lines of communication open so that sufficient supplies will reach us. Augereau should be able to send several divisions across the frontier from north Germany, to assist in maintaining our hold on Vilna and Vitebsk.'

'Should we denude Germany, I'll warrant that country will blow up behind our backs.'

'To replace the garrisons there, His Majesty might decide to withdraw further troops from Spain.'

'Could he afford to do so? Are things going better in the Peninsula?'

'Alas, no. Suchet alone seems to have read the Spanish riddle, and Valencia remains peaceful under him. Soult has again fallen back on Seville, and has come no nearer to taking Cadiz. As you must have heard, after the fall of Badajoz, poor Marmont was heavily defeated outside Salamanca, and grievously wounded by a cannon ball. He brought his defeat upon himself by being too impetuous. Had he waited but another three days before giving battle, he would have had under his hand another fifteen thousand men that King Joseph was bringing up from Madrid. As things were, he came near to losing his whole army. It was only owing to the skill displayed by General Clausel, who took over after Marmont became a casualty, that a good part of the army was saved. But it received a terrible battering and, even with King Joseph's fifteen thousand, was in no condition to give battle again. Our latest information is that our people are still retiring, and milord Wellington advancing on Madrid.'

To Roger this was excellent news, but he naturally concealed his pleasure at hearing it, and simply said, 'Then things go really badly for us at both ends of Europe, and I know not in which army I would rather have to face

the future. But you must excuse me now. Having but just returned I have a number of things to see to.'

His several conversations had each lasted only a few minutes. Mary was standing where he had left her, and he took her across to another big building in which his room was situated. All he wished to do for the moment was to show her where it was, and make certain she could find it again. When he had done so, they walked back the way they had come and into the main block. There he led her up to the second floor and along to the room in which the Mess waiters had their quarters. Halting outside, he told her to go in, ask for Sergeant Loriel and tell him who she was. She would then be given supper, and when she had finished it she was to go to their room.

The next thing he had to do was to deal with the soldier servant, a man named Greuze, who had looked after him since he had rejoined Napoleon at Vilna. Walking back to his quarters, he found Greuze there, unpacking his valise and the panniers from Mary's horse, which had been brought up from the stables by his groom. Greuze was a lad of only seventeen, and Roger had selected him from a number of applicants, because he came from a respectable family, so kept himself clean, and was by no means robust. For the latter reason Roger did not want to send him back to normal duty, which would mean a much harder life for him; so, having returned the lad's greeting, he said:

'While I was away from Moscow, I acquired another servant, a Flemish youth named Hipé Abrail. He has worked as a valet in a good hostelry, so will look after my clothes better than you can.'

Seeing Greuze's face fall, he went on with a smile, 'But that is a private arrangement, and I am still entitled to a soldier servant, so I intend to keep you on. My new lad is having supper now. He will be over here in half an hour or so. When he comes in, you are to show him where you

352

keep your cleaning things, and tell him about the routine we normally follow. Then you can go to your quarters. After you have cleared up here, I'll not need you until tomorrow morning.'

Having established Mary in her new position in a way that he hoped would protect her from unpleasantness, he went back to the Mess and had a drink with Rapp. Soon afterwards they went in to supper and, as Roger had expected, he found himself the centre of interest. All his companions wanted to know about his journey and what St. Petersburg was like. Sitting over their wine, they continued to ply him with questions but, as soon as he decently could, by pleading fatigue, he got away.

In his room he found Mary, not in bed as he had expected, but curled up under a blanket on the straw palliasse that he had ordered to be brought. When he asked her why she had not made herself more comfortable, she said:

'I didn't dare undress and get into bed, in case that nice young servant of yours came back, or someone else came in.'

'You could have locked the door.'

She shook her now boyish head. 'No, darling. Servants don't lock themselves in their master's rooms. Anyone finding I had done that would have thought it very queer.'

'You're right,' he agreed. 'And I was stupid to suggest it. Bless you for starting off in your new role so conscientiously. How did you get on with Sergeant Loriel?'

'Very well. And with the others, too. They made me tell them about St. Petersburg and said I was a fool ever to have left it. But they were very pleasant to me, and think me lucky to be your servant. It's nice to know that you are so popular with the Mess orderlies.'

'Oh, that's only because I am civil to them, and many officers don't bother to be.'

'Nevertheless, it's going to be a big help to me. I'll reap the reflected benefit of their liking for you. Young Jean Greuze is nice, too. He comes from Pontoise, near Paris, and his father owns a little news sheet and sweet shop. He absolutely worships you for having taken him from the hard life of an ordinary soldier.'

'He's a good lad, but delicate and not up to the hard life of the rank and file. As an officer's servant, too, he gets more and better food than he would if with his regiment.'

'The food I was given for supper surprised me. There was a good choice, it was well cooked and there was plenty of everything. I'd gathered from you that the troops in Moscow were half-starving.'

'They were when they got here. Since then they have not done too badly, but supplies are getting short again and you must not take the fare that Sergeant Loriel gives his boys as a criterion. Mess servants are the lucky ones, they feed nearly as well as the officers. The men in the regiments have to make do on biscuits, cheese and stew with only a few bits of meat in it. But come, my love, we must get some sleep.'

The room was one of many hundred in the vast Palace which, before the coming of the French, had been occupied by Court officials and officers of the Imperial Guard; so it was well furnished in the heavy Russian style, and they were soon snuggled up in the big, four-poster bed. The thought of what Mary might have to face by being brought to Moscow as his servant had greatly worried Roger. But he dropped off to sleep with the comforting thought that things had gone much better than he had expected.

When the bugles sounded the réveille, they got up. He told Mary where she could fill the water cans at a washroom along the corridor, then they washed and dressed and crossed the square to have their breakfasts. Before

he left her he said that, as soon as she got back, she had better set to work polishing one of his pairs of field boots, so that when Greuze arrived he would find her busy.

On his return he found them both in his room, talking cheerfully and making the bed together. When they had finished he said, 'I am going out to make some purchases, and I wish you both to come with me.'

There were no longer shops in the city where one could buy things, but there was a strange market in the big square outside the Governor's Palace, where a part of the Imperial Guard was billeted. The vendors in the market were troops of many nations and camp-followers. When they needed money or drink or clothes, they brought pieces of their loot there and bartered them for whatever they wanted.

Many of them had small carts that they used as stalls, and Roger persuaded a Pole to part with his, which was a good, solid one in sound condition, for a tempting sum of money. When the man had emptied it of his things, Greuze placed himself between the shafts and pulled it along for Roger to put other purchases in.

Going from one stall to another, he bought high boots, sheepskin breeches, long fur coats and fur mittens for Mary and Greuze. His own clothes were of good, stout cloth, and he had a fine fur that he had bought the previous January in Stockholm, so he needed only a muff for himself when he bought muffs for them. His next purchase was two large fur carriage rugs and, after that, a good supply of flints, tinder and six dozen candles. The choice of goods at the food stalls was limited; there was little meat or game, but he was not looking for perishable goods. There was plenty of tea, so he bought several pounds quite cheaply, but a supply of sugar and half a stone of oatmeal cost him a lot of money. By chance, on one stall he saw some boxes of candied fruit, so he bought

them all and from another stall a dozen bottles of brandy. His final purchase, as an afterthought, was a block of salt. Except for the furs and the tea, he had had to pay from five to twenty times the normal price for the things he had bought, so he had spent the greater part of his money; but he had big arrears of pay on which he could draw and he knew that if he had waited until the afternoon, by which time he thought it as good as certain that it would be announced that the army was leaving Moscow, he would have had to pay three times as much.

Back at the Kremlin, his two servants carried all the things upstairs, then he said to them, 'You, Greuze, are to come with me and wheel the cart round to the stables. Then return here and give a hand to Hipé. I want the two of you to sew together the sides and one end of the two big fur carriage rugs, so that they will serve as a large sleeping bag.'

Ten minutes later he was talking to the Guards Sergeant-Major, who was in charge of the horses belonging to the Emperor's entourage. Producing all that remained of his gold, he pointed to the little cart and said, 'I want you to get me a small horse or, better still, a mule to draw that.'

The Sergeant-Major made a face. 'That won't be easy, sir. You know how terrible short we are of horses. The number we lost on the way here doesn't bear telling; and fodder being so short, a good third of the poor beasts that did get here have died from lack of it since.'

'I know, Joux,' Roger replied. 'But an animal I must have. Procure me a good one—a good one, mind—and there are thirty napoleons for you. If all else fails, commandeer a mule from the Italians.'

'You shall have your beast, Colonel,' the Sergeant-Major grinned. 'Leave it to me.'

In the A.D.C.s' Mess, Roger learned that the members of the conference the Emperor had called had wrangled

for three hours, but the meeting was now over and the decision he had anticipated had been taken. The army was to evacuate Moscow and winter in Smolensk.

Opinion on the wisdom of retreating was sharply divided. Several of the younger A.D.C.s were young nobles: ex-émigrés with famous names, whom the Emperor had taken on his staff for his own aggrandisement. They were all in favour of retreat. The Niemen, which formed the frontier, was some six hundred miles distant, and Smolensk was getting on for half-way to it; so, like Duroc, they argued that, being so much nearer Poland, it would be much easier both to keep open the lines of communication and keep the army supplied.

But the older A.D.C.s who had served through many campaigns, did not agree. In such conditions the army could not be expected to march more than fifteen miles a day. That meant that it would be the first week in November before it reached Smolensk. Just as the summer had proved exceptionally hot, so the autumn weather was unusually fine and sunny. But could it be expected to last? If the snow came early, it would slow down the speed of the march and, as the troops would have to sleep in the open, it would inflict terrible hardship upon them. A great part of Moscow was in ruins, but so was Smolensk, and it was a far smaller city, so was much less easy to defend. Even if the army was cut off and Moscow besieged, they could somehow hang out there. The hardened campaigners had tightened their belts before; up in the Alps, during the siege of Genoa, on the retreat from Acre to Egypt, and many other places. They could do so again, and stick it out until reinforcements reached them in the spring.

The midday meal over, everyone set about his preparations for departure. Roger had already made his, so had only to see the Paymaster and refill his money belt with gold. In the evening he went again to the stables.

Sergeant-Major Joux had got for him a sturdy mule. Having made 'a careful examination of the animal's hooves, Roger willingly paid over the sum he had promised.

Over supper he learned that the Emperor had decided to leave Mortier and his Young Guard in the city, to give the enemy the impression that he meant only to strengthen his line of communication with part of the main army, then return. The Young Guard was to follow a few days later.

On the morning of October 19th, after occupying Moscow for thirty-nine days, the Grand Army began its evacuation of the city.

But it was a very different army from that which had entered it after Borodino. Then the battalions had marched in, column after column, in impressive military formation. Now, it was one vast horde, in which troops were mingled with camp-followers. The men were determined to take their loot with them. Many of them were wearing women's furs, or had costly brocade curtains draped over them. There were hundreds upon hundreds of wagons, carts, carriages and hand barrows, in fact everything left in the city that had wheels. All of them were piled high with furniture, bronzes, pictures, china, carpets, clothes, cooking utensils, antiques, jewel-encrusted weapons and sacks of food. On the top of many of them were perched women, mostly Russian whores who, unlike the vivandières, were unused to foot-slogging. About a third of the carts and carriages were drawn by horses or large dogs. The rest were pulled and pushed by groups of men wearing the uniforms of many nations: French, Italian, Polish, Prussian, Czech, Hanoverian, Swiss, Hessian, Dutch, Westphalian, Croat, Wurtenbergs, Albanian with, here and there, groups of Russian prisoners.

Only the Old Guard marched out in good order, with bands playing and tricolours fluttering beneath the gilded Eagles.

Of the five hundred thousand men and women who had crossed the Niemen toward the end of June, fewer than one in five were destined to live to recross it in December.

CHAPTER XXIII

DEATH TAKES SOMETHING
ON ACCOUNT

On the advance from Kovno to Moscow, the Grand
Army had cut a great swathe through the country, leaving
not a thing to eat behind it and very little shelter. But
the swathe did not extend for much more than twenty
miles on either side of the highway, owing to the limited
distances that forays of horsemen could cover and be back
by night with the main force, secure from capture by the
Cossacks. Well aware of this, the Russians had refrained
from scorching the earth outside the limits within which
Napoleon's troops could commit their depredations.

The Emperor had therefore decided that, instead of
retreating by the way he had come, he would march
south-east to Kalouga, as that would enable the army to
march through unspoiled country, where there were still
inhabited towns and villages, hay-filled barns and, with
luck, a number of horses and cattle.

The thought of new territory to plunder greatly
cheered the men, but the Generals and Staff were not so
happy. They knew that Kutuzov's main army lay out on
that flank and, only the previous day, Murat's cavalry
had suffered a severe defeat in the neighbourhood of
Tarutino, which was not far off the route they were to
take. But, after five weeks of inactivity, everyone seemed
to have taken new heart at again being on the move.

Napoleon, riding his grey, wearing the plain uniform

of the Guides and his undecorated tricorne hat, rode between two battalions of the Guard, immediately followed by his staff. Behind them, under Duroc's quartermaster, came the headquarters' baggage train. In addition to its own wagons, a number of others had been commandeered to carry the trophies, loot collected by the staff and a big supply of food reserved for the entourage. A number of them had also secured small vehicles to transport their personal belongings. These followed the wagons with, among them, Mary on her mount and Greuze walking beside the mule.

At midday the Emperor, his people and the Guard halted for a picnic meal at the roadside, clearing the highway for the endless stream of mixed units to continue their march. As Roger watched them going by, he decided they were in better trim than he had judged them to be earlier that morning. Although, at a casual glance, they had the appearance of an incredible rabble, their officers had got them into some sort of order, so that different units were at least distinguishable and, if attacked, could swiftly be called on to leave temporarily the motley collection of vehicles carrying their loot, supplies and women, and get into fighting formations. In general, too, the health of the men appeared better than it had after their long march to Moscow and the terrible battle of Borodino. The majority of those whose wounds had not been too serious for them to stagger as far as the city had since recovered. While in Moscow, for the first few weeks they had enjoyed an abundance of food and, even recently, their rations had been reasonably adequate. Rest and relaxation had put new spirit into them. Many of the groups were singing as they marched and, as they passed the Emperor, they cheered him with something of their old enthusiasm.

The worst weakness of the army was its shortage of horses. Roger noted that in most cases artillery units had

had to leave behind their second-line ammunition limbers and, in many cases, the guns and first-line limbers were drawn by only four or two horses, instead of the normal six. A great part of the cavalry, too, was no longer mounted, but now sharing the lot of the foot-slogging infantry. However, as relays of remounts were constantly being sent up from Poland, at least the French cavalrymen could hope to be in the saddle again by the time they reached Smolensk.

On their first night out of Moscow, the miles-long column bivouacked at the roadside and had an opportunity to try out such arrangements as they had made to secure for themselves as much comfort as possible. The Emperor sent Roger and his other A.D.C.s to ride some way along the road and see how the men were faring. In the neighbourhood there were many woods of pine and larch, among which fuel could be collected, so the hundreds of bivouac fires blazed merrily, and the A.D.C.s were able to report that morale was good; also that nearly everywhere, in addition to the rations with which the troops had been issued, they had brought with them stocks of food of their own.

But early in the morning the news that the staff had feared came in. Strong Russian forces, possibly Kutuzov's main army, were advancing toward them, so the Emperor, being most averse to fighting a battle at that moment, sent orders to the head of the column that it should leave the road for Kalouga and turn off to Malo-Jaroslavitz. Nevertheless, many attacks by Cossacks had to be beaten off, and it was clear that they were not going to be allowed to continue their march in immunity.

Then, on the 25th, Kutuzov launched General Dokhturov's division against the centre of the marching column as it was passing through Malo-Jaroslavitz. The French were taken by surprise and the action very nearly proved fatal to the Emperor. Early that morning he had ridden

out, accompanied by some fifty officers, to make a personal reconnaissance. Suddenly a horde of Cossacks broke from a wood, yelling their war-cry, '*Hourra! Hourra!*', and came galloping toward the little cavalcade.

Napoleon had never lacked for courage. He drew his sword and his companions followed his example. Next moment the Cossacks were upon them. The French were outnumbered three to one. There ensued a wild mêlée. Several men on both sides were killed or wounded. Roger escaped being run through with a lance only by throwing himself violently sideways. As he did so, he slashed out with his sword and severed the Cossack's arm at the elbow. Rapp was less fortunate. A lance dealt him his twenty-third wound and he was thrown from his horse. The fight raged furiously; but only for a few minutes. The Hetman of the Cossacks sighted a convoy of wagons in the near distance. Having failed to recognise the Emperor and realise what a prize he was forgoing, he called his men off and led them toward the wagons, more eager for loot than slaughter. At that moment, having heard the shouts of the combatants, two squadrons of Chasseurs and a troop of the Cavalry of the Guard came charging up. They fell upon the Cossacks and routed them. But the battle was on. Dokhturov was attacking all along the line.

For several hours the units of the Grand Army in the area were in grave peril; then Eugene arrived with his Italians and was followed by Davout. By then Kutuzov had brought up his main forces and a general engagement took place. All day there was desperate fighting. The battle continued until long after dark, and it was not until close on midnight that the French succeeded in driving the Russians out of Malo-Jaroslavitz.

Frantic with anxiety, Roger went in search of Mary. At last he found her. She and young Greuze had taken refuge under their cart. Twice they had been charged

over. Only one Russian had spotted and attempted to kill them; but Greuze had brought up his musket and shot him dead at close quarters.

The Emperor was now faced with a question of paramount importance. Should he renew the battle next day and gamble everything on succeeding in breaking through to Kalouga—or should he abandon that route and take another?

It was known that General Tchitchagov had now brought up his army from the lower Danube and this reinforcement made the Russians much superior in numbers. On the morning of the 26th, Bessières went out on a reconnaissance. His report was pessimistic and decided the Emperor to retreat north on Mojaisk. The decision was fatal. It drove the last nail into the coffin of the Grand Army.

In taking it, Napoleon had supposed that, though he must abandon the advantage of marching through country that had not been scorched, he would be compensated by the depots of stores that he believed to have been established in every town and village through which the army had marched to Moscow. Throughout August, September and the first half of October, thousands of head of cattle, quintals of wheat and tons of flour had been despatched from Poland. By this time they should have been available at intervals all along the road, in readiness to supply the army should it be forced to retreat. But many of the depots had never been filled, and many more were empty. Millions of pounds' worth of supplies had simply vanished.

In many cases they had been carried off by raiding Cossacks before they reached their destination; but there had been a far more serious drain upon them. During the advance, the Grand Army had left in its wake tens of thousands of wounded and deserters. The wounded had had to be fed, and the deserters were determined not to

starve as long as their weapons could obtain for them food and liquor. As bands of them had made their way toward Poland, they had attacked the depots and carried off their contents. The Grand Army, still eighty thousand strong, and making up for the casualties it sustained by being joined by the troops who had guarded the lines of communication, must now retrace its steps along the scorched-earth swathe in which neither food nor fodder was to be found.

Until the last days of October, the weather remained sunny; but then the skies became overcast, a biting wind got up that swept across the plain and the first flurries of snow gave a warning of what was to come. At Mojaisk the head of the column debouched on to the road by which it had marched to Moscow, and turned west toward Poland. Forty miles further on, the army suffered the most terrible blow possible to its morale. It had to cross the battlefield of Borodino.

For miles round lay the evidence of the cost of the Emperor's insatiable ambition: the price that comrades had paid and that, at any time, each man of them might be called on himself to pay. In every direction, as far as the eye could see, the grassy slopes, furrowed by countless cannon balls, were dotted with thousands upon thousands of seven-week-old corpses of men and horses, and below the great redoubt lay a solid, tangled mass of them. Lacking legs, feet, arms or heads, with broken skulls or disembowelled, their shrunken lips drawn back in hideous grimaces, their eye sockets black, empty pits, clusters of white worms feeding on their rotting flesh, they lay there in the awesome stillness of death, beneath a dark and threatening sky.

Even the most hardened of the old 'moustaches' who had followed the young Napoleon in Italy and Egypt and later fought at Marengo, Wagram, Jena, Austerlitz, Eylau and Friedland, had never seen such appalling

365

destruction: so many smashed guns, overturned limbers, shattered wagons, abandoned muskets, swords, lances and pistols, or bloated horses, the ground beneath them dyed red with their blood. And the unburied humans were not alone in silently demanding vengeance for the cutting short of their lives. The rains had washed away the soil from the shallow graves in which the minority had been hastily interred. Among the litter of cuirasses, helmets, dolmans, *sabretaches,* saddlebags, knapsacks and entrenching tools, from the earth there stuck up solitary protesting arms, odd legs and grinning skulls.

The Grand Army passed on its way with bowed heads, heart-stricken, weeping and with many of the men vomiting. Soon afterwards the first snowflakes drifted down.

Death now began to stalk the endless, snake-like column. Horses rather than men were the first to be stricken, because, while no fresh supplies were obtainable for either, there were very few wagons containing fodder and this small quantity was reserved for the mounts of the senior officers. Before leaving Moscow the troops had scoured the city and brought with them all the livestock they could lay hands on: pigs, goats, tame rabbits and crates of geese, ducks and chickens; but these had now all been killed, cooked and eaten. A daily ration continued to be issued to all the men, although it had become a meagre one; and those who carried private supplies of food were now jealously hoarding them, so everyone was hungry. In consequence, whenever a horse staggered and, its knees giving way under it, slumped to the ground, a score of the nearest men fell upon it. With knives and bayonets, they hacked away the flesh before the body could become frozen by the fierce cold, and caught in their pannikins every drop of blood.

By the beginning of November there were sufficient biscuits left only to provide a small ration for the Guard, and horseflesh had become the staple diet of the army.

Berthier ordered all the cavalry that remained up to the van, so that no horse should die in the rear and remain uneaten. Through drinking horse-blood, the beards that had sprouted on the faces of the men were soon stained red.

Apart from brewing tea, it was not until they actually began to feel the pangs of hunger that Roger permitted any of the private supplies he had brought to be broached for himself, Mary and Greuze. Moreover, much as he disliked horseflesh, whenever he could secure a hunk of it, he made Mary stew it for their supper, in order that their stock of special food should last longer. For such grim meals he was now thankful that he had bought the big slab of salt, as it counteracted the unpleasant, sweetish flavour of the meat.

The temperature had dropped to five degrees below, and was dropping further every day. The wind howled over the flat, desolate countryside, searing any portion of exposed flesh like fire. The flurries of snow increased to storms and, as each ceased, the sky was blue-black, with more snow to come. The ground became one great sheet of white, with patches of snow-covered trees in the distance. At night the men sat on their knapsacks, crouching over their bivouac fires, worn-out and wretched; then slept either huddled in groups for mutual warmth, or sitting with their backs propped against the wheels of vehicles, for fear that if they lay down in the snow they would never wake up.

Owing to Roger's foresight, he and his two companions fared far better than the great majority. He had given his own sleeping bag to Greuze, and slept with Mary in the big one he had had made from the two fur carriage rugs. As a staff officer he still received a daily ration of cereal, a small portion of beef or pork, a potato and sometimes a carrot or other vegetable. The cereal he gave to the mule, in order to keep it alive as long as possible. The meat

and vegetables went into the pot when they had a stew of horseflesh. On other nights Mary made a porridge out of their oatmeal or the flour that was issued to the N.C.O.s and men in the Emperor's entourage, and they nibbled a small piece of preserved fruit or marzipan, slowly so as to prolong the pleasure it gave them.

Apparently assuming that the men of the Grand Army would as soon die fighting as wait to be killed by cold, and would, therefore, put up a desperate resistance, Kutuzov husbanded the lives of his own men by refraining from launching a full-scale attack. But every day and often at night the column was harassed by Cossacks; and, now that such horses of the Cavalry as remained were too weak to be spurred into more than an amble, and so could no longer charge, the raiders became ever more daring.

Men who had brought food of their own were now more than ever loath to share it with their comrades; so, to escape being begged for a trifle, or having to fight to keep what they had, many of them formed the habit of going off into the woods, where they lit small fires and cooked themselves a meal. But they did so at their peril. The snow muffled the sound of approaching hoofbeats; so even in broad daylight any man who was out of sight of the column was liable to be surprised and slain by the Cossacks before he could get back to it.

Head bowed against the piercing wind, the Emperor rode, or often walked. The weaker men had to rest more frequently than their comrades. This was daily causing the units to become more inextricably mixed, and discipline had broken down to a point where many of the commanding officers had given up trying to keep their men together. Instinctively, they collected round Napoleon, spontaneously forming a body-guard that, from lack of other occupation, helped to erect the headquarters' marquees every night and to collect fuel for

the fires. As there was no organised fighting, the A.D.C.s had no duties, so Roger rode up to join the staff only for a short while two or three times a day, and was able to spend the rest of the time with Mary and Greuze. Both of them were well nourished so were able to keep going as gamely as the stronger men; but young Greuze felt the cold so badly that his face was often blue with it and, although Mary kept her hands in her muff whenever she could, she suffered severely from chilblains.

Ever since the battle of Malo-Jaroslavitz, the army had left behind an increasingly-thick trail marking its passage. There were the skeletons of horses and, as more and more of them died, wagons, limbers and carts had to be abandoned. As the wounded and the less robust of the younger conscripts became weaker, more and more of them dropped behind to be butchered by the Cossacks. The men now had no use for women. As the number of carts that had to be pulled by hand increased, and the strength of the men declined, the Russian whores who had ridden out of Moscow were forced to walk. All but the most robust among them staggered on for a day or two then, fatigued beyond bearing, collapsed and died at the roadside. Even the toughest of the old soldiers found themselves unable to continue to carry the great loads of loot with which they had started out. Boxes, bundles and baskets were thrown down with bitter curses, and soon covered with the all-pervading snow.

At last Vyazma came in sight. The pace of the column quickened. Eagerly the men hurried forward, expecting to find food and shelter. But the town was a burnt-out wreck, the stores in it had been greatly depleted to maintain the garrison, and they were busily employed in sharing out what remained among themselves before joining in the great retreat.

The General commanding the garrison there had bad news for the Emperor. On the left General Tchitchagov

had chased Schwarzenberg right back to Brest-Litovsk, and on the right St. Cyr had been driven out of Polotsk; so both flanks of the main army were now unprotected.

To escape the danger, Napoleon pushed ahead with only the Guard and the Westphalians. Miloradovitch attacked the corps of Poniatowski and Davout as they hurried after the Emperor, leaving behind hundreds of stragglers who were too weak to increase their pace. Ney's corps, hotly pursued by Platoff's Cossacks, was the last to get through the town, and, only by setting fire to what remained of it, succeeded in temporarily checking their pursuers.

The first week of November took a terrible toll of the marchers. At times blizzards of blinding snow made it impossible to see more than a few feet ahead. The roads became icy. Scores of men slipped and broke ankles or legs and had to be left to perish where they fell. The troops were also afflicted by a strange sickness for which no-one could provide an explanation. Men who were still comparatively hearty would suddenly appear to become drunk, stagger on for a few paces, then pitch forward, dead, into the snow. On the 7th of the month fifty of Ney's men perished in this way.

By then the road ahead was clear of obstacles only for the vanguard. Increasingly, toward the rear, men had to step over, or go round, others who were dead or dying; abandoned carts and wagons had been left in the middle of the highway because everyone was husbanding his strength and no-one would give the effort needed to haul them off the road. Every step had to be watched by the marchers, who trudged on bent nearly double against the driving blizzards, otherwise they would have tripped over the endless variety of items, already half-hidden by the snow, that had been cast aside as too heavy to carry any longer.

Often at nights their blood was chilled by the eerie

howling of wolves, and sometimes in the daytime they caught a glimpse of their grey shapes in the distance, or slinking through the trees. As men were constantly dropping out of the column to die, the packs had any number of newly-dead bodies to feed on, so they never attacked those who were still capable of defending themselves. But it was a horrifying thought that, at times, men and women who had given up from exhaustion might be savaged and half-eaten while there was still life in them.

From Moscow they had started out with eight hundred Russian prisoners. Not one of them now remained alive. Gruesome stories were in circulation that many of them had been taken into the woods by their Czech and Polish guards, murdered and eaten.

The 7th November proved a most unlucky day for Roger and his companions. Mules are much more sensible animals than horses. If driven to it, a horse will go on until he drops dead. Not so a mule. When he feels that he has done as much as can be expected of him, he will stop and refuse to go another step, even if severely beaten. Greuze had started out leading the animal, but after the first fortnight of the march, the youth had become so pallid and hollow-eyed with fatigue that Roger feared he would soon die; so, to keep him going, he had told him to walk for two hours and every third sit in the cart and drive it. He was driving it when the mule came to an abrupt halt.

Scrambling down, he endeavoured to pull the animal forward by its bridle; but it refused to budge. Roger knew that it would be useless to whip it, and resorted to the classic way of making a mule move on. Taking his tinder box from his pocket, he struck a light and held it under the mule's tail. Greuze had seen perfectly well what his master was about to do but, probably bemused by the cold that racked his thin frame, he did not step away quickly enough from the mule's head. The little beast leapt for-

ward like a Newmarket winner from the starting post. One of the shafts of the cart struck Greuze a frightful blow in the chest, sending him sprawling, and the cart ran over him.

Galvanised into a final spurt of vigour, the mule covered thirty yards at a gallop, knocking down two marching men and scattering others. When a sergeant grabbed at its bridle, in an attempt to stop the terrified animal, it swerved and carried the cart over a steep bank. Roger, fearing to lose the stores on which their lives depended, rowelled his mount into a fast trot. On riding up the bank over which the mule had disappeared, he saw that the cart had overturned and that one of the poor beast's forelegs was sticking out from under it at an acute angle, so was obviously broken.

The episode had roused a number of the marchers from their semi-stupor. Half a dozen of them were already scrambling down the bank, intent on looting the cart and killing the mule. Drawing his pistol, Roger yelled at them that he would shoot the first man who laid a hand on either. Then, as they reclimbed the bank, panting, the breath from their exertions making little clouds of vapour in the frosty air, he picked on a stalwart corporal and ordered him to stand guard over the cart while he rode back to look to his injured servant.

He found Greuze lying at the roadside with his head in Mary's lap. The poor youth's breastbone had been broken, and his jaw had been fractured by one of the cartwheels which had bumped over it. He was bleeding profusely and it was obvious that, in the low state to which he had been reduced by cold and hardship, he had not long to live. Roger poured enough brandy down his throat to dull his pain; then, in spite of Mary's protests he insisted that they must leave him and get to the cart in order to salvage the things it contained.

When they reached it, they found that a group of gaunt,

bearded soldiers, grotesquely muffled up to the ears in the rags of blankets, saddle cloths and looted finery, had knocked out the corporal whom Roger had left in charge, shot the mule and had already started to flay it. Drawing his pistol again, he drove them off, then promised them shares in the animal if they obeyed him. All of them were weak from privation and lacked the courage to attack an officer who appeared to be still full of vigour; so, with chattering teeth, a big fellow who appeared to be their leader told the others that they had better have patience.

Fortunately the cart had overturned completely, and the contents were under it, so none of the soldiers had had the chance to steal anything during Roger's brief absence. Fearful that, when they saw the food, desperate craving might lead one of them to attempt to kill him, he made Mary, whom he had armed with his second pistol before they set out, remain mounted a few yards back and keep them covered. Then he told two of them to turn the cart right side up.

When they had done so, he rummaged among the things until he found two bottles that had held brandy, but had since been filled with melted snow. Emptying them of the half-frozen water, he had the big fellow open a vein in the mule's neck and drained off the blood into the bottles. He then cut a large hunk of meat from the saddle and told the men they were welcome to the rest of the beast.

While they fought ravenously over the carcass, he sorted out the stores they could take from those he must leave behind. The big sleeping bag was essential, and he strapped it under the saddle of his charger. They had used up most of the oatmeal, about a third of their tea, sugar, marzipan and preserved fruit and four of their bottles of brandy. By emptying the panniers hanging from Mary's saddle of all their spare clothes, they managed to cram into them all the provisions except the hunk

of mule flesh, which would soon be frozen by the intense cold. That, and the remains of the block of salt, Roger lashed to the pommel of his saddle. Drawing in an icy breath, he heaved himself up on his horse and told Mary that they must now hurry on in order to catch up with the headquarters' cavalcade.

But she would not hear of it. The liking she had formed for the gentle young Greuze and pity for him had determined her not to allow him to die alone. Roger protested that the temperature now being twelve degrees below zero, the youth must soon fall into a coma, so to remain with him would be pointless. But Mary only shook her muffled head and turned her mount in the opposite direction to that in which the column was slowly plodding. Annoyed though he was by her stubbornness, Roger had no alternative but to follow her.

When they reached Greuze he was still conscious; but he had already been robbed of his fur coat, muff and stout, sheepskin-lined boots. Mary wrapped his feet in a blanket that she took from under her saddle, and asked Roger to let her have their big sleeping bag to cover his body. But Roger refused, because he knew that it would be no kindness to prolong the lad's life and, had he been on his own, he would have covered him up to the chest with snow, so that he might the sooner become numb and oblivious to the fact that he was dying.

For over an hour Mary sat beside Greuze, holding his hand and endeavouring to comfort him. Now and then he opened his eyes and gave her a little, twisted smile; but gradually the gasps of his agonised breathing became less frequent, until his head rolled on one side and his grip on Mary's hand relaxed.

When she stood up, she was so cramped with cold that her legs would not support her. Roger had to shake and beat her to restore her circulation. For most of the time she had been crying and, as he helped her on to her

horse, he saw that the tears had frozen on her cheeks, already red and peeling from the biting wind.

As they set off again, he faced the fact that their future was now grimmer than ever. Over two hours had elapsed since the accident and, by this time, the Headquarters Staff was several miles ahead of them. Both their horses had lost so much flesh that their ribs could be plainly seen, and to force them into a pace which would enable them to catch up would almost certainly result in their dropping dead. It was a risk he dared not take; but it meant that they would no longer be able to draw their ration which, up to that time, had provided about half their frugal sustenance.

Alternately leading their horses and riding, two days later, on the 9th, after having been twenty-one days on the road, they at last reached Smolensk. To the immense relief of everyone, the news soon spread that there were plentiful stocks of food in the city. But the great multitude of shivering marchers, many of who were now suffering from frostbite, was so famished that the men would not wait for rations to be issued in an orderly manner.

The ravenous troops thrust aside the sentries who had been posted to guard the warehouses, broke down the doors and helped themselves to everything they could lay hands on. In this mêlée, great quantities of food were trampled underfoot and ruined. Much was also wasted as nourishment, owing to the shrunken stomachs of the men rejecting quantities such as they had been unused to for so long, so they sicked it up. Others gorged themselves to a point where they were racked with such frightful indigestion that they died from it.

The garrison in Smolensk was in good shape, as they had lived well on a number of the convoys coming up from Poland, instead of letting them go on to Moscow. They also made a valuable replacement of the casualties that had fallen on the way from the capital, greatly

strengthening the Grand Army's fighting power to resist further attacks by the Russians. After a few days with ample food and liquor and the shelter of the many buildings in the big city that had not been totally burned out, the scarecrows bundled in rags who had staggered or limped into it became different men. The Headquarters Staff and the Guards were quartered in the better mansions that remained undamaged, the remainder of the polyglot horde cheerfully set about making half-ruined buildings into snow- and wind-proof snuggeries, in which to spend the winter.

Then the terrible blow fell. The awful news came in that Vitebsk had been captured by the Russians. The supply route from Poland had been cut. If they remained in Smolensk for more than a few weeks, every man Jack of them would starve to death.

CHAPTER XXIV

THE GRIM REAPER GIVES
NO RESPITE

FORCED to take a new decision, the Emperor told his staff that he now intended that the army should winter in the undamaged towns behind the Dvina and Dnieper. With this in view, he sent Poniatowski's Poles and Junot's Westphalians ahead with the trophies, on the road to Krasnoi. On November 14th, with the Guard and all that remained of the cavalry, he followed in a carriage.

On reaching Smolensk, Roger had thankfully rejoined Napoleon's staff and, with Mary, had for a few days fed well. He had also succeeded in getting hold of enough oats for their horses to fill one pannier and, for themselves, half a side of frozen bacon. The other pannier held most of their remaining stores; the rest were distributed in their saddle-bags, pistol holsters and pockets.

Apart from unceasing harassing of outposts by the Cossacks, the Russians had for some days ceased attacking, so the three corps with the Emperor got away from Smolensk with few casualties. But Prince Eugene was less fortunate. When crossing the little river Vop, his corps had already suffered severely at the hands of Miloradovitch and now, as they followed Napoleon toward Krasnoi, it was again ferociously attacked.

Although Eugene's mother had been divorced by Napoleon, he had remained unshakeably loyal to his stepfather. As a boy of fifteen, the young General Bonaparte

of those days had taken him on the first victorious campaign in Italy, and he had since had many years' experience in commanding troops. Unlike the Emperor's troublesome, treacherous and futile brothers, who were incapable both of waging war and ruling, Eugene, as Viceroy of Italy, had shown himself to be a most capable administrator and an able General. Apart from the Imperial Guard, his Italians rivalled the Saxon corps—which had been trained by Bernadotte and had been largely responsible for the victory at Austerlitz—as the best-disciplined and most reliable troops in the Grand Army. Now in this present campaign Eugene was proving himself to be, with the exception of Davout and Ney, the equal of any of the Marshals.

By the afternoon of the day that Eugene left Smolensk, he realised that Miloradovitch's force was only the vanguard of the main Russian army, and that he was faced with impossible odds. Nevertheless he fought his way on. By the time he was half-way to Krasnoi, he had lost eight thousand of the twelve thousand men who had left Smolensk under him. To continue the battle for another day could only mean complete annihilation. He then decided to attempt to save the remainder of his men by resorting to a stratagem, although it meant risking being caught flank-on to the enemy, which would prevent him from even making a last stand effectively.

In the night, leaving his camp fires burning, he led his troops by a circuitous route round the enemy. He was challenged by a Russian sentry. The next hour might have seen his force cut to pieces, but he was saved by the quick wits of his Polish orderly, who at once rapped out, in faultless Russian:

'Quiet, you fool.'

The sentry then took Eugene's corps for another body of his own countrymen moving up to the front for a night attack, and let them pass.

378

The Emperor had reached Krasnoi on the 15th, and waited there for the main body of his army to join him. He then learned of the Russian advance that threatened to cut the road from Smolensk and divide the Grand Army in half, which would enable Kutuzov to defeat first one part, then the other. Temporarily regaining his old initiative, he at once directed the three corps he had with him to return along the road to Smolensk, and set out to free the way for Eugene, Davout and Ney.

He met the remnants of Eugene's corps, which had escaped the previous night; but Davout was still a day's march away, Ney had only just left Smolensk and both were desperately defending themselves in a pitched battle against Kutuzov's main army, which had by then come up.

Despite his greatly inferior forces, Napoleon decided that he must gamble everything to save the two corps separated from him, and hurried forward to attack. But, fortunately for him, the old 'fox of the north' preferred to save his men and let the devastating cold continue to destroy his enemies; so, rather than sacrifice further troops against Davout's fierce resistance, he let him get away.

Napoleon was now in a quandary. He had been saved from a battle that might have ended in the complete destruction of the Grand Army, and Ney was many miles distant. He could be rescued only by again challenging Kutuzov's eighty thousand Russians and defeating them. With great reluctance the Emperor decided that discretion was the better part of valour. Leaving Ney to his fate, he retired on Krasnoi.

There he realised that his plan for wintering in the towns behind the Dwina and Dnieper was no longer feasible. It had been only another pipe-dream. If the Grand Army was to be saved, a new plan had swiftly to be formed. His choice was to cross the Dnieper at Orcha,

join Schwarzenberg, by way of Minsk, and winter behind the Berezina.

During the campaign Ney had already surpassed himself, eclipsing even the brilliant feats of arms he had achieved in Austria, Prussia and during Masséna's retreat from Portugal. For having stormed the Great Redoubt at Borodino, the Emperor had recently made him Prince of Moscow. On leaving Smolensk, his corps had been reduced by having to leave behind six thousand wounded. As his men had hurried out of one side of the city, the Cossacks had come galloping in at the other, and had since never ceased to savage his rear battalions. Now, cut off from any hope of help, with exhausted troops, no cavalry and very few guns, he was called on to face the greatest challenge of his career.

He was beset by the whole Russian army, and it was rapidly closing in round him. Still fighting a heavy rearguard action, he battled his way toward Krasnoi; but, as he advanced, met with increasingly violent opposition. On his second day out of Smolensk, he launched an all-out attack, in a forlorn hope of breaking through. But it failed, and he realised that his last chance of rejoining the Emperor was gone.

The Russians were well aware that they had him in a trap, and orders were sent out that in no circumstances must he be killed, but taken prisoner, so that this most famous of all Napoleon's fighting Marshals could grace a triumph for the Czar in St. Petersburg. Miloradovitch, who greatly admired Ney, sent an officer to him under a flag of truce, to impress upon him that his position was hopeless. The Russian General even offered a temporary armistice in which he would personally conduct Ney on a tour of the Russian front, so that he could see for himself the tremendous odds that were arrayed against him, and promised that, if he would surrender, his men should receive the honours of war. Ney's reply was:

'A Marshal of the Empire never surrenders.'

On Napoleon's right, up in the north-west, there had been severe fighting along the Dwina ever since July. Wittgenstein had had the better of it, capturing Chasniki and Vitebsk and forcing Victor to fall back on Senno. To the south-east Tchitchagov now had under his command Tormasov's army as well as the one he had brought up from the Danube. He had easily beaten off a half-hearted attack by Schwarzenberg's Austrians, and had captured Minsk; thus frustrating Napoleon's latest plan of retiring on that city. The Emperor's situation between these two forces, and with Kutuzov's main army at no great distance from him, was, therefore, now very precarious.

Believing the bridge over the Berezina at Borisov was still guarded by the Polish General Dombrovski, he planned to cross that river instead of the Dnieper at Orcha, and ordered the pontoon bridges that had been assembled at the latter place to be destroyed. But on November 21st Tchitchagov arrived before Borisov and, faced by heavy odds, Dombrovski abandoned the town.

While retreating, Dombrovski ran into Oudinot's corps, by then reduced to eight thousand men. On hearing that the all-important bridge had been given up, the Marshal was furious and, in spite of the odds against him, hurried forward to attack Tchitchagov. However, the Russian had become obsessed with the idea of the glory that would be his if only he could capture Napoleon; so he had marched off at a furious pace toward Orcha and, in his hurry, neglected to order the bridge to be destroyed.

This stroke of good fortune enabled Oudinot to save the line of retreat. In addition, Tchitchagov had set off at such a speed that his baggage train was far in his rear, so Oudinot captured it and was able to feed his hungry men and horses well for several days.

Meanwhile, the Emperor had reached Orcha and everyone at the headquarters there had accepted as inevitable

that Ney's corps must have succumbed and that the Marshal was either dead or on his way to St. Petersburg as a prisoner. Napoleon constantly reproached himself for having abandoned his old friend, and could not be consoled for his loss, exclaiming from time to time, 'I can never replace him! He was the bravest of the brave!'

But on November 20th, to everybody's amazement, Ney appeared out of the blizzard, leading nine hundred men—all that remained of the eight thousand who had left Smolensk with him.

In the two days of gruelling conflict that had followed his leaving the city, his already sadly-depleted corps had been reduced to three thousand five hundred men. Realising the impossibility of breaking through the eighty thousand Russians who barred his way to Krasnoi, he had assembled his senior officers at night, and said to them;

'*Messieurs*. There is only one course open to us. We must do a right-about turn, strike north and find a place where we can get across the Dnieper.'

They had all protested that it could not conceivably be done. There were no roads. Such an attempt meant condemning his whole force to die in the wastes of snow.

'Very well, *Messieurs*,' he had replied, 'if you will not accompany me, I shall set off on my own.'

Invigorated by his indomitable courage, they agreed to his apparently crazy plan. The camp fires were left burning. Everything on wheels was abandoned: wagons, cartloads of loot, even such guns as remained to them. They then marched north into the illimitable forests.

In the morning, when the Russians realised that Ney's battered corps had made off during the night, Platoff's Cossacks and Miloradovitch's regular cavalry followed in hot pursuit. Day after day Ney and his men fought them off until, at last, they reached the Dnieper. The broad river was frozen over, but only lightly. Hundreds of officers and men crashed through the treacherous ice and

perished in the icy water. On the far bank, when they headed left, the survivors were again harassed night and day by Russian horsemen. As often as they could they kept to the woods, but every few miles they had to cross open spaces. At such times they formed square and continued to repel their enemies while still marching.

The most determined attack of all came when they were within a few miles of Orcha. It seemed that they were fated to be completely wiped out; but a Polish officer, mounted on one of the very few horses that they had got across the river, managed to break through the Russians and reach the town.

As he rode into it, shouting that Ney was coming but needed immediate help, the weary, starving troops in the streets were suddenly galvanised into activity. That Ney had fought his way through seemed impossible to believe, but they grabbed up their weapons and ran from the town to his assistance, cheering like madmen. Eugene and a handful of horsemen were the first to reach the nine hundred haggard men who, a few months before, had been a twenty-thousand-strong Army Corps. The remnant was not the full strength of a single battalion, and there was scarcely a man among them that was not wounded; but the epic feat that these brave fellows had performed put new heart into the despairing army.

Only the day before, in his distress Napoleon had exclaimed, 'In the Tuileries I have millions in gold. I would have given it all to save Ney.' Now the Emperor of the French threw his arms about Marshal Ney, Duke of Elchingen, Prince of Moscow, Bravest of the Brave, and burst into tears of happiness on his strong shoulder.

On the day following Ney's return, the Grand Army left Orcha, and headed for Borisov. For the first few days the weather improved, but a rise in temperature brought new afflictions. The ice on the roads turned to slush, water seeped into the boots of the many men whose foot-

wear was worn out, and the driving sleet created greater distress than the snow, because it soaked into clothes and, when the temperature fell at night, they froze on the men's bodies. But the thaw was only temporary. On the third day intense cold again made iron red-hot to the touch and inflicted frostbite on the unwary. By then the supplies they had obtained in Orcha were nearly exhausted. Famine again stalked the miles-long, slowly-moving column.

Alternately the wind howled like a hundred banshees, tugging at the wraps of the marchers and blowing little puffs of newly-fallen snow from their feet with every step they took, or the myriad of big, white flakes fell steadily in utter silence. No-one uttered an unnecessary word, or made an effort of any kind that was not essential to keeping alive and on the move. It was now mostly the younger conscripts who had joined the column from the garrisons along the route who fell out and died. But now and then one of the older soldiers, who had marched all the way from Moscow and for forty days and nights endured almost unbelievable suffering, could stand it no longer, put his musket beneath his chin, pulled the trigger and so committed suicide.

The Emperor and his staff were about half-way to Borisov when ill-fortune again struck at Roger. While on the march, he now rarely left Mary's side, except to ride forward each afternoon to draw his miserable ration and to pick up from Rapp such news as had come in.

On this occasion the early winter darkness was already falling when he dropped back to rejoin Mary; but she was not riding as usual among the headquarters baggage wagons, so must have fallen out, for some reason. Suddenly the hush of the gently-falling snow was broken by the sound of distant shouting, followed by a shot. Spurring his horse into an amble, he rode a hundred yards in that direction then, through the drifting flakes, glimpsed

a number of men fighting. By then the units had become so mixed up that a cluster of Prussians were marching not far behind the headquarters wagons. A minute later he realised that Mary was among them, and the centre of the commotion.

Thrusting forward on his mount, he took in the scene. Three days earlier they had fed their horses the last of the oats he had managed to get hold of in Smolensk. Since then they had had only a few vegetables and some frozen thistles that he had found and cut for them. From lack of fodder, Mary's horse had become very weak. Although she led it for most of the time, it had now collapsed and lay dead in the road.

Like a flock of vultures, half a dozen Prussians had fallen upon it to get themselves a meal. Not content with that, they were pillaging the panniers of the priceless stores. Mary had evidently made a gallant attempt to stop them, and had shot one of the would-be robbers with her pistol. But another of the brutes had knocked her down.

Berserk with fury, Roger whipped out his sword, rowelled his horse and charged the group. Before they realised what was happening, his slashing blade struck one of the men from behind, slicing half through his neck, then its point pierced the breast of another. The remaining four, maddened with rage at the thought that they were about to be deprived of their feast, instantly attacked him.

Fortunately for Roger, the eagerness of all of them to grab as much as they could of the spoil before their companions got it had led to their throwing down their muskets; but, flinging themselves at Roger, they strove to drag him from his horse.

During the next few minutes it was touch and go whether he would succeed in driving them off or if they would pull him to the ground and kill him. He was able to keep in his saddle only because each of his legs had

been seized by men on either side of him, and neither was strong enough to tug him away from the other. In an attempt to free himself, he urged his horse forward by digging his knees into its flanks, but a third man had grabbed the animal's bridle. Instead of responding normally to the jab of Roger's knees, it reared, almost lifting off his feet the man who grasped its bridle.

The fourth man had picked up his musket and was raising it to shoot Roger. Swiftly he lunged over the shoulder of the man who was hauling on his left foot. The stroke took the would-be murderer in the mouth. His eyes bulged. His mouth, full of shattered teeth, gaped wide but, choked by his own blood, only a horrid gurgle came from it. Reeling back, he staggered a few steps and fell, a gush of his blood turning the snow beside his head crimson.

As Roger lunged, he yelled '*A moi! A moi!*', praying that some French soldiers would hear his cry for help and come to his rescue. But only Prussians—notorious for their excesses and the most brutal of all the troops forming the Grand Army—were within earshot. Most of them, their heads bowed, their ears muffled and their brains numbed by cold and misery, shuffled on. The few who heard him turned to stare for a moment and, no doubt feeling too weak to risk themselves in a fight, resumed their monotonous bid for life by forcing themselves to keep on putting one foot in front of the other.

Only seconds had elapsed after Roger had slain the man with the musket. With his left hand he pulled his pistol from his sash. Straightening his arm, he aimed at the man who was holding his horse's head. It flashed and there was a loud report. The Prussian's forehead was smashed in. The top of his skull lifted. Blood and brains spurted from it, his knees gave and he fell backwards in the snow.

Again Roger drove his knees with all his strength into

386

his charger. Freed from restraint, it now trotted forward, dragging with it Roger's two remaining assailants who were still clinging to his legs. Before it had covered twenty yards he had brought the barrel of his pistol cracking down on one man's head and the hilt of his sword on that of the other. As their grip gave and they fell away, he pulled hard on his mount's reins, so that the animal reared, turned and came down facing in the opposite direction. Within a minute he covered the short distance back to Mary. She was lying face down in the middle of the road near her dead horse.

His mind was in a whirl of agony. Was she dead or only injured? And, if injured, how badly? Would she be able to continue on their terrible march or, in a day or two, collapse and die by the roadside?

From the day she had attacked the *guarda* with her parasol outside the British Legation in Lisbon and enabled him to escape into it, he had known that she was a girl with courage; but, until they had made this ghastly trek together, he had not realised how steadfast and splendid that courage was. All through the exhausting days of alternate riding and foot-slogging in bitter winds or blinding blizzards, and nights when every limb ached and it was agony to expose hands or face to the blistering cold, she had shown extraordinary fortitude. Not once had she complained of the overwhelming weariness that everyone felt during the last hours of a day's march, or the pain of twisting stomach muscles that, at times, they had had to endure before giving in to the temptation to stave off their hunger with some of their reserve of special supplies. Only the fact that she had been in excellent health when they left Moscow, and the occasional titbits with which he had been able to supplement her miserable rations, could have kept so small and frail a body alive for weeks on end in the terrible rigours of a temperature that had sometimes fallen as low as twenty-five degrees below

zero. So he knew that her sufferings must have been worse than his; yet she had never faltered in her belief that he would bring her safely through their ghastly ordeal.

Her companionship on the seemingly endless days of tramping along the icy, snowbound roads, and during the frustrating halts when, somewhere ahead, a small bridge had broken down, or for some other reason they had had to stay stamping their feet and flogging themselves with their arms because the column had become snarled up, had been a constant tonic to him. Determinedly she had insisted on maintaining her role as his servant, cooked their scanty meals and, after Greuze had died, rubbed down his mount as well as her own. Time and again she had brightened the days by her cheerful chatter, not only for him and young Greuze, but also for the other officers-servants.

Then at nights they had been pressed body to body in their big sleeping bag. When they had not been too drained of energy to kiss and fondle each other, she had been sweetness itself. On other nights, when the sky was clear and the wind had dropped, side by side they had gazed up at the myriad of stars in the frosty sky, while they talked of things that had happened to them in the past.

These weeks of shared dangers and difficulties had brought about an intimacy between them that is often not achieved by couples who have been married for many years. He loved her little body and merry, piquant face, but he loved far more her sterling worth, her active, inquiring mind and her unfailing gaiety. The thought of losing her made tears start to his eyes. He could not bear it. He would rather have died himself.

The second he came up to her, he threw himself off his horse, thrust his arm through the bridle and knelt down, his eyes searching her face in terror that it would confirm his worst fears. One of the Prussians had hit her,

probably with the butt of a musket. There was a big bruise on her forehead above her left eye and, although she was unconscious, that eye was open, bulging and bleeding.

Round about were scattered in their blood the four Prussians he had killed, the one Mary had shot and the two whose skulls he had fractured. The rest had passed on. For about fifty yards the road was empty. Approaching on it was the remnant of a battalion of the Guard. Thrusting a hand under Mary's furs, he felt her heart and gave a great sigh of relief. It was still beating, and strongly.

As the officer leading the Guards came up, Roger called to him, 'Be good enough to tell one of your men to hold my horse. I've trouble here that I can't handle by myself, but I'll not detain you long.'

With an eager eye on Mary's dead mount, the officer willingly obliged and halted his squad of men, while those of other companies tramped past them. Quickly Roger got out from one of his saddle-bags the small first-aid kit he carried in it. Again kneeling he swabbed Mary's injury with disinfectant lotion. The pain brought her to her senses and she began to moan fretfully. Covering her eye with a piece of wadding, he put a bandage round her head, then got out his flask of brandy and made her drink as much as he could get her to swallow.

Like ghosts the guards stood round, hollow-cheeked and sunken-eyed, watching him and already savouring in their minds the good supper they could make of the flesh of the dead horse; but Roger knew that they were still too well disciplined to attack him. The animal lay on its side, one pannier hidden beneath it, the other, exposed, had been nearly emptied by the Prussians. Having opened his furs so that the officer could see his A.D.C. sash, Roger said to him :

'Tell some of your men to roll the horse over, then get those panniers across the withers of my charger. Is there

any chance of my wounded servant being given a lift in one of your wagons?'

The officer shook his head. 'There's no hope of that, Colonel. We've had to abandon more than half of them already, and those that remain to us are now drawn by only two horses apiece. Even the weight of another sack of biscuits could prove too much for a pair of the poor beasts to draw for long. If we'd given lifts to one-tenth of the wounded we've passed, all our supplies would have had to be left with them scores of miles back, and the lot of us would have died of starvation by now.'

It was the reply Roger had expected. With a shrug he said, 'I'm fond of the lad and would like to save him. We'll get him up on to the saddle of my charger, and secure him there. Your men can then set about flaying the carcass.'

Without waiting for an order from their officer, the listening men readily freed the panniers and lifted them on to Roger's horse. Into the nearly empty one he stuffed the fur sleeping bag. Then, having hoisted Mary, who had again become unconscious, on to the saddle, they tied a cord that was attached to both her ankles under the horse's belly and another, tied to her wrists, under its neck; so that she could not fall off. Immediately the men had done as Roger asked, slobbering ravenously they attacked the dead horse with bayonets and hands, tearing strips of meat off the back, haunches and belly until, within a few minutes, it was reduced to a bloody skeleton.

Roger had already taken the reins of his charger and joined the ragged stream of men who were blindly trudging forward. Darkness had now fallen. Many of the marchers were lighting little fires at the roadside to cook bits of horsemeat they had managed to get hold of during the past few days; others, who had nothing to cook, were still doggedly tramping on, in the hope that they would reach some village that had not yet been stripped

as clean as an empty iron cauldron of everything edible.

That, too, was Roger's hope. From time to time he glanced back to make sure that Mary was still securely in the saddle, and saw how her bandaged head swayed from side to side with the horse's motion, her face brushing its mane. The jerking movement must, he knew, be very bad for a head wound; but he dared not stop until he reached some place where she would be under shelter and he could tend her.

When he had walked for something over a mile, not far off the road he saw a ruined farmstead. Light coming through gaps in the shattered wooden walls showed that it was occupied. Every night any such protection from the cutting wind was always eagerly seized upon and, at times, groups of soldiers of different nations fought for such meagre shelter. He thought it certain that he would find the place crowded to suffocation, but left the road to investigate.

As he approached, he was challenged by a sentry. In reply he called out, 'I have a wounded man here. I pray you, in God's name, let me take him inside.'

'No room,' the man called back gruffly. 'Be on your way, soldier.'

'I beg you, think again,' Roger pleaded. 'I've tea and sugar with me, so can pay for my lodging.'

At that the man told him to wait a minute, then went into the house and returned with another man who proved to be a young French Lieutenant. After a brief conversation he agreed to let Roger join the eight men who were all that were left of his platoon. Between them they untied Mary and the Lieutenant and the sentry carried her inside. Roger remained with his horse. It was irreplaceable and, without it, he knew that he would never be able to get Mary out of Russia; so it was essential to give it all the care that was possible.

The moon was coming up and the light reflected from

the snow made it almost as light as day. Leading the horse round to the back of the farmhouse, he saw that the stabling had been burned down; but he found a large woodshed that still had about a third of its roof left. He was naturally loath to leave his mount, in case it was stolen in the night; but it was still uncertain whether Mary would live or die, so the first consideration was to be with her.

When he had tied up the horse, he gave it a drink from a bottle containing melted snow that he kept hung from his saddle, then he fished about in the still-full pannier until he came upon a canvas bag nearly full of crushed army biscuits, upon which he had fed the horses when no fodder or cereal were available. In two journeys, he then carried his saddle-bags, the panniers and the big sleeping bag into the only room in the house which still had a roof.

The soldiers had made Mary as comfortable as possible in a corner on some empty corn sacks that had been left there, and were now huddled round a fire on which an evil-smelling stew was simmering. Roger learned that they belonged to a regiment from Dijon; hardy fellows whose homes were in the Jura mountains. They liked and respected their young officer, so had agreed to remain together under his leadership, although they now treated him as one of themselves.

Trembling with anxiety, Roger knelt down beside Mary. As her uninjured eye was open, he saw that she had come round, but she was breathing in little, short gasps, and when he laid his hand on her forehead he found it to be burning. In a whisper, she said:

'I . . . I killed one. I shot him. Then . . . then another of them . . . struck me down.'

'I know . . .' He was just about to add 'darling', but checked himself in time, and substituted, 'Hipé. Yes, I know. You were splendid.'

'My eye hurts,' she murmured. 'Oh, it hurts terribly.'

Rummaging in one of his saddle-bags, Roger produced a small pot of opium ointment that he had carried all the way from St. Petersburg. Removing the bandage, he gently massaged some of the ointment on to the big bruise on Mary's forehead and all round the injured eye. The eye was a terrible sight, and he feared she would never see with it again. Having replaced the bandage, he got her into their sleeping bag and said :

'You must try to sleep, Hipé. Go to sleep if you possibly can. I know your eye must be very painful, but you have escaped any other injury and you'll soon get back your strength. You're quite safe here.'

She gave a slight nod, and obediently closed her good eye.

He now had a chance to find out what had been stolen from the panniers and, with his back turned to the soldiers, went through them. The remainder of the vegetables that he had hoarded for the horses was gone, so were a small bag of flour and a piece of salt pork that he had been given for rations, one of his cones of sugar and the last of the preserved fruit. There remained three packets of tea, two cones of sugar, the marzipan which they had hardly touched, most of the side of bacon that he had got hold of in Smolensk and six potatoes. They had used up six bottles of the brandy and two had been smashed when the horse had fallen on the pannier; but two remained unbroken and he had two more in his pistol holsters. There was also the bottle of blood that he had taken from the mule. Keeping out one packet of tea and about a quarter of a pound of sugar to give to the soldiers, he packed the rest of the things back into the panniers.

The Lieutenant and his men invited Roger to share in their stew and afterwards talked to him for a while in low voices, while the wind whistled outside; and, presently a wolf began to howl dismally. For a moment Roger feared

393

it would attack his horse, but reassured himself with the thought that there must be the dead bodies of plenty of humans within the pack's range.

The Dijon men spoke bitterly of their sufferings during the past seven weeks; but they were still hypnotised by the personality of Napoleon and, apparently, it did not occur to them to blame him. Roger told them some stories about the Emperor and his brilliant Court, then they all settled down for the night.

Early in the morning they roused up, ate a frugal meal from supplies they had obtained while in Orcha, then made ready to set out again on their terrible journey. By seven o'clock, although it was still dark, they wished Roger and his wounded servant well, and went on their way.

In the early part of the night Mary had become delirious, but latter dropped asleep. Now she was again delirious and evidently in a high fever. For her to be moved that day was clearly out of the question. Roger bathed her eye, massaged some more of the opium ointment into the flesh round it, and put a cold compress round her head. Then he went out to see to his horse.

As daylight began to filter through the big hole in the roof of the woodshed, he was able to take stock of its contents. A big pile of logs, sufficient to last for the rest of the winter, filled one end of it. He was already deeply concerned about how he and Mary could remain at the farm in safety for at least two days. It was certain that another group of men would seek shelter there for the coming night, and they might not prove friendly as had the men from Dijon. Even more to be dreaded was the following day, when the last of the Grand Army would have passed and the pursuing Cossacks enter the area. Somehow he had to hide his horse and stores before nightfall; and, the day after, Mary and himself as well.

It then occurred to him that the logs might serve his purpose. Soon, he was hard at work carrying them from

the end of the shed where they were stacked to build a four-foot-thick wall across the other end, leaving a good space behind it in which he could conceal the horse and, later, also Mary and himself.

Three times during the morning he went in to see how Mary was, and found her much the same. For the rest of the time he laboured on the logs and, half-way through his task, he met with a most welcome surprise. The owner of the farm had evidently had the same idea of using his stack of logs to conceal a cavity. Behind the pile, Roger found a space and, in it, two bales of hay and a sack of oats. There was enough fodder there to last for a fortnight, with care. At midday he was happily able to give his charger a luxury meal.

By this time his wall of logs was completed and the horse stalled, so he was able to return to and remain with Mary. She was still in a fever, but conscious. As he bent over her, she asked in a low voice :

'My eye, Roger. Will it recover its sight ?'

He had not the heart to tell her that he doubted it, so he said, 'It is impossible to say as yet. We can only hope so.' Then, as there was no-one else present he was able to kiss her gently, hold her hand and use endearments as he talked to her; but he would not let her tire herself by talking much.

The embers of the fire the soldiers had made were still glowing, so he put more fuel on them and some of the bacon to boil in an iron pot that he had found in the burnt-out stable. Knowing that Mary would not be able to get down anything solid, he poured half the bottle of mule's blood into another bottle, filled them both up with brandy and fed her some of the mixture, a few sips at a time.

To his great relief, in the afternoon Mary's fever abated and she slept; so, for a long time, he sat looking out through a rent in the wall at the marchers on the road,

which was no more than fifty yards distant. For once it was not snowing and the light was good enough for him to see the endless stream of men clearly.

Now they looked much more like a whole nation of gipsies on the move than an army. When they had had to abandon most of their loot, many of them had kept richly-embroidered silk and satin robes which they had intended to take home to their wives and sweethearts, and now wore them round their shoulders for extra warmth. Many wore furs that were either too large and trailed along the ground, or too small. Others wore sheepskin kaftans or the padded jackets of peasants. Under this strange assortment of garments it was no longer possible to distinguish infantry from dismounted cavalry or gunners from sappers, let alone tell whether individual men came from the sunny shores of the Mediterranean, the rugged cantons of the Alps, the forests of the upper Rhine or the flat, windy plains of Poland.

Here and there a group of them had harnessed themselves to a gun or limber and were pulling it with the aid of a single horse. Now and then an officer passed, still mounted on an apology for a charger, consisting of little more than skin and bone. Hands buried deep in their pockets or muffs, and heads thrust forward at an unnatural angle, the marchers tramped soundlessly onward through the last fall of snow. To conserve their strength they looked neither to right nor left, and maintained complete silence, not uttering so much as a word to their companions. Under fur hats or shapeless busbies, their faces were swathed in wraps of wool, cloth or silk. Occasionally Roger caught a glimpse of long noses sticking out from pinched features above matted beards. They had been reduced to from three-quarters to half their normal weight and were little more than living skeletons. Many of them had bandaged heads, arms in slings or were limping

along, supported by sticks or crutches. Only the inherent urge to survive kept them moving.

Yet even that could not impel many of them on indefinitely. Every quarter of an hour or so one of them would stumble and fall down in the snow, never to rise again, or just give up and sit down at the roadside on his knapsack, waiting for death to end his misery. Half a dozen times Roger saw a man halt, drop his musket, unfasten the bandolier carrying his ammunition and, with a sobbing curse, throw that down beside it. These arms and other objects that the men no longer had the strength to carry constantly added to the litter on the road. Along it, every fifty yards or so, there were mounds of snow covering the dead of yesterday or of the day before. And he knew that the road was like that for the whole of the four hundred and fifty miles back to Moscow.

In mid-afternoon it began to snow again. Soon the heads and shoulders of the slowly-moving figures on the road were powdered with it. Then the fall increased to a blizzard and they were hidden from view. Suddenly apprehensive that the big, driven flakes would not provide a permanent and sufficiently thick curtain to conceal the farmhouse from the road, and that a group of men might seek refuge there, Roger hastily began to make preparations against that possibility.

First he took the panniers and saddle-bags out to the woodshed, then he carried Mary there. In his wall of logs he had left a hole low down, large enough to wriggle her through, and he settled her behind it with the saddle-bags beside her, and the panniers for a pillow. He then watered and fed his horse, and fed Mary for the third time on the warmed-up mixture of mule's blood and brandy. It had been his intention to remain there, but he feared that to have got into the sleeping bag with her would have prevented her from sleeping. After sitting with her for an hour, he became so cold that he was taken

with bouts of shivering and his teeth began to chatter. Having decided that he must return to the fire that he had left burning in the farmhouse, he told Mary why he was leaving her and promised to return once or twice during the night to see that she was all right.

It then occurred to him that if a group of men came to the farm and brought a horse with them, his own horse might neigh and give away the hiding place, so he tied a strip of sacking round his horse's muzzle. After crawling out through the hole, he camouflaged it with some loose logs and more sacking that he had left there for the purpose, then hurried into the house.

He had let the fire there die down, as he had not wanted the light from it to attract possibly unwelcome visitors; but he felt that he must now take that risk, for he judged that the temperature was in the neighbourhood of twenty below and, with no sleeping bag, he feared he might otherwise freeze to death in the night.

Having made up the fire and warmed his chapped hands at it, he pounded up some of the oats he had found in the woodshed and cooked himself a meal of porridge, washing it down with a swig of brandy. Then, for a long time, he sat over the fire wondering for how long he would be able to keep Mary and himself alive. When it became dark outside, he decided to try to get some sleep under the sacking on which Mary had lain while in the house; but first went out to see her. The weather had worsened and on his way to the woodshed he was almost blown off his feet by the driving snow that was piling up in a drift against one side of it. He was thankful to find that Mary was asleep, so remained in the shed for only a few minutes, then fought his way back to his fireside.

He was still arranging the sacking when he caught the sound of voices. The door of the room was hanging on one hinge. A great hand forced it back, and an enormously fat man pushed his way in. Roger judged that before this

human barrel started on the march he must have weighed at least twenty stone, and would still turn the scale at fifteen. The man's features were hardly distinguishable in the firelight, as his heavy eyebrows and beard were so thickly rimed by the frost; but his face was round and looked as if it would normally be cheerful. Stamping his feet to shake the snow off his wraps, he addressed Roger politely in Italian:

'*Signor*, for the past three hours, my companions and I have been lost and walking round this accursed white wilderness in circles. I know it, for we have passed this place before. Can you tell me, please, where is the road?'

Roger smiled and replied in the same language, 'It is no more than fifty yards in front of this building.'

The fat man considered for a moment, his eyes on the fire. Then he said, 'That is good, but all the same I think I and my men will stay here for the night. I am Sergeant Giuseppe Balderino, of the Second Mantua Regiment.'

Giving a nod of agreement, Roger replied, 'You are welcome, Sergeant.' Then he put into operation a plan that he had formed to win the goodwill of any soldiers who might arrive and take the place over, by adding, 'I am in the fortunate situation of being able to offer you a meal.'

Balderino's dark eyebrows shot up, 'But, *Signor*, this is most unexpected, most generous. You are a Prince. My men and I are your servants.' Then he turned and shouted through the half-open doorway, 'Come in! Come in! The good St. Anthony of Padua has led us here. Be not deceived by the looks of this place. In reality it is a palace. We are invited to dine here, and our host can be no lesser person than the magician Cagliostro, for he conjured up food in a land where there is none.'

Roger had realised that his single horse could not possibly carry Mary, the sack of oats, a bale of hay and all

their other things, so he had decided to give half the sack of oats to any soldiers who might come to the farm.

The Italians stumbled in. They were grateful and garrulous, politely shaking Roger by the hand before crowding round the fire to thaw out their clothes, which were frozen stiff. With them they had some onions, a piece of pork and four pig's trotters. Adding these to the pounded oats they made a savoury stew that they sucked down with delight, followed by much belching.

Not long after they had all made themselves as comfortable as they could for the night, they were roused in a most unwelcome manner. A number of men emerged out of the darkness and endeavoured to force their way in. The Italians believed the would-be intruders to be Montenegrins, but their fierce war cries gave no certain indication of their nationality.

Roger quietly slipped out of the back door to defend Mary should any of the menacing newcomers go round to the woodshed. He found her still asleep, and she did not even wake when several shots were fired. There followed a silence that lasted for a good five minutes. Gathering from it that the attackers had been driven off, Roger returned to the room and found that the Italians were settling down again. Sergeant Balderino chaffed him for his lack of courage, but he took no umbrage, being only too glad that Mary's safety had not been imperilled, and replied with a laugh that his guests owed him protection for having given them hospitality.

The only other disturbance during the night was the terrible hacking cough of one of the men named Carlo. Towards morning it ceased and, when the others roused, he was found to be dead. After carrying his body out, they made breakfast, which Roger shared with them, off some more of his oats; then, on departing, with the optimism of their carefree natures, invited him to come to see them in Mantua when the war was over.

Only too well Roger realised how fortunate he had been in the two groups of men who had shared the farmhouse with him during the past two nights; for, had either of them been Germans, their inbred brutality being so stimulated by their hatred for the French, they might well have killed him, and Czechs, Albanians or Poles could also have proved hostile and dangerous. For the night to come the chances were against his luck continuing, so he was hoping that Mary might have recovered sufficiently to take the road again with him that day.

When he went out to her he found that she had had a good night and was much better. Her eye still pained her badly, but when he had redressed it she said she felt well enough to get up. However, when she did, had crawled out from her hiding place and started to walk, she was very unsteady on her legs, so Roger reluctantly decided that she would not for long be able to ride the horse and they must remain there for at least another day.

By then the Emperor was well over a day's march ahead, and the bulk of the Grand Army had followed him. During the morning not even an apology for a formation went by. On the previous day there had been occasional irregular squads travelling in company, or a few guns and limbers led by an officer or N.C.O., but now there were only stragglers.

Soon after ten o'clock, Roger heard distant gunfire. Hour by hour it grew nearer. Presently a body of a hundred or more men came up the road. They bore no resemblance to a company on the march, as they were not in fours or even attempting to keep step. All the same Roger realised that they were a unit and probably all that was left of a battalion. Several more groups of roughly the same size passed at about ten-minute intervals. They were obviously the rearguard, falling back to take up the next position where the ground offered possibilities for a

good defence, while other units continued to hold the line from which they had retreated.

Within an hour of entering Orcha, the gallant Ney, with his nine hundred men, had offered himself to the Emperor as Commander of the rearguard for the army. No man was better suited for the task, and Roger well remembered how persistently the Marshal had fought off the pursuing British when he had commanded Masséna's rearguard in Portugal. Napoleon had gladly accepted Ney's offer and allocated to him about a division of his best remaining troops.

But Roger did not wait to see the red-headed Marshal go by. It was certain that he would be commanding the last unit of the Grand Army to fall back, and if the Russians were not actually engaging him they would be following up within a mile of his retreating men.

Roger had already taken everything he possessed into the woodshed. Now, having put out the fire, he went there himself, crawled through the hole he had left in the wall of logs, then filled it up behind him.

Soon after he had stretched himself out beside Mary, a succession of explosions sounded quite near the farm, and he told her that a French gun must have taken up its position nearby. There followed other explosions of various intensity, as the Russians shelled the French and their cannon balls exploded. Then there came bursts of musket fire. Once a man screamed and later they heard the wild war cry of charging Cossacks. The sounds of battle continued for half an hour, then faded away in the distance.

While the fighting had continued in their immediate vicinity, they had dreaded every moment that the farm buildings might be used as a strong point, bombarded and blown to pieces. Now they could breath again. But Roger was wondering if he had not been foolish to have refrained from mounting Mary, weak as she was, on the horse the

402

day before and joining the half-frozen scarecrows of the Grand Army who had then still been passing.

Now there was no possible hope of rejoining them. He and Mary were cut off behind the Russian front. How, in the depths of winter, with only one horse, very little food and surrounded by illimitable wastes of snow, could they hope to survive?

CHAPTER XXV

OLD SOLDIERS SOMETIMES DIE

WHEN the silence had continued for an hour or more Roger went out to reconnoitre. Snow was falling again, so visibility was bad. But through the ever-moving curtain of flakes he could make out blocks of infantry marching along the road at short intervals in good order. Even had he not been able to see them, he would have known them to be there from catching the sound of the melancholy Russian marching songs they were singing.

His dread now was that some body of signallers or a small battalion staff would decide to doss down in the farmhouse for the night. To have relit the fire would have drawn attention to the building, so there could be no hot meal for them that evening. Even though they found it difficult to get their teeth into the semi-frozen bacon so had to hack it in bits and suck it, they made do on some of that and small pieces of the marzipan; but Roger gave his horse as much oats as it could be persuaded to eat.

He was now anxious to get away from the farm; as, apart from the risk of remaining there for another night, it was quite probable that next day the Russians would notice it and come there, not for shelter but to chop up the building for fire-wood.

The pain in Mary's eye was now no more than a dull ache. In all other respects she was again as well as she

had been when they left Moscow. By the light of a single candle they made their preparations. It was essential to travel as light as they could, so Roger decided to leave behind his saddle and, instead, tie the sleeping bag on his horse's back for Mary to ride on. As they would be moving only at a walking pace, she would not need stirrups. Into one of the panniers he packed the rest of the bacon, the sugar, tea, marzipan and a bundle of candles, and into the other oats and hay for the horse, three and a half bottles of brandy and another that had mule's blood mixed with it. He then fastened his sword belt round Mary's waist, in order to be free of his sword.

As he did so he recalled his civilian suit and greatly regretted having parted with it when the mule had died. If they ran into a *sotnia* of Cossacks and he had been wearing it, he could have persuaded them that he was a Latvian business man, for his fur coat did not disguise the fact that he was a French officer.

Knowing that they no longer dared follow the road, and he must plod through deep snow, he would have given all the gold in his money belt for a pair of snow-shoes. But even if he could have procured a pair, what of the horse? It was far heavier than he was and its hooves would sink deep into the snow. Still, Ney and his men had not had snow-shoes when they had left the road to Krasnoye, and made their great detour round to Orcha. Perhaps the going would not be so hard as he expected.

After he had pulled away enough logs in the wall to get his horse through, he led it out and mounted Mary on it. The snow had stopped falling, but that by no means pleased him, as there was a rising sickle moon, and it gave enough light for them to be seen at some distance. But as some consolation there was no wind, and the sky was clear. So, with the help of the stars and the map that had been issued to him, he hoped to be able to keep direction. Returning for the last time to the woodshed,

he passed round the back of his neck the thick strap that joined the two panniers, so that they hung down on either side of him. Taking the bridle of the horse he led it away from the refuge that had served them so well.

As they crossed the now deserted road, Mary asked, 'Where are we heading for?'

Roger gave a grim little laugh, 'For the Baltic coast, my dear. From here we go due north until we strike the river Dvina, then we follow its course until it reaches the sea at Riga.'

'How far is Riga?'

'The better part of three hundred miles.'

'Oh, Roger!' Mary exclaimed. 'We shall never get that far.'

'I think we shall,' he replied tersely. 'That is unless we fall in with some Russian troops and they find out that under my furs I am wearing a French uniform. We have already travelled nearly twice that distance.'

'But, darling, it will take us weeks, and our stores will give out long before we could reach Riga.'

'My sweet, it is the only course open to us. To go east would take us deeper into Russia. To go west would bring us again into the battle zone, with the risk of being killed by one side or the other, or murdered for such supplies as we have left by some of those poor devils who are being driven mad by hunger. I tell you, Mary, that is our best chance, and I am determined not to die in this damnable country.'

The going proved easier than Roger had thought would be the case, because the intense cold froze the snow solid within a short time of it falling. The country was well wooded with larch, pine and fir trees, so there were plenty of small fallen branches to make fires with whenever they halted. The woods, too, were a god-send in enabling them to avoid other people. After the first night and day they had little to fear from the Cossacks, as the

Russian army had passed on in its tireless pursuit of the enemy. But every hour or two they discerned in the distance solitary figures or groups rarely exceeding half a dozen who, although clad in the wierdest assortment of garments, they knew must be deserters. Whenever they were crossing an open space and such dubious characters came in sight, Roger quickly took the horse by the bridle, turned it and headed for the nearest wood, in which it was easy to disappear.

In order further to minimise the risk of dangerous encounters, they decided to travel mostly by night and lie up in a wood, snug in the big sleeping bag during a good part of each day. In the woods, too, they could light a fire where they halted, without its being seen from a distance and attracting unwelcome attention.

On their second day out, after having a meal they were both in the bag and Roger was just dozing off, when he was suddenly roused by a wail of misery from Mary. She was half sitting up, had got out a small mirror she carried, pushed up the bandage round her head and, for the first time, was examining her injured eye.

As Roger was unhappily aware after having dressed it each morning and night, where her eye had been there was now only a black pit containing a multi-coloured scab. Dropping the mirror, Mary burst into a passion of tears.

Wriggling up, Roger threw an arm about her shoulders and drew her to him as he said quickly, 'Don't cry, darling. Please don't cry. I know it is a terrible misfortune for you. But it might have been worse. You're not blind. You can still see with the other one.'

'It's not that!' she sobbed. 'It's not that. I'm hideous, hideous; and you'll never love me any more.'

'You absurd child.' He kissed her cold cheek. 'Say that again and I'll slap you. Of course I'll go on loving you. Your face has nothing to do with your personality, and

it's that I love. Besides, when we get back to England we will have you fitted with a glass eye, and no-one will realise that you've lost one of your own. Unless . . . yes. Stap me, I have it! You shall have a bright blue one. The contrast to your green one will prove most mightily intriguing, and make you the toast of the town.'

His attempt to take her mind off her misfortune by a joke brought a half-smile to her cracked lips. But she could not stop crying, and it was a long time before his comforting and caresses persuaded her that her disfigurement would make no difference to his feelings for her.

That night the moon was obscured by clouds and they virtually stumbled on a little town that, from his map, Roger believed to be Zepel. If he was right they had covered twenty-five miles in a little over two days and nights, which he considered to be good going. The town was burned out and, having made a cautious reconnaissance, they reached the conclusion that it had been completely evacuated. The cold was almost petrifying, as a wind was blowing from the east, so they decided to seek shelter among the ruins. Near the far end of the single street they came upon a hovel that still had a roof, but from it moisture had dripped down during the daytime to form a curtain of icicles, two feet long, over the open doorway. Breaking them off they went inside, lit a fire and spent the remainder of the night there.

The next six days and nights were uneventful. At times they saw small towns or villages in the distance, but as soon as they entered still-inhabited country they were careful to keep well away from them. The greater part of their way lay through forests where more icicles hung like stalactites from the branches of trees made feathery and sparkling by the snow, and an utter silence reigned. Even on nights when the moon was hidden, the all-pervading snow gave them enough light to see their way without diffi-

culty between the trunks of the trees, and these at least broke the force of the wind that never ceased to blow across the open areas. But they found the absolute silence, broken only by the occasional howling of wolves seeking the bodies of dead deserters, eerie and oppressive, and the climate tried them sorely.

Only when, still wearing their furs, they huddled together in the sleeping bag, were they really warm; and they came to dread having to leave it. Frostbite was a constant menace. Even a short exposure numbed their noses, ears and fingers. Not an hour passed but they had to rub these places on one another vigorously, with handfuls of snow, to restore the circulation. When they were on the march, Roger's beard and the eyebrows of them both were always rimed with frost. Often they had difficulty in keeping their teeth from chattering, and Mary's chilblains caused her agonies.

Just before dawn on the eighth day they reached the frozen Dvina. When they had followed its southern bank westward for a few miles they saw at intervals across the broad river palisades running along the lower part of big, snow-covered mounds, and Roger realised that the mounds must be the earthworks thrown up to form von Phull's great redoubt, behind which lay Drissa. Since there had been constant fighting in that neighbourhood until fairly recently, Roger wondered for a moment why they had not come upon broken gun-carriages and other debris that always littered old battlefields; then he realised that such jetsam would long since have become mounds covered with snow, and that some of the smaller ones they had passed over probably concealed the bodies of men and horses.

By reaching the river they had accomplished nearly a third of their terrible journey and since, apart from the constant gnawing of the cold, they had suffered no ill,

they were cheered by the thought that, if their luck held for just over another fortnight, they should reach Riga. But misfortune was about to strike at them again.

With all the other things he had to carry, Roger had been able to bring only five days' rations for the horse. He had counted on coming upon some means of renewing the supply—perhaps a solitary, still-inhabited farmhouse with a barn he could raid, or a barrow of turnips buried for the winter. But such hopes had not materialised, and they had not dared go near any of the villages that were inhabited.

At the time that the Prussians had attacked Mary, Roger's horse had already become pitifully thin; and they had not been long enough at the farmhouse for the plentiful supply of oats there to put much weight on it. So, although Mary had walked for a good half of the time, the hundred-mile trek to the Dvina had again reduced the animal to a living skeleton.

When they woke from their daily sleep on the third day they had been unable to give the poor beast any food, they found it dead. This blow necessitated a redistribution of the things on which their lives depended and, although the panniers were considerably lighter than when they had left the farm, much as Roger would now have liked to take the meat from a whole haunch of the horse, he had to limit himself to cutting off only a few pounds, as he would also have to carry the sleeping bag.

Following the course of the river, but now and then taking short cuts across the bends, they trudged on. Neither of them could decide whether the snow storms that half blinded them and sometimes caused them to lose their way but made the atmosphere a little warmer, or a clear sky under which a knife-like wind often cut fiercely at their chapped faces, was the greater affliction. Mary's chilblains itched intolerably, then broke and bled and, for

a time, Roger was stricken with snow blindness, so she had to lead him.

Their thirteenth day brought them within sight of the city of Daugavpils. With terrible longing they gazed at the spires and towers. There lay food in plenty, warmth, rest and comfort. But such joys were not for them. To have entered the city would almost certainly have meant death for Roger. Turning away, they made a great detour round it.

With the detours to avoid towns that they had had to make and, from time to time, losing their way in blizzards, they were now averaging only about ten miles in each twenty-four hours, and they still had about a hundred and thirty miles to go before they could hope to reach the coast. Neither said so to the other but, at times, both of them began to wonder if their strength would last out long enough for them to complete the journey. Apart from the horseflesh, which they had not yet touched, their supplies were getting low and, although that lightened their burdens, having to ration themselves more strictly was undermining their stamina.

On their sixteenth day they at last had a piece of luck. They were by then passing through the country that Macdonald's corps had fought over and, here and there, the skeletons of burnt-out farmhouses rose starkly from the white sheet of the almost level plain. Since setting out they had come upon and searched a score or more of such ruins, but found nothing of use to them. On this occasion, they spent, from habit, a few minutes rummaging among the charred beams without result, then walked on through a hedge-enclosed plot that had once been the garden. At the bottom of it there was an orchard, the trees now bare and the snow on the branches glistening in the sunlight; but, among them, there were a number of beehives.

Assuming that they would be empty, Roger would have

passed on, but Mary opened one and peered inside, then gave a cry of delight. The hives had not been taken in for the winter, so the bees were long since dead, but there were several combs of honey. Eagerly Roger set about hacking out lumps of the frozen honey, with his knife, then they happily sucked pieces of the sweet, sticky, life-giving food, devouring the wax as well. Having satiated their ravenous appetites, they started on a round of the hives to collect their contents. As they were about to open a third hive an angry, gutter-bred voice shouted in French :

'Hi ! Lay off there, 'less you wants a bullet. That's my 'oney.'

Swinging round they saw that a tall, ragged figure had come up behind them and was pointing a musket at them. As the man had spoken in French, it was obvious that he was a deserter; so Roger called back :

'You have no more right to this honey than we have. But I've no wish to quarrel with you. What's your name ?'

'Sergeant Gobbet, Sixth Grenadiers,' the man replied promptly. ' 'Oo are you ? Sounds from yer lingo as though you was an officer.'

'I am,' said Roger, and gave his name and rank.

The Sergeant grunted. 'So you're one of the bloody gilded Staff, eh ? Well, I wouldn't give a cuss if you was a Marshal. We're all equals now. No difference 'tween you an' me if the Ruskies get us. They'd soon settle our 'ash. No difference neither if we freeze ter death in this bleedin' snow. What you got in them panniers ?'

'Supplies of more value than this honey. Still, we might have a talk. I take it you're living in what is left of the farmhouse.'

'No. In the barn. It's got a bit of roof on.'

'Very well. Let's go back there.'

Sergeant Gobbet lowered his musket and they accompanied him to the barn. A low fire was burning there, and

412

they squatted round it, gratefully warming their half-frozen hands by the glow of the embers, while the heat thawed out their frost-stiffened furs and water from them made little puddles on the floor.

The Sergeant was a big, burly man with a full beard, small, piglike eyes, a receding forehead and a wonderful, flowing moustache. Roger discussed with him their respective aims. The main difference was that, while Roger had a plan for getting out of Russia, the Sergeant had not. He had simply made off, thinking that on his own he would stand a better chance of remaining alive than if he stayed with the Grand Army. Before the opening of the campaign, he had been stationed in Germany for the best part of two years and had picked up a smattering of the language. Knowing that to enter a Russian town in a French uniform was to ask to be set upon and killed, for several days past he had been keeping a look-out for a solitary Russian peasant whom he could shoot and rob of his clothes. Then he had meant to go into a village and hope to pass himself off as a Rhinelander. But no peasant had crossed his path. Half-starving, he had reached the farm the previous day, found the honey, and meant to stay there for a few days, building himself up on it.

With a grim chuckle, he admitted that as Roger's uniform had been hidden by his furs, he had taken him and Hipé for Russians and, had either of them been alone, he would by now be dead; but he had not liked to risk shooting as, had they been armed, the survivor might have shot him before he could reload his musket.

Roger then spoke of his project of trying to reach the coast and getting away in a ship. Gobbet objected that, on arriving in Riga or some similar port, they would still be in French uniforms, so would either be killed or sent as slave labour to some camp where, before the winter was out, they would be knouted unmercifully and die of

privation. To that Roger replied that to raid an inhabited house to obtain civilian clothes before they neared the end of their journey would be foolish, as a hue and cry after them might be started; but when they did come to the outskirts of a port, they must take that risk and bury their uniforms. He added that both he and Hipé could speak Russian well enough to pass as Ukranians, and that he had ample money to buy passages in a ship for them; so if only they could come by enough food to keep them going on the way, he had good hopes of his plan succeeding.

The Sergeant's objections having been overcome, he became enthusiastic about the idea, so it was decided to pool their resources and travel together. Roger produced some strips of horseflesh, the fire was made up and twenty minutes later they were chewing the hard, unsavoury meat with as much gusto as if it had been chicken. Gobbet was a garrulous man and, while they ate, he gave them an account of how things had been with the Grand Army when he decided to desert.

'I was with Oudinot's corps—"Old Blood and Guts" as we called 'im,' he told them. 'And a cracking good soldier 'e were, too. One what led 'is men in battle an' took good care of 'em other times. Back in the summer 'e got us all these sheepskin coats, like wot I'm wearin'. The weather was that 'ot then we didn't 'alf curse 'im. But come the autumn an' the snow, we was a durn sight better off than the chaps with the other corps.

'Things didn't go too bad until early November, then the Ruskies got atop of us an' pushed us east. Arter the middle o' the month we was down on the Berezina. Some dam' fool Polish General at Borisov 'ad given away the bridge over the river. But we got it back. Might 'ave made a stand there, too, if only Victor 'ad backed us up. But that red-faced drummer boy's a bad General an' a bad friend. 'E took 'is chaps across the river without a thought

of anyone else. But our man, "Old Blood and Guts", 'e waited for the Emperor.

'About the 24th or 26th, wouldn't say which, the days 'as got a bit muddled in me mind, the main army came along an' started ter cross. The town bridge weren't the only one. It were said that General Eble—'im wot's the chief sapper—'ad 'ad orders ter burn 'is pontoons back at Orcha; but 'e 'adn't, an' 'e got two of 'em across the river 'igher up. All the same, things couldn't 'ave been worse wi'out 'em.

'The 'ole bleedin' Russian army came chargin' up, screamin' blue murder an' dead set ter finish us off. Old Kutuzov an' both 'is pals who'd been out on the wings. Both sides of the river, they were. They flung at us everything they'd got : cavalry, infantry, them bastards of Cossacks on their little ponies, thousands of cannon balls an' Gawd knows that. Davout's boys managed ter clear the far bank, then the crossin' began. Us lot an' the old sweats further along managed ter 'old the Ruskies off, but a 'ole mass of troops panicked. Jus' meant to get over the bloody river at any price an' devil take the 'indmost. There was lots of women among 'em. Yes, an' children they'd 'ad on the march, too, though 'ow they'd managed to keep 'em alive beats me. Any'ow, the 'ole lot stampeded like a 'erd of cattle, 'undreds of 'em were tryin' to force their way across the bridges at the same time. Consequence was 'alf of 'em got pushed off the bridge inter the river.

'Gawd, yer never see such 'orrors in yer life. 'Ole divisions panicked. Wouldn't wait fer a chance ter cross by the bridge, but tried ter cross over the ice. The river weren't frozen all that 'ard. It cracked up under their weight, an' there was the poor devils strugglin' in the icy water. Tryin' ter climb on one another's shoulders ter get out, they was. But not a 'ope. Couple of minutes was enough. The freezin' water got 'em in the 'eart. They slipped back an' drowned.

'Then the biggest bridge, the one wot the vehicles was goin' over, gave way. Weight was too much fer it. You jus' can't imagine the nightmare ter be seen then. Screamin' men, women and kids was all mixed up in an 'orrible 'eap wi' the icy water closin' over 'em. We was all bein' shelled cruel by the Ruskies, so all them wot 'adn't got no discipline any longer was frantic ter get across the river. Them be'ind pushed them in front till the bloody river were so full of corpses you could 'a walked near dryshod over 'em. An' the Ruskie shells blowing' them wot weren't drowned ter bits every minute. Then, ter put the lid on everything, the foot bridge that I an' my pals were about ter cross caught fire.

'That's when I opted out, that was. I says to myself I says, "Baptiste Gobbet, you old sod. You bin in Italy an' Egypt an' 'Olland an' Austria an' God knows where else, an' you always got away with it. But this 'ere's too much. Among that mob of 'owling perishers you won't stand no chance. You'd best take care of Number One." Night were fallin' by then, so I jus' slipped away quiet like, an' 'ere I am.'

When the Sergeant had finished describing the awful scenes of chaos that had taken place during the crossing of the Berezina, it emerged that both he and Roger had been wounded at Marengo, so they talked about the old days for quite a time before settling down for a sleep.

On waking they ate another meal, then hacked all the frozen honey out of the hives and packed it into the cooking pot that Mary always carried. Leaving the farm they followed the course of the river, for most of the time walking along its hard-frozen surface, but where that was too broken by boulders and piled-up floes of ice, taking to the bank. The honey greatly benefited Roger and Mary, putting new energy into them, but the climate remained arctic. Just as the past summer had been exceptionally hot, so this winter was proving exceptionally cold.

For three days, accompanied by the Sergeant, they continued on their way north-westward, travelling mostly by night and, whenever they sighted a village, leaving the river for the woods. During their halts, when they ate their miserably small meals before sleeping through the middle of the day, Roger and Mary said little about themselves; but Gobbet proved a great raconteur and never tired of telling stories about adventures he had had during his many campaigns. He was typical of the old soldiers who had joined up in their youth as volunteers when the young Republic had been in danger of being overrun by the Monarchies. Tough, resourceful and unscrupulous, his language was foul and he was a born looter and lecher. Most of his stories and his accounts of how, when sacking cities, he had raped grandmothers and schoolgirls indiscriminately would have made Mary blush to the roots of her, now, six-inch-long hair had she not become accustomed to hearing such talk during her weeks with the Grand Army.

On the fourth evening after they had met Gobbet, they had not been on their way long when, in the distance, they discerned a town; so, in order to go round it they left the river and entered a forest. Darkness fell soon afterwards and, several hours later, they ran into grave danger.

It was not snowing at the time and a now waning moon gave just enough light to see by. Suddenly, among the tree-trunks ahead, Roger, who was leading, caught sight of low, moving shadows. Next moment the silence was shattered by a loud baying, and the shadows came bounding toward them. In terror they realised that they were about to be attacked by a pack of wolves.

Many times during the march from Moscow, and in recent weeks, they had heard the howling of wolves and seen them prowling in the distance; but the beasts had never threatened to molest the living, at least as long as

they showed they had the strength to defend themselves. That was because, all through the winter, there had been innumerable corpses for them to feed on. But now, the three weary, half-frozen travellers had left behind the country that had been fought over.

At the first sound made by the pack, the three had come to an abrupt halt. Fortunately they were within a few feet of a big birch tree, the lowest branch of which was within reach. Seizing Mary by the waist, Roger lifted her so that she could easily grasp the branch and swing herself up on to it. With a swift jump, he followed. Gobbet had unslung his musket. Aiming it at the leader of the pack, he fired. The beast leapt into the air, twisted and fell. Instantly the others were upon it, tearing it to pieces. To take his weight off the lowest branch, Roger had scrambled on to another, opposite it and a little higher up. With a blasphemous oath, the Sergeant clambered up between them, into the fork of the tree.

After tearing the dead wolf to shreds, the rest of the pack loped up to the base of the tree and milled round it. There seemed to be between fifteen and twenty of them. After a while they settled down on their haunches. Lifting their heads, so that their yellow eyes glistened in the faint moonlight, every few minutes one of them gave a blood-curdling howl.

For a time the besieged travellers stared down in dismay, wondering how they could rid themselves of the menacing beasts. Then Gobbet muttered, 'Only thing ter do is to 'ave 'em feed on one another till they can't eat no more.' Reloading his musket he shot another wolf. Within five minutes it had been devoured by its companions.

In the half-hour that followed, he shot three more and Roger shot three with his pistol. They, in turn, were torn limb from limb by the snarling pack, and their more succulent parts eaten; but there still remained nine of them

and they showed no sign of going away. Giving vent to a spate of curses, Gobbet announced :

'Ain't got no more bullets. Wot fricking luck to 'ave run out. Their bellies must be near full by now. Bet another couple 'ull do the trick. Let that big grey brute 'ave it wiv yer pistol, Colonel.'

Roger had just reloaded, but he had only two bullets left, and he was loath to use them in case they were needed for some other emergency. Then he remembered that Mary was carrying his other pistol, so he called across to her, 'How many bullets have you got, Hipé?'

'I had eight,' she replied quickly. 'But they are in a little bag tied on to the pistol, and when you swung me up into the tree it fell out of my belt. I dropped the cooking pot with the honey, too.'

Turning to the Sergeant, Roger said, 'When we get near Riga and break into a house to get clothes we'll need both weapons, in case we are surprised and have to use them to get away, so I'm against firing the two bullets I've got just yet. We'll wait for another hour or so, in the hope that the brutes will tire of sitting there and leave us to return to their lair and sleep off the big meal they've already had.'

The hour that followed seemed never-ending. Occasionally one of the wolves would whine and prowl round for a few minutes. But for most of the time they were silent and remained sitting on their haunches, staring upward with unwinking eyes. From time to time Gobbet muttered an impatient curse and shifted restlessly, then he committed a terrible act that he had evidently been contemplating for some while.

Suddenly his hand shot out. Seizing the collar of Mary's fur coat, he gave it a swift, violent pull, designed to throw her backwards off her precarious perch, and snarled :

'Boy's no dam' good to us. The brutes can 'ave 'im, an' we'll save 'is rations.'

With a scream, Mary overbalanced and slipped from the branch. But as she fell she managed to catch hold of it. Next second there was pandemonium. Howling, the wolves hurled themselves into a solid mass and began to snap at her feet.

Roger's heart gave a lurch. He still had his loaded pistol in his hand. Yelling, 'You bastard!' he swung it round and fired straight into Gobbet's face.

Had there only been one wolf it would, by then, have buried its fangs in the calf of one of Mary's legs. But, as they leapt at her, they knocked one another aside. The moment Gobbet fell out of the tree, they swerved away from her and fought to get at the human flesh for which they had waited so long. Roger threw himself forward across the now empty fork of the tree and, with his free hand, seized Mary by the wrist. A moment later, sobbing and half-fainting, she was hauled back to safety.

He had hardly done so and clasped her in his arms before the wolves had ripped away the Sergeant's clothes and were beginning to eat him. But their eagerness to gorge themselves had abated. They seemed satisfied to have secured a fair sample of the prey they had been determined to feed on. Almost with indifference they gnawed the flesh of Gobbet's limbs, then, as though instinctively obeying a common impulse, wandered off.

It was not until Roger had recovered from seeing Mary in such dire peril and the effort needed to rescue her that he realised that another misfortune had befallen them. As he had thrown himself across the fork of the tree, the two panniers had slipped from his shoulders and fallen to the ground. Anxiously he peered down to see what had happened to them. But the moon was now down, and the light had become so dim that he could make out only the hump that was the remains of Gobbet's corpse.

For quite a time, in case the wolves returned, he and

Mary did not dare come down from the tree; but when it seemed safe they slithered to the ground. The panniers were there, but had been ripped to pieces, which were mingled with the Sergeant's half-eaten limbs. To their great distress, there was little among the stores that could be salvaged. What remained of their sugar and tea had been spilt. The wolves had eaten most of the precious marzipan and chunks of honeycomb. Their last piece of horseflesh had been chewed and, as a final blow, their last bottle of brandy had smashed as it hit the ground.

Sadly depressed, they walked for an hour until they came upon a deserted charcoal-burner's hut. Dawn was approaching. As they were by then famished, they lit a fire and cooked the mangled piece of horseflesh. Then they crawled into the sleeping bag which Roger had been carrying strapped to his back, and fell into a sleep of exhaustion.

They had been so tired after their ordeal with the wolves that it was not until the early twilight fell that they moved on again. The trek they made during that night was the worst they had ever endured. After their many days of travel they were desperately weary. It did not snow, but the cold was excruciating. They had had nothing left to cook before they set out, so they tried melting a candle and lapping up the fat, in the hope that it would warm them; but it was so greasy that it made them feel sick. They could not get it down, and their empty stomachs rumbled with hunger. Their faces were chapped, their feet bruised from stumbling on the uneven surface of the frozen river. Every time they stopped to rest, Mary was shaken with shivering fits and whimpered, 'It's so cold! Oh, it's so cold.'

At first light they came to a bend in the river. Boulders protruding from the ice showed that when the water was unfrozen there was a cataract there. When it had frozen in the late autumn, ice floes had piled up on top of one

another, making the going very difficult and dangerous. Dreading, as he had so often during the past week, that one of them might slip and break an ankle, Roger led Mary to the bank of the river. It was steep, but they scrambled up it and continued on their way. The bank gradually rose, until it became a hundred-foot-high cliff. It had begun to snow again so, when they reached the summit of the rise, they decided to halt. Roger had been hoping that they would come upon a wood in which he could gather sticks for a fire, but it was barren ground. They sucked half of the few chunks of honey that the wolves had left them; then, silent and utterly miserable, crawled into their sleeping bag.

After a while Mary fell asleep, but hunger pains prevented Roger from doing so. He had to face it that Riga still lay at least seventy miles away, and that without further supplies it would be impossible for them to reach it. That left three possible alternatives. He could break into a house; but, if he were caught, he was too weak to put up a fight or, if he shot anyone, run far without collapsing. So, to adopt that course would be to risk leaving Mary alone and starving. They could give themselves up. Mary would be saved and come to no harm. But for him it meant death, and a far from pleasant one. Russian resentment at what the French had done to their country was so great that, when they saw his uniform, the odds were that they would kill him out of hand. If some humane official did protect him and send him to a prisoner-of-war camp, the chances of his getting a message to the Czar—as he had realised all along—were infinitesimal, and it was as good as certain that he would suffer a lingering death from hardship. The third course was to throw in his hand and just lie down and die in the snow.

Had he been his normal, vigorous self he would never even have contemplated giving up and not making a last desperate endeavour to reach the coast. Had he been on

his own he would still have elected to embark on that forlorn hope. But he had been sadly weakened by privation and he had Mary with him. The thought of seeing her fall by the wayside and die of starvation was unbearable, So he decided that he would save her if he could, and die himself.

About midday he eased himself out of the sleeping bag only temporarily disturbing her, stood up and looked about him. Although still freezing as hard as in Dante's lowest depth of Hell, the weather was fine and the atmosphere extraordinarily clear. From the top of the high cliff he could see a town down on the river, about four miles way. It was, he felt sure, Plavinas. For the first time in days his features, made rugged by the cold, broke into a smile. Their being within easy distance of it perfectly suited his intention.

But next moment his face had become sober again, at the thought of how difficult it was going to be to persuade Mary to leave him. He had no doubt that she could manage the four miles to the town on her own, and she had nothing whatever with her that would connect her with the French; so, out of charity, she would be taken in and cared for. Besides, although he had many times contemplated lightening his burdens by throwing away his money belt, he had resisted the temptation. The gold in it was sufficient both to enable her to reach Riga by sleigh and from there secure a passage home. His problem was that he did not believe for one moment that she would agree to walk off, leaving him to die.

After a while, the solution came to him. He must leave her. To make her do so would necessitate his playing a horrid part, and it greatly distressed him to think that, to the end of her life, she would believe that he had not loved her enough to remain with her but had sent her off on her own in order that he might have a better chance of saving himself. But there seemed no alternative.

Kneeling down beside the now almost empty panniers, he looked through their few remaining stores. There were a few bits of mangled honeycomb, about a quarter of a pound of marzipan and half a bottle of the mule's blood mixed with brandy. Taking off his money belt he put it with the stores.

When he had shaken Mary until she came out of her semi-coma, he said, 'My love, I have come to a decision. This is the parting of the ways.'

'What . . . what do you mean?' she stammered.

'That we are reduced to such extremities that I mean to leave you.'

Her one eye opened wide with fright and through her cracked lips she whispered, 'Leave me! Oh, no, Roger, you can't mean that.'

'I do,' he replied in a firm voice. 'We are still over seventy miles from Riga. For us to attempt to reach it together would be hopeless. We'd both be dead within the next few days. But if we separate there is still a good chance that we may both survive.'

'No, Roger!' she burst out, her face becoming panic-stricken. 'No! Please! Anything but that. I . . .'

'Mary, you must be sensible.' He cut her short sharply. 'My life depends on this as well as yours. The town of Plavinas is down the river, only a few miles off. If I went into it wearing a French uniform, that would be the end of me. They would never believe that I am an Englishman. But there is no reason why they should harm you. I am going to give you half my money. That will easily enable you to get to Riga.'

'But, Roger . . . Roger, what about you?'

'There are plenty of villages along the river. I mean to break into a house each night and raid its larder. With luck, I'll also be able to steal some clothes.'

'Then I'll come with you. How can you ask me to go into that town, where there are warmth and food, while

I know you still to be nearly starving and out in this freezing cold?'

'I am not asking you, Mary. I am telling you what you are going to do. To take you with me is out of the question. To be frank, you would be an embarrassment to me. I'd be worrying all the time that, if I were caught, you would be caught, too. I'll not risk having you tried as a thief and sent to a Russian prison.'

'But, darling, I just can't bear the thought of leaving you. I love you. I love you terribly.' Tears were running down Mary's cheeks and her face was the picture of misery.

Roger could hardly bear the sight of her distress. He was greatly tempted to give up his plan, take her in his arms and tell her that they would remain together. But he knew that would be fatal for them both. Anxious now only to be finished with playing his distasteful role, he decided to end matters, and said almost brutally :

'You say you love me. Very well then. Prove it by doing as I wish and give me a chance to save my life. I told you long ago that I was determined not to die in this damnable country.'

Choking on a sob, she remained silent for a moment, then said in a small voice, 'I see now that I was being selfish. Instead I should have thanked you for having borne with me all these weeks. If you had sent me into a town much earlier, you would by now be in Riga.'

Her pitiful surrender distressed him beyond measure, but he dared not show his feelings. With an effort he raised a smile, and replied hurriedly, 'That's better, Mary. Now, we have no time to lose. You must be in Plavinas before the light falls. While you were dozing I divided our things. I've put enough food in my pockets to keep me going for a day or two. You must take the rest. And here's my belt with half the money in it.'

425

With a word of thanks she took the belt, but added, 'I'll not need any food. You must keep it all.'

He shook his head. 'No. You must eat these bits of honeycomb and marzipan while you are on your way, to give you the strength for your long walk. I want you to take the mule's blood and brandy, too. There's just a chance that you might not reach the town before dark, and there is no moon now, so you could lose your way and have to spend the night in the open. You won't have the sleeping bag, but drinking this stuff will keep the life in you until morning.'

Submissively now, she agreed to do as he wished, stowed the things in her pockets and, a few minutes later, at his urging that she must make the most of the light, was ready to start. Tearfully, she looked at him and asked, 'Are you not coming with me for part of the way?'

'No,' he replied hoarsely. 'I did not sleep at all this morning, so I must get a good sleep this afternoon in order to be at my best for breaking into some farmhouse tonight.'

Now that the die was cast, he felt that he could afford to show his true feelings. Holding out his arms, he took her into them and said gently, 'Mary, my darling. Please don't think I am being altogether selfish about this. I do love you. For a long time now you have meant everything to me. But this is our only chance. Given a little luck, I'll get through, then in a month or so we'll be together again in England.'

She returned his kiss and murmured, 'I can only pray for that.' Then she suddenly broke away and added bitterly, 'But you don't love me as much as I love you, or you'd have let us die together.'

Turning her back, she stumbled away. He repressed his impulse to run after her; and, with an aching heart, watched her small figure until it was out of sight.

When she had disappeared down the slope, Roger did not get into the sleeping bag. Having resigned himself to death, he saw no point in prolonging his life, and the stomach cramps from which he was suffering, for a few additional hours. But, as he lay down in the snow, he instinctively drew one end of the bag over his head, to save his lips and nose from becoming frostbitten.

Now that he was lying still, his hunger pains eased and he was able to think more coherently. As there was no likelihood in the foreseeable future of his having been able to marry Georgina, and it was now out of his power to marry Mary, he decided that he did not greatly mind dying.

After all, he had had a wonderful life. He had met the majority of the most famous men of his time, travelled far and wide and, for many years past, had had more money than he needed. He had also been blessesd more than most men in that many lovely women had found him very attractive. Amanda had been a sweet wife to him, and they had been happy until she had died in giving birth to Susan. Then there had been his dear Clarissa. What a tragedy that he had lost her when she was still so young. And Pauline. It was an intriguing thought that he might have married the sister of an Emperor. But Napoleon was really only a cardboard Emperor and, but for his remarkable achievements, Pauline would have remained only the little Corsican whore she was at heart. Yet nature had endowed her with the beauty of a fairy-tale Princess.

Other women drifted through his mind, not only ones he had loved, but his dear mother and young Susan. What a pity that his mother had not lived long enough to know Susan. She would have been so happy at having a charming grand-daughter. What a pity, too, that until he returned from abroad as a grown man, he had so hated his stern and uncompromising father. Admiral Sir Chris,

as King George used to call him, was really a very like-
able sort of man. What a tragedy it was that so often
young people and their parents failed to appreciate one
another's good qualities, sometimes until it was too late.

He could take pride in the fact that both his father and
himself had served their King well. Was the poor old
madman still alive? But where would England be now
without Billy Pitt? Frail and ill for a great part of the
time, for over fourteen years, with indomitable courage he
had fought to save Britain and all Europe from self-
seeking demagogues and spoliation under irresponsible
mob rule.

Would Talleyrand and Metternich replace him, and
destroy once and for all the demon power of Bonaparte
to inflict untold misery on millions of men and women?
What a good friend Talleyrand had been, and dear
Droopy Ned, who had been closer than a brother to him,
ever ready to welcome him back to London and help him
with shrewd advice.

Then there were his friends the enemy, who had blindly
followed the dynamic Corsican's star: Duroc, Rapp,
Lavalette, Bourrienne, Lannes, Bernadotte, Eugene, and
the rest. Several of them were now dead, the others
Princes, Dukes and Counts. What a glorious company!
Unrivalled in all history, they had fought and laughed
their way into Brussels, Amsterdam, Mayence, Cologne,
Milan, Rome, Venice, Madrid, Vienna, Hanover, Berlin and even Moscow.

What had happened to the Grand Army? That fabulous host that Napoleon had led across the Niemen six
months ago. How many of them would recross it? From
the scene Gobbet had described of the crossing of the
Berezina, probably not more than a few thousand. How
many of them had left their bones to crumble and fertilise
the Russian soil? Well, he, Roger Brook, was just one of
them.

428

Then it seemed as if the fur over his eyes dissolved and he saw Georgina standing beside him. She was enveloped in a halo of light. He wondered if she was dead and had come as an angel to carry his spirit away, united at last with his own. She was smiling down at him. In the warmth of her smile, he fell asleep.

EPILOGUE

ROGER had a terrible nightmare. He was being beaten unmercifully. Someone was alternately smashing fists into his ribs and slapping his face and thighs. Groaning and moaning, he made a feeble attempt to escape the blows by turning his head from side to side. Then he managed to open his eyes. Candlelight told him it was night.

An ugly giant of a man, naked to the waist and with beads of sweat standing out on his forehead was belabouring him vigorously. The ugly man grinned and said in Russian :

'That is better, friend. I feared we were going to lose you.'

Roger's breath was coming in painful gasps, so he could not reply or ask any questions. The pummelling and slapping continued. He became conscious that he was lying on a bed, nearly naked, and that there were hot-water bottles at his feet and behind his neck.

Apparently at last satisfied with the result of his exertions, the giant stood back, covered Roger with blankets, then went to the door and shouted something. Two minutes later a middle-aged man and a portly, well-dressed woman came into the room. She was carrying a pewter mug that held a steaming liquid. While they stood on either side of Roger, the lady fed the brew to him with a spoon, and he found it to be mulled wine. After he

had had a few sips, he had the strength to ask in Russian:
'Where am I?'

To his surprise the man answered in English. 'My
name is William Colgin. I am a fur trader and you are
in my house. Our coachman, Jan, has been massaging
you. We feared you dead, and are greatly pleased that
you have recovered.'

Full realisation of the past then flooded back to Roger
and he asked anxiously, 'Have you seen aught of an English girl? She was wearing men's clothes. We parted up
on the cliff, a few miles east of the town.'

It was the lady who replied. 'Yes. You have no need
to be concerned for her. She now lies in bed in the next
room. It was she who took my husband and others back
the way she had come, to find and bring you in. By the
time they returned she was near overcome with exhaustion and distraught with anxiety. I'd not have wagered a
penny herring that we'd succeed in reviving you, but I
told her I was confident we could; so she was persuaded
by me to imbibe a sleeping draught. When you have
finished this wine, I am going to prescribe one for you,
too.'

It was daylight when Roger was roused by a soft kiss
on his lips. Mary, clad in a dressing gown much too large
for her, was smiling down at him. Quickly she told him
how he had been rescued.

'After you had sent me off on my own,' she said, 'I
suddenly had a feeling that 'twas not really your intent
to try to get to Riga. My belief was confirmed by looking at
the bits of honey and marzipan you had made me take.
I felt certain you had given all we had left to me. You had
already become so weak that, without sustenance of any
kind, I doubt if you could have walked another ten
miles, let alone muster the strength to break into a house
and rob a larder. I was much of a mind to turn back.
But I realised you were giving your life for me, so I de-

cided that I ought to accept it and do my utmost to save yours as well.

'On the outskirts of the town I met a pedlar and enquired of him the whereabouts of the town hall. He kindly took me there, and I asked if there was an English family living in the town. Good people there gave me hot soup and drove me in a sleigh here, to Mr. and Mrs. Colgin. To them I told the truth about you; that, although wearing a French uniform, you were an English gentleman in disguise. A party was quickly assembled and we went out with lanterns to search for you. In the dark I don't think we should ever have found you, but we saw a most strange light, like a will-o'-the-wisp, and we walked in that direction to find out what it could be. As we approached, it vanished, but below where it had been hovering was your body.'

Roger felt certain that the light must have been an emanation from Georgina's spirit, and that by the strange psychic link between them she had saved him yet again. But he could not spoil Mary's belief that she alone had been responsible on this occasion; and, indeed, his guardian angel could not have caused his half-frozen body to be recovered and revived. Taking her hand, he squeezed it and said :

'My spendid Mary. 'Twas stupid in me not to have thought of sending you ahead of me, into a town earlier. But until we had been reduced to such desperate straits I would have been loath to allow you to face the dangers of the road alone. As long, too, as we were in the heart of Russia, we could scarce expect to come upon any English people who could believe me to be their countryman and give me their protection. It is to your courage and good sense that I owe my life.'

She shook her head. 'But, my love, 'tis to you that I owe mine. It was your willingness to die, so that I might live that saved us both.'

432

An hour later a doctor, who had been sent for to examine Mary's eye, arrived. Roger knew nothing of this until Mr. Colgin came in to tell him the result. Whether she would regain the sight of the injured eye was very dubious, but it was just possible. If so, that would be due to the fact that ever since she had sustained the injury she had kept a bandage over it, and no attempt had been made to remove the great scab that had formed in the socket above the eyeball. The doctor had eased off the congealed mass of dried blood and tissue and at once put on a new bandage, which was not to be taken off for a week or more, except for brief intervals in a darkened room.

For three days they remained, recruiting their strength with the hospitable Colgins. By the end of that time, when removing the bandage, Mary could distinguish the flame of a candle; but the doctor would not encourage her to believe that the sight of the eye would ever be fully restored.

Now that they had recovered from their terrible ordeal Roger hired a sledge to take them in to Riga. On Boxing Day they crossed the Baltic to Stockholm. Bernadotte was in residence at the Castle. He received them most kindly and from him they learned the fate of the Grand Army.

Far out on the Eastern flank Schwarzenberg had retreated across the frontier of his own country, having lost comparatively few of his men. To the west, the bulk of Macdonald's corps had escaped down the Baltic coast, and out in that direction St. Cyr had also got most of his troops away. But the whole of the rest of the army had piled up at Borisov on the Berezina.

That it had not been totally destroyed was due to four things: Kutuzov, cautious as ever, had ignored the Czar's order to launch an all-out offensive; he was content to let the weather continue to do its worst and drive the enemy out of Russia. The Generals under him were hypnotised

by Napoleon's unique reputation and, fearing to fall into
a trap, had failed to press home their individual attacks.
The Emperor's genius for waging war was no myth; his
energy and initiative returned to him; within the limits
that were possible he handled magnificently such units
as were still capable of putting up a resistance. The tireless energy, the skill and the valour with which, with his
rearguard, Ney held the Cossack hordes at bay.

But the bridges for the crossing of the Berezina were
hopelessly inadequate. Only a few thousand could cross
each hour, while tens of thousands remained massed and
waiting to do so on the eastern bank. Platoff, Maloradov-
itch, Tchitchagov, Wittgenstein and Tormasov had all
closed in from different directions. For three days and
nights their hundreds of guns shelled the helpless host,
sending it stampeding on to the ice of the river, which
broke under their weight. Sergeant Gobbett had not
exaggerated in his account of the ghastly scenes that had
been enacted there. On the banks of the Berezina and in
its icy waters Napoleon left thirty-two thousand dead.

By December 2nd the Grand Army had been reduced
to eight thousand eight hundred effectives. There was
no longer any talk of wintering behind the Berezina. The
only hope left to the survivors was that the Russians
would not pursue them across the Niemen into Poland.
On the 3rd Napoleon prepared the world for his defeat
by issuing the 29th Bulletin. In it, he blamed the loss of
his army on the early commencement of the Russian winter. After admitting that the greater part of the greatest
army ever assembled was dead, the Bulletin ended with
a statement the cynicism of which can rarely, if ever, have
been surpassed, 'The Emperor's health has never been
better.'

Shortly afterwards he received news from Paris that
a small group of conspirators, led by a General Malet,
had sought to take advantage of his absence to launch a

coup d'état. He used this as an excuse to leave the remnant of his army. On December 5th, he assembled those of his senior Generals who were available at Smorgoni and told them that he was returning to Paris to raise another army. Then he drove off in his sleigh, leaving Murat in command.

As the leader of a cavalry charge, the King of Naples had no equal, but he had no stomach for the task with which he had been entrusted. Without even appointing a successor, he made off as swiftly as he could for Poland. Realising the utter hopelessness of further attempts to stem the Russian tide, Davout, Eugene and Mortier went with him.

Brave Oudinot managed to keep a thousand or so men together, and Ney continued to perform prodigies with his rearguard. With him remained old Lefebvre, whose washerwoman wife had once laundered Lieutenant Bonaparte's small-clothes for nothing and who, for old times' sake, the Emperor had made a Marshal and Duke of Danzig. In the retreat he displayed all the finest qualities of the courageous Sergeant-Major he once had been, and above which rank he was never qualified to be promoted.

From the Berezina the rabble fell back on Vilna. When it left the ruined city the Grand Army numbered only four thousand three hundred men. By then everything that the French had managed to drag with them, the last guns, baggage and trophies, had been lost. The suffering of the men was beyond description. At times the temperature fell to forty-five below zero. From Vilna twelve thousand boy conscripts, most of whom had only just left their schools, came out to reinforce the army; within four days nine out of every ten of them were dead.

On December 14th a starved, freezing remnant reached the Niemen at Kovno. Of all the vast host that had crossed it in June, only one thousand of the Old Guard

and Ney's rearguard, which numbered fewer than that, remained disciplined units. Up to the bitter end the Russians continued to attack, but they had received orders from Alexander that they were not to invade Poland. During those desperate weeks Ney's deeds had won for him immortality. Musket in hand, he was the last man of the once *Grande Armée* to cross the bridge at Kovno to the safety of Polish soil.

During the campaign one hundred and fifty thousand reinforcements had reached the Grand Army, so the total number of men who took part in it was in the neighbourhood of six hundred and fifty thousand. Only thirty thousand survivors succeeded, one way or another, in reaching Poland. Of these only the corps on the flanks escaped the holocaust, and only some ten thousand had made the journey to Moscow and back. To the dead must be added about one hundred thousand camp-followers. Horses to the number of one hundred and sixty thousand had been lost, and over one thousand guns. It was the greatest military disaster in history.

When Bernadotte had given these particulars, acquired through his intelligence service, to Roger and Mary, he told them that the Swedish army would be ready to take the field in the spring, and would join with the Austrians and Prussians in a final campaign to crush the monster murderer. He then invited them to stay as long as they liked in Stockholm and promised, when they wished, to send them safely home.

Next day Roger took Mary into the city, to buy her suitable clothes, and an outfit for himself. In the Castle they had naturally been given separate rooms, and he observed the proprieties by not going into hers—until the morning of the fourth day of their stay.

He then went in to her carrying an enormous cardboard box, put it on the bed and told her to open it. Packed in layers of tissue paper, it contained a magni-

436

ficent wedding dress, which he had secretly ordered after the dressmaker had measured her. Mary had been sitting up in bed, a pink eye-shade now covering her injured eye. At the sight of the dress she could not contain her delight, and kissed him fondly, as he said :

'Although you are a widow, I should like you to wear this today.'

For all their lives his relationship with Georgina would remain a thing apart; but he had no doubt whatever that she would be happy for him, and during the past four months he had come to love Mary very dearly. She had no dowry, no relations who moved in high society, was no great beauty; but she had courage, steadfastness and gaiety. He knew that she would make him a wonderful wife.

Later that morning, New Year's Day of 1813, when they met in the chapel of the Castle, Roger caught his breath with surprise and delight when he saw that Mary was no longer wearing pink eye-shade. The only remaining sign of her injury was a white scar severing her left eyebrow, and she assured him that her sight was improving every day.

With the Swedish Royal Family as witnesses, they were married by a Lutheran pastor, and the Prince Royal of Sweden gave the divinely happy bride away.

*This book
designed by William B. Taylor
is a production of
Heron Books, London*

*Printed in England by
Hazell Watson and Viney Limited
Aylesbury, Bucks*

A Collection distributed by Heron Books

D1634083